THE
ACADEMY FOR
SOULS

THE ACADEMY FOR SOULS

by

JOHN O'HARA COSGRAVE

© 1931 John O'Hara Cosgrave
ISBN: 978-0-9559090-9-2
Book Studio 2013

Front cover:
"Sunset Over South America," courtesy NASA

British Library Cataloguing in Publication Data.
A catalogue record for this book is available from the British Library.

To my wife, Jessica G. Cosgrave, and to A. R. Orage, who have borne much of the heat and burden of this book

PREFACE

I gather from my editing of the proofs of this book that the irascible Martian and his behavioristic vis-a-vis are convinced that the Universe is self-conscious and that humanity may be redeemed from anonymity. Glad tidings, undoubtedly for whoever can guess what is meant by it, but these must be in a minority since for most of us the Universe is no better than stellar scenery, and our identities derive from our forbears. There are those who contend that the members of our race should long ago have supplied themselves with more accurate biographies than the superficial accountings of biology and geology, but men are practical folk devoted to the end of staying put where they have found themselves, and so their indifference deprives them of nothing they could eat, drink or wear. In fact, it figures rather as an advantage, since if we discovered that our identities were greater or less than is taken for granted, it might devolve on us to change our viewpoints or technics, which, obviously, would make for trouble and confusion.

On the other hand, if the Universe is self-conscious, it must be responsible for our presence on Earth, and aware of our plight. As thus far it has shown no disposition to alter the errors of our ways, save by periodic removal of our units from their contamination, perhaps some need of its own is served by our being as we are. Maybe this world is a reformatory for refractory or abnormal souls, and exposure to the rigors of its experiences has educational as well as punitive values. The theory that another purpose than sustaining our own lives is being developed here, though speculative, should not be rejected because of its novelty. Today all the old moorings are adrift, and between Einstein and Eddington, Jeans and Whitehead, not to mention Sir Oliver Lodge, or the upsetting postulates of Walter Russell, the character of the Universe is any man's guess. So though the Martian's epistemology seems at variance with prevailing texts, who knows but that tomorrow or next week some local authority may not confirm or advance his predications? In the meantime it may be said for his version that despite a flavor of the occult, it involves neither faith nor the old Fourth Dimension. Yet though the argument is based on mechanics it is liable to displease the disciples of automatic determinism as greatly as it will disturb the Fundamentalists.

It's a realistic view of the cosmos he propounds, less picturesque than Revelation and more matter-of-fact than the offerings of our philosophers. He depicts it as a large-scale power plant whose activities are devoted to maintaining the existence of the creator who materialized his ideal of his entity in its works. He would have us accept the revolving aggregation of stellar satellites as constituting the physical body and person of this Being, assume its motivation as in fulfillment of his obligations, and regard the vital organisms which pervade all its spheres as instrumentalities for the conduction of his self-consciousness. Life, he construes as the ebb and flow of this awareness, kindling to action the forms devised for its commitments, and developing in each that power of exchange with environment which enables the assertion of individual birthrights. Thus he establishes premises anterior to phenomena, and design as precedent to performance. Consciousness, separated from structure, becomes the executive principle for coordination and supervision in a mechanical system. Rank, therein, is graduated according to capacity to understand processes and objectives, and in ability to participate in management of relations, but all that move sequentially in the orbit of its ordination return some moiety of energy to the unit of control.

To the failure of men to discriminate between consciousness as the positive factor and the organisms which it both inspires and pilots, this Martian attributes the ills that canker our civilization, and he is offensively derisive of what he calls our ignorance of meaning, identity and origin. In the development of his fantastic hypothesis this audacious intruder revives all the discarded notions of animism, dualism and design, and goes far beyond Eddington, Jeans or Millikan in insisting on the inevitability of an administrator God.

Thus we are invited to exchange for the comfortable assurances of natural selection and the survival of the fittest in which experience had demonstrated there remained scope for personal aggrandizement, an almighty determinism in whose colossal dimension men shrink to insignificance. We are mere looking and listening posts or messengers for conveying the will of a Galactic Entity. The freedom we presume we exercise in going about our affairs is likened to that which we impute to the wild ass, and our most precious inherencies, including self-preservation, indicated as installed on behalf of an Interest that is forwarded by the activities set up in pursuit of food for the maintenance of our bodies. On the same terms, pain, sorrow and suffering are made to appear as ferments for engendering in instinctive races the growth of a latent property—intelligence—which will drive them to apply its native functions of recognition and reasoning in removing their woes. This latter might be construed either as a scoff at the doctrine of vicarious atonement, or an attempt to deprive our populations of their primordial alibis, for in the type of mechanical framework delineated, good and evil would be reduced to misconstruction, maladjustment, mishap or insubordination. Morals, in turn, fall into the category of prescriptions for regulating conduct and associations among animal organisms confined to a common environment.

Without straining my imagination, I can hear the ancients and the Fathers spluttering at so facile a disposition of their pet embarrassments.

Yet, for all his animadversions, our censor admits that the state of our peoples is not so lowly as to be irremediable. We wear to him the aspect of ducks that might, if they had the will, be swans. He declares us scions of a loftier ordination, not fallen from a higher estate, but who have failed to realize and redeem their prerogative. He reviles us because we loll lazily in a servitude of instinct and habit which might be relieved by enlarging the conception of our mission in the scheme of things. Princes, he says we are, content to eke out existence as paupers rather than exert the energy required for grasping the rich inheritance of our endowment.

In the bodies of men, this Martian alleges, the Master of the World invested the powers he would have his subjects apply to the conduct of his work, but though he retains first call on their services, provision had been made for their comfort and the enhancement of their stature. If they have omitted to observe the conditions of tenure or the trends of his requirements or have not entered into such command of the noble vehicle of Being as would return control of its faculties and forces, the blame for their unhappiness is not on his head, but on their own shoulders. Have they not eyes to recognize, and legs to deliver them from temptation?

In the pages that follow, this bumptious oracle parades his theories at full length. He may flatter himself that the proof he advances of the reality of the element, Consciousness, is irrefutable but until the Association for the Advancement of Science makes formal recognition of mind force, of what avail are his wisecracks? That Mankind at large should heed the utterances of one, who saddles its errancy on the racial inertia, is ridiculous. If the episode and the argument were not palpably fictitious, grounds would appear for resenting their effrontery. Setting down the achievements of humanity as the products of unconscious cerebration amounts to impertinence. Stigmatizing our civilization as instinctive is sheer impudence. Moreover, the idea of projecting the tutelary deity in the role of an executive director is churlish. Denuding him of the familiar and endearing attributes of love, and mercy, and placing his administration on a strictly business basis, is something akin to blasphemy, or, at least lèse-majesté. And that those precious emotions whose indulgence lends inspiration and color to our lives should be accorded no higher than an endocrine rating, deserves the reprobation of all who cherish sentiment for its own sake.

Who, may I ask in all seriousness, would exchange the glorious privilege of kicking up his heels in the wilderness of his imagination for a precisely ordered, paved and sewered universe such as is presented by this Martian? Is it not enough that in commerce and mechanics we must observe and conform to the depressing laws that govern process and work? Bounds should be set against the encroachments of whoever would limit the horizons of our fancy. Without its worries our race would be as devoid of topics for disputation as a dog, deprived of his fleas, is of use for his leisure. So I urge banishment to any country in the throes of politico-economic revaluation, of all persons who threaten hereafter to resolve our perplexities.

As Editor of this record, it is stipulated that I am not obligated to subject my own person to the disciplines required for the establishment of that Self the Martian declares may be found by hard seeking. The being I think I am, even if he be no better than the subject of his own activities, is probably more tolerable as friend and companion than his internal prototype, who if developed into a positive, could hardly refrain from instituting invidious comparisons between himself and his contemporaries.

JOHN O'HARA COSGRAVE

CONTENTS

itarian and that they are not alive for their own benefit. Races ignorant of their identity or rights are servile. Freedom the offspring of knowledge. Cryptic defense of religion and of Mrs. Eddy.

templative apes. Pursuit of the Lost Factor. Dual
environments. No activity its own occasion. Is
the individual his occupation? Industry no end
in itself. Our philosophies just juvenile culture.

Men do not deserve their digestions. Tibetan
Sage on earth because of a miscarriage. The culture of escape. Occidental vs. Oriental creeds.
Captains of Industry as Mahatmas of the environment. Original version of the Garden of
Eden legend. Does experience belong to him
who has gained it or to him who created the opportunity? Subject matter of discovery predates
its identification.

Martian scientists analyze the properties exhibited by living organisms. Life something other
than energy, and does not design its habitations.
Plants and animals live off the country and follow
the same conventions. Man and amœba, incarnate
appetites. Trends and course of human activities.
The problem of conscious participation. Morality dismissed as having no existence in itself. The
crucial question—is man just a body, or does an
entity pervade his parts? Civilizations exist independent of their memberships. Consciousness
the coordinating factor and the causative agent
in organic evolution. A protean power that has
escaped classification in knowledge.

up. Life's joys and sorrows arise from circumstances that accelerate or retard the motions of its bodies. Gold as subject, object and medium. The credit system. Divergent reactions of opposite categories. If someone kicks your dog, where do you feel his foot? The structure of identity. How oysters feel about the tide.

Dispassionate consideration of the phenomena of hypnotism. Only mind can measure the imponderable. The uncontrovertible facts: you are here, and you know it. Functions consciousness contributes to organism. Significance of the mechanics of a simple action. The problem of etheric exchange. Perception as factual as enunciation. How human beings overcome their isolation and insulation for the purpose of communication. Identity of the Universe resides in its unity, and is expressed in self-realization. Our Cosmos as the embodiment of a Logos whose obligations lie in the preservation of his own entity and orbit. Men as agents for the maintenance of His awareness. Go look for your own soul.

Tribulations of a bestseller. Cosmic speculations in a smoking car. Looking the facts in the face. The rough frames of living. Men, servants and victims of their circumstances; their identity geographical, their institutions, outgrowths of

economic need. Life's meanings, external to mediums and motions. Functions of an Intelligence
factor and how they are conducted. The Power
to Be, and Being. Has the Universe an invisible
government? Phases of reality. Man lives off the
equilibria he disturbs. Expansion of understanding as the means of altering relations. To be what
I am, more wonderful than to do what I do. Bird
and cage. Life an artifice. Human behavior as
electrolysis. Futility of progress without comprehension. Inequality and determinism. Is there a
Book in which the Fates of men are written?

XVIII. THE CHARTER AND CONSTITU-
TION OF IDENTITY

Minds play tricks on their owners. Development
and operations of an unpremeditated talent.
Dual structure of man. Life, the product of machineries organized for its delivery. Role of the
individual prescribed by organism and defined
by public opinion. A plot with all creation for
accomplice. Looking and Listening-posts of the
All-Consciousness. We are not party to the conditions that enfold us. Characteristics of the Ordainment external to our senses. If the Universe
is a unity, events are fulfillments of purpose.
Commercial practices as analogues of cosmic
mechanics. The process of evolving executives.
Man's career, the dramatization of innate tendencies. Mother Nature attends to her exchanges, indifferent to controversy.

THE
ACADEMY FOR
SOULS

THE
ACADEMY FOR SOULS

The Martian introduces himself. How he reached Earth. Pattern of his individuality projected here by powerful etheric waves. Recovers consciousness and faculty, and integrates an invisible organism. Superiority of Martian culture, and knowledge of the laws of energy and matter. An arrogant and supercilious personality. Declares the race of men benighted, and our scientist's ignoramuses. Life on this planet a muddle.

MY encounter with the Martian occurred in this manner. After a solitary dinner I had settled down in my library with a book on Behaviorism which I expected to finish before retiring, when at my elbow I heard a strange, thin voice: "It's a shock to be addressed by a being you cannot see," it began, "but a blind man would think nothing of it. I'd like to talk to a rational human."

Sharply I turned in the direction of the sound. I saw no one.

"If I stay here long enough I shall institute classes in gland and nerve control," the voice continued contemptuously. "Here are you presumably sensible—your ear registers spoken words, but because neither lips nor a microphone is in sight your whole organism is panic-stricken. Exert your mind. Calm yourself. I am no ghost even if I am outside the radius of your visual apparatus."

"Who and where are you?" I asked with an effort to regain composure.

"At your elbow," was the reply, "anxious to interest you—also to sit down if you'll pull over one of those armchairs as near your own as possible. I've managed to tune my voice to your auditory range, but the effort is exhausting. In this heavy atmosphere I tire easily."

There was assurance in the tones of my extraordinary visitant, and though it was hard to subdue my palpitations I moved a chair into the position designated, and faced the voice.

"That is better," it said, in the manner of one sinking among cushions. "Now get a grip on yourself and be prepared for surprises."

Literally I saw nothing. The voice came out of the air a few feet from my ears. It was as though there was a radio nearby, but there is no radio in my house.

"I am an inhabitant of Mars," the voice began, "by profession an engineer and inventor especially interested in etheric communication—what you here call radio. By the application of physical principles possibly beyond your capacity to understand which are extensions of the potencies you are still using as a toy, I have bridged the gap between our worlds. Your sense of probability is outraged, but bear with me further. Perhaps because Mars is an older solar entity or that our skull insulation is less thick, I have found that our knowledge of physics and of the properties of energy and matter greatly exceed your own. We use voltages so powerful that literally we have been able to make over the surface of our planet. Martian telescopes of immensely higher magnification than your best have been for ages focused on the earth as our nearest neighbor in space. Our curiosity

about your ways of life—the degree of your mental acquirements—is enormous; we have bombarded you with waves of
low and high frequencies without eliciting response. Just as
your learned bodies discuss projected flights to the moon,
ours debate possibilities of visiting this planet.

"It was my good fortune to discover certain laws that revolutionized the old methods of generating and transmitting
power. About the same time researchers found the principles
underlying the integration of forms—you will yet learn that
all life bodies are based on an etheric mold just as a building
is supported on its design. Out of these and other findings
I derived clews that set me thinking of a way to realize my
greatest ambition—to be the first Martian to visit the Earth.

"I reasoned that, if one could release the positive pattern
of a physical being, there was power available to project it
to the Earth and be sure it got there. But how to reintegrate
it without special mechanical receptors puzzled me. For ten
years I experimented. I believed the magnetic charge on the
pattern would ensure a reassembling of the psychic organism
with its faculties, but that without its correspondent matter it would be equivalent to a ghost. In search of the laws
that underlie the growth of forms, I studied plant and insect
life and the transmutation of soil, sap and sunlight as exemplified in leaves and flowers, and the miracle by which the
cells of the caterpillar within the cocoon are converted into
the butterfly. Still, there appeared no way of evading the
planetary conditions that condemn all growths to the slow
processes of fertilization and cell division in the terms of the
environment. There are no passports in interstellar space.

"After years of study of what you call occult practices but
which are none other than exercises for developing the positive potential in the organism, I learned a method of leaving

my body at will, retaining consciousness while outside it, and with the aid of my associates, had this psychic entity transmitted by etheric waves directly to stations on our own moons and returned to base by the same agency. There my physical frame awaited me, and temporary dissociation had not affected its mechanisms. By accident, on one occasion, the carrier waves were deflected and fell on a large sheet of ice. The glacial surface turned out to have the properties of a detector and coherer and I recovered objective consciousness to find myself stranded in a region remote from all habitations. On Mars we are far advanced in the art of communicating by telepathy, and I generated energy to acquaint my associates with my plight. While they were transporting the apparatus to return me to my laboratory I discovered that long exposure in that frigid atmosphere had in some strange way changed the atomic pattern of the psyche, and it was with difficulty that later I adjusted myself to the cellular structures of my body. From this harassing experience I reasoned that the psychic organism must possess capacity to sustain itself through other agencies than those with which we were familiar.

"After the illness that followed this mishap, I found my mind had gained resiliency and definiteness of focus, and that literally there had occurred a shift in the seat of consciousness, which conferred a keener sense of identity and an unbelievable ascendancy over my physical organism. I learned how to control even the subtlest of its processes and, in the exercise of this power, widened and deepened the scope of my intelligence. When assured that this inner integration had proceeded as far as seemed necessary for my purpose, I decided to make the great experiment.

"Though there was tremendous opposition to overcome,

I eventually prevailed on the Supreme Council of Engineers who form our governing body (of which I was the head), to harness our greatest power generators in such fashion as to furnish rays strong enough to carry across the space abyss and penetrate the wall of your atmosphere to a frozen mountain lake in the Andes, which the chief astronomer had located as best suited to my purpose. However extraordinary it may seem, I am at your elbow by virtue of an ingenious use of forces which are as natural as the oxidization of blood in breathing or the utilization of food in the bodies of men."

"Interesting but implausible," I broke in. "Hitherto Martians who appeared in fiction on this planet came in rockets and emerged here with their bodies intact. Apparently you lacked the ingenuity of Mr. Wells' heroes since you had to leave your corporeal parts behind."

"At least you regain self-possession," returned the voice, "if I may so construe this attempt at humor. Incidentally some of the imaginative literature produced here, and a few of your moving pictures are rather good—I speak of course from the point of view of a higher civilization."

There was so much arrogance in the tone of this remark that I started, raised myself in the chair, and again looked intently at the spot from which the sound seemed to come. Listening, I had persuaded myself that I was plunged in the depths of a vivid dream and should wake later and regard it as no more than an unwonted experience. With a sharp gesture I passed my arm over the chair at my elbow, but there was no resistance.

"You are wide awake," the voice commented, "at least as conscious as an undeveloped mind can be. Try to realize that he who speaks is as definitely a denizen of your earth as yourself. Give him the attention and consideration due a stranger in your home. I do not ask you to believe what I say, so accept me as a guest with a strange story. Your arm passed through me just now, and, curiously I was unaware of any sensation. Conceive me a bodiless photo-electric cell capable of converting intelligence impulses into sound waves and you will have a distorted negative of my physical constitution; otherwise I represent consciousness without force, which explains why I can pass my hands over your face without effecting nerve response. Perhaps though," this with a little sigh, "it is difficult to persuade a Behaviorist that the universe contains anything he cannot weigh or measure."

At last the reality of the situation penetrated my mind and I summoned my faculties to bear on it. There flashed into my consciousness the sentence:

"The highest achievement of man is to exercise self-control in an emergency." So I said:

"All this is extravagant. I don't know what to think or to say."

The voice interrupted.

"Remember the patience and restraint of Balaam when his ass spoke. Probably he was just as shocked over the affair as you are now, but he listened and remembered, which is the full extent of the tolerance I seek from you."

I bowed towards my invisible vis-à-vis.

"Balaam shall have nothing on me—though it's surprising to think of a Martian quoting a fable from the cornerstone of Fundamentalism."

"Not more surprising than to hear a voice from the void in full light," was the reply. "However, since you are now equal to the occasion, I'll proceed."

"On the understanding that none of the premises already submitted are to be taken for granted," I replied—

"For instance; the idea of entity being separate or separable from the physical organism, or having an independent existence, is at variance with the conclusions of scientific authority."

The Martian emitted a sound resembling a chuckle.

"Thank heaven," he replied, "an ethereal body can register a sense of humor. I am laughing. Many ages ago Martians believed that the legs walked the horse—every planet has to explore itself out of its delusions. Just now your scientists are coagulated in a mechanistic eddy from which they will not emerge until their intelligence catches up with their information."

"By which you mean what?" I asked sarcastically.

"You have the alphabet and vocabulary, and you talk, but science has given you no grammar. You apply the general laws of construction and development but have not yet realized that the basic principles of all creative work and growth are the same. The knowledge you have piled up so carefully is not coordinated. Though you know better, you ascribe to matter properties it is incapable of exhibiting. You live in a world which you have partially made over by the exercise of an innate creative faculty, but, though you know exactly the series of processes and practices by which your structures and machines are brought into being—made to run or push, pull and carry, you believe that the innumerable plant and animal organisms surrounding you, including your own bodies, are natural products. Evolved! Like Topsy they just 'growed' that way. You deny magic and it's your creed."

"Surely you'll admit a distinction between a natural and an artificial product," I objected. "To classify a plant or an animal in the same category as a motor or house is far-fetched."

"Only intelligent," responded the Martian. "If you see an

extraordinarily ingenious machine whose efficient operation represents a grasp of chemical and physical laws perhaps beyond your own comprehension, don't you describe it as a marvelous invention and credit its development to an exceptional mind? It does not occur to you that it sprang out of the ground? The light that illuminates the pages of your book and distributes its beams throughout this room is the fruit of years of experiment by human beings. If someone explained that the energy and resistance through which it is developed had harnessed themselves for your benefit, would you not laugh?

"Your race has lived on this Earth thousands of years and yet scientists and philosophers have failed to grasp the fact that what is called nature is merely the raw material for mind. Wherever you find two agencies harnessed in a form to produce a third, take it for granted that the same type of intelligence that developed your phonographs, your automobiles and your radios has been at work."

"The world created in six days, etc.," I remarked sarcastically. "I never expected to encounter the Messiah the Fundamentalists have so long sought—but I hail you—incidentally, I prefer our own to the Martian brand of fairy stories. Where and who are these gifted chaps that invented plant life?"

There was a moment's silence.

"Obviously I've committed a cosmic blunder," the Martian exclaimed. "This shows how deluded the inhabitants of one planet may be about the intellectual development of their neighbors. The purpose of my foolhardy excursion was to gain knowledge. Because the Earth was larger than Mars and nearer the sun, I had persuaded myself that your information about the laws and principles of the universe and your application of its splendid and obedient energies might be greater than our own. What do I find? A race just budding into self-consciousness, accepting appearances for realities, incapable of logical classification of the phenomena amid which it lives, and unable and indisposed to realize its errors."

"It must be disappointing after so long a trip," I said, making an effort to be sympathetic. "Really I did not intend to be offensive; but to hear a voice out of the air retailing fables that our authorities have exploded so many years ago, is irritating."

"I understand," the Martian replied in a more cheerful tone. "I knew the worst before I talked to you. Since my arrival I've done considerable reading and exploring, and discovered long ago that I had fallen into an arrested development. It was just to confirm my conclusions that I accosted you. You were alone, reading a pseudo-scientific book. It was an opportunity to test my voice and my English. To my own satisfaction it has been demonstrated that an etheric organism in a foreign atmosphere can attach to itself sufficient energy to be capable of creating and projecting sound waves in orderly succession without the agencies of lungs, larynx, tongue and lips. So I will say good night."

"Now that you have broken the ice and excited my curiosity, don't fade out on me," I exclaimed with some alarm, for, though I had been rude to my invisible guest, his strange conversation had deeply interested me.

"Besides," I added, "you have nowhere to go."

"You fail to appreciate the privileges of invisibility," retorted the Martian, "I go where I please since this body of mine has all the properties of its etheric constituents. So far as you are concerned I cease to exist when I stop speaking—

but I may remain here among your cushions as long as it suits me. I have spent days and nights in the White House, in Buckingham Palace, in the mansions of millionaires and in the slum houses of your paupers. I know more of humanity than any living being who ever visited this earth. A pretty mess you have made of things."

"Perhaps I should be more comfortable if you were a little less superior," I suggested as gently as possible.

"It's churlish, I'll admit," the Martian replied with the first touch of graciousness he had exhibited, "but excusable under the circumstances. Your fear, hostility and incredulity irritate me. I'm filled with resentment over the condition of affairs on this planet, and allowed myself a psychic body's equivalent of blowing off steam. However, we are both engaged in a rare experience, and, if you care to have me do so, I shall regard it as a privilege to offer a view of the cosmos that does not seem to have occurred to your philosophies."

"My ears are at your service then," I bowed toward my visitor.

Trees as inventions. Mechanical determinism on Mars. The hierarchy of Science. An iconoclast asperses the fabric of its faith. Matter denied capacity to create forms. Natural selection called wishful thinking. Universe peopled with conscious beings of various development. Cults and heresies. A tyranny overthrown by propaganda. Renaissance. A civilization of reason and intelligence.

"I SHALL avoid mystery as far as is practical," the Martian began, "but do try to realize that this earth of yours is no more than a village in the universe, and, that elsewhere, are beings to whom your intellectual attainment would seem but little better than that of bees and ants.

"Perhaps I should begin by describing my sensations and observations when self-consciousness returned and I found myself on the icy surface of the lake in the Andean gorge that had acted as coherer of the etheric waves on which my egoic organism was projected from Mars. Above snow level, surmounted by jagged white peaks, there was a sparse vegetation and a fairly large insect colony flourishing in spite of the brief hours of light and the chill winds of the locality. My faculties, undimmed by cell tissues, discerned the inner structures and processes of these forms, and I recognized that the methods of transmuting the chemical constituents of the soil and fixing solar radiation to manufacture products suitable for the digestive apparatus of higher organisms, were similar to our own. Like yourselves, we live off the country, though we have a better understanding of the expert craftsmanship through which every atom of earth, air, fire and water is made to contribute to the sustenance of the planetary life.

"When my subtle frame had drawn to itself from light and the atmospheric gases ions essential for its reintegration, I descended to the lowlands and saw the magnificent spectacle of the great forests of that region, so rich in their profusion of noble forms and graceful contours. In comparison with these exuberant specimens of multiplied cell development our Martian vegetation seemed vague and shadowy, and I realized the superiority of your place in the Sun and the potency of that proximity. I spent some time thereabouts, analyzing the molecular fabrics and the physiology of these superb organisms, and found the atomic patterns of far greater density and the ratios of transformation, combustion and respiration slower than our own. I wondered then to what degree the higher beings I knew inhabited the Earth would be affected by the strength of this superabundant, radiant energy that had generated such resistant tissues in its vegetative population."

"Why population?" I ventured.

"Surely plants are living beings," insisted the Martian. "They are born, grow and die like yourselves. I regard the tree as one of God's greatest inventions."

"From your own scientific standpoint, objection to using the term in such a connection is well grounded. Some 600 years ago—at the period of your middle ages, if someone on Mars had alluded to a tree as an invention he would have been derided by the mechanists and behaviorists who made the opinion of that era. We were then committed to the theory of automatic evolution and development of species by natural selection. We had found that the instrumentalities,

which conducted lives on our planet carried agencies that explained and accounted for their performance. In intellectual
mechanical and social ascertainment we were abreast of your
present attainment.

"Our scientists were satisfied that they had got rid of superstition and had found the working basis of things as they
are. It was the apex of our own age of materialism and in
our schools and colleges this doctrine had ousted the creative myth and all other supernatural traditions. Belief in a
God or in soul, mind and consciousness—or any agency imperceptible to the senses, or which could not be weighed or
measured or tested, was as unpopular then as it is here today.

"Among our engineers was a minority which clung to the
notion that the accepted explanation of phenomena took
more for granted than the rigid standards of science justified.
Their leader was a distinguished and wealthy inventor—a
man who united to the genius of an Edison something of
the dialectic skill of your old Socrates. He made a practice
of attending the congresses of the great scientific bodies and
propounding awkward questions. If a Martian be no more
than a protoplasmic mechanism, a product of carbon oxygen, hydrogen and a few other elements, he would say—by
what natural agency were these elements so associated as to
achieve that miracle of architecture, the Martian body? Its
knowledge and use of subtle and complicated chemical processes were far beyond the consciousness of the race. If the
physical texture of the brain held and accounted for all the
operations a being performed, why was it unable to penetrate the secrets of its own works and the mode of its operations? Martians had devised out of inert matter—the same
materials that composed living organisms—a multiplicity
of tools and engines for an infinity of purposes, but these

were planned and not planted, did not grow but were put together. None of our agencies could propagate themselves or determine their own performances; to each it was necessary to add a conscious being to guide and compel their accomplishments. If matter carried creative and directive capacity without any visible agency of direction, as it seemed to do in nature, why did it withhold inspiration from us?

"Then this iconoclast would go on to beg the pundits to explain where and when the atmosphere and the Sun, the recognized forces of nature which, according to accepted doctrines, were accountable for the flora and fauna of Mars, had lost the capacity of inventing forms and of combining gases and minerals which they exercised when this our world was young. Of course the age of miracles was over, but he wondered if there were no other instrumentalities at work that exercised faculties akin to those we applied when we made gasoline explode in a cylinder to cause wheels to revolve. As an engineer, he found it difficult to believe that such simple agencies as stimulus and response really accounted for the phenomena represented by a field flower or a Martian.

"Since he had helped in the development of aircraft he accepted evolution, he is further quoted. Had he not conducted countless experiments in the adjustment of this machine to the medium it traversed? It originated in a mental conception, took shape on a draughting board, was metamorphosed into a form of wood and canvas, equipped with a motor to revolve a propeller and finally made to fly. The original aeroplane was a crude appliance beside the graceful shapes that now swarm the air. If these machines could speak, doubtless they'd attribute the changes in their formation to natural selection—adaptation to environment and so forth, but he and other engineers had performed this natural selection through their own brain and hand agencies, which fact led him to think that the potency of nature to create and animate moths, butterflies and birds, and endow them with the several instrumentalities of flight, direction and digestion with which they were equipped, might be exaggerated.

"You can imagine the resentment such unorthodox remarks excited among our old time materialists. Here was an expert assailing the very basis of their faith. He was asked to name the agencies responsible for bird flight and insect movement, or who taught plants to convert carbon and store sunlight in sugar and starch? He explained that he saw none but, being a good mechanist and knowing something of the properties and characteristics of the substances of organic growths, he realized these lacked the imagination, ingenuity and knowledge essential to devising such forms and processes as they exhibited. He possessed no more information about what mind was than anyone else, but some faculty inherent in him as a self-conscious being enabled him to manipulate matter into a form and animate it with energy to perform a task, and he thought it logical to believe that every effect must have a causal being commensurate with the phenomena it developed.

"Another distinguished skeptic created a still more rancorous dissension because in an article in an important periodical, he set forth that, since it had been established that the same elements composed the universe, the same laws must prevail in all parts of it, varied only by the physical circumstances of their application; that since Mars was the home of innumerable life forms in successive stages of development, it was childish to presume that the same conditions did not obtain elsewhere throughout the cosmos. Elsewhere, then, there must be self-conscious beings with similar instincts and aptitudes, dealing with each other and the exigencies within their worlds much as we did at home. Like ourselves, they must sustain themselves off the lands of their birth, and generate energy for their activities by burning in their bodies substances derived from their soils.

"However unlike us in appearance they might happen to be, their position in the scheme of things must turn on the degree and freedom of their intelligence, and intelligence plus its vehicular life force, he argued, need not be dependent on a particular type of body, because it could adjust itself to function in whatever organisms were prescribed by the tensions, pressures and proximity to the Sun of each individual sphere.

"It was this skeptic who advanced the proposition that a Martian was more than merely an inhabitant of Mars. He was a citizen of the universe. He ranked there according to his knowledge and sense of identity, and while it was probable that many of his fellows on adjoining globes were less civilized than he, it was possible there were others who had advanced much further.

"Our history also records the development at this period, of a heresy which seriously disturbed the Martian medical profession and aroused anger and ridicule among scientists. Sects had arisen that were practicing magic rites on their members, claiming that the mind controlled the body and that disease could be cured if you believed it did not exist. This was akin to the Christian Science and New Thought theories which seem to exasperate your best thinkers. The worst of it was that the types of treatment applied by these practitioners were often successful and the creed proved an extraordinary source of consolation to those who had adopted it. Obviously such methods contravened the established order of things, since our greatest men had proclaimed there was no such agency as mind. Mention of a creator or of the soul in intellectual circles, proclaimed one ignorant or old-fashioned.

"You are aware how hard it is to change public opinion here, and, that it is practically impossible to persuade a mechanist, a behaviorist, a psychologist or any of the other experts on life that there is anything in the scheme of things for which they are not able to account. However, the old inventor I mentioned was a shrewd propagandist, and, in about ten years our whole country was in revolt against the scientific orthodoxy. Religion, which had been chastened during the naturalistic régime, had a great boom following this exposure, and its priests and ministers who had been despised as disciples of outworn tradition, were again sought and given attentive hearing.

"This was the beginning of our renaissance. Science, humbled by the rejection of its authority, threw off its inhibitions and, instead of taking for granted the phenomena of objective life as isolated aspects, began to study them in relation to the world as a whole. Automatism and coincidence were abandoned. Of the prodigies of the faith-curists the ablest men took cognizance seeking to find the basis for the changes in physical tissue wrought through fixation of ideas. Psychic investigation became a serious study, and all the strange practices of occultism, to which millions in our backward races adhered in spite of the contempt which labeled their creeds superstition, were scrutinized for clews to the nature of that kernel of reality of which it began to be obvious that appearances were no more than the shell. Released from prejudice and formalism, physicists and chemists tackled anew the problem of life, and thereafter was evolved a civilization of reason and intelligence.

"We are realists administering life in the interest of its characteristics. Health and comfort have been standardized. Races, boundaries and creeds were abolished centuries ago.

"We have a common language and religion. Our golden rule is anchored in the behaviorism of the atom.

"We believe in the continuity of individual being and that physical existence is to be regarded as an enjoyable opportunity for the development of wisdom through the extension of consciousness.

"Industry is no more than a means for the enhancement of living, so the distinction between work and play has ceased.

"Rank is defined neither by possession nor in intellectual attainment, but in capacity to apply knowledge to service.

"Aspiration is enlisted for the good of the whole.

"Happiness to us is profit on the right investment of talent, and its currency is growth.

"We know not wars, poverty or slums."

In defense of Orthodox Science. Its rescue of mankind from superstition. We are creatures of the environment. Martian ridicules theory of spontaneous generation of life. Location does not explain function. The fallacies of Behaviorism. A causal agent required for every phase of phenomenal activity. Engineers suggest objective study to find what life is about. They draw up statement of principles and elements coordinated in the production of work.

STANDARDIZED health and comfort—the drab words lingered in my mind. I wondered if there were good restaurants on Mars? Did the Atomic Verities mean that every human electron had to stay in its own orbit—or what? If rank represented mere utility—perhaps the government of our neighbor was composed of the presidents of public service corporations. As these disquieting queries streamed through my consciousness suddenly I bethought myself of a host's responsibilities to a guest, which set up the problem—if the guest is invisible and uninvited is there an obligation? It's a nice point but before it had half a hearing I heard myself saying:

"Refreshments are in order after that flight—but I'm embarrassed what to offer. There's neither nectar nor ambrosia in the icebox—only proteins and carbohydrates. What you may have, you can take."

"Alas," responded my visitor sadly, "an appetite is among the other physical effects I had to discard before leaving

Mars. But don't worry:—The void sustains its own voices. Remember I am *vox et præterea nihil*."

"Since convention is out of order we'll resume controversy," I said. "The attitude you set forth is so foreign to our own scientific thinking, and your ascription of personality to agencies we are accustomed to consider material so opposed to the soundest views held here that I can't grasp the bearing of your argument. Assuming that it implies criticism of our ways of thinking," I went on, "the inhibitions you allege to limit the investigations of our biological experts, psychologists, neurologists and physicists do not exist. They are free and conscientious men searching for the truth. I am convinced most of them would be gratified if their researches revealed evidence of God and a soul, and it is with reluctance they have recorded the conclusion that there is no warrant for believing in the existence of supernatural agencies or beings.

"For ages Earth's populations had been dominated by superstitions. Through our religious mentors we were taught the preposterous doctrine of a world created out of the void in six days, whereas geology shows us life has existed on this planet for millions of years.

"No one of intelligence doubts the evolution of the being, Man, from a unicellular organism back in the ages beyond memory, and our bodies in their prenatal development carry the patterns of this ascent from the lowest forms of organism through the chain of fish, reptile and mammal to human. Thus man is no more than the ranking animal who having developed an organ of reason, the brain, has by painful process of trial and error built up the form of civilization under which we live.

"You find we have made a mess of things—it is less of a

mess than when science began to take leadership of humanity away from religion a hundred years ago. We have ascertained some of the truth about our world and discovered the working principles of the living forms that surround us. We know something of the transforming forces through whose interactions the food needed to generate the energy we use is produced. We dare look up at the sky when lightning flashes and the thunder roars without fear that some angry god is proclaiming his wrath. Disease, we realize, is not a punishment for our sins, but the penalty of our errors.

"Since we find ourselves an integral part of the vegetative functions of the sphere on which we revolve through space, nourished by its foods and drink, exercising our faculties on the resources it offers, and stimulated to exertion by the will to adapt these to the finer fulfillment of the needs engendered by our circumstances, surely it is logical to assume that these visible, compelling and restraining agencies account for our place in the scheme of things, and represent the motivation of our activities.

"What is a man anyway, but a mammal equipped with instrumentalities to keep his footing in the environment of which he is a part? Since its stresses have supplied him with organs to deal effectively with its stimuli and reactions, he is on the way to conquest of its resistances. All I gather from your discourse is that you wish to plunge us back to the magic and terror which we have so mercifully escaped."

A gurgle that sounded like applause from the Martian.

"My attempt at 'hear, hear,'" he said. "That I take to be the note of the emotion you call approval. An etheric organism imperfectly localized is limited in its capacity to exteriorize its reactions. If this apparatus of mine keeps growing,

I may yet develop into a cheerleader. In the meantime—assume enthusiasm."

"Thanks for your consideration," I returned.

"Consideration is exactly what is implied," my visitor continued, raising the pitch of his voice a trifle higher. "Your points are well taken, and the defense admissible as far as it goes.

"The trouble is that mankind, intellectually, is in the situation of a swarm of semi-conscious bugs who, having penetrated the mechanism of a plant sprinkler system, are satisfied that the rich rainfall of their vicinity is no longer a mystery. Acceptance of any environmental phenomena in the terms of their immediate causes is but a single remove beyond the superstition of the savage that the thunderstorm to which you so feelingly allude represents the wrath of an offended deity.

"Of the aspects of your curiously abnormal lives nothing has amazed me more than the idea which so obsesses your thinkers that motion is an adequate explanation of movement, or that the revolution of worlds and wheels is an end in itself—in other words, the mechanical theory of the universe. Since you know the nature of the atom and have allocated your planet in the solar and stellar system, it is obvious that your earth can be no more than an infinitesimal cog in a mammoth engine and must partake of its mechanical constitution; but there is more to an engine than its parts. Its dependence on the location in which it is set up does not really control or account for its functions.

"For my God I prefer a Being commensurate with the performances that issue from him—and the deity called Environment, most favored by the intellectuals among you, lacks the several resources the role requires. I chuckle over the wholesale scrapping of miracles, including the virgin birth, by your pundits, who yet cherish the touching faith that in some inscrutable way sunlight and warm seawater beget life. Just an accident, like the detachment of the planets and the establishment of our solar system by the agency of a maverick star that had broken out of its gravitational field and hit our pleasant luminary a glancing blow in a soft place.

"Of course we are entitled to guess about the universe according to our notions, but considering the manner in which heavenly bodies keep their distances, these hazards seem better imagination than physics.

"Now on Mars we are real mechanists. According to our code, in analyzing a phenomenon it is obligatory to require an agency for every phase of the activities it represents. Applying that prescription to vehicular traffic in New York, for instance, instinctively I segregated the several elements combined in its movements. First, that the carriages and trucks bore passengers or freight and preceded in different directions, which indicated use, intentional divergence and destinations. Next the character of these conveyors—automobiles—heavy appliances in swift progression—I took it for granted that one of the many energies you have learned to use had been harnessed to their wheels. I discovered that the agent of propulsion was gasoline artfully exploded in cylinders to set pistons moving inside. I said to myself—Contraction and Expansion-the ancient stand-by—force confined in a frame to develop motion.

"I observed, also, that the lines and structures of all these machines were adapted to the strains and tensions of the environment—character and inclination of streets and planetary atmospheric pressure—and that their various parts, transmission, starter, wheels, brake, lights, had their reflex arcs on the dashboard. Discretional and directional apparatus being absent, I deduced that the processes of use as initiating movement, steering, turning and stopping were centered in and performed by a detachable agency—the driver.

"Thus I accounted for the several elements represented in this movement of wheeled appliances—its reasons, the method of effecting it, and how it is fulfilled. The pervasive trilogy present here as on Mars, I concluded. Probably the same principles prevail throughout the Milky Way—the inevitable sequence of the law—so if I should find myself on a satellite of Sirius, beings would be discovered operating natural agencies on precisely parallel terms."

"One does not have to be a Martian or a Messiah to follow that kind of reasoning—in fact you record what every school boy sees and knows—by use of his eyes. Where's the occult significance?" I interrupted.

"The old problem of unconsciousness and consciousness," replied the Martian. "You do what you know how to do, but don't know why or by what means. The flights of birds south, the marvelous functioning of ants, are ascribed to instinct. If it were possible to interrogate a bee on his flight and demand of him the purpose of his trips between the flowers and the hive, he would tell you he was storing honey and knew just where to get it and carry it to the comb. Everyone did it and certainly no general principles he ever heard of need be cited. Now, in separating the several elements entering into the movement of traffic, I discriminated clearly between the roles of user and the instruments employed for effectuating the purpose of the user. I hoped to provoke in you realization of the commonplace fact that though man and apparatus might be conjoined and are made of similar substance; they belong to opposite poles of the universal mode.

"Another truism, you are about to suggest, forgetting possibly that the philosophy most widely accepted in your learned institutions today, recognizes no such difference in categories. Behaviorism describes the human being as a biological combination of three interactive systems of response to environment—the muscular, the visceral and the cerebral. It interprets the business of living as interchanges among these systems as they react to the strains and stresses of the external world that surrounds them.

"Life, its advocates conjecture to be a fortuitous incident contrary to all the interests and principles of the vicinity in which it occurs (an immaculate conception) but which, persisting in the face of prejudice, has cumbered the Earth with its several kingdoms. After innumerable experiments at adapting itself to the pioneer elements of sun, wind and water, it has evolved a universal-jointed appliance called Man whose organism unites the best qualities of the substances which it has filched from its parents and presumes an independence it does not possess.

"In reality, they say, the set of interactive muscles with which this machine is equipped no more than parallel the interactive system of the elements and has no purpose, save to interpret in its individual behavior, the forces that birthed, nourish and play around it. Its real achievement is self-preservation; its works, including the paraphernalia it calls civilization, mere byproducts which further condition and complicate its being.

"When this conception is put into plain language, it conveys the theory that life is a species of spontaneous combustion generated by the impact of the sun's rays on the earth and that after aeons of exposure, without the interposition of other than the several original forces, there occurred or were bred, the vegetable and animal forms among which is Man. Man, then, is the protoplasmic equivalent of a barometer-thermometer linked with an internal combustion engine to which is attached a combination radio receiver, phonograph and broadcasting apparatus plus an automatic moving picture camera which develops its own films and files them for reference.

"The business of this strange instrument is to find fuel for the motor from which its power as a going-concern is derived in the terms of the stimuli imposed by the environment as registered by its barometer-thermometer, ear receiver and camera. Furthermore, this little community of appliances, through its nerve connections, reports all its internal and external creaks and strains to its phonograph, which broadcasts them through its laryngeal sounding-board in an arranged series of noises it calls speech. Thus language is no more than verbalization of the whirring of the bodily machinery, the heart beat, blood circulation, lung inflation, the flexing of muscles, digestive and structural adjustments and all the other interchanges among parts in pursuance of their obligation to the paths they pursue. When one remembers that each of these separate organic instrumentalities with all its properties, *sprouted* through the mediation of an ultra mechanical force known as adaptation—it is possible to grasp the basis of the expression—'ain't nature wonderful!'

"Every now and then I have to recall the fact that you earthlings carry fourteen and one-half pounds atmospheric dead weight on every square inch of your bodies including the head. Under so much pressure, intelligence is seriously handicapped.

"A thesis or conception which assigns general effects to local causes is, to a Martian, incompetent or childish. Time is not more widely separated from space than form from force, or function from mechanism. At what place in the scheme of things does knowledge or information, which certainly condition most of your habitized responses, become factors of the environment? Or, have they no reality exterior to the words in which they are verbalized or registered, or the circumstances to which they are the instinctive reaction? Rather too many premises and far more phenomena outside the vehicle of your scientific method than it has accommodation for, in the opinion of a disinterested observer—but primitive thinking always entertains me.

"Not so long ago I enjoyed myself listening to a discussion among a group of Zulus investigating the corpus of a tenantless aeroplane that had fallen from the skies upon a remote South African veldt. It was a miracle, but its inexplicable advent did not prevent these savages exploring its engines, propeller and structures. They agreed it was not a bird though it had traveled in the air, but the conjunction of its parts told them nothing of its purpose, destination, method of propulsion or a single fact about its invention or development. Because it was beyond the radius of their information they characterized it as a mystery and of divine origin and hauled it off to the nearest Kraal, where it does duty as a god. Yet, they gathered from their rough analysis as much and no more than an autopsy furnishes of the identity, character or achievement of the man whose dead body the surgeons dismembered.

"Earlier in this discourse I sketched the story of our own intellectual revolution on Mars and the havoc wrought by a leader whose ironic interruptions set the academies at loggerheads. He was the spokesman for an organized movement among the engineering fraternity who had become

convinced that the mechanical determinism of the old scientific hierarchy was out of date. Their contention was that,
though force did move matter, the carrier was powerless to
redistribute its content in sequential order or in a definite
place. Further that, matter being inert and force casual, their
conjunction in a form was impossible without the interposition of some catalyzer; therefore an hypothesis that omitted
from its equation this quantity was fundamentally unsound.
To hold that life is a product of haphazard interaction between these elements is absurd, since life represents a divergent and independent principle, and it is axiomatic that
neither matter nor force can transmit a property it does not
possess. To ascribe potency to sterility is superstitious, they
argued, and they demanded formal scientific recognition of
the agency Mind, with its attributes of awareness, initiative
and integration, as the determinant factor in all creative activities.

"Imagine a protest of this character formally lodged with
the National Association for the Advancement of Science by
a prominent engineering society in New York, and you parallel the sensation it precipitated on Mars. Official science
was aghast at the presumption. To entertain propositions
so subversive of the established order meant the sacrifice of
the honorable structure of evolutionary development which
biology and physics had reared. It involved revaluation of
cherished formulas, scrapping adaptation, survival of the fittest and all the careful magic of automatism which accounted
for the existence and functioning of organic forms on the
score of response to environment. In fact the whole scientific
philosophy.

"The great Associations did not deign to reply, where
upon the engineers issued pamphlets aspersing the fabric

of this scientific faith, ridiculing its tenets, proclaiming its apostles to be no better than witchdoctors. Institutions they said, which could uphold the theory that a Martian represented no more than a tendency among protoplasmic cells, that these divided and multiplied to furnish him a form, such senses as he used and the faculties he applied in his job of subduing nature to his needs—such institutions, they declared, were capable of believing that automobiles assembled themselves and that skyscrapers came into being by magnetic attraction.

"In due course the malcontents unfolded a philosophy of their own which however crude, they asserted gave due weight to the several elements present in the performance of work. Roughly, it ran thus:

" 'We members of the race called Martian, are alive and are surrounded by the evidence of our own and our ancestors' achievements in making life supportable on the surface of this planet. We are builders of lofty edifices, have dug great canals and made magnificent machines and in these creations that we have imposed on the environment against its resistances, there must be represented the principles that underlie all achievement.

" 'Let us look at this world of our making from the viewpoint of honest mechanists and analyze the practices and transformations that enter into the organization and development of the structures that exhibit our powers. However minute our sphere or insignificant in the system in which it is a quantity, it shares the uniformity of law that regulates the precise movements of the great universe, so its own beat and rhythm must be in consonance with the cosmic measure.

" 'Since our knowledge of the nature of things proves that there can be no sequence without plan and no unfoldment save in furtherance of design, let us set it down as basic that where order is found, purpose is being manifested. Whose purpose and why, may ever be beyond our reasoning, but let us no longer be deceived by the delusion that our existence is happenstance, or that the physical vehicles in which we find ourselves at the beginning of consciousness were not made, but grew. Rather we must face the mystery of our being in the terms of our experience and, by observation of such arrangement and coordination as our lives exhibit, make a commencement at finding the truth about ourselves and our actual relation to this planet.'

"To this challenge the academies of physics and biology responded with the sneer that the rebellion was a revival, and that the objective of the engineering schism was no better than the reestablishment of God and religion. The reformers retorted that if by ascertainment it should be proved that God was essential to explain the operations of the universe they would as cheerfully believe in Him as they accepted the periodicity of the elements, the precession of the equinoxes, or the constitution of the atom. In the meantime they urged—'Let us examine what we do and how we do it— mayhap like bees and beavers, we are building better than we know'; and thereafter, they issued a statement of principles addressed to all the learned bodies on Mars, a statement for which serious consideration was asked. Transposed in terms of your thinking and language it ran about as follows:

"We deal with power and machines according to the character and capacity of two of the factors involved in the production of work. In order to accomplish any of the tasks of human activity, the first of these must be harnessed to the second and the sum of their interaction should represent a third—the intention or purpose for which power and machines were combined. In all performances

of our race these factors, each distinct from the other, are present and it is in their coordination, in the true terms of their individual properties that the science and the art of our profession are engaged.

"Thus all the works undertaken by us must be molded in the raw material our world furnishes, but it is their function and their results, not their form or substance which explain and justify their existence. So our edifices and utensils bear a dual identity—first, as prescribed by shape and weight as things in themselves, and second, as tools of use. We take it for granted that the structures and machines which we have made are no more than agencies to accommodate the needs inseparable from the nature of beings— living under the physical circumstances and conditions that prevail on Mars.

"Life is the creative principle which originates and animates the organisms that exhibit its character. It operates consecutively and continuously in a medium and atmosphere resistant to its nature, but whose properties are convertible to its needs. Though the predominant factor on our planet, Life itself is invisible; its individuality and quality are disclosed to us by the variety and development of the species that possess it and through which it is maintained.

"Men's operations are ever in the interest of a hidden employer, and in a hidden organ we call mind, we frame plans which subsequently are reborn in material form. All our acts are determined in the invisible and are neither perceptible nor tangible until invested in the clay or wood or metal of the environment in which they are devised to work. In the process of objectivization, designs and the energies essential to transfer them over our threshold of reality disappear: so that the things we see and touch and do are no more than the reflections and reactions, in physical substance, of plans and forces beyond the range of our sense organs.

"Since no thought or idea may be reborn into our world save

it comply with the conditions exacted by the gravity and pressure of its mass and atmosphere, there is implicit in all the works of engineering, information about the tensions, stresses, resistances and chemistries of this sphere. Our achievements are developed from the facts men have ascertained about the pattern and habits of the matter and force elements which must be coordinated and framed before the simplest task of construction and delivery may be accomplished.

"The body of this information is knowledge. Knowledge exists independent of its application, but has no value apart from its use. It is the key to the secrets of the environment's contents, but like the properties of the matter it defines, is inert unless motivated by some purposive and propulsive agency equipped to employ it. Though it be the instrument by which one compels his homeland to yield up its resources for the sustainment of his being and the erection of his edifices, it serves no end nor need of its own.

"Three diverse principles confront us—the nature of being—the life force through which it is transmitted and the physical world, the stage on which it expresses its inherent characteristics.

"In his own organism Man is the unit that integrates the special qualities of these factors, for in his work and the modes of his existence must be represented the instincts and demands of his being, which the stream of life transfers and reproduces in the exact conditions required by the properties of the theater in which the performance is given. Because the limitations of his sense organs exclude man from relation with the source of his actions, he is inhibited from responding to other stimuli than the effects that arise from them. So he is both actor and audience. He personates the role of First Cause in his environment but is unaware of the drama, the prompter and the setting, save as his identity is unfolded in the part he sees himself playing.

"Consciousness—that attribute of man's nature through which

he apprehends the visible and tangible world conveyed by his eyes, ears and touch, and memory—the record of his contacts there-in—make the continuity through which he traces his individuality and his potency. They are the clues by which he may realize the separateness of his vehicle, both from the results of its efforts and from the physical circumstances that envelop it.

"Thus man," the Engineer's statement went on to say, "is submerged in his works. By semi-instinctive processes he has forced this physical environment to yield its secrets to his needs and has erected structures that exhibit the character of his entity. Yet from all these he himself is apart, a blind instrument of the power that works within him. But of the nature of his identity enough evidence has been accumulated to enable us to diagnose its quality and type.

"The time then has come for a stock taking, a fresh examination through which the anomalies and obscurities that retard our progress as a race may be lifted and our true stature and relation to the scheme of creation determined.

"We urge that man and his works be studied in the same spirit of objectivity we devote to the analysis of an insect's habits or the atomic pattern of an ore. Prejudice, tradition and superstition must be discarded. To everything that moves sequentially must be applied the rigid formulas we have learned to follow in all instances of mechanical propulsion. No longer shall dynamic values be denied to forces exterior to our perceptions, for if we are to find the right proportions, accurate equivalents must be attached to every phase of our activities.

"In conclusion we may say that our experience indicates, that where organization and sequential operations are found, purposive intelligence is being revealed; where order, ordination; where process, administration. And, since every substance, object and life form of which we have cognizance both plays its own part and contributes its own quota of utility to the world as a whole, it is incredible that man does not share this common lot and yield some meed of value to whatever invisible but inevitable causative principle it is that originated and sustains his being."

"Rank dualism I call it," was my comment on this long exordium.

"*Inconvenient* dualism would be better," returned the Martian. "Your scientists and philosophers have merely excluded a natural principle to accommodate their hypotheses. One might mention the duality of the poles, of electricity, of the atom, even of the sexes—but—"

"To dream of a messenger coming all the way from Mars to unload such a farrago. In comparison with such elderly trappings of thought, psychoanalysis is sensible and Christian Science conservative."

I had interrupted with some heat, for though the stream of my strange visitor's argument had carried me a silent victim of his eloquence, his mythological absurdities had stirred my indignation. I was minded to give no further ear to his vagaries.

"Fortunately our own scientific formulas are so stoutly anchored on rock bottom ascertainment that we can laugh at such maunderings. A Martian prototype of Conan Doyle, I suppose, was chairman of the committee that drew up these findings."

"No," replied my visitor, "the leading spirit at the conference at which this modernistic credo was prepared was the great contractor who cut the first of the colossal canals which now seam the surface of Mars. The men who rallied to the support of this movement were the notable industrialists—the group of millionaires who then piloted our affairs. Hitherto engaged at amassing fortunes and absorbed in the details of occupation and pleasure, like their kind here, they had never faced the facts of their own experience.

"Business is realistic and when these sound minds were forced by the exigencies of a crisis at this period to compare what they knew about the way things happened with the scientists' explanations of origins and development, they recognized the underlying fallacy and joined the revolt.

"But, as among yourselves, science on Mars was sacrosanct. It was the established religion; for through its ascertainment of the laws regulating force and matter in the spatial area of life, it had contributed so magnificently to the comfort and knowledge of the race that to asperse its hypotheses represented atheism. Your own reaction at my mild attempt to lift the threshold of your understanding exhibits the tight grip of the academies on your mind. Eventually you will realize that this elaborate structure is no more than an intellectual doll's house and, in its relation to the truth, about as limited as a worm's notions of the chemistry of soils. 'Ah,' says the curious child, having picked its new watch to pieces, 'the uncoiling of this spring moves cogs which imparts motion to wheels, and the hands register time.' "

I yawned. Really, I could not help it. I interrupted:

"Interesting the way you tell it—picturesque, too, so far as color goes, but I can't see that a six hundred year old difference of opinion about the origins of life among Martians especially concerns me. Besides, you've been talking for three hours."

"Forgive me," the Martian replied contritely. "It is rather a load I'm saddling on an unaccustomed brain. Go to bed— let me come in tomorrow night and tell you more."

"But about yourself. What will you be doing in the interval? You can remain here of course—all I have is at your disposal."

I spoke with some solicitude. It seemed to me my visitor's lot must be lonely.

"Thanks for your thought," he returned, "but I'm to be envied rather than pitied. Sleep is the least of my needs and this gauzy thought body of mine is quickly wafted wherever I want to take it. I'm not yet tired of terrestrial scenery or cities, and as an anthropologist I'm picking up a lot of useless but entertaining information about the manners and habits of a rich primitive society."

"Shall I turn out the light?" I broke in.

"Do," replied the Martian. "It suddenly occurs to me that a sunrise on Lake Como might be worth looking at."

The Sun as kindler of Earth's machineries. Nature waste-
ful or economical, according to the observer's viewpoint.
Confused details assemble into patterns when the mind has
fathomed their proportions. What one wants—ever out of
reach; and why. Prohibition and morality on Mars. Sin not
in substance but in violating relations. Earth's business—
food production. Eat and be eaten, the universal law. Processes involved in converting a house in the mind from a
dream to a domicile.

THE sense of my visitor's personality was so strong, and
our clash of ideas had so interested me that I got to sleep
without realizing the strangeness of the affair. Next morning
my mind awoke to the extraordinary nature of the incident
and throughout the day recollections of his statements
kept recurring to my memory. To one's fellows one dares
not mention incredible adventures, so I was silent about
the experience, but it amused me to think of the responses
that would be aroused if I told what had happened to my
associates in the publishing house which is the scene of my
daily tasks. No one would take seriously a syllable of my
story—perhaps I should be reminded that dreams were not
fit subjects for conversation or that fiction is more convincing
to the eye than to the ear. Towards evening I found in myself
an eagerness for the Martian's return and made sure that
our séance should not be interrupted by the telephone or by
stray callers.

I was in my study by eight o'clock, arranged the chairs in the position that the Martian had designated as best befitting his intangible organism, and sat smoking a few minutes before I heard the thin, high-pitched, but exceedingly definite voice of my visitor at my elbow.

"I've had an interesting day," it said. "That sunrise was worth the trip. A clever arrangement of clouds set off the rising light—and there were magnificent colors. I prefer dawns to settings. To Earth the Sun is an excitement—the universal stimulant. He puts plant chemistries to work, leaves and grasses to their eternal tasks of extracting moisture from the soil, carbon dioxide from the air and at sugar making. All vegetable and animal tissues react joyously to his vital presence and everywhere the processes of life are awakened from the slumber of darkness and set expanding and contracting in compliance with the laws of their being."

"Rather mechanistic than poetical," I commented. "One might suppose a Martian gifted with the capacity to see the nature of things as they are would have something to offer about natural phenomena more picturesque than what is apparent to an ordinary observer."

"Unfortunately lyrical outbursts are not in my line," replied my visitor good humoredly. "I suppose I should have hummed a bar or two of the music of the spheres. Unfortunately my vibrations are not attuned to those melodies, if they exist. I find the large-scale manufacture of products carried on here by the agencies of nature so diverting that symbolism seems unnecessary. I might point out how admirably the series of processes at work on your planet utilize the energies of the innumerable agencies engaged, how sedulously they attend to their duties as converters of earth into food, or of light into fuel, or as scavengers disintegrating or removing decayed matter and useless surplus. So prolific, yet so economical. And withal, so beautiful. If only you humans had intelligence enough to grasp the magnitude and skill of the structure of which you are the material peak, how much more entertaining the spectacle and living of your lives would be."

"Nature economical—did you say," I hooted. "Why, she is wanton in her wastefulness. Think of the profusion of seeds she provides for the few plants that survive, or of the sparse hundreds of fish that escape into the waters from the millions of ova she spawns, of the multiplicity of the varieties of trees and shrubs that cover her areas, of the hordes of birds and beasts, of reptiles, of insect plagues—mosquitoes and boll weevils, useless and futile, far beyond our own or their food needs, cumberers and ravagers of the land, serving no use that intelligence can ascertain."

"Agreed," retorted the Martian. "Probably the aspect of your earth and its fullness does arouse in you the same emotion that an Eskimo would experience in a New York department store. He might marvel at the ingenuity invested in the multiplicity of strange and disparate articles of no use that he could imagine, and wonder at the character of beings who waste time on the creation of such quantities of fripperies. But compare his reactions with your own in a similar scene, in which every object is a thing of use, an appeal to the eye and the pocket; or with the attitude of the owner of the establishment to whom all these are but goods for sale—their variety prescribed and limited by demand, their place and display calculated, each a thing-in-itself, tagged as to price, and the history of its acquisition. Further, they exist as exhibits of some buyer's judgment of salability, are enumerated in inventories, are factors in the purpose of the institution and minister to its function as a machine of profit.

"Your authorities are agreed that there is no design in nature, but is there no suggestion in contrasting the primitive impressions of a savage about a subject which is strange to him with the inferences that occur to you? He sees all that you do, since he has the same organs of vision, but your eyes are the agents of the information your mind has gathered through its contacts and experiences in the surrounding civilization. With none of that learning did you enter this sphere but you have acquired it during the years of your sojourn. Its possession as definitely differentiates you from the Eskimo as my wider knowledge of the life exterior to the range of your enlightenment precludes real exchange of understandings between us.

"This is not a declaration of superiority since it only represents a variation in opportunity. I am merely illustrating, that confused details assemble into patterns when the mind has fathomed their proportions. A sightseer who surveys New York from the spire of the Chrysler Building sees a larger picture than he whose outlook is limited to the corner of 42nd and Broadway. And both viewpoints are narrow in comparison to that which his altitude affords an observer in an aeroplane."

"All of which indicates that you discern a purpose underlying the confusion and superfluity in the midst of which we have our being," I remarked. "It would be interesting to hear what you think it is?"

"The path to comprehension is not by revelation but through exploration," replied the Martian. "You are capable of being a mathematician, and of speaking Russian, but unless you devote attention to acquiring the matter of the science and the words of the language, you cannot do either. It is easy to lift the mind to a mountain top but you cannot take it there without its container, the body. For that purpose there are legs and nerves to release the muscles which move its bulk to the destination the mind has set. I have no magic to offer. This is the physical world. What occurs in it must be assimilated in its terms before it can be expressed through its means. It is realization of the facts about our beings and their structures that makes us Martians true mechanists. We are not satisfied that in defining their chemical relations we have conferred properties on things. We ask, where they got them and for what, bearing in mind that use is only the purpose of him who applies it. Like force, it enlarges with the information of the user. So I can tell you nothing; but I can show you where to look so that you may see for yourself."

"Sounds like a correspondence course personally administered," I murmured. "I had rather expected to be taken to the top of a high mountain and shown the countries of the world. There's an encyclopedia on the shelf through which I might satisfy most of my curiosities. Why should I submit to aural instruction that may be had more quickly by turning over its pages?"

"You'll get nothing there that I'll tell you," declared my visitor. "My interest is in viewpoints and vistas, not in mere facts. But if by turning to a given section you could find exactly what you seek, you must transfer the words to your brain and distil the meaning and its bearings by a process parallel to that by which your body converts food into animal tissue and extracts energy for its needs. Only by converting the substance of what the eyes record into a part of oneself is it possible to use information as material for speech or application. I am no better off than yourself. Life in any world is always uphill. What one wants is ever out of reach, and must be sought and taken by dint of mental or muscular effort. It is one of the Creator's tricks to keep us moving onward. If I did not know the contempt for their owners that cats would express if they could speak, I'd say that only the days of a domestic pet are truly happy.

"At this moment I am wondering what justification there is for usurping your ears and disturbing your complacence. Except that I'm exercising my voice and displaying my acquirements, I'm subserving no need of the type of being that I represent. Perhaps there's no real motivation other than suction—nature's unfailing response to the vacuum. Forgive me—really, I was but talking to myself."

"I'm sure you need a drink."

I blurted this out without the slightest consideration of the invisibility of the speaker. Something tragic in his tone excited fellow feeling.

"I do," replied the Martian mournfully, "but I've nowhere to put it. However, I can get the essentials of stimulation from odor, so help yourself, and you'll be helping me."

"Then prohibition is not the rule on Mars," I remarked after I performed the office indicated.

"From that error we recovered centuries ago," my visitor replied with an access of cheerfulness. "It is among the throes of the births of all civilizations. Throughout the innumerable solar systems which surround us, wherever minds occupy bodies, experiments at controlling appetites have been conducted. No particulars are as yet accessible, of course, but since our remote neighbors can be no other than human beings whatever forms they function in, at one time or another, depend upon it, they have made the same mistakes.

"As long as man believes himself to be no more than a

body, he will enact laws which, if he were no more than a body would correct the defects they are proposed to relieve. But in reality he represents a diverse principle—Mind—which unconsciously revolts at exterior attempts to usurp its own functions, so that denial, instead of a restraint, becomes an incentive. We on Mars have learned by experience that morality consists in holding all relations within the terms of their constituents. An engine being fed more gas than its carburetor can ingest is only drunk as a man who has imbibed more alcohol than his system can accommodate. The sin is not in the substance, but in violating the proportion that regulates their affiliation.

"This is merely by the way, however. The ascertainments of other civilizations are useless to one's own. All races learn by experiment—the trial and error route. There's no instinctive common sense. The reason why building codes or regulations prescribing behavior in relations to dynamos, machines and traffic are more effective than the Decalogue, is that these define properties and characteristics which take immediate vengeance on him who disregards them. Compare the respect and devotion a locomotive driver or the attendant of a dynamo lavishes on the mechanistic monsters whose power they direct, with the attitude these same individuals insensibly adopt towards religion or government or the other abstractions they are given to regulate their lives. Conviction, or the accretion of experience in the one instance—in the other, revelation. People know only what they've felt, and don't believe what they are told. It's futile railing at the obtuseness of populations. The conduct of life here represents a phase in the evolution of the race of which you are members. All the knowledge necessary to render you intelligent and even happy has been assembled, but you can no more take what you are not equipped to receive than a forty-five caliber cartridge can be adjusted to an air gun."

The voice subsided and ceased. For all I knew my visitor might have thought himself back to some celestial ceremony in Turkestan or wherever else the sun was beginning his round. I raised my voice a bit and exclaimed:

"There are still cakes and ale. Youth and beauty dance valiantly in the night club round the corner, unaware they are blind and dumb. Outside, the moon disperses her old-time silver currency, and in the park, trees flaunt their spring liveries regardless of biochemistry, local politics or the number of light years that separate the Earth from Sirius. Ignorant and foresworn though we be, admit we have made ourselves comfortable in this worst of all possible worlds. At least we can lay hands on most of the things we want. Health and the term of life increase, so there are additional years and wider opportunities for the enjoyment of the food and warmth within the pleasant structures wherein we entertain ourselves. Our control of the forces which science has trapped for us confers ease and abundance, together with a little splendor on our lives. Benighted perhaps, but how much better off than our ancestors. You indicate life to be more mysterious than it appears—if there be cards up its sleeve it will produce them in due course, so why anticipate? If we really are going anywhere, which I doubt, we are on the train. In due time we'll hit where we're bound for."

While I spoke I was aware of the Martian gurgling protests, but politely, he kept still until I had finished. Now I could hear him assembling his voice from whatever interstices it resided in, and when he spoke its intonation was vibrant with indignation.

" 'Give me a sunbeam and an open garbage pail,' cried the

fly, 'and I care not if tomorrow I die, or what flies are for.' There is more under the lid than you realize. I'm no evangelist, only a spectator watching your game. If you lacked the equipment to do better, I should regard the performance as being of the same quality as the gambols of lambs at play, or the caperings of monkeys in jungles. But, men are endowed with latent potentials through which to discover their true identity. Inherent in their equipment is the faculty of reason—a compass to guide them to realization of their part in the great scheme of things. To rest satisfied with being assigned the role of No. 1 among carnivore in the midst of circumstances and achievements that exhibit you as intelligent beings of higher species, seems to me akin to the complacency of pigs wallowing in sties, grateful for the bountiful mercy of swill.

"What immaterial agency profits by your stupidity is outside my range, but depend on it you are earning keep for some one. Lift the variegated coverlet of your genial environment and you'll recognize that the business that this earth is in is food production. With the aid of Father Sun the great mother nourishes all the progeny of the life that encumbers her. Suckers, mandibles and jaws in perpetual motion—universal mastication—perhaps it's the noise of eating that is the music of the spheres. At birth you enter this giant cafeteria, feed and expand out of the carefully prepared proteins and carbohydrates you consume therein, and, on leaving, your carcass is returned to the maternal bosom where her scavenger worms reshuffle its elaborate fabrics back to their original molecules. And on every linear square inch of Earth's surface there is a busy tenantry struggling to sustain and extend its material existence, every member furnishing some moiety of chemical or organic conversion and transformation to its immediate neighbor. Eat and be eaten, is the common lot.

"I merely sketch an aspect of the submerged spectacle of cosmic cannibalism that flourishes beneath your unseeing eyes, but I whisper to your skeptical ears that the rental of any body is in proportion to its equipment. Opportunity is always costly. Nothing is for nothing either here or on Mars—probably nowhere else among the constellations."

"I smell hell hereabouts," I remarked. "No wonder your engineering Luther's were suspected of revivalism by their contemporaries. Really, I am at a loss to know what you are spluttering about. In one breath you admit a mechanical world in the terms of my own knowledge. Yet you protest that to accept the natural order of affairs is to incur some mysterious form of damnation. Why not be frank and say that a divine mission has been given you to save my soul? Then I'll know where we are at. Religions I have always regarded as the most picturesque of the aboriginal delusions. Your version will undoubtedly have the latest pseudo-scientific trappings."

"You score," the Martian returned in tones of good humor. "There's a superiority complex to be reckoned with, and I have been waving my arms in the air—metaphorically speaking. Religion is exterior to my thesis and your salvation the least of my concerns—but your stupidity irritates me. In the carpet of life beneath your eyes is a pattern you don't see. Now if I were to escort a Patagonian Indian through a great automobile plant I know that his senses would register a spectacle of revolving wheels and shafts, of huge traveling cranes, of swarms of men dancing attendance on metal monsters, of confusion, whirl and blare. Nothing resembling this exhibit would be within the content of his experience, and reasonably he might be forgiven if he construed the performance as rites of the worship of the god of machines. He would not relate the turmoil to its product—that graceful vehicle which bore him to the scene of its own birthplace. You, on the contrary, are aware that the automobile is an arrangement of diverse parts assembled to produce a foreseen result, that it embodies collated facts and forces and that it is the means to the end for which it is used. What the Patagonian perceived as disorder is present in your mind as process, one of thousands of similar proceedings for fashioning out of earth's rough stuffs the utensils of business or pleasure. In every separate instance the same principles are repeated, yet your race has failed to enunciate them in a code or recognize their existence save as rule of thumb."

"Still hovering over my head," I commented. "What are these principles we use and don't see? If we did fix them in a code how would it alter our lives?"

"Nothing alters life, but recognition of bearings does broaden horizons," my visitor corrected. "The laws that regulate work are incorporated in the statement of our Martian engineers which I quoted. Therein are set forth the several elements that are present in performance—subject and plan, force to enact it, with environment the stage of materialization. Subject is man's interest or requirement, plan is his prevision of the conditions of construction in the sphere of its application; force is the energy required to transfer and reproduce the plan in space—environment—the chemical region, is your earth, with all its own tensions and resistances, as represented by mass and atmosphere."

"The three represent the cards—let us follow the play—for instance, in the building of a house for your own occupation. The character and dimensions of this house are prescribed by needs peculiar to yourself, and capacity to pay for their satisfaction—your nature and your circumstances. These exist independent of any activity you engage in, though they color all you do, as reflection of your personality. In your brain all preliminaries to the fulfillment of the proposed house are wrought. Within that secret chamber the building begins. Pictures of it appear to you, dream pictures that, as they are dwelt on, take the aspect of reality.

"But no other human being can see what you are looking at. It is an air-fabric, this house—however concrete. As this idea-image grows definite, it seems to gather desire-force enough to be born into the world where you and your body reside, and you take it to an architect. Then from your brain for the first time the picture is lifted, converted into words, and conveyed to his brain-receptor. Therein he carries the information as to how dream-houses are made real, for he is agent of the nature and circumstances of the environment in which the home is to be set up. As he listens, perhaps he sketches on paper the image, so that it assumes length and breadth before your eyes. Thus it becomes visible as a thing-in-itself, and is out in the light.

"Now the architect becomes initiator—his task the pro-creation and delivery of your idea into the world. He knows the resistances that gravity, air pressure and climate oppose to houses, and how to offset them. So he designs an erect structure whose parts are arranged in a pattern calculated to withstand the forces whose law it defies. This design is an exact picture on paper of the house to be. The settings and dimensions of each brick, beam, tile, pipe and plank that will enter into it are represented. Thus it is the embryo, the mold of that which is now ready to be organized and coupled to the site. It is handed over to the builders—the masons, carpenters and plumbers whose occupation is recopying plans in material substances. They know the art of bricklaying, how to attach and make posts stand up on foundations, how to articulate roofs and walls to be immune to wind and rain. Every step of the process is informed by exact knowledge of the constituents wrought into the structure. Steam-power, muscle, noise and sweat are interwoven, and there comes a day when the house stands out in the light, a tenant of space.

"It is concrete, objective, a thing-in-itself. Enter and inspect its fabrics. It is in the image of your dream and the architect's design, but seek as you may with test tubes and scales, not a trace of thought stuff or blueprint plan can you find. Density and weight are present, but the days of the architect's scheming and calculations, his hours of negotiation with contractors have disappeared, together with the actions of the score of artisans who for months have made the place resound with their labor. All have been swallowed up in this mere scaffolding and frame of material. And it may retain this identity of being a house, only for a brief period. As soon as you move in, it becomes no more than your home. It is a chattel, known by your name—a background for whatever activities are generated behind the shelter of its walls."

"Maybe a bit symbolic, but a fair picture of the procedure of building a house," I commented. "Its bearing on the eternal verities I miss."

"Is there no significance in the facts you have admitted, that the determining factors in the production of the house were immaterial?" demanded my mentor. "In a womb no anatomist has found, was born an impulse which accreted round itself an imperceptible embryo of pictures, words and resolves, and developed in the likeness of the home of your desire. As you organized its parts, apportioned its spaces,

colored and furnished its surfaces, did not the plan evoke
sensations of pleasure? Were not the problems related to the
formation of this apparition solved before you sought a col-
laborator to aid its rebirth in the world? Was the thought
stuff, of which the house in the non-spatial area within the
brain-womb was fashioned, less real than chemical substance
of the order of wood, brick and plaster which the architect
and the artisans subsequently assembled round it? Was not
the fact of weight, the sole difference between the matters?
Are sight, hearing, touch, the only evidence of reality? You
are aware these are no more than reporters of sensory impressions—reflectors of environment to agent—yet, according to your curious logic, Man, the originator and subject of
actions, has no substantiality save in the same terms as the
things he causes to be reproduced in material form.

"You deny maker and accept product, though you know
the latter is the offspring of the former and without its interaction could not have been born. Is it not absurd to contend
that because the house was contrived and set up out of the
earth, and adapted to its climate and conditions that environment is responsible for its being? Surely the earth did not
need and does not profit from it."

I was about to break in.

"Not yet," protested the Martian. "You propose to tell me
again that I am still tramping the cobbles of well traveled
highways and that you are still in the dark as to my meaning.
There is a proverb—one does not see the wood for the trees.
Again I repeat—there are no revelations; only patterns that
reassemble themselves under keener inspection and better
information. I ask you to assign specific gravity to the thinker and the matter of his thought, and to realize both as dom-

inant over and apart from the physical activities they define and energize."

Fundamentals of materialism. The ostrich explains a railway train. One thing evolves from the next, but rotating axles do not account for revolving wheels. Automobiles unaware of chauffeurs. Martians discover that the Cosmos is utilitarian and that they are not alive for their own benefit. Races ignorant of their identity or rights are servile. Freedom the offspring of knowledge. Cryptic defense of religion and of Mrs. Eddy.

A STRAIN of self-satisfaction rang in the Martian's voice as he summed up his argument. He felt he had demolished my defenses but, though I had to admit mentally that there were values in his thesis, the fundamental absurdity of the whole magical contention aroused my irritation.

"I wonder," I ejaculated ironically. "From this rigmarole I gather that, though I do what I do, it is not I that does it, but something else. If I admit that another agent transacts my performances through my person, how does that alter the sum total of the proceeding? It seems to amount to the same thing. This dragging in of immaterial powers to explain open-air effects is waste motion. Thought is a function of the living brain as flame is of a candle. Man carries the necessary parts for what men do. His behavior represents the reactions of his biological inheritance within the social and physical environment that adapted him to its circumstances. Continuous interactions color circumstance and response, but otherwise neither varies. Man's conduct no more than registers the pressures of the civilization that envelopes him. Education is just the process of adjustment."

"The Materialistic credo in a nutshell," the Martian exclaimed exultantly. "Now that you have defined it, we can examine its works to see if there are parts to cover the phenomena life exhibits. I'm reminded, though, of the elderly ostrich I heard consoling a terrified grandchild who had just seen a railway train thunder past the family feeding ground. 'Hush child,' said the wise bird, 'there's nothing to fear. It's just one of nature's interesting manifestations. It arises behind yonder hill and disappears in a cloud of dust. Its members are neatly adjusted to the steel pathway it laid down for itself. Since it belches smoke and flame and has never been seen to stop and feed, probably it is a type of volcano. It has no use and is harmless unless you get in its way. Since it recurs at regular intervals, it is easy for ostriches to avoid.'

"In this argument, train stands for biological inheritance, its passage for interaction with the environment, the track for adaptation to its circumstances—all sound deductions from the viewpoint of an ostrich who explained what he saw in the terms of his information.

"Literal interpretation of surface phenomena does, I concede, exhibit the world as the mother and motive of all the actions and inventions that swarm over her broad bosom. As cogs in gear engage corresponding teeth in a transmission system, so does one thing evolve the next. Believe the eyes, and there are immediate causes for visible effects, as rotating axles account for revolving wheels. By the same token, clothes and architecture derive from climate, silk stockings and leg-shows from the lower limbs of females, carts from horses, streets from houses—it's a wise child who knows which came first. The inevitable dualism. In action and conduct, as in mechanism, subject and object must be in correspondence. There can be no appearances save in the terms of the environment, for it is here the representation is being made. So each individual deed and word is a thing-in-itself, as well as the bearer of the purpose it expresses. If your point of identification is that of the thing-in-itself, the act you engage in is the corollary of the equipment you carry to perform it. As key to lock.

"Endow an automobile for instance, with consciousness and a rough capacity for reasoning—would it not find on examining its parts, the same unfolding of cause and effect we discover in our own physical organisms and in the processes we perform? A motor car biologist, exploring his chassis, engine, clutch, gears, wheels and brakes, would locate in the carburetor, magneto and gasoline tank the source of his movements. The set of appliances on the panel, he would figure as brain and nerve ganglia—reflex arcs—the agents of starting, guiding and stopping. Since the character of his organism was adapted to traversing highways and the mode of his life running back and forth over their surfaces, inevitably his existence was related to theirs. They provided the food, gasoline, which circulated through his veins and in his carburetor, mixed itself with air and supplied the power which forced his pistons to perform their offices within the cylinders. This general structure, equipped with its three systems of interaction with environment, satisfactorily explained behavior; habitized response would be achieved through clutch, wheel, horn and brakes.

"Doubtless there would be inexplicable passages. No one could agree why some motor cars should be better than others—why there were classes and masses such as Lincolns and Rolls-Royces and Fords and Chevrolets. Still, that was how they came. Heredity, evolution, economic determinism or some specific force, the laws of which were not yet fully established, must account for these divergences. No automobile remembered its youth or parentage or the circumstances of its birth, but that would be because its memory retained only the tracery of its travels. No self-respecting or tough minded automobile capable of facing life in its true terms would give consideration to rumors of the existence of immaterial agencies such as chauffeurs.

"It never occurred to you that unicellular organisms might suppose themselves lords of the world of their vision and be in ignorance of bi-cellular existence. Depend upon it, where there is consecutive movement and function—life—some glimmer of awareness glows. Instinct is but rudimentary consciousness—so even the humblest among the amœbæ knows the world for its oyster, explains its existence as the need for sustaining it and is blind and indifferent to the superimposed life of which it is the foundation unit. Accept as a further fact that every member of genera and species on every step of the long ascent up life's scale feels superior to its inferiors, takes itself and its horizon for granted, counts its own activities as ends in themselves, and entertains no more definite conception of human beings than a flea does of a dog show."

"The light you throw on the intellectual inhibitions of the protozoa and their brethren will be a boon to science," I ventured. "Perhaps it would be embarrassing to ask how you know? Intuition, doubtless."

"Intelligence," retorted the Martian. "When I find beings performing methodically tasks, the nature and bearings of which are recognizable, just because they are structurally adapted to their jobs and live off them, I don't infer the job created them. I assume them to be cogs in a transmission system and admire the cleverness of the mind capable of adjusting them to its purpose in such fashion that its fulfillment becomes both the means and end of their existences. I admire the economy of the procedure and, realizing myself to be but a larger and more ingenious fabrication of the same substances and forces, ask—to whose load am I hitched?

"When I arrived here and discovered it was a benighted race that inhabited this planet, I marveled at the incongruity between the creative capacity of men as evidenced by their mechanical and artistic achievements and their servile conception of the place they occupied in the scheme of things. Perhaps, I said to myself, it is because of some anatomical deficiency, the lack of an essential cerebral link that prevents them from connecting and cognizing their experiences.

"As I entered more deeply into the life of the environment I began to smell the manipulation of extraterritorial powers. I'm telling tales out of school, but it cannot be for nothing that your successive civilizations have reached heights only to be swept back to abysses, nor that the seed of some disintegration is always inherent in your achievements. It never of course occurred to you that the power which made your running-gear might be serving some purpose of its own by holding your noses to its tracks. You use blinkers on horses!"

"That's too absurd," I protested. The suggestion that we are deluded by malevolent deities is even more ridiculous than the presumption that deities of any kind exist.

"Biologists admit that the race of men does not use even half its brain capacity," my visitor went on, "but I fear the trouble is graver. When we on Mars tackled the problem of our existence, it soon became clear that the Cosmos was a stranger organism than our imaginations had conceived or religious traditions had led us to expect. There appeared grounds to suspect that we were not alive for our own benefit, but, like the protozoa and metazoa and all their plant, fish, bird and beast descendants, we were part of a system.

"The thought that we might be no more than blind employees earning a living by the sweat of our brows, subserving some unknown and mysterious purpose not necessarily in our interest, came as a bitter shock. Remember we too had heavens and hells and the other paraphernalia by which primitive peoples attempt to mitigate the hardships and maladjustments of life. Roughly speaking, it began to dawn on us that our particular world must be like any of the enterprises we ourselves organized—an institution engaged in attending to the business that was its function. Probably conducted for the purposes of the overseers, to whose interests the workers were subordinated.

"The Martian who first propounded this novel suggestion became so unpopular that the government secluded him on a remote island like your own St. Helena. From there he bombarded the newspapers with letters arguing that there was nothing extravagant in his theory, since it represented principles familiar in our own systems. He asked us to remember our attitude to the inferior animal organisms we bred and fed to furnish us meat and clothes; such as your own sheep and cattle, for instance. How solicitous our provision for their wellbeing and sustainment and that they be sheltered and inspected, yet, without scruples about utilizing their carcasses, skins or wool for our necessities. There must be powerful Intelligences in the Universe, he reasoned, to whose greater lives unconscious beings, such as men, bear the same relation as livestock to our own.

"Assuredly they did not eat us or tan our hides, but perhaps our existence in the state of virginal innocence of identity and purpose that characterized our race might furnish some essential chemical or conductive element of value to the cosmic grind. And, as no going-concern of which we had cognizance could operate without the direction of its most efficient members, was it not fair to assume that a colossal enterprise like the Cosmos must also be administered by beings equipped with the requisite knowledge and power for their great engagements?

"To the protests aroused by this audacious hypothesis, our Martian reformer replied that this outcry surprised him. Obviously our world was part of a system and it was logical to assume that the modes and practices of the inhabitants of all the spheres were versions of the same principles.

" 'In every large institution,' he went on to say, 'are men who learn the details of the affairs it transacts, comprehend the laws that regulate its activities, acquire the technique it practices, and so become capable of controlling its functions. According to the degree of their capacity such individuals are made foremen, superintendents, governors or presidents. What they apply is the knowledge they have attained, and its possession alters the character of their participation. They become partners in the processes under way and gain an interest in the proceeds.'

"Since preferment here represented the application of intelligence and will to the circumstances of the environment, and this seemed to us both legitimate and inevitable, 'why,' he asked, 'assume that affairs elsewhere beyond the pale of our senses, were or could be conducted on a different basis? It seemed but natural that we at home, should do the thinking for our illiterate and backward races who had not learned enough to protect their own rights—must not the same rule apply to the inhabitants of planets who came, lived and went in ignorance of their origin, identity or part in the scheme of things.

" 'We Martians belonged in this category condemned to sub-consciousness by our indolence and servility, so we deserved the type of overseer-ship that obtained. Self-emancipation was no one's but our own business. The knowledge Martians had already acquired that had made them free of the air, land and water had been piled up by the sweat of their brows; so we must take it for granted that enlightenment and self-determinism could only be gained by the same processes of thought and experiment. The information existed. To become aware who we are, what we are about and where bound, represents a racial coming-of-age. Thereafter our obligations might be intensified, but we should be on our own feet, entitled to look the universe in the face.

" 'Let us then,' he urged, 'go forth on the greatest of all quests, cease supplicating and debating, cast aside all superstitions, including morals, chance and coincidence, and seek the facts in the same spirit of dispassion that we apply to the properties of a gas. A master mind designed and operates the magnificent plant of which we are inhabitants and the prophets have told us that his ways are manifested in his works.'

"Call it revivalism, evangelism or any other opprobrious term that occurs to you—this Martian's plain talk proved the best propaganda our intellectual revolution developed. The character of the civilization we evolved I have already outlined. The example is open to your embrace."

"Gorgeous poppycock but a good story," I commented as my visitor halted for a rest. "Cosmic mythology is not among our inventions unless you include Genesis. But with due respect to the untenable pretensions of your presence, is not this particular episode, together with its grotesque imagery, rather a large draft on the credulity of a mere mortal? As folklore and fairytale stuff I admit its values—but methinks I discern an underlying aroma of Christian Science. If for one moment I had imagined you were leading me into the lap of the late Mrs. Eddy, I should have stuffed my ears two hours ago."

"I do tend to fly high for a fledgling to follow," the Martian responded with a note of sarcasm in his tones, "so let us return to Earth.

"To judge by the multiplication of its triumphs and the increase of its flocks, the devotees of what you call Christian Science must be persuaded they are getting something for their money. In a sensible world the phenomena it offers would have engaged the attention of the savants of science and medicine who, I note, content themselves with denying and deriding them. Why this sage woman and her adherents should be singled forth as marks for exceptional ridicule in a country in which the Bible is the accepted basis of faith, I cannot yet understand, especially since two thirds of your population secretly subscribes to someone or other of the pseudo-esoteric cults that pervade these states. A disposition is represented here that points the way. You are not fool enough to believe that if there did not exist an underlying pith and reality beneath the institution you call religion—if this did not subserve some property of the nature of the human race—that it could have persisted throughout the ages of which you have reckoning. Even if some of the faiths that attempt to point the way to the Kingdom are floundering, having lost captain, compass and sextant, do not forget that the Poles still work their ancient magic, and that both Sun and North Star haunt the selfsame orbits."

Gradually I had been losing such patience as it had been possible to maintain against the airing of these fantastic heresies. It was time for further protest.

The delusion of speed. Communication not an end in itself. Development of machinery extension of intelligence, but its exaltation over man, perversion. No market here for inventions that do not discount mind. The error of taking the framework of Earth and life for granted. Credit due primordial chemists for great achievements.

"HELP, help!" I cried, raising both arms aloft. "My brain is awhirl in a futile attempt to get the pitch of your gyrations. In one breath you offer vistas of an orderly universe proceeding by law, in the next my veneration is invited for the worst charlatanry of the time. I'm willing to be entertained by any one's Utopia, but consistency has not yet lost its franchise in intelligent circles. As for your notions of the verities, no jury would find guilty of murder one who publicly aired such convictions, even if he had cut his own mother's throat. It's the most hospitable philosophy, I'll admit, that has yet got by the intellectual customs, but there are more holes in its texture than a good telescope discloses in the Milky Way."

"If astronomers sought no more than holes they would never have diagramed the myriads of separate and distinct solar systems that in their aggregate constitute the colossal pattern of the Milky Way," suggested the Martian in his mildest tones. "Most sciences," he continued, "are based on collections of isolated or fugitive details which when properly assembled exhibit relationships in common. The detectives of knowledge continuously pursue resemblances in search of correspondences. Analogies! Species and variations are synthesized in genera, and all forms and types are traced to the interaction of the selfsame forces. What seems fortuitous or inexplicable today, is tomorrow pinned and tagged in some familiar category. The giant web comprehends every stitch and phase of every pattern it carries, and those bright strange threads that seem at loose ends as the loom weaves on, in due course drop into appointed moorings as the design unfolds its richness. If I go farther afield than your information warrants, remember I draw from a wider perspective. The incredible is no more than the undiscovered.

"Imagine yourself back a century, an invisible voice from today pouring into some critical scholar's ears the spectacle of such commonplace marvels as aeroplanes, 60,000-ton ocean liners, and millions of automobiles. What reaction might you expect, were you to describe a president talking into a microphone to twenty million listeners? In justice to his sanity such an auditor would have no better recourse than your own, to attribute the message to a lying illusion. If it were germane to my purpose, I could cite wonders to which your loftiest flights would seem no more than the gymnastics of grasshoppers, but it is not the rate of progress of your race in discovering and applying natural forces that gives me concern—rather it is that its members are in danger of being submerged by the mere multiplication of appliances.

"You earthlings seem incapable of shedding the delusion that communication is a goal in itself. He who flies to Europe is exalted as a superman, though nothing is involved in the achievement save that it was made in a medium hitherto untraveled. No one is a whit wiser or better, nor are peace and understanding promoted among your warring clans. 'But we have conquered the air,' say your savants—'to what purpose?' I ask tearfully. 'You can neither eat nor drink the gained hours, nor has one among you invented a better use for time than the age-old routines prescribed.' If it were true that ends were inherent in means, and that every fresh vehicle brought into the world new destinations, I'd applaud the enthusiasm with which successive novelties in transmission are welcomed. Alas, I notice that trucks and trains are loaded with the selfsame cargoes that were moved in carts, that wires carry old ideas in the ancient currency of identical words and that the burden of the ether waves is still the trivial interchange of song and story as among your ancestors.

"Endowed with the priceless gift of intelligence, alive for countless ages in one of the most luxurious terrenes in the universe, in possession of the secrets the generations that preceded you so laboriously mined from nature's store—the sum of your reaction to the power that birthed and sustains your being is—speed. Compassless conquerors of time in space—motiveless motes in the beams of Eternity!"

"Jeremiah had nothing on you," I burst in as my visitor paused. "All along I've been convinced that you were a fundamentalist, who had found no more than a new vein of lamentation. Just why a Martian who began by boasting of the mighty engines his countrymen had devised to make over the surfaces of their planet, should object to inventions of the same character here, I cannot fathom. Admit at least, that this machine age is more convenable to live in than that of the cave-dwellers, for instance."

"Not a syllable I've uttered can be construed into an indictment of machinery," contradicted the Martian in indignant tones. "Machines are legitimate extensions of men's muscles and represent the use of his intelligence in adapting natural energies and a hostile environment to the modes of his physical organism. But when, through ignorance and greed mere mechanisms are exalted above man and he tends to be degraded into a servitor of some such engine of power as a loom, a locomotive, a lathe or a dynamo, I fear for his future and his fate. Implicit here is perversion, the dishonoring of humanity. Service without knowledge is slavery. Dumb and uncomprehending labor is for beasts. There is no market among you for inventions that do not discount mind. You say 'men are endowed by their Creator with inalienable rights,' but is not a stranger justified in assuming to be morons and robots the inhabitants of a world, the slogans of whose merchants and manufacturers is *'fool proof'*?

"The information that represents the achievements of the human race is lodged in a few minds. The bulk of your populations are button-pushers, tap-twirlers, disk-twisters. Is the man with an automobile or a radio a better friend, husband or citizen—wiser or more temperate because he has speeded-up his movements or may listen-in to standardized and sterilized music or talk? Has his intelligence been increased by better lighting or heating? He has only been deprived of initiative, the opportunity to use his own faculties, without compensating him with a corresponding understanding of the forces that ingenious mechanics have harnessed for their own profit. And do not forget the sinister side of all these triumphs: those lordly steel mills may tomorrow be turning out artillery, and the giant motor companies, armored cars. What boots a leakless roof that is not proof against the bomb from an aeroplane? Tomorrow you may be dead with the bullet of an unseen and unseeing invader in your heart with no inkling of why you have lived or for what. Ponder the privilege of dying on behalf of economic determinism, or because some oil or tobacco monopoly is dissatisfied with the tariffs another nation has set up in defense of its own life, liberty and of happiness."

"That dirge needed a chaser, and you topped it with a draught of pacifism," I observed with mock gravity. "I had hoped to be urged to organize suicide clubs, or to propagandize on behalf of universal sterility, so nature might have space for her next reincarnation."

"Suicide clubs are superfluous where the institution of war is maintained," he remarked, ironically. "As to sterility, birth-control provides a preface to the regulation of propagation but decades must elapse before it affects the masses for whose creative needs childbearing is the instinctive outlet. Your remark indicates ignorance rather than cynicism. Again, you have missed the point of my argument. I keep forgetting how long it took one of your professors to induce an experimental monkey to fit two sticks together to gather a remote banana."

"Surely a respondent is entitled to express dissent," I returned.

"But the exponent is entitled to a greater measure of intelligent apprehension than your replies denote," he insisted, angrily. "Still as I look across the surfaces of this planet and note you all at each other's throats, living in armed camps, poisoned with envy and detestation of each other, it occurs to me that perhaps this is the wrong market in which to distribute my brand of common sense. I might as well try expounding the Steel Trust to a savage examining an ax-blade, as attempt interpreting truths to an unawakened mind."

"Patience greatly becometh an apostle," I reproved. "Besides, why relinquish one's hold on sound home truths for foreign importations?"

"The point is well taken," the Martian admitted, in a tone

of reluctance. "I keep forgetting our divergent logic; and miscomprehensions unnecessarily irritate me. Fundamentally, the trouble is due to the error of your philosophies in taking for granted the whole framework of earth, life and being, and assuming the interaction of its parts as the end and aim of its existence. Here is a giant sphere woven of an intricate fabric of gases and metals, revolving on its own axis, following an exact orbit round a central power-station from which it derives energy, illumination and heat, bearing an infinite cargo of passengers who are sustained from its substances by their own exertions; all according to principles so mathematical, so efficient that they are classed as immutable laws—and in the face of a system so obviously a mechanism designed for a purpose, your wiseacres declare the whole business an accident! It's absurd.

"If, in some remote and inaccessible valley of your world, an explorer should find a conjoined laboratory, plantation and mill, manned by an infinite variety of sizes and shapes of robots fitted with appliances so subtle and dexterous that in gathering fuel for the operations of the establishment, they generated not only the energy necessary for conducting them, but means and incentive for their continuation, he might well marvel at the genius of the managers. That he could see no overseers, nor trace the output of the busy workers would not lessen his certainty that here was a set-up—a factory turning out articles in response to need and *on behalf of* its administrator's pocketbook.

"Would you not dub an innocent, that Eskimo in the aforesaid department store who, in examining the diversified contents of its shelves and counters, the pottery, the groceries, the textiles, furniture and utensils—each article the flower of intricate processes, imagined they had been picked off trees or dug out of the ground? So when I hear your sages gravely discussing the fitness of the environment, the felicitous properties of oxygen, hydrogen, nitrogen and the carbon compounds which enable plants and animals to sustain life; the adroit instrumentalities that organisms have developed and adapted for themselves to extract power from the elements in which they occur, I realize that the Eskimo's faith in the magic of nature is shared by the most enlightened of your race.

"Why persuade yourselves that before your own advent in this sphere, matter was more responsive or cohesive than it is today, or that gases ever formed intricate patterns for social reasons? New alloys do not happen by wish, but of the purpose and by the will and persistence of men who know chemistry and physics. So why deprive the primordial chemists who arranged the elements of primordial substance into the periodic table, who loaded each with its characteristics, who invented bacteria and set them at fitting the earth for organized life, who made and propagated the original amœba and planned this succession of plant and animal structures which a visitor finds here—why deny them the credit due for a great performance?

"Apply to the form and substance of the planet on which you are living and laboring and being carried around in space the bitter lesson of your own experience with force and material—that their behaviors are always conditioned by mind and will. Awake from your trance and stop dreaming that things happen—they are made to happen."

Physiological thinking is in defining performance in the terms of the instrument that effectuates it. The human being a mechanical cryptogram. Standardized bodies as biological Ford cars. Phenomena floating in space without physical anchorage. The Mystery of Identity. Key to biography not in biology. Man the focal point of a relationship with environment; his existence dependent on his organism. Texture of living lies outside agent who conducts it.

WHAT a sensation this Martian evangelist would make at an ecclesiastical convention, I thought to myself. His mixture of cosmology, mythology and theology excelled offerings of the kind our own holy men had put forth, and there was color and vivacity in his fables. Perhaps, though, the blend of mechanism with which he adulterated it might be as unpalatable to good Christians as the whole argument was to my own thinking, and to scientific authority in general.

"It's impossible to discuss these theories of yours seriously," I said, "they sound like theology to me. As long as men accepted a divine origin for the universe, they took everything as fixed, and did nothing about it. Step by step our chemists are unlocking the patterns into which you declare the original elements were fused by their predecessors and that's enough of a task for science today. Where there are no patents recorded or handiwork visible, it prefers to ascribe the facts to nature and go on with the job. Were it not for laboratory investigations, we should never have known how wonderfully we and our world are devised. The theologians

were satisfied to take what they saw and tell us to be good—
or be sent to hell."

"It's always a new world upon which kittens and infants
open their eyes," my visitor responded with that suavity he
exhibited whenever he was about to score a point. "But, just
because one discovers he is organized to live within the precincts of this particular planet, why set up the location as
divinity and say It did it? Fantastic notions are only important to the degree that they divert minds from the facts of
the case. Environment is a cul-de-sac. There was hope in
behaviorism until its adherents declared it a philosophical
panacea."

"A concession," I declared. "Your damnation of that particular theory still rings in my ears."

"It began with objective observation of human performance and ended by declaring that mind is a delusion," the
Martian expostulated. "Assume a road, a plate of roast beef
at the end of it and a man heading towards it. The man's legs
derive from the road, and his movement is conditioned reflex to the smell of beef which sets up an urge in his viscera
stimulating both to saliva and the muscles of locomotion—
what could be simpler? The deduction that man's physical
system operates in reaction to the environment, before it
finds words to explain what it does, is equivalent to recog-
nizing that the earth revolved on its axis before there were
maps. One may call all such crude assumptions physiological
thinking. It defines performance in the terms of the instrument which effectuates it—as though you spoke of its bed
as the river, or ascribed a telegram to the wires by which it
is conveyed. Everyone knows that the bed is not the river,
though it be inseparable from the circumstances of a volume
of water cutting its way to sea level, by gravity and the wire

is no more than the messenger by means of which sender and recipient communicate.

"Now a human being is a mechanical cryptogram. His true entity is buried in the physical tissues of his body. To be born here he must conform to the conditions prescribed by the atmosphere and gravity of this planet. So he is clothed in a protective texture of protoplasm, a sensitive compound capable of retaining and responding to the etheric fabric which carries his racial constitution and degree. This represents the design or architectural plan that sustains and pervades the frame in which Man, the entity, functions; and it is also the conductor of the life energy which vitalizes its organic parts.

"The outward transactions, through which the entity expresses his nature, fall under the same conditions that ordain this material armor. Masked himself, he operates in a masked world of substantial and resistant forms of the same staple, property and quality as his own body. His relations with this world and with his fellows must be transmitted through the medium of this prevailing stuff, and in its terms alone. So he is created a complicated piece of engineering; outfitted with devices by means of which he establishes equilibrium, registers light, sound, movements and the spatial demarcations of the locality in which he must direct his way.

"A being thus organized is a child of two worlds—that of his origin and character, and that of the environment which supplies his corporeality with food and air. So he partakes of the nature of both—he is an animal in whom is infused the positive intelligence of an entity; and the unconscious struggle between the two orders is the story of the development of civilization."

I arose from my chair and turned derisively in the direction of my visitor. "And I've been listening all this time for a revelation," I exclaimed with mock sorrow. "Good old neo-platonism with a few mechanical trimmings. As plausible as ever, but as incapable of proof. Even I would rejoice in having a spirit identity forced on me—but all the authorities are on the other side and there's no tangible evidence to uphold the case."

"Putting aside the testimony of prophetic character witnesses who might be supposed to speak by the card," returned the Martian gravely, "there remains a sound physical basis for this contention. Without some such thesis it is impossible to explain the phenomena represented by human behavior."

"Go on," I urged, "but remember I'm from Missouri."

"It's common knowledge," he continued, "though the average man galloping in pursuit of his individual concerns does not realize it, that he and his fellows are conducting the affairs of their lives in a standardized machine whose parts are the same for king and beggar, Nordic and Hottentot. The human body is just a biological Ford car. There are weak and strong motors, graceful and awkward chassis; but by and large, all the distinctions that mark the races and conditions of mankind—rank and class, wealth and poverty, culture and barbarism, are registered through the same make of conveyance. Despite this uniformity, no man concedes that he is the counterpart of his neighbor or anyone else, and, in reviewing the qualities that mark his own personality, discounts the fact that all have lungs, limbs and brains in common. Minor divergences in the pattern and dimensions of his organism—height, shape, weight and color, he cherishes as vindication of his own sensations of uniqueness.

"Here, then, are some two billion citizens of this world of yours, suffering from the illusion that, though accoutered in the same protoplasmic costume, each is dissimilar to all the others. Furthermore, no two of them have the same history, or energy rating, or look at the objects of life from the same angle. Conscious, articulate, capable of supplying the needs of their beings, of finding their own way through the vicissitudes of life, their forms and faces offer not a single indication of their accomplishments or their experiences. The corpses of a king, a shopkeeper, and a crook laid side by side naked on a slab would look the same to a spectator unfamiliar with their status. Neither anatomy or biology has discovered a trace of identity in human flesh or bone, nor have the psychologists yet deciphered a man's name among his brain cells. Your best authorities agree that all these differentiations are imaginary, and that there is little more variation in the ways and paths of men than occur in the lives of peas and oranges, but not even the theorists themselves accept that conclusion, because each is convinced that it is not true in his own case.

"Here then is an immense body of phenomena floating in space without physical anchorage. Your ancestors, lacking instruments of precision, lodged the activities associated with the achievements and accomplishments of the human species in an organ they called Mind, but your savants have discarded this as aboriginal, because no one has ever seen a mind nor has the highest powered microscope disclosed its existence. I ask in all fairness, is it not reasonable to assume that this freight of individuality, experience and information conveyed around in the comings and goings of your race must be borne in some sort of a vehicle?

"Another anomaly is the transcendental character of your business organizations—those large corporations through which the affairs of your own and other nations are transacted. Their names appear over buildings, in advertising, on stationery, in sky writings, but no one has ever seen one in body. About their structures, dispositions and operations, there is extant as large a literature as that of biology and anatomy, but it is concerned with intangibles such as supply and demand, product, distribution, accounting, and so forth. Similarly, the form of government and the frame of the law cast no shadows in the sun, and have no more weight or dimension than a thought. Yet all these abstractions have individualities, offices, executives and employees, shift and carry burdens over the world, exercise power but are as discarnate as ghosts.

"Confusing to the stranger from afar is the way identities shift here. No one is either his body or himself save in a purely private capacity. Soon after birth he becomes a scholar, an artisan, a tradesman, a farmer, a clerk, or a member of some learned profession. His entity is swallowed up in his occupation as a building is in its tenants. Though the scientists assure you a man is just the locomotory apparatus bearing his name, I find names and reputations existing independently of their appliances. Houses dissolve into homes, women into mothers, daughters, cooks or seamstresses, lovers into husbands, and vice versa; blondes into vampires, devils into saints. Order and classification underlie these tangles and shuffles undoubtedly, but they perplex a conservative mechanist like myself."

"Nothing abnormal or extraordinary about all that," I assured him. "Just social classification, growing out of the ways that men have invented to sustain their lives. Dazzling, perhaps, to a member of a simpler civilization, but reflecting no more than the ingenuity of our peoples."

"Such optimism is commendable if disconcerting," responded the Martian. "Perhaps the motes that dance in a sunbeam believe they are being drilled. What I'm attempting to demonstrate is that classification of identities by their occupations betrays the lack of a rational philosophy of being. The key to biography is not contained in biology. Curious it is so hard to make you realize that the warp and woof, the texture and pattern of living lie outside and are apart from the physical agent who weaves it."

"I begin to grasp what you are driving at," I said—"that there actually are two bodies, an interior and an exterior—the former an apparatus in which originate the motives, the latter the instrument for executing the former's projects. An original and a clothed copy. Strange that the biologists find no sign of this buried treasure! Also, how dependent are the lives of men on the condition of this protoplasmic counterpart. If a wild taxicab or a stray bullet disrupts the casing or the fabric of its brain, there's an end to its existence, however much the accident interferes with my plans. *I* may be the hand within the glove, but if the window-sash breaks and bruises its fingers, I cannot write. If the real *I* is something other than my body, why this dependence on its mechanism? If *I* actually be of celestial origin, why this concern of mine with mundane affairs?

"I seem to be the focal point of a relationship with an environment which furnishes the circumstances and the facts that have made me what I am and with which I and all other humans must deal. The ideas that enter my mind are born of these circumstances, as they bear on the course I travel, and their subject-matter is of the same texture. My interest is centered in feeding, sheltering and diverting this body, so it may be comfortable and pleased, and the great variety of occupations you describe have no other objective.

"That there is need to drag in an additional agent, when the conduct of the organism's own business furnishes adequate incentive and purpose for its being, I can't concede. That's what it is outfitted for and what it achieves. I'm omitting all the imaginative fancywork, such as religion and philanthropy, and holding to brute reality. Besides, if there be an impalpable substratum as you suggest, it would have, on leaving me, nowhere to go but out, and the wind would give it short shrift."

The Martian chuckled.

"Considering the number of physical circumstances this room contains that you cannot see," he said, "there might be spaces in the Universe in which a ghost could find tenement. Right here are gravity, air, light, heat, sound and moisture— neighbors occupying the same space area without a clash or a by-your-leave. As to the dependence of function on body, one recalls the tenets of that highly successful sect which calls disease error, and denies it exists.

"Since you are an inhabitant of this sphere, you have no recourse except to deal through the circumstances of the environment. It provides the mise-en-scene, the costumes and the properties for the life-drama in performance, but remember, you contribute the motive power, the action and the pantomime. An actor assumes but is apart from his role. He conceals, under his masquerade, a private identity. Does it occur to the bridge or the poker-player that he is the subordinate of the fifty-two pasteboards of the card pack or the rules of the game? Are not these but tools, to whose conditions he conforms for the fun of using his skill?

"An injury to a finger may stop your writing, but does not diminish the faculty of formulating what is in your mind to express; nor impair knowledge of the art. Loss of your limbs does not remove the need or capacity for locomotion—you substitute wheels for legs. A chauffeur accommodates, to his sense of direction, a crippled steering gear. A wobbly gait does not imply a feeble brain. If his car is junked in a collision, his ability to continue driving is demonstrated in a new vehicle. An insoluble blood-clot in the cortex may cause you to forget your name, but does not deprive you of identity. Nor does the surgeon who lifts the depressed skull of an idiot, confer on him sanity—he merely clears the intelligence channels. An overcharged wire blows out a fuse and breaks an electric circuit, but the fuse was not the force it interrupted, nor was that force the light that failed.

"Physical disablement interferes with and handicaps the expression of faculty and the use of intelligence, but does not remove them to a greater degree than an accident to a carburetor affects the constitution of gasoline."

My visitor's voice had dwindled to a whisper. Though his sentences had followed fast on one another it was evident that the mysterious dynamism that motivated the invisible apparatus of his speech was exhausted.

I looked at my watch.

"There's much to object to, but the hour is late," I said. "I need sleep, being just a benighted mortal; and your vocal organ is worn to a shred. I suggest your inspection of one of the numerous sunrises being unveiled by your friends, the Cosmic Authorities, at various points west of Suez. Too bad the spectacle at Mandalay is over now, but there are excellent backgrounds for the performance in Switzerland."

"The suggestion is not amiss," the Martian responded feebly. "I hate to leave an argument half finished, but the truth is, the energy I use is solar, and my system requires hours of exposure daily to his rays. After I've treated myself to a due allowance of scenery, I'll depart for the Sahara Desert and bask there in the higher octaves of the spectrum. Tomorrow night I promise myself the privilege of upsetting a few more local superstitions and offering interpretations of the human organism more logical than are entertained hereabouts."

"And I shall continue to play Sultan to your Scheherazade," I replied, amiably.

CHAPTER VIII: IN SIGHT—UNSEEN

Anthropomorphic paradoxes. Instinct, dumb knowledge. The flaw in mechanics. A determinant missing. How homo sapiens lost his self-consciousness. Revised Darwinism and contemplative apes. Pursuit of the Lost Factor. Dual environments. No activity its own occasion. Is the individual his occupation? Industry no end in itself. Our philosophies just juvenile culture.

I HAD no sooner disposed myself in my chair after dinner next evening when I heard the familiar voice. It began with a question.

"By the way, what do you know about anthropomorphism?"

"Attributing the human form to divinity, or human characteristics to lower animals—tongues in trees, books in the running brooks sort of thing," I replied, "but why?"

"If I told you I had heard two elms exchanging statistics about the amount of starch their leaves had converted out of sunlight and carbon dioxide that day, it would represent anthropomorphism, because I had ascribed to trees a capacity for which they lacked the instrumentality."

"That covers it," I replied.

"But if I stated that trees had acquired from earth, air and sun a faculty of converting the chemical elements contained therein into sugar, starch, cellulose and chlorophyll, to combine them into organisms with power to breathe, grow, excrete and reproduce their kind, that would be in strict accordance with the findings of science, would it not?"

"Trees certainly possess the properties you mention," I assented, "but, though science has traced the processes by which they conduct the intricate chemical interactions that make them what they are, it does not know how, and contents itself with describing the modes of their growth. By following these it can condition the development of plant life."

"Virtually, a tree, though it can neither speak nor move, is as alive as a human," continued the Martian. "Its body, like your own, is an arrangement of cells which derive, from solar radiation, the energy they use to transform mineral substances into the right nourishment to sustain their business of living and growing. Though the modality differs from the more complicated processes at work in the animal body, they are parallel. Yet, because trees have no tongues and occidental plant-biologists have been unable to discover in their physical texture aught corresponding to brain or senses, they are pronounced *unconscious* organisms. A plant may know enough to manufacture a structure by means of which it can eat, drink, breathe, gain strength and girth, and propagate its kind—all activities requiring practice and information; so it would be fair to say a big tree possesses real knowledge and wisdom—yet because it is rooted to its home and is silent, you call its noble attainments *instinctive*. Why, if a tree's life is but a few removes from a man's, is anthropomorphism such bad philosophic form?"

"More pettifogging," I remarked, a bit exasperated. "Anthropomorphism is an aboriginal superstition, a caveman creed. To institute correspondences between the constitution of a tree and the human organism is childish."

"Such fine distinctions are drawn here it's no wonder that a visitor is confused," replied the Martian apologetically. "I gather that if a tree could explain its arts, it would emancipate itself from the reproach of being instinctive and would rank as intelligent. I infer then, that speech is the insignia of humanity, if it be in a language you can understand. Months ago I talked with a Tibetan monk who possessed great erudition. Save that his body is of the standardized type, you and he have little in common. He lived in a cold cave on the side of a high mountain, wore a ragged robe, subsisted on oatcake and water and told me what life was about. Since you are ignorant of his dialect, to your ears his words would be but a succession of unmeaning sounds. Truly no apparatus for mind or consciousness has been found in trees—but your eminent authorities have searched in vain for appliances of this type in Man's physical structure.

"Just because you are aware of yourselves, of the world in which you reside and have formulated methods of communication with one another to affirm it, why this glib assurance that a tree is an ignoramus? Knowledge, foresight and memory are ingrained in tree structures—they are orderly, equable, tolerant of each other's leaves and branches, adapted to environmental strains and stresses, for they are better equipped to withstand the rigors of nature than yourselves—why this superiority? Because you can talk to a tree and it can only reply in the rustle of its leaves, why assume it is unaware of your presence, or is dumb?"

"Prattle," I announced aggressively.

"On the contrary," pursued the Martian gravely, "I'm but attempting again to demonstrate the insecurity of the foundations of your philosophy and to help realization of the fact that, in the terms of accepted conventions, an understanding of the truth about life, being and nature, is impossible. That competent physicists, as the large accomplishments of your race exhibit you to be, have failed to grasp in their totality, the principles involved in the performance of work astonishes me. Though the first factor is necessarily implied, it figures in none of your calculations. In consequence, mechanics here begin with the disturbance of equilibrium and omit the character and function of the determinant, whose interest initiates whatever displacement is produced or retarded. Though this determinant carries the information through which the second factor is applied in the right measure to the third, whose place or state is the subject of change, and is the beneficiary of the transaction—its part does not appear in the record. This ignored constant makes the false quantity in your logic. Failure to identify, and to allot it proportionate value in the scale of magnitudes, is the cause of the lopsided culture and civilization that prevail on this planet."

"Doubtless a meaning lurks hereabouts," I commented, "but it is out of my reach."

"Nothing mysterious is involved," the Martian insisted. "I am attempting to convey that, in your engineering, there are no specifications which cover the relation of the I, at whose behest the forces applied in work are released. A while ago, I showed you the preliminaries that preceded the building of a house disappearing in the finished structure; but the truth involved in this dissolution is not realized. Nor is it recognized that the object created—the assembled material form, and the agencies which inspired, combined and operate it—belong in opposite categories. The profit and interest of human beings is implied in all performances, but, though every man knows he is of a different order from the stuffs he molds—official silence sanctions no such discrimination. This is primitive thinking and characterizes all races that have not emerged from instinctive culture.

"When *Homo Sapiens* woke upon the earth and looked around he discovered himself in a hostile country which cared nothing for his pedigree and was heedless of his wants. His organism was unsuited to the climate and its preservation required provender. Meeting these initial obligations made him cave-dweller and hunter, and, though later, he has emerged as architect and agriculturist, his bitter experiences as pioneer had warped his self-consciousness. Because all these early problems concerned his body but were outside it, they had to be solved on the outside, with the result that he identified his being with his body, hands and visible results of their application, and grew up to manhood oblivious of the magic of his own machinery and of his essential separateness from the activities he inspired—the structures he reared. This is natural enough, for it is easy to dream, and hard to build against the gravity and pressure prevailing here, so the job is more important than the idea until the agent reaches the age of self-identification."

"Always the same nigger in your woodpiles—concealed divinity," I yawned. "How much simpler, more probable and more natural the revised Darwinian thesis. A contemplative ape, piling up supplies for a forthcoming winter accidentally realized that four cocoanuts lasted longer than two and started arithmetic and the development of a brain. He survived his fellows and his descendants extended the discovery. A coincidence established fitness as the derivative of accumulation, and memory began with competition among gatherers of cocoanuts; speech and writing, with the need to protect scores and stores. Self-preservation generated self-interest and blossomed as individuality. Personality is in the degree of ability to acquire, be it material wealth or knowledge. Our civilization is the structure of possession, of every man's right to spend or protect what he has, including his health and his life. The Ten Commandments have the same concern. The capacity to get and keep is the seal of wisdom. Of course environment is God, because it furnishes source, substance, medium, law and consequence. Life is probably a sort of cancer among the cells of the Earth's organism and our existence, in reality, as fortuitous and meaningless as a maggot's. If a trained flea were soliloquizing about his relation to a dog he would embroider some such plot as you offer."

"Most apposite," the Martian returned. "My contention adequately illustrated: character of the determinant who originated and utilized the energy and profited by the result, is omitted. Your picture takes for granted a self-starting and self-propelling engine equipped with senses—the complicated instrumentalities that enabled it to convert light into awareness of trees, cocoanuts and its own kind—to distinguish itself from its fellows and to know its enemies. Your contemplative ape was installed in a machine which synthesized energy from air and carbohydrates, and was fitted with locomotory appliances to pursue its fuel, and with organs to reproduce its species. All these intricate processes it performed instinctively—it, too, took itself and the other life agents—the animals and plants of the neighborhood—as matters of course. If, inherent in this organism, had not slumbered the faculty, plus the apparatus, to realize the larger values of four cocoanuts over two, the coincidence would not have been noted. No telescope ever discovered a star, for instance, nor are scales capable of understanding the theory of weights and measures. If capacity for flight were not installed in an aeroplane, it could not take the air."

"There's no need to drag in the entire problem of organic

evolution whenever one mentions a problem of behavior," I grumbled.

"In discussing the appearances and use of buildings it is unsafe to leave out foundations and architecture," my visitor objected. "Or the bodies and habits of occupants. Behaviors can't be studied apart from the instruments that exhibit them or the conditions that evoke them. Remember that the superiority of four cocoanuts over two, as means of sustaining life, was fact before the ape realized it. He merely discovered its relation to his own body, and began subordinating the environment to his use, thereby isolating himself from the circumstances by which he was affected. A nerve end, discharging in an inert brain, excited its sensibilities, and opened neuron tracts to the records of experience. The profit on the transaction was information—an intangible derivative available for the use of all monkeys who could acquire and apply it."

"But what's all this talk about, and where are you heading?" I demanded, impatiently.

"I'm just tapping on your skull, trying to accomplish what you declare coincidence did for the contemplative ape—establish a connection," he responded, amicably. "It's a charitable attempt to extend the horizon of your reason and to induce more accurate evaluations of the factors and forces that go to the making of Life. For instance, there's all this palaver about environments, and yet you do not realize that a man born here enters not one but two environments—the Earth, and the civilization erected upon its surface. He is equipped for the first, but this equipment must be adapted to the second. He might still sustain himself on a desert island, but must know how to earn a livelihood in New York. This civilization is the incorporation of the facts that men have ascertained about themselves and their habitat during the ages of their occupation, and, like its physical foundation, is a structure independent of and apart from the beings who must fit their existences to its framework.

"Since there are no definitions extant prescribing his part and identity, a newly born being is no more than an addition to a population. As he is allowed nothing of his own but his body, he grows up no more than a citizen-servitor of the civilization of the State whose laws and customs he must memorize to conform to. Hence standardization, and stereotyped living. Only by according him stature commensurate with his gifts can an entity gain the opportunity to deliver them."

"Even if he be laden with mystical significance, your entity is still stranded in the Earth's mud," I argued. "It matters little how many environments there be, if all the stimuli to which men react originate, and may be traced to the locality of which he is native. Obviously, he is the subject of his own energies, and his maintenance the object of their exertion. Where's the unknown quantity? When the factors in sight balance, and explain the product—why go further?"

"The factors in sight always balance, but never explain the product," insisted the Martian. "A watch keeps but does not use time. No activity is its own occasion; not even exercise. In every transaction the motivating interest is external to the tools it uses. It's not the loom that needs the cloth it weaves. While it is true that the stimuli to which men respond may be traced to their habitation, the fact is no more a clew to the identities concerned, or their objectives, than the movement of electrons in a copper wire is to the contents of the message being conveyed."

"Rather a puzzle, your intangible," I scoffed. "Where does one seek this mysterious quantity?"

"It lies in the nature of man himself," said my visitor firmly. "Decode that nature; define and allocate its attributes and you'll have the basis for understanding relationships in the scheme of things. Remember that, though use is knowledge, its application is instinctive until information is subtracted from practice. All the factors and bearings are familiar because they are embedded in experience. Since the seeking and the isolation of this potential are the means and the art of developing it, the individual must do his own looking."

"Does one look under the bed for it? Or where does one begin?" I said.

"By putting the reasoning faculties to work," he replied. "For instance, assume yourself the agent of a Boston shoe factory stationed in Berlin for the purpose of extending the firm's trade in Germany, and, in the light of the exposition I have offered, analyze the situation. You are an alien in a foreign land, an uninvited guest, proposing to exploit your hosts for the benefit of the country of your paternity. You are handicapped by ignorance of the German language, of her trade conventions and of the natives' taste in footwear. So, before the market may be entered, you must master the vernacular, learn the customs and become acquainted with the national attitude as regards shoes. It may be your offering is superior to the home product, but you are powerless either to plead or prove the fact except through the mediums of common understanding established there. So your previous experience in shoe-making and selling is ineffectual until you have converted them to Teutonic usages. Meanwhile, the soil, the air you breathe, the food consumed, the home you live in and the laws that regulate your intercourses and comings and goings, are all German. It follows, perforce, that the stimuli to which your behavior is response, must be Germanic also.

"Here, then, are involved the circumstances of a complete transplantation but in thus adapting your individuality to conform to the conditions of a strange environment, have you lost your identity as an American? Alteration of a system of communication has not changed you or your objective—the advancement of your own interest in furthering that of the Boston shoe firm. If the enterprise is successful, the profits accrue directly to its pocket and you share the proceeds. If not, the effort has, even so, enriched your mind with knowledge and experience.

"Now survey the involutions comprised in this transaction and note the divorcement of its agents, both from the activities they actuate and the background which furnished the site and the properties for the engagement. As, in a play the actors preserve their own identities and interests, apart from the roles they assume, so all the participants in this little drama of business conducted private lives independent of and separate from the making and exploitation of shoes. This was but means to the ends, not only of sustaining the energies of their bodies but more especially of using and enjoying life itself.

"All the relations involved in your situation are embodied here—what do you make of my allegory?"

"No mystic significance appears to me," I declared. "Events followed precedent; business as usual. Action confined to environment; earnest workers striving for monetary enhancement; proceeds of industry invested in keeping the game going and having a good time. Pure materiality throughout. Men are what they do. To suggest that they can be something else, is just wishful thinking. That cancer whose symptom is faith."

"Then time is a clock—a banker, money—a head of steam, the fly wheel it revolves—a writer, pen and ink or prose and poetry, as the case may be," returned the Martian, in tones of resignation. "Just blind cerebration; on a par with the mental processes of the bee and the ant.

"If someone accused *you* of being the books that issue from your press, you'd laugh and think him mad; or, if he suggested that books write and print themselves, and get distributed to readers by gravitation or some other impersonal force. You recognize yourself as a creative agent, combining ingredients into a format, animating each step of the process with energy—all for the purpose of entertaining or informing the minds of prospective readers on behalf of your own pocket. Now, a book is only a medium for the transportation and exchange of ideas, and is mental—not physical currency— though it be a thing-in-itself having shape and weight. Its existence implies establishment of a series of conventions covering language, type, and paper, and the presence of beings familiar with these terms, whose minds derive profit from reading. The raw material alone, the substance of the bookmaking ingredients, is derived from the environment, but so changed is it in texture, that Nature, if she had eyes or an interest, would be unable to identify her progeny. In reality, the significant components of the transaction, as in the case of the shoe-salesman in Germany, belongs in the mental world, miles removed from its earthly origin.

"And as to the reinvestment of the proceeds—have you inquired of yourself, what motive inspires your own devotion to work? Industry may be praiseworthy, but it is not an objective. Is it not for escape?—Labor is just the price of leisure. From the application of energy, you have derived the means to assemble a background for that private *I*, the being who, in other hours, masquerades as a business man. This *I* is a lover of form and color, and expresses his real nature in the pictures and draperies and rugs which he has gathered around his person. Action and profit do not enter here, for it is the retreat of a mind withdrawn from the rough contacts of the world for the delectation of its secret qualities."

"Thanks for the compliment—even if the definition does not fit," I returned.

"I can imagine nothing more irritating than the inconsistency of materialistic thinkers," the Martian retorted. "Organisms, vital or mechanical, can transmit only what is implanted in them. No car will return more speed than its horsepower indicates—each petal of a rose is specified in its seed cells. The conduct of a human being, you say, represents the behavior of a type of biological engine, but, since its own parts cannot determine its actions or professions, responsibility for its preferences must be allotted to some latency inherent in its constitution. Evidence, in your own instance, is in the selection of an especial mode of living.

"Doubtless you'll insist it was by deliberate option this course was adopted, but since the doctrine you avow denies freewill, use of such faculty cannot be claimed. At best, freewill offers no more than the privilege of choice among alternatives. There remain heredity and environment, but no microscope has disclosed identification or proclivity granules, in either sperm or ovum cells. If you assure me you accommodate the inclination of your personality, I reply that, if your personality is only your body, it has no physiological need for seclusion, beauty or scholarship.

"Exact thinking requires an adequate agency for every

phase of physical effect an organism registers. On the part of an insect, rational behavior—employing means to the ends of its own interests—is ascribed to instinct. It is logical to assign to the same instrumentality, any conduct on the part of a human being for which he has no more adequate explanation than inclination.

"Incidentally, the gamut of instinct, which is merely use, without cognizance, is wider than your savants dream. It comprises the philosophies of beings who have not yet learned to distinguish between their minds and their bodies."

The last sentence rang out exultantly.

"Your third-degree stuff is breaking down whatever measure of cerebration my personality unconsciously exercises, so I ask adjournment for the night," I exclaimed wearily.

"Too bad," said the Martian a bit resentfully. "I'm just at the top of my stride. Get your resistances into good trim for tomorrow—my heaviest artillery is still in reserve."

"Off for a new sunrise?" I murmured, as I turned out the light.

"I'm not in the mood for scenery tonight," he answered. "I shall switch over to Tibet and exchange cosmic gossip with a Mahatma I know there."

CHAPTER IX: AN INTERLUDE IN MAHATMA LAND

Men do not deserve their digestions. Tibetan Sage on earth because of a miscarriage. The culture of escape. Occidental vs. Oriental creeds. Captains of Industry as Mahatmas of the environment. Original version of the Garden of Eden legend. Does experience belong to him who has gained it or to him who created the opportunity? Subject matter of discovery predates its identification.

AFTER a hard tussle, unconsciousness mercifully supervened and I slept. Through my tired brain filtered a disorderly confusion—of shoe salesmen spending their profits in Berlin beer-gardens, of monkeys counting cocoanuts with a hand each on stomach and forehead, of winged books flying out of presses and into libraries. Civilization and environment wrestling, throttling one another. Equilibrium was a sleeping beauty, and for some reason or other, I was disturbing her. A chaotic night, and it was long past the ordained hour when I awoke. In spite of my intangible nocturnal adventures, I felt refreshed and ready to give battle to whatever delusions the day developed. In fact, my partner thought me overly harsh with one of our bestsellers, who had based the plot of his new novel on a premonition.

And I was in the full enjoyment of that delectable placidity which is the reaction to the free, full glow of gastric juices, breaking down the proteins and carbohydrates of my late dinner—a meal of broiled tenderloin and onions, and broccoli and peach pie in which I had done myself very well indeed, when my invisible guest announced his arrival.

Suddenly I remembered the penetrative power of his singular vision, and it occurred to me the Martian might be following the intimate processes of my digestion tracking its successive steps along the route of the alimentary canal. I experienced a twinge of resentment at the idea of the hidden machinery of my system being exposed to an alien and critical eye.

"Don't worry," he began. "I'm torn between admiration and envy. As an engineer, I am marveling at the surpassing ingenuity of those primordial chemists and physicists who developed that extraordinary method of disintegrating and converting fuel into energy, which your stomach and intestines perform so efficiently. When I listen to some sarcastic savant railing at the mild miracles ascribed to your Christ, and remember that the changing of water into wine is simple in comparison with the synthesizing of elements proceeding in his body, I smile. To me the transmutation of meat and bread into lymph and blood, the manufacture of bile, saliva, pepsin and enzymes, and the subtle separation of oxygen from nitrogen in the lungs, are far more amazing than the raising of Lazarus. The fact that all these, and the innumerable other complex arts this silent and secretive engine within practices so deftly, are conducted without the knowledge or cooperation of the human passenger, is a cosmic joke. But, forgive me; the contentment of your expression awakens memories of my own body in cold storage on Mars, and I covet every phase of the sensations you are enjoying."

"If your satisfaction be mixed with malice, it is good to know that at least one of our human properties is approved by so superior a being," I remarked.

"Yes, but it's wasted on you," the Martian returned bitterly. "Now if I were where you are, I should have derived ten times the pleasure out of the operations. Sense of smell and taste in humans is almost vestigial, because you have not coupled your minds to nerve-ends of nose and tongue. To a connoisseur of organic processes, the operations of his body afford a succession of enjoyable reactions which grow in intensity with the growth in awareness of function."

"In this instance, then, ignorance is bliss—" I responded. "I'm feeling fine and I know it. But why this animosity?"

"That confounded Tibetan irritated me," replied my visitor more placably. "It happens that the Mahatma I went to visit was off on an etheric excursion into China, and I got talking with a celebrated Sage who is an object of veneration in the vicinity. Actually he is a most cultured person and knows more about the real nature of things than all the academicians in Europe, but he suffers from the complex that he is on Earth because of a miscarriage, and that he may only secure release and restoration to the serene realm of his former existence by holding the thought that matter, being unstable, does not exist. His body he considers a prison, the penalty of his exile, so—though it must be sustained—being a badge of shame, it should be maltreated. Use of its faculties he construes as acceptance of earthly conditions; so act, speech and effort spell anathema to him. He makes himself as uncomfortable as possible, lives in mire in a cold cave, begs his food, spends his days in contemplation and acts as far, as circumstances permit, as though he were somewhere else rather than here. Personally, I regard him about as misguided as your scientists, who imagine the sole business of life to be preserving itself, or the religious driveling about love, and praying to be saved by some superior power willing to take over the tasks they are too stupid to attend to themselves."

"It's a most distressing time you are having," I commis-
erated. "Not so long ago you declared that in Tibet there
was a true understanding of life, and here you are back, full
of denunciations of a system I thought had much to recom-
mend it."

"It has, and that's the measure of its guilt," the Martian
insisted. "Ignorance is an excuse for error, though it does not
avert consequence, but he who knows the law and violates it,
earns condemnation. A visitor to this world confronts two
orders of civilization—that prevailing in the East and that
in the West. The first is based on introspection; the other
on information. The information is being applied; the introspection is short-circuited. Gifts, in this very pragmatic universe, are for use, and woe be to him who, having knowledge
and means, employs neither.

"Now this holy man I described had so sensitized his mind
that its range far transcends the limitations which spatial geography imposes on the human species. Though his physical faculties were no better than your own, he had perfected
them into instruments of penetration and precision. Lift
no eyebrow at me—for nothing more is implied here than
what pianist, acrobat and conjurer apply in pursuit of their
callings. Early in life an adept had selected him as promis-
ing raw material for development, and his young days were
rigorously devoted to exercises adapted to the awakening of
his faculties. In the process of subordinating the properties
of his bodily organism to his will, he convinced himself that
the interests of the twinned organisms were not identical. In
fact, he was a bird, and it a cage. So his culture became that
of escape. Life was vulgar, to be endured as an ordeal; not to
be accepted as an experience. He was an expatriate.

"This view of his circumstances I expounded, to his dis-

gust. Since it was an ordered world, he must admit it represented the intentions of the Founders. Since he was billeted
here, it indicated an assignment, so he was not present on
his own affair, save as the agent of the authorities who had
conscripted him. He shared faculties and vehicle with the
race into which he had been born, so he must be part of
an incarnation without personal privileges. What his intellectual endowments had enabled him to attain, insight into
the Ordination of Life belonged not to himself alone, but
to all his brethren. Therefore, use of his power for personal aggrandizement was treason. Though he derided western
civilization as barbarous, and compared its industry to the
bustle of maggots in cheese, I argued that its concern was the
amelioration of its members; and, that individual enhancement lay in contributing to the common cause. Knowledge
therein was not secret doctrine, for all ascertainment and
every improvement in utensil was for collective service.

"Let him contrast the crudeness of his own life, and the
wretchedness of his poverty-stricken and ignorant countrymen, with the comforts and conveniences to which western
peoples had access. In the practice of non-participation, to
avoid some immediate law of consequence, might he not be
challenging the mandate of a higher jurisdiction? It would
be a shock, eventually, to find his cherished Karma loaded
with the sufferings of those compatriots whose mean physical needs he had not deigned to relieve.

"What most deeply irked this eminent sage's superiority
was to be reminded that men were of one breed, anchored
to the same locality, and that, however different in development, their equipment was uniform. All had faculties to reason, to perceive and to create, together with hands for work,
and legs for locomotion. Whatever the task, its attainment

called for correlation of all the powers of the outfit. Perhaps Mind lent itself more readily to creeping than to climbing, but, adapting the environment to the physical needs of the individual exacted employment of the identical qualities the individual must apply in the effort to release himself from its claims.

"Agreed, that stabilization of Mind was a higher achievement than the blind exercise of its potency to generate buildings, corporations and other physical engines for outside purposes, yet, since it was double-jointed, and worked as well in the open as on the inside, perhaps it no more than fulfilled a functional obligation. To this latter he cried heresy, but was too logical to deny that growing a great mercantile structure required of its creator devotion and concentration, as single-minded and intense as ever he had applied to the development of super-consciousness. I added that the virtue he most prized in himself—subordination of appetite, temper and self-interest—was engendered in the executives of large institutions by the discipline of their evolution. In ascending to control, perforce they had acquired the technique of the processes they conducted, had learned the laws governing the relation of product to need and needs to conditions, to exercise authority with reason and justice, and to subdue their personal interest to the responsibility they sustained. Unconscious agents of the environment they might be, exercising wisdom without sensing its significance, and ignorant of the nature of their being, yet their training differed from an adept's, in subject rather than in degree."

"Representing captains of industry as Mahatmas is picturesque," I commented, "though I'm not sure Big Business would relish the compliment, or know what you meant—but what did your sage say to this onslaught?"

"With exemplary patience he pointed out my error," answered the Martian. "However efficient, he insisted that instinctive culture was without standing in the universe; industry was not an end but an attribute; concentration of faculty in an objective exterior to the self, though it involved self-sacrifice and all the other virtues, was as chasing after wind; man was no more than a tool of life, and so must remain until he recognized his own identity. Since this wisdom was unattainable without faculty, for if the gift were not inherent in the seeker its pursuit was vain, and since it was impossible to show a man the way who had not eyes to see, the better part was to attend to one's own business of *Being*, in preparation for the bliss of non-being at the end of the chapter. What I construed as a civilization was shell—and the more structures man built around his body the harder the escape from it. What seemed betterment to me was compromise—cowardly surrender of spirit to matter. I had mistaken periodicity for progress, whereas stream and source were one, and their course, a circle.

"Men, he went on to say, were life's actors, circling with the Earth around the Sun. Death was night, and birth—re-emergence into day. The garb of existence changed with the seasons, but its pattern and color never altered. The generations traveled the paths the feet of their predecessors had worn, stumbled over the same obstacles, ever moving onward but never arriving; because for such as these, there were neither destinations nor ends. Effigies they were, driven by wind and weather, sweating and groaning under the yoke of imaginary obligations, the greatest of which was their delusion of the need for self-preservation. History repeated itself because the constitution of the characters committed them to reproduce identical blunders. Monotonous iteration—same plot, situations, scenery and dialogue. What a spectacle!

"An eloquent old gentleman—he made behaviorism seem mellow and old Ecclesiastes an optimist. He entertained me with the original version of the legend of the Garden of Eden which he said the Israelites had stolen from India and transposed to fit the crass conceptions of lovers of flesh-pots. This paradise was no happy hunting ground for a first man and his wife. It contained no birds or beasts, or fishes; nothing material—not even gravity, light or air. These were aftereffects—consequences. In this ideal realm, remote from time and space, dwelt spirits blissfully unconscious of existence. Here was Being without becoming, Sensibility without sensation, Knowledge without knowing. Beauty had no form and music was free of sound. Around them played Possibilities innocent of probability, and Qualities unaware of properties. The Shapes of all The Things that are, flourished there in luxurious intangibility—except Error. So every prospect pleased and monotony was undreamed of.

"In this version, the snake that entered and tempted Adam, was Experiment; and the forbidden fruit of the tree of knowledge was Experience. It occurred to our first parents that it would be interesting to invest some of the lovely ideas that surrounded them with shape and weight, and they expressed the notion. That broke the spell. An indignant divinity, who knew evil when he saw it, cast them forth into realization, clothing their naked souls with bodies, implanted memory in these, as a scourge, ever to remind them of the lost elysium. Thus Work, the primal curse, came into the world together with cold, heat and sweat.

"There was a saving clause, the Sage concluded. If, among the descendants of these degenerates, there appeared men brave and constant enough to reclaim their true identity, they might be shown the path of attainment. It was a long, rough road, up which the aspirant must drag his body, deaf to its appetites and blind to distraction. But the goal was liberation, and there was welcome for the prodigal son, returned to the house of his father. *His* feet were on this path, and he had reason to believe that he was nearing the end of the passage."

"A sensible man," I commented. "At least there is nothing vague about his mysticism. According to his lights an honest mechanist."

"Being able to disappear, I had the last words," the Martian continued. "His was a picturesque tale, I told him, more entertaining than what western philosophy offered to cover the phenomena in evidence, but too colored by his own preoccupations to fit the perspective. His evaluation of the premises seemed superficial to me. A universe was spread before the eyes of men and they had come to know that the traveling planet which carried them in its revolutions was a tiny item in the constitution of a great system. Its place, orbit and speed were prescribed in relation to the mass of this organization, and that it and its neighbors kept their courses, must be due to the efficient administration which governed vehicular traffic in stellar space. He was cognizant of an orderly sequence of unfoldment in the succession of living organisms, of which man's body was the peak, and it was reasonable to assume that, since all the beings who clung to the surface of a planet partook of its nature, they were subjects of the Power that maintained and regulated its momentum. He would agree that an immense and elaborate pre-arrangement must have preceded the entrance of his entity into this sphere, because he knew, better than the ruck of men, the marvelous properties of the physical vehicle in which his life was conducted. To the design of this body he had contributed nothing, though he animated, sustained and utilized its agencies. Sojourning therein, through its sense appliances, he had become aware of the world, his fellows and of himself, and of the isolation of each from the other. Undeniably this information was the fruit of the contacts incurred by his presence, just as the control he had achieved over his thoughts, nerves, muscles and limbs was due to the application of his will to the instruments to which it was yoked.

"Since the crux of his accomplishment within the period of his stay was represented by a consciousness of entity, apart from both his body and the Earth that had furnished the forms and materials of his experience, was it not logical to assume this was the result of the ordeals to which he had been subjected? Might not use of the mastery he had attained, fairly be claimed by that Power which had predetermined and arranged the resistances he had encountered and survived? The sharpness the razor derived from the hone belonged to him who evoked it. And this concern over sorrow, disease and transiency? Surely these were no other than the pangs inseparable from change; incidents of the way—not reasons for rejecting it.

"Non-being, cessation, freedom, were delusions. How could one blot out an episode of his life by denying it?—there were neither alibis nor truancies in the universe. In the great nexus of cause and effect, which made the warp and woof of that gigantic going-concern the Cosmos, how could any thread declare itself out of the pattern?

"Perhaps he had been deceived. His own development might have been hastened by his devotion, but I feared he had no more than pushed himself into a more difficult job, before he was sufficiently weathered and tempered to carry on with it. And in the interim, by shunning the objects of desire, he had deprived himself of legitimate pleasures provided to lubricate the throes of evolution.

"Before my sage could discharge the words that burned on his lips, I retired from the vicinity and whiled away the remaining hours of the Sun, perched on a monument at Memphis, meditating on the futility of all superiorities."

"Transpose a few passages and you have the foundations of Behaviorism," I remarked. "But you flit so swiftly from sheer mechanism to crass supernaturalism that it is hard for one whose feet are on the ground to follow the loops of your flight. I subscribe to the allocation of identity as product of contact—encounters of man with society and the environment—but it is preposterous to allege these are predetermined."

"In a millionaire's garden nearby—it is on the roof of a Fifth Avenue apartment, fifteen floors above the street—are tulips," parried the Martian. "In grace and beauty each lovely flower sits proudly on the column of its slender stem. With the glimmer of consciousness that glows even in the lowliest of life's organisms, they feel they have fulfilled themselves, and attribute to the nature of their being the evocation of their charm. To you, they represent the art of some gardener who enfolded in a bulb the pattern of stalk, leaf, petal and color, and in a culture of fertilized earth set sunlight and warm air to develop his design.

"Perhaps it is asking more than humanity is now capable of, to demand it awaken to resemblances, while it is still asleep amid familiarities. Comparisons are based on a positive, and until that is identified, recognition of likeness or divergence is impossible. In nature, cause blends so subtly into effect that for diagnosis, detachment is essential. Direction, as your relativists perceive, is determined from the point of view. That which you interpret as progress onward or upward, horizontal or perpendicular, may be circular. When the humbled Martian savants took up the task of resurveying our planet and its inhabitants and their works and ways, from the plane of objectivity, the resolution lifted them out of subjectivity and beyond the orbit of the phenomena they scrutinized. They had stepped from the parade, and were spectators. As their perspective widened, the facts which had seemed so nicely adjusted within the circumference of their former convention extended themselves into the open, as the streets of a city are revealed from an aeroplane to be highways of communication into the surrounding country. Old patterns took on new aspects. Connections hitherto invisible, became apparent, and it was obvious that all the ancient truths must be reassembled to fit these larger coordinations.

"Perhaps this sounds symbolical, but recall the ruin wrought in the structure of your own physics by Einstein's announcement of the law of relativity. Your scientists are still gasping from the shock, and have not yet begun the adaptation of their bearings to this fundamental."

"Adding Time to the dimensions lends no planks to your platform," I interrupted. "Thus far Einstein has not interfered with the multiplication table nor with everyday applications of force to matter. Gravitation still operates as of yore and evolution is untouched."

"Your unconcern is not shared by the more eminent scientists of this world," the Martian replied. "To their thinking, the old anchorages are afloat, and even the reality of reality at stake. Yet, relativity is itself relative. It complicates the calculations of astronomers, but upsets no digestions. The Earth rotates at the same pace, the stars cling to their accustomed courses, and you sleep as soundly as if Einstein had never raised his voice.

"Discovery, one may repeat, has nothing to do with creation. What investigation discloses was present prior to its detection. There was America before Leif Ericson or Columbus. Circulation of the blood antedated Harvey. The endocrine glands were not news to the bodies of men, even if unmasking them did extend the horizon of physiology. Knowledge is the environment in which the mind functions, but, like food, information is ever exterior to the individual, and must be absorbed if he would be nourished by it. He can digest only what his brain has been conditioned to accept and he may use no more than his interest demands. Eventually the findings of the German mathematician will penetrate the laboratories, the colleges and the schools, and in unsuspected ways influence the behavior of the race. Until the principle becomes a direction point, and is brought within the range of the average mind, it and you will be untouched by its implications."

"More metaphysics," I intruded sharply, irritated by this digression. "I'm curious about the objective survey. What did the Martian savants see from the sidewalk that was not visible to those who marched in the procession?"

"As if physics was ever more than metaphysics materialized," responded the Martian, "but though you have not admitted that the springs of your attention have run down, your aura is losing color and consideration bids me withdraw. Bolshevism arouses my curiosity and I shall employ the interval between this moment and tomorrow night, examining aspects of that naive experiment in accelerating economic evolution."

"You'll be bored stiff," I remonstrated.

"There's always pleasure in inspecting the ruins wrought by another's error," he returned. "And I pledge that not a syllable of my experiences shall burden your ears."

CHAPTER X: THE QUEST FOR THE TRUTH ABOUT LIFE

Martian scientists analyze the properties exhibited by living organisms. Life something other than energy, and does
not design its habitations. Plants and animals live off the
country and follow the same conventions. Man and amœba,
incarnate appetites. Trends and course of human activities.
The problem of conscious participation. Morality dismissed
as having no existence in itself. The crucial question—is man
just a body, or does an entity pervade his parts? Civilizations
exist independent of their memberships. Consciousness the
coordinating factor and the causative agent in organic evolution. A protean power that has escaped classification in
knowledge.

"ADVENTURES in political economies, like narratives of
dreams, bear hardly on the attention of audiences," began
the Martian as we foregathered the following night for our
conference.

"In spite of my promise," he continued, "I'd like to tell
you of the sights, sounds, smells and nightmares of Moscow,
but entertainment must be sacrificed to the fulfillment of
responsibility. I'm no more than a parasite on your patience,
but as I've nothing better to do than talk, nor you than listen,
no obligation is incurred on either side. I'm about to plunge
back into history, and unroll the dull record of the ancestral
controversy between our Martian scientists and their engineering persecutors. For convenience, understand me, as
substituting English for Martian terms.

"As I was saying," he proceeded, "my ancestors began by

extending the boundaries of their conceptions but, finding themselves in cloudland, agreed first to determine the quantities, proportions and perspective of their problem. Living was the product of an engine, called Man—what relation did the various activities its texture exhibited bear to the apparatus from which they flowed? This protoplasmic organism generated the energy applied in the conduct and movements of its parts by the combustion of food, but, beyond fuel, shelter and fair treatment of its corpus, had no needs of its own. Yet it transacted great affairs, had reared noble edifices and had developed industries whose scope was as wide as the planet. However different in nature from a locomotive, a mill or a clock, in principle the machine belonged in the same category, because it was not the object of its own use. This implied the presence of another agent—a beneficiary, whose power and character the achievements in sight expressed, but since none was visible, perhaps the apparatus carried his constitution in addition to its own—as a telephone wire conveys conversation, a radio wave, words and music, or a current of air—heat, moisture and sound. In support of the existence of a latent habitant, was the fact that though this physical organism was standardized throughout its parts, the interests expressed were never identical."

"The same tune in another key—just rationalizing from a fresh angle," I expostulated angrily. "Even a half-wit would dispute the dissimilarity of interests you stress."

"This survey was not in search of novelties but of bearings," the Martian corrected. "As here, all the facts were familiars of too common acceptance to be weighed and measured. For instance, it does not occur to you to consider the dynamics and mechanics involved in the act of lifting the cigarette you are smoking to your lips. Now our savants had progressed to the point of discriminating between utensil and user—the first step in emergence from the realm of the instinctive. It was in order, next, to examine the property called Life, as exhibited in the multiplicity of animal and vegetable organisms on Mars, and it became evident that Life was something other than energy. Life grew and conducted the work of the structures it animated, but invariably these were equipped with engines, to generate from the environment, the energy their activities required. So it appeared as a factor endowed with capacity to expand, from seed or egg, the characteristics of the genus or species which carried it, and to inspire and sustain the processes through which the power essential to vital functioning was developed. Since the forms of the vegetable and animal kingdoms were all standardized and had been for ages, it was plain that current life did not design its habitations. Literally, it materialized, out of the elements at hand, plans rudimentary in the sperm and ovum-cells it entered at birth. Or, it was a transient, that set in motion the laws which executed the specifications for each particular tenement it occupied, and in departing destroyed it. Amœba, plant, flower, tree, fish, reptile, bird and mammal assumed the properties and fulfilled, without variation, the role assigned to each. All lived off the country they inhabited, and rank and file were dependent on the same type of apparatus, consumed the same fuels and followed the same conventions, in maintaining their business as going-concerns.

"In one aspect, the planet was no more than a giant laboratory, in which complex chemical processes were being conducted for no other purpose than the sustainment of the innumerable armies of vital organisms that swarmed all over its broad surfaces. This orderly array of living forms con-

ducted a vast business of exchange with environment, converting, transforming and renewing its substantial elements,
extracting minerals from its soils for the fabrics of its vegetable structures, storing heat from the sun for consumption in
the engines of its animal populations. Within this self-contained and self-sufficient circle, all relations were derivative
and dependent upon each other. The same building material
entered into the constitutions of the inhabitants. The large
organisms were multiples of the smallest, and, in the unfoldment of their forms, retraced their own evolution. Survival
amid the circumstances of the terrene defined the types of
anatomies, and their behavior was guaranteed by the adjustment of their mechanisms to the locations in which they
functioned. The perfect chain—cause linked with effect—as
wheels to axles—all in the open.

" 'To what end?' the awakened Savants demanded. 'None
of the elements entering here furthers a purpose of its own,
but since there is organization, sequence and consecutive-
ness, some definite interest is being served. Of what nature
are the profits, and to whom do they accrue? Since there is
no beneficiary in sight, and we are ignorant of what is in the
making, perhaps examination of the premises and processes
of the institution may yield a clew to its objectives.

" 'The site of operation is a revolving planet with its accessories of atmosphere and sunlight and the employees are
the innumerable living organisms engaged in converting its
elementary raw materials into fuels acceptable for burning
in their several types of engines. On the surface then, these
organisms seem to have no other use than to consume what
they produce, which is absurd. Imagine a great railway ter-
minal with trains shuffling in and out, puffing locomotives,
passengers arriving and departing but neither going nor

coming, all performances confined within the boundaries of the yards without either direction or deliveries. Such affairs are incompatible with reason and experience.

" 'It may be fallacious,' argued our Savants, 'to conclude that the sole purpose of all these vital organisms, the employees of the system, lies in the preservation of their own lives. Among them is an infinite variety of forms and properties, and they have in common only the cellular texture of their bodies, appetites and access to the communal sun, air and food stores. Each species and subsection had its peculiar characteristics, a particular mode of conducting its existence, and member-parts graduated to its role. Though they preyed on one another, they held independence, bred true to type, and confined intercourse to their own kind. All subscribed to the incessant chemical interchange with the environment—their ground rent—but it was blind tribute rendered involuntarily, without realizing requital of obligation.'

"To grade all these employees on the score of common origin and means of subsistence was to omit from consideration the marking factor in the ascending scale of multiplied organisms—degree of participation in their own activities. Here was an avenue that might yield a clew. Evolution of form, it was evident, accompanied, and was in correspondence with, development of consciousness, use and control. In so far as the business of living was concerned, the life history of an amoeba paralleled a man's, but protozoa's consciousness was rudimentary—impassive dynamic adjustment—whereas human beings were aware of entity and location, cognizant of their own faculties, and able to apply them.

"Without the equipment represented by his organs and senses, man would be as impotent as the amoeba, but the accomplishments of the race could not be ascribed to the character of the apparatus its members employed. These denoted no more than a gift of power, tools and materials; circumstances of the environment imposed on all entrants the task of using them; but the individual must supply initiative and direction. Eyes and ears were essential to find bearings in time and space, but each entity had to establish his own relation therein and make his private way. Routes were labeled, because there had been accumulated a store of facts covering the nature of the world, the character of men's physical machinery and the arts of combining and coordinating the elements of the first for the benefit of the second; but this information, though it figured as the racial inheritance, was isolate and inert—like food, it had to be sought and absorbed before it could be turned to account.

"Man's capacity to bend the processes of nature to his purpose, was no more than a potential, and lessened not a whit the need of exertion. In the ascent from the depths, he had acquired stature and vision; could help himself with his hands and speculate about his prospects; but advancement of knowledge of the technic of living, and the multiplication of the mediums of shelter and locomotion increased, rather than lessened, his responsibilities. Nor did these cultural gains relieve his obligations to the routine of life, growth and death, or illuminate the cause or use for his existence.

" 'Wherein lieth the advantage of participation?' our Savants asked, at this stage of the survey. 'Both man and amoebas are incarnate appetites. The amoeba does not know it, and finds its needs without looking; man does, but may only satisfy his needs by both looking and finding the right means to supply them.' "

"Shocking," said I, with mock sympathy. "So, objective

inspection again discovered the obvious. Fumbling among familiar facts may be exercise, but amounts to no more than waste motion. Say the universe exists because it exists, and it is unnecessary to go further."

"If obtuseness were talent, you'd be a genius," responded the Martian pleasantly. "Perhaps the universe exists because you exist and in that instance there are long distances ahead of you.

"Being committed to their survey, our Savants next proceeded to review the trends of the attainments of men, and register their direction. What, in reality, did men do? The human race fed, clothed and sheltered its bodies, reproduced its kind, talked, walked, traveled and flew, and engaged itself in the exchange of commodities that ministered to the conduct of these occupations. From this it was deduced that living consisted in the establishment of contacts and communications among beings, and the sustainment and preservation of the agencies by which intercourse was conveyed. Except for squabbles about destiny, the activities thus engendered covered the range of the performances of men, for they included the institutions of property and government which, in themselves, were no more than traffic regulations. All assemblages of the planetary population as nations, communities, classes, castes, fraternities, unions—gregariousness in general—could be set down as human trends; also the passion for motion and speed. Though these might have no significance, they deserved note as characteristic of the animal under investigation."

"But what about morality?" I suggested. "Good and evil—and so forth."

"When the Savants published their preliminary findings," replied the Martian, "their attitude on this subject gave offense both to the religious minded and to the lawyers. The moralities were summarily dispensed with as having no existence in themselves, being involved in the interactions between Martians and their surroundings. They admitted inadvertence, incompetence and ignorance, all of which carried their own consequence.

"Society was as subject to malignant growths as the physical organisms of its members, and must protect its own metabolism against infection and derangement. Crime therefore was only infraction of civilization's immediate code of self-preservation, erected to secure life and property against invasion. Punishment was not to deter, but to eject and exclude rebels against accepted conventions.

"Virtue, they suggested, lay in observance of the laws prescribed by the nature of man's body in its relation with the properties of his environment, and had no mystic significance. Goodness was only sound pilotage; an able steersman, in ordering the way of his craft, held in mind her speed and dimensions with respect to the breadth and depth of the channel to be traversed, the rights of passing vessels, and the state of wind and water. Sin, therefore, is in circumstance, they concluded. Call it maladjustment, inaccuracy or error, and class all such disorders with leaky roofs and shoes, hot-boxes, loose bearings, misspelling; losses and accidents as failures of intention or frustrations of purpose—bad calculation as products of maladroitness or obstinacy; and, though nothing will be changed, one source of confusion will be removed.

"As for religion, though its inclusion in the category as a definite characteristic was debatable, consideration of its bearing and place in the constitution of man must await light on the basic problem, which was the actual nature of Martian beings. If a Martian was no more than his body, discussion of a divine order or of immortality was mere chasing after wind."

"That's the best news your story has carried so far," I interrupted. "It's kicking superstition downstairs with a vengeance. But if in this country an important scientific body declared God a delusion, all the churches would unite in denouncing it."

The Martian smiled. "But science has done that very thing," he declared. "Religion in this country has no standing before the intellectual court. As you have told me, it is vestigial—a tradition of the period before men took stock of their surroundings. Though God survives in your constitutions and courts, it is as a symbol, not as a fact. Even if religious institutions persist among your populations, and billions are spent constructing or adorning temples of worship, no one takes the subject-matter seriously. The ministry is a profession, faith a crying aloud in the dark, churchgoing one of the imaginary obligations."

"You flatter us," I corrected. "We are more fettered than you think. And though it is true that intelligent men have discarded revelation, the Scriptures and the preposterous beliefs that so handicapped the old civilizations, our clerics have transferred their sanctions to enforcing the moralities and are more of a nuisance than ever."

"The blessed certitude of ignorance—how I envy it," the Martian observed. "Our Savants were no less positive when they began the quest. As they looked and listened, so many mysterious lights showed up, and strange sounds became audible that their assurance diminished. But that's the story and this a digression."

"Bring out the concealed assets," I said with all the derision my voice could carry. "It's time for a buried treasure to come forth."

"At this stage of the inquiry the Savants called for a conference with the leaders of the militant Engineers who had initiated the survey, and confided that, though the inquiry had not been barren, the avenues explored all proved cul-de-sacs. Life they knew to be something other than energy, but confined to the forms it grew and animated. Consciousness was among its properties, having the quality of spectator and reporter of sensory impressions. There were grounds for assuming that man might be more than his body, but since that was the medium through which his nature was actualized, his identity was represented by its record. Why seek an invisible agent in the presence of the cause and object of the effects in evidence?

" 'Interesting but disappointing,' was the verdict of the Engineers after listening to these disclosures. Somehow the problem had slipped through the Savants' fingers, they said in effect. At base and throughout, man is a machine. Regarded simply as a device to do what he did, he is a great invention. He grew, but did not plan his own parts. The designer, whoever he might be, knew more about mechanics and chemistry than any physicist on Mars. Explaining that a Martian evolved from an amœba, meant no more than to say a skyscraper represented the ultimate development of a hut, or a dynamo the unfoldment or multiplication of a magnet. Museums were filled with embryonic motors and aeroplanes, and whoever pleased might trace the processes of adapting the ideas represented by our devices of work and communication, from inception to operative practicality. When one could follow a transaction from start to finish it was fashionable to call it architecture or engineering; when one confronted living organisms, whose structures exhibited skill and knowledge in comparison with which our most ingenious fabrications were awkward bungles, one mentioned evolution, survival of the fittest, or some other blind or mystic term.

"To bestow gratuitously on Nature, the degree of intelligence and purpose in evidence, was guesswork. To refer the credit to God, was speculation. If God were responsible, it behooved men to learn more about his ways and show greater respect for his works; if Nature did it, this Power should be identified and deferred to, since it had secrets to impart which would help us to better living. Facts are wanted.

" 'But what facts?' chorused the Savants.

"The Engineers told them:

" 'Find, to begin with, who does what a man does, and what for? Is he just his body, or does an invisible entity animate and utilize its parts? If he be no more than his body, then life is an interaction between an organism and an environment, and it begins and ends here and now. If this be so, let us face the truth and make the most of our span. If Man be this entity, then his body is a vehicle—discover the character and mode of the affiliation: who confined him in its frame, and what is being done or demonstrated during his occupation of it?'

" 'But such determinations are beyond the resources of science,' the Savants declared.

" 'Since scientists have never faced the subject as a problem, that remains to be demonstrated,' the Engineers replied. 'The world you deal with is that which Martian beings have made. It is full of intricate organizations and complex institutions. Nowadays, Nature's best stuffs are the raw materials of our factories. More transmutations separate a silk stocking from a silk thread than exist between an amœba and the caterpillar that spun it out of mulberry fiber. We carry on the creative tradition—what is it and how do we do what we do?'

"Back to their task the Savants retired. Such definitions, they agreed, were outside the field of their professions. Human relations were abstractions—so laboratories were useless. X-rays could throw no light on behavior, nor would it sit still under a microscope. Yet in view of all the circumstances of Martian occupation of this planet, admittedly the report they had submitted, was superficial. No account had been taken of the works of the race, or the order and organization of its societies. As to the internal nature of beings, it had not been touched upon. Martians lived by their wits as well as by means of the physical activities put forth in providing their needs. There were, then, other avenues for exploration that might profitably be followed. If, however, an unknown factor existed, such as the Engineers suggested, since its presence is unsuspected, its operations would be subjective. Its influence would have to be traced by the character of the capacities exhibited by Martians, the impulses to which they responded and the trend of their actions.

"This mode of approach eventually brought them to the heart of the problem, and their next summation was significant. They began with a consideration of the social order which, though it again led to an impasse, opened the way to decisive conclusions. Epitomized, and converted into your own terminology, their report ran thus:

" 'Life has a structure; for men have resided on this planet through ages beyond computation and have an order of living which comports with their needs, that they call civilization. This, then, is the racial framework, welded of tradition, habits and laws and it exists independently of its members, but owes its mobility to their presence. Into its patterns the passing generations fit their activities, and since it is a continuity, and they transients, its authority transcends their passing relationship. Under stress of internal pressures its contours change, but its constitution endures. Though inert and oppressive, unquestionably it accommodates the dispositions of its passengers.

" 'It is absurd to call this civilization. Rather is it a system for the naturalization of the anonymous newcomers who enter this planet's precincts by the gate of birth and tenant its spaces for the terms of their leases. These aliens are classified according to the location of their delivery, and being all of the same shape and make, are designated by the names of the progenitors who provided their bodies. Their identities are derived from these parents' circumstances and subsequently are merged in their own occupations. The system holds the communal assets of food and information and, through ownership of the resources of life, controls conduct. In return for service, it provides its subjects with food and protection.

" 'There is nothing esoteric here. About the same set of principles may be deduced from the operations of the Metallic Trust or any other large going-concern on Mars. All are converters of raw material into objects of use. Shape and use carry identification of product. Invested in the corporation itself are the powers it exercises; its capital, plants and practices are separate and apart from the lives of the executives who administer them. The institution prescribes the terms of its employees' service and sustains their energies with its wage. The purpose of its existence is to supply the requirements of its customers for the profit of its stockholders. All of which leads to the conclusion, already well established, that inspection of phenomena affords little information about their origins.

" 'Prior to further research the commission summed up its findings and, in re-plotting their position, found the long sought clew.

" 'A globe turning on its axis, encircling a sun from which it derives light and heat. This sun, center of a system of planets and itself an atom in the constitution of a universe. All hanging and rotating in space, without reason. On this globe, unorganized beings calling themselves human, arriving from nowhere and returning there. Transients—who enter bodies provided for a timed passage and, on retirement, leave behind their remains. They bring and take away life. For these appearances and exits, no explanation is obtained.

" 'In evidence of their occupation—their work, the buildings, implements, vehicles contrived to accommodate their needs. These needs of humans arise from the character of their bodies in juxtaposition with the physical circumstances of their planetary habitation. Hence all inventions—things-in-themselves—the tools, machines and goods which owe identity to men's use.

" '*But the form and order of such accessories represent the exercise of faculty and power extraneous to the conditions that evoked their application.*

" 'In machines, the function of pilotage is exerted from the outside, and implements and apparatus are equipped with accommodations for the person of the operator. Without such driving and regulating attachment no work is performed. In living organisms the directive power is indwelling, but as the forces in conjunction are of identical order, the same principle is being manifested. *It follows that the basic agent of cause and effect, in all physical phenomena, is the coor-*

dinating factor that has power to collect, hinge and vitalize the elements through which it reveals its purposes.

" 'Such faculty and power is inherent in the nature of the beings in whose interest it is employed.

" 'Humans are aware of themselves apart from their environment and, through their gifts of initiative and integration, have created a pattern of living adapted to the peculiarities of their physical state. *Since such activities are due to the presence of these potentials in individual organisms, it may be assumed that the internal constitution of these beings must be blent of a factor of which such potentials are characteristic.*

" 'Accepting behavior as indicative of character, the nature of this submerged organism is defined by the province and manner of the services it renders. It identifies and interprets its own principle and is the agent and convoy of its communications. Pilotage of a vehicle entails knowledge of its weight, dimensions and needs, of the course on which it is bound, of the resistances to be overcome en route to the destination set for the voyage. So its entities carry faculties to learn and remember the facts that bear on the problem of adjusting carrier to medium, together with will to employ them—powers which represent the properties called awareness, curiosity, memory, initiative, balance and control—universal factors valid apart from application or use.

" 'Defined herein are the inherent characteristics of the two complementary principles—use and medium—which, though united for need, are divergent in essence. Joined in the same body, they do not mingle; for their alliance is that of content to carrier, tenant to house, player to instrument, aim to gun. Identity and impulsion are the contributions of the purposive factor. Medium furnishes scene and properties for performance.

" 'What is true of the bodies of men applies to all vital organisms that maintain factual existences by changing the state of matter in the environment to which they are native. Each must be a unit of a factor capable of energizing the functions that identify and fulfill its own nature. These are adaptability, growth, sustainment, mobility and reproduction; attributes of life, whether it be of bacterium, animal or man. And however simple or primitive such exercise, or limited its scope, it implies presence of consciousness of circumstance, and power to convert these to the interest and need of their subject. Since the degrees of consciousness and volition are proportionate to the development of the structures through which they are expressed, there is reason to conclude *that these dynamic factors are the causative elements in organic evolution.*

" 'Though this assumption is contrary to the hypothesis of automatic adaptation according to which science has classified its ascertainments, at least we have defined agencies whose properties correspond to the effects registered.

" 'We conclude Consciousness to be an effective element, or power that motivates all the agencies and institutions in which its inherent qualities are expressed. Like other forces, it acts in expansion against resistance, and so it must be confined to perform. The degree of its pressure is defined by the capacity of the container-cylinder through which it is released. It establishes and sustains the patterns of the forms wherein it functions, but its individuality is dissolved in their fabrics to reappear in the issues of their processes: As power does in work. Where doer and deed are united in volume, sequence and sight, scrutiny is voided because source has masked itself in effect.'

"So this, the most fundamental, familiar and protean of

all forces, has escaped classification in knowledge, because the eyes of its entities, being turned outwards rather than in, have deceived them into the belief that they *were* what they *did*. The true nature of their being has been obscured by the smoke of their activities.

"We have but broached the outlines of the next field for research, but, since pursuit of its complexities requires both reversal and refocusing of vision, it is offered for the investigation of minds more capable of objective self-exploration than our own."

"Sounds like the report of a spiritualistic séance, rather than the findings of a body of scientists," I commented acidly. "Anyway it's long past midnight and this especial agent of purpose is in need of sleep."

"Try during the night to recharge the batteries of your mind," retorted the Martian, "and tomorrow night I shall enjoy the society of a more intelligent auditor."

The function of pilotage. Etheric organism declared superfluous. New facts affect only those who digest them. Topsy-turvy reasoning. Segregating the principles and interests present in the construction and operation of railways
and business corporations as bearing on the nature of man.
Physics and metaphysics as involved in the production of
The Moonlight Sonata.

"PILOTAGE"—the word kept ringing in my brain. A
profession, of sorts, practiced by seamen. Pilots were able
to steer ocean liners in and out of harbors, because they had
learned the way from their mouths to the docks. There was
always a channel to whose course, width, depth and current
the dimensions of the traveling steamer had to be adapted.
So "pilot" was an agent of transfer, whose knowledge of the
conditions involved enabled him to adjust one to the other
on behalf of the interest he represented. Though inferior
in magnitude and value to a ship, her bulk was subordinate
to his force and obedient to his touch. He had professional
and private identities, the latter, though dominant, being
dependent for sustainment on the wage of the former.

It occurred to me that my own relation to the publishing concern whose revenues I helped make, was of the same
general character as that of pilot to craft. My occupation is
that of producing books, so adjusted to the tastes and desires
of the people that they exchange their money for my wares,
and in my brain is carried information, derived like a pilot's,
from study and experience which enables this conversion

to be accomplished. In return for certain hours in applying this equipment to its task, I acquire the means to purchase goods, shelter, and pleasure. And, it is true that in the gratification of these individual needs I exercise private preference, and call the leisure to which they are dedicated, "my life"—though my identity among men is derived from my profession. So I am what I do, but also I am myself. And this self is, in a way, isolated from the agencies through which it is sustained or expressed.

Pursuing thoughts so foreign to my convictions irritated me. It was going Martian with a vengeance. What difference did it make in my affairs who, and what, I might be? I was an agent for the delivery of certain goods—my rank in the book game was based on my capacity to make profits—my stature in the community had the same foundation. So why entertain theories for which no practical application appeared? Such conjectures were remote from the interests of my associates, who were also my friends. Keeping up with the procession engrossed their days and nights, as it did my own. Against casualties and death we were insured. There was neither use or value in reviewing the past, or peering into a future which would mature in due course, and on terms our attention could not affect.

As I sat awaiting the Martian that evening, the same train of ideas began their reflexes in the association centers of my cortex. As I followed their play, the voice of my invisible visitor broke in.

"An hour ago I listened-in on the unconscious cerebrations of a couple of philosophical worms who had collided in a lump of mold, and their conclusions about life were of the same tenor as your own," he remarked. "They too agreed that one did what one did, because one had the parts and the arts for doing it. One went where one was going, in search of nourishment, and made history in the form of tunnels en route. And to them, good weather was wet."

"And wisdom in avoiding the beak of the early bird," I rejoined. "Be that as it may," I continued, "though the cogitations I've indulged in take me part-way along the line of your argument, just what's in the making I can't see. To admit the existence of an underlying organism, would not change my relations to a single circumstance of life. Your savants agreed that men's actions derived from their physical constitutions. So, logically, what they do is because they are what they are. Our progress is due to that conviction. Since we have quit listening for God's good tidings we have gone ahead. No authentic instance of celestial interference for or against the race is on record. There are legitimate and tangible causes for every effect registered and one does not have to look heavenward, to find them."

"Incidentally," interrupted the Martian, "it would be interesting to know how, in a physical environment which conditions not only stimuli but their receptions and reflexes, effects could be registered, save in apparent and tangible terms. You live in a thought-world in which all ideas, advice and suggestions are suspect, lest in accepting and delivering them, some other interest than your own be served. An act is an impact. It has been pushed or pulled from under cover into the light. And in a sphere thus motivated and construed, inhabited by beings as transparent as glass, porous as sponge, and suggestible as monkeys, you tell me there is neither place nor space for unknown influences. The universe, my friend, is a cave of the winds whose currents are not all set in the direction of your own destination."

"All of which, however picturesque, does not answer the

question—what availeth the existence of two bodies when one is but the reflext of the other?" I persisted. "Science describes man as an animal, equipped with organs that translate the environment to his self-interest, which automatically interprets itself in the steps it initiates to maintain the status and further the cause of its subject. He's a receptor, with mechanisms for adjustment to change: his character is determined by the blend of his constituents and the accuracy of his reflexes: his individuality is the sum and record of his responses. In an engine of this type there's no need for a submerged outfit, which, if it were there to function, would register the same reactions."

"Your faith in the irritability of protoplasm touches me," the Martian replied. "But it is carrying a larger burden under your system than its nature fits it to endure. One of these days an experimentalist will stumble on the trick of manufacturing it, and you'll be shocked to discover that the stuff cannot behave like a human being. As for the role assigned environment in this conceit, it's a bit too anthropomorphic, even for my tastes. The idea of scenery developing a medium in which to exhibit and review the perfections of its own outlines, is novel. Hitherto it had never occurred to me to attribute a publicity-sense to inanimate Nature, but if your theory be right she must have decided back in the primitive slime-period that she was not born to blush unseen, and therefore created Man to mirror her charms. Or, the elements, developing temporary self-consciousness, through the violent interactions of those early days, agreed that organizing a world without witnesses was waste motion, so were delivered of Adam and Eve, to give testimony.

"As to the problem that disturbs you, let me ask—to what degree does the existence of the force called gravity affect your personal equilibrium? Or, in what manner has the knowledge of the constitution of the atom changed the business of bookmaking and selling? The functions of certain glands that control the structure and workings of the human organism were unsuspected until recently, but, though the information has revolutionized biology, it has not disturbed your metabolism or quickened your pulse. Yet this lofty house in which you are sitting is poised on Newton's laws: the textures of most of the materials and fabrics used in your work have been transformed in the few years since industry learned from physics and chemistry the laws that regulate the combinations of the elements. If you would know what bearing endocrinology has on your individual system, ask a physician. He'll tell you it has profoundly influenced his practices. It has provided information about obscure processes of the body that enables him to recognize and to cope with physical conditions of which previously he had no understanding whatever.

"Since you are unconscious of the reactions on your personal concerns of the immense array of facts that have swum into the vision of this generation, facts that, illuminating the nature of the world and its relations in the universe, are already transforming the character of your civilization, rest assured that the inclusion of an etheric counterpart in the structure of your knowledge will not add to your girth or modify your attitudes. The fact that the clever and flexible arrangement of bone, muscle, tissue and blood—your hand—initiates no movement of its own and is unaware of what it does or why, has not occurred to you; nor that the fingers of any burnt child are likewise ignorant of the information about heat which its sensory nerves so swiftly transmitted to central."

"Not one whit of which affects the fact that the burnt child reacted as an individual organism, to a stimulus from the environment, and that the interaction represented no more than the disturbance of the molecules of protoplasm, by temperature above its normal resistance-rate," I returned. "Communicated as pain, its self-interest unit interpreted the message as danger, and, automatically, the efferent nerves reacted to contract the muscles, which withdrew the injured member from a relation to which its constitution was not adjusted."

"Thereafter, neurons in the burnt child's cortex classified and recorded the episode as dread," replied the Martian cheerfully. "Considering the susceptibility of fleshy tissue to changes of temperature and other hostilities, it's in order to establish a society for the protection of meat from ovens. In reply to which, it is on your lips to tell me there's a difference between a live organism integrated for self-preservation, and substantial elements of similar texture released from its system—in other words, that a steak cut from a steer being no longer in communication with the neurons of the departed animal's cerebral cortex, is automatically transposed into beef."

"Humor, presumably," I interrupted.

"At the expense of the topsy-turvy reasoning, so popular in your midst," the Martian retorted. "Why logical minds should ascribe to any substance, or set of mechanical parts the motives they actualize, or skip blindly the fact, so thoroughly established in experience, that no medium is the cause of its own activities, is beyond my comprehension. Failure to realize that relations within the human organism must parallel the relation that organism bears to the world outside its own nature and needs, is anomalous. The divergent interests of differentiated dynamisms are apparent in all transactions. Consciousness of it is represented in the constitution of every device through which Man adapts his body to its circumstances."

"Still the record stands unchanged," I persisted. "Converting the organism into twins won't lessen their dependency on the environment, or enhance their potency to deal with the problem of everyday living. It amounts to nothing at all."

"Spoken like a tumble bug," proclaimed the Martian. "What amazes me, faced by the indifference that inhibits the normal exercise of faculty here, is the magnitude of the achievements of your race. As elsewhere, doubtless there are live and dead minds—a few that are fertile coordinate forces and rear skyscrapers, cut canals and subways, make motor cars and aeroplanes, harness water power, design and operate huge business machines, while the infinite majority are drones and parasites who feed on the harvests these others have sown."

"Why avenge the inadequacy of your own explanations on this involuntary listener?" I protested. "Do recall that the complicated theory you advance, though it be the basis of oriental creeds, has been examined and discarded by the Science of today. Let us step one pace off the path of ascertainment and we'll be plunged back, into the jungle of old superstitions. Representing the body as coverage of a power greater than itself, reopens all the ancient avenues of myth and fraud. At least our feet are on solid ground. You'd take us back into unplumbable waters—and to no end save confusion."

"Pardon," the Martian said, "I keep forgetting that ghosts are forbidden in these shades. Where instinct holds the fort, information is the enemy. However, I note a growing con-

cern among scientists at an accumulation of knowledge beyond the mental viscera of its receptors. Wisdom begins to
despair that the kind of folk available here can ever be made
safe for democracy. That there's an intellectual impasse, com-
mences to creep into the consciousness of the race and, before long, there may be opened a market for enlightenment.
Probably, up-to-date psychology interprets such phenomena
in meteorological equivalents. Interaction of an integrated
organism with environment, in due course charges the neurons of its cortex with electrons, in the form of information.
When these accumulate to the saturation-point of the receptor, they must expand its field, and be released as activity or
discharged as an explosion—as heated air, rising, condenses
as moisture, coheres and appears as cloud, attracts electrons
which overflow in lightning, and disperse their temporary
nests in rain."

"Sound reasoning, it seems to me," I affirmed. "And if any
analogy is worth a whoop, that is it. Holds the phenomena
within the field of the energies and mechanisms involved,
and saves dragging the cosmos for super-causes."

"It is as though one explained the impulsion of a shell
from a cannon by declaring it due to the sudden conversion
of substance into gas ignoring the requisites and prearrange-
ments represented by gun, powder, percussion and aim," returned the Martian. "However, if my mind, in interaction
with your own, has failed to overcome its resistances, obviously my energy has not been applied in the right terms to
its objective. Let us re-examine the premises and the agencies from a different angle."

"If you have anything I can use, I want it," said I, perhaps
with forced cordiality.

"Suppose then, we take that familiar of communication, a

railway, and segregate the principles and interests involved in its birth, being and operation," continued the Martian.

"Suits me," I agreed.

"To begin with," he proceeded, "if bodies weighed no more than thoughts, ideas and desires, there would be no need for railways. Unfortunately, your identity, its aspirations and its needs, are tied to a heavy physical vehicle, which must be carried to every destination you wish to reach. Since the locality in which your life is conducted abounds in resistances and distances, and the muscular appliances with which this body is equipped for its own and your transportation are weak, devices to supplement its energies have been invented. The railway is one such invention. So railway is a mechanism which owes its origin and existence to a difference in the speed-capacity of two conjoined agents—identity and organism. It reinforces the latter's legs and arms, in the affair of swiftly conveying identities and supplies across the spaces that intervene between their organisms and their objectives."

"Again, why separate identity and body?" I interrupted. "Both are going to the same place."

"Are you the taxicab which brought you to the office this morning, or the subway car in which you were snatched from 42nd Street to the City Hall at noon today?" the Martian replied. "Bend to this matter the kind of logic you bring to the solving of crossword puzzles, or, that a mechanic employs in calculating the amount of force and the mode of application necessary to remove an obstacle in the path of a plan. Anyway, a railway is a contrivance to accommodate a need for the expeditious movement of weights over intervals of space, and represents response to the nature and circumstance of the type of entity that designed and uses it.

"Whenever a race evolves the art of supplementing from

outside sources, the energy generated in its own organism, the speeding up of its processes intensifies its capacities, but confines their expression. To utilize its new franchise, requires exact information about the ways of procuring, releasing, and harnessing the power, and the contriving of vehicles through which it may deliver work. So the field of knowledge and concern is narrowed to the environment, and the problem of the members is to learn how to convert and adjust its properties to their new instrumentalities. Thereafter, the attention of that race is fixed on materials, mechanics and foundations.

"In the building of a railway, speculation is replaced by ascertainment. The task requires advance determination of focal points, such as terminals; of routes, of methods of adapting surface to track, and track to motor appliances, and all these in relation to capital, cost, service, patronage and profit. Chance, supposition and generality give way to calculation, survey and definition; opinion, to measurement. A new decalogue emerges, in which resistance of strains and stresses appears as virtue, and sin as failure to adjust edifice to the tensions and pressures it is its obligation to endure. When technique becomes purpose, subject disappears in object; so Being is Becoming, submerged in the activities it initiates; and identity is fused with its professions. Incidentally, that is why members of your generation have lost the sense of their own reality and interpret their individualities as their jobs."

"Come out of the ether and back to time and the track," I implored. "You promised me physics, and here you are, turning hypothetical somersaults."

"Calculus is more in my line than arithmetic," pleaded the Martian. "Anyway, a railway is a graded foundation of tight packed earth and rock, to which steel rails are so fastened as to facilitate the swift passage of wheeled vehicles. Over this stabilized bed, locomotives pull cars. Rails are adjusted to wheels or vice versa—cars are carriers imposed on axles; motors convert and impart energy through which movement is delivered. At the base of the structure, two organisms in interaction, whose product is distinct and separate from its parents. Here, then, is the physical body of the railway, integrated for its office, but inert until animated by dynamic factors from outside, whose own interest is subserved by stimulating its functions. These agents, transforming its potentiality into service, are the engineers, trainmen, depot clerks, freight handlers, mechanics and track-gangs who initiate and motivate its processes and repair its premises.

"I am not amiss in representing the aggregate of this manpower as the vital body of the system. So to render this or any other organization capable of transacting business, there must be set up a stabilized frame, equipped with reciprocal parts for interchange and maintenance, together with energy converters (vital organisms), for internal stimulation, before it is able to discharge the task for which it has been assembled.

"Though outfitted for its role with physical and vital bodies conjoined, our railway is ineffectual without other factors to sustain, superintend or direct its performance. To feed the organism its fuel of passengers and freight, requires a traffic agency; for supervision, an operating department; and for direction and finance, an executive board—each a contributory but independent body—correlatives of management and essential to the functioning of the whole."

"Dualism overboard and pluralism on the bridge!—the

plot thickens," I murmured ironically. "Any more bodies up your sleeve?"

"If I've persuaded you to consider the complexity of the familiar organizations, through which are transacted the commonplace affairs of your lives, I shall have established a fulcrum for larger realizations," returned my visitor in a graver tone. "As aid to comprehending the conditions of operation I've sketched—rehearse the system of the institution to which you are attached and note the parallel. Publishing is no other than the business of communicating information and entertainment through the medium of books. Its field— the brain and optical organs of the literate public. Its physical parts—the corporation's offices, furniture and stocks; its vital body—yourself and partners, who form the supporting and directing factor, together with the force of readers, clerks, secretaries, printers, pressmen, salesmen and packers, who carry through the processes that precede and follow the multiplication of manuscripts into merchandise.

"Duplicated here, in a field remote from the transportation of goods, are the factors associated in the constitution of the railway. The same formula applies to all commercial and manufacturing structures—banks, department stores, or mills—always premises and plant, integrated and energized in material terms, with living entities sustaining and motivating their mechanisms. Invariably, interest and plan preceding development of organism; fabrication of apparatus preceding function; and product—the issue of interactions among parts adjusted to deliver the design which was the objective of their conjunction."

"But how else could things happen," I asked, plaintively. "What you describe so pedantically is the natural order of events—calls for no other agency than what appears, and certainly throws no light on my own being, nor adds an inch to my stature."

"I'm not attempting to endow you with a soul," the Martian responded, gently, "or, to take over any prerogative of your own intelligence. If there be a purpose in this discourse, it is to awaken a latent mind. I may be wasting energy, but I'm practicing the use of language. Besides, the vibrations that eardrums register do alter the patterns of brain cells; and strange ideas do disturb tissues, like stray bullets."

"Add to list of painful predicaments—being reasoned with by a garrulous ghost loaded with a mission to explain what life is about," I retorted. "A unique experience truly, but voided by the ghost's delusion that he and his incredible theories may be sanctioned by prosaic argument. For a change, return to that Martian referendum about which you waxed so eloquent last night: The Savants agreed that though life might seem to be what it was about, inherently it was something else. One lived with it but never met it, like an elephant and his tail. It eluded capture, by being both the object sought and the seeker. Like lost spectacles astraddle one's own nose. Imagined itself a cocoon, when it was really a caterpillar; or a pea persuaded it was its pod. Having located this cosmic introvert, they abandoned the search."

"Even if there be a glimmer of understanding in that latter commentary," my visitor responded, "the tenor of your criticism indicates that the logic of my ancestors did not penetrate your mental threshold."

"I felt like a Rotarian at a symbolistic drama," I explained. "The profundity impressed me, but the meaning was out of my reach. It's some sort of a puzzle, I suppose—what's the answer?"

"The key is at hand," said the Martian cheerfully, "but

again be reminded, that the language of specification is clear enough to those whose business it is to interpret designs. The statement is simple, in comparison to the verbiage employed in the will of a multimillionaire, and translucent, as against an astronomer's exposition of incidents in interstellar space. But here is the whole business in household terms. Nearby are an open piano, Beethoven's Moonlight Sonata and you. Music and instrument are inert but potential. To transfer the pattern described by the notes, to the taut steel wires that convert them into an ordered series of sounds, requires connection, coordination and energy. You make the contact, and furnish the understandings and information the operation requires, together with the interest, power and hands to activate it. You are at once the cause of the performance, and the beneficiary of the effect. The piano is equipped with accommodations through which an energy circuit can be established between the cortex of the player and its keys. Impulses arising in your brain are conveyed through nerves to your hands, to release vibrations which air waves return to your ears in a sequence you identify as the Moonlight Sonata. For ages, men have engaged themselves perfecting instruments—adapting certain stresses and tensions arousable in material substances by impact of touch or breath, to produce that order of tone they recognize as harmony. Exterior to the physics involved in its evocation, are the music and you."

"I might burst into song and invalidate all your facile mechanics," I suggested.

"My hearing appliance is sensitive," exclaimed the visitor hastily, "so, if you have not conditioned the instrument you occupy to that form of air compression and emission, please don't. Try to realize, that the problem of tone production is not altered by the character of the medium in which it is excited. Because men are equipped with lungs, a larynx, a pharynx and a mouth they are not thereby constituted singers. Each of these organs must be trained—to cooperate in the task of stimulating vibrations, of the quality and order prescribed by the intervals of the scale. Thereafter, this protoplasmic outfit becomes an instrumentality for the broadcasting of some composer's arrangement of sound waves. Violinists and pianists spend long years, disciplining arms and fingers to be adroit conductors and reporters of the frequencies in which musical meanings are pitched and enunciated.

"Music then is set up in a frame conveyed by force and delivered to the auditory apparatus of the being who imposed, on its flow, the harmonic pattern that it carries. The interests involved in its inception and recognition, are the coordinator's. Since subject and object, together with the values received, are outside the orbit of the elements and appliances used in materialization, it is fair to attribute the phenomena to an intangible source, and assume a primary agent, present but invisible, capable of reintegrating correspondences to answer an inherent need of its own nature."

"At affixing ponderous meanings to innocent pleasures, you win," I said, plaintively. "Hereafter, whenever I hear a tune I'll feel like stopping my ears for fear that someone is trying to put something over on me. However, I'm willing to call it a night."

"As for me," my visitor remarked as I arose to leave him, "I shall occupy this comfortable chair till early morning and then set forth to explore your great city. I spent yesterday afternoon examining civilization as exhibited in the behaviorism of a large ant-colony in Venezuela and was impressed with its fine organization and orderliness. Now I shall observe the movements of the members of this community, as they swarm in and out of their subways and into the anthills of Wall Street, for the purpose of comparing the modes of the two species, as represented in the affair of sustaining life. The divergence will be in degree, of course."

"No doubt you'll find evidence to sustain whatever thesis you expect to establish," I returned. "Surveys here as elsewhere invariably return predetermined conclusions."

CHAPTER XII: A STANDARDIZED BODY FOR PROPHETS,
GENIUSES AND FOOLS

Men direct their own movements; ants do as they must. Real
significance of the terms evolution, installation and behavior. Every natural form, a design. Personality also requires
a structure. Life, the adventures of an Entity undergoing
experience. Other catalyzers than enzymes. Aliveness, the
tide-swell of energy in organic structures. Protoplasm, a
material compound. Messiahs and geniuses work their wonders wearing the same fleshy habiliments as ordinary men.

AWAITING the arrival of my visitor, I recalled the comparisons
he had suggested between the habits and characteristics of
ants and human beings. It occurred to me that the Martian
underrated the character of a race capable of the loyalty, ardor
and adaptiveness exhibited in the behavior of our citizens.
Rail as he might, he must concede the magnitude of men's
accomplishments. Remissions and errors one admitted, but
on the whole a nation of sound hearts and willing hands.
There was more here than met the captious eye. If we were
uncertain of our destinations, our ignorance was balanced
by our worth. A good world, when all was said, and life a
glorious experience.

On hearing the preliminary chuckle with which he announced himself, I greeted him with more cordiality than
usual.

"How were the ants?" I inquired. "The Wall Street variety you inspected today."

"Incoherent, confused, restless, timid, as one might expect," he replied. "From your expression I gather that you took seriously the correspondences I alluded to last night. Obviously, the behavior of a subconscious race must be inferior in efficiency and effectiveness to that of instinctive organisms."

"Implying superiority on the part of ants," I challenged. "Another exhibition of Martian humor!"

"On the contrary," he returned tranquilly, "the planes of being are so remote from one another that there is no basis for such differentiations. Humans are separated from the hymenoptera by ages of development. Consider for a moment the characters of their respective equipments—the complex sensori-motor mechanism of men, engineered for the variety of experiences that befall the race, and the simpler apparatus of the ant, so exquisitely adjusted to transact the minor activities of its lot. In hymenoptera, the swarm is the unit, and the great physiological functions of life are divided among its members, much as protoplasmic cells in the development of the human embryo assign themselves to the organic parts which it is their mission to form and sustain.

"Imagine a society of individuals comporting itself in the terms of the cell colonies composing the bodies of its members; its natives would be self-confident, realistic, reliable and law-abiding; by nature, not by selection. Their community would be an Utopia, but without humor, sentiment or joy. To a philosopher, the spectacle I witnessed this morning—that muddled, lusty, half-savage mob of egos, fighting and scrambling their way to work, however primitive, was magnificent and beautiful, because it represented human beings on the path to the attainment of self-consciousness and responsibility. Crippled and fettered by conventions and superstitions, blind to their real identity, but lodged in a noble vehicle and endowed with the potentiality of free control, they were finding their way on their own feet. No, my friend, I should not dream of comparing creatures whose behavior is installed, with men who direct their own movements, however imperfectly they transact their affairs. They are equipped with organs to learn better; ants do as they must."

"Again you imply an order exterior to objective reality," I remonstrated. "Use of the word *installed* as applied to behavior, the mystic distinctions you infer between men and ants and so forth, suggest an extra-mundane agency that, for some end of its own, shapes life and fixes the roles of its organisms. Is this the divinity's job in your system, or is there an hierarchy that attends to minor details?"

"Not so long ago," my visitor related, "I tried speaking to an Airedale. He was not troubled by my invisibility, but listened, with cocked ears and an air of sympathy. After a while he began to bark at where the sound came from, as much as to tell me I was taking him beyond his mental depth. You can hear and understand, but because it's the shibboleth of your faith that goods are made and get into packages by evolution your mind is reduced to the dog's level. It is inhibited from the exercise of the inherent faculty for reasoning. Centuries ago, the creed of this race had it that the world was flat, and the sun revolved around it. He was damned who did not so believe. Now you have emerged from that delusion to be plunged into another futile hypothesis, enforced by the sterner penalty of ridicule. *Evolution* is no more than the course and sequence of adaptation, and why the form and manner of any development should be deified as its cause, is beyond my comprehension.

"As to my use of *install,* a behaviorist would resent it, but any intelligent mechanic would grasp the implications it conveys. In the basement of a great newspaper nearby, is a large and exceedingly complicated piece of machinery, called a press. It is capable of printing and folding 30,000 forty-two page papers per hour. The capacity of this instrument to execute so difficult a task so speedily was *installed* in it cog by cog, bolt by bolt, lever by lever, roller by roller, by the men who designed and built it. Performance of the work turned out by it is its *behavior*. The other day I saw a boat gliding down the Hudson River at a pace of 60 miles per hour—it did not occur to me that a miracle was being exhibited. I realized that a metallic vehicle had been so adroitly adjusted to the medium which carried it, and the force which conveyed it, that an exceptional yield of speed had been returned to the designer.

"This speed was the product of the means compounded to deliver it. It was installed in the lines of the hull of the boat and contained in the power of the engines that propelled her. Thereafter she *behaved* on the water at the rate of a mile a minute, and raised a wave of foam in the process.

"Why not apply the common sense of mechanics to living organisms? Neither bird nor beetle could do what they do, save through the physical equipments with which they are outfitted for the lives they conduct. Their bodies and their locomotory and digestive mechanisms, are surely as indicative of design as the frame and parts of printing-press and speedboat. Why assert they *evolved,* in the same breath in which you admit these devices of men were *made?* And as to the identity or purpose of the designers, it would be reasonable to infer that both must be external to the instrumentalities through which they are expressed, in the same way that the personality and intentions of the makers of speedboat and press are other and outside these appliances. To a Patagonian, both machines would be marvels and inexplicable; beyond his conception, the needs that inspired their invention, the agencies employed in their construction and the character of the beings who used them.

"No one," he continued, "has assigned a sound reason for the appearance here of men or life itself. If the race be merely the offspring of continuous interactions of energy and matter, or sun and soil, the identities of its members would surely be as standardized as their bodies. That consciousness of personality which converts the motor mechanism—your body—into an 'I' requires a structure as complex as the set of physical parts through which it is expressed to your neighbors. What is here called your *life* is just an individual enactment in time and space of the character and nature of the entity undergoing experience. To the degree of his power he gains knowledge and command of the means to mold its circumstances in relation to his aspirations.

"Surely the ebb and flow of human society, the rise and fall of status show the dispositions of catalyzers other than enzymes! Leadership in civilization is not determined by the physique of those who exercise it, but is gained by an indwelling capacity to ride or control the flow of events. If only your own scientists could be persuaded to reason about the affairs of humans, according to those familiar tenets of mechanics which rule the application of force to matter, some inkling of the working principles of vital existence would be extant here.

"I cannot understand why, in the study of living organisms, no discrimination is ever made between their behaviors, as representing the characteristics of genus and species, and the energy used in conveying and exhibiting them. This

energy is derived from the oxidization of proteins and carbohydrates and, though the volume of the dynamic flow varies
with the number and arrangement of cells in the systems
in which it is generated, an amœba—in pursuing and wrap-
ping itself around a prey—uses force of the same quality as
that which keeps your heart beating, your lungs breathing
and your muscles contracting and expanding. What you call
aliveness is no more than the tide-swell of energy in organic
structures, adjusting to the usages to which they are devoted. It issues therefrom as conveyor—of predetermined deed-
and-word patterns.

"No engine or motor prescribes the use of the steam, gas
or electricity that is developed within its parts. Purpose and
method of application, together with the apparatus in which
design is imparted to material, are always systems separate
from the power-plants that revolve their shafts and wheels.
In seeking the secret of the convolutions traced in metal cogs
by a screw-making machine, it would not occur to you to
look for it within the interstices of the instrument, or among
the cylinders or armatures of its motor equipment. It would
lie outside, and be found in the character of the civilization
which required and had devised screws and nuts to sustain
its structures. Embodied in their designs, execution and in
the molecular arrangement of their atomic constituents, is
the status and degree of that civilization. To attach history
to a screw is absurd, you think, yet its form and texture carry
the record of the struggle of your race to adapt its environment to its needs."

"But since the sum of an action is the actor who discloses
his nature in that which his physical person effectuates, how
is it possible to separate the doer from the deed?" I objected. "It's an old adage that actions speak louder than words,

which means that a deed is a truer avowal of individual interest than conversation about it."

"It's that same unfortunate error of mixing psychology with physics, which keeps your heads in the sand," my visitor replied. "Do realize that all changes in the state of matter, even of gray matter, imply the action of force. Not a habitized response can issue into the world from its individual neuron nexus save on an energy-current. The sum of the sciences whose study is the human body, proves it to be a physico-chemical engine. That it is the subject of its own activities does not exempt either its organism, or the movements of the parts through which it exhibits its individuality from the ordinary laws of mechanics and thermodynamics. However mysterious or complex the protoplasmic components of this body, their substance is no less a material compound than wood or metal. It is passive, save in contact with an energy-source and its province is that of transformer of the power transmitted through its medium. It is a factor in the processes it conducts, but no more contributes to the design of the structure it composes, or of the use to which that is put, than does brick to an architect's plan for a house.

"Considered objectively, that weighty piece of apparatus which represents the body of a man, is simply an arrangement of matter shaped and equipped to transact the functions of being a man, in opposition to the gravity and pressure that retards motion in space. As is plain from its annals and experiences, it is never other than the vehicle of the invisible coherer, contained in and disguised behind the fabric of its appearance. In reality, it is a screen on which the inhabiting entity projects that moving picture he calls his life."

"Which seems to justify my old contentions that man *is* what he does," I broke in.

"If man be what he does," my visitor resumed triumphantly, "the potential of the race must include the varieties of expression and achievement which its members have at any time exhibited. That flexible protoplasmic contraption, within which you and your neighbors plod their unseeing ways, has accommodated Plato, Shakespeare, Dante and Goethe. Also Balzac and Dostoievsky, Beethoven, and Wagner, Newton and Einstein, Alexander and Napoleon, Velasquez and Phidias, Washington and Lincoln. Today, among others, it carries Gene Tunney, Mordekin and Nurmi. Henry Ford and Edison look through the same type of eyes, and manipulate arm-and-hand implements parallel to those that serve the humblest of their workmen.

"Here then is an infinite range of qualities and accomplishments, evoked and exteriorized through the standardized parts of the human organism. And, in full appreciation of the fact that Buddha, Christ and Mahomet wore the same fleshly habiliments as their worshipers, you continue to parrot—'man is his body.' Because looms and lathes have wheels one might as well declare a bolt of velvet to be a turned steel bar.

"Sleep on the formula, my skeptical vis-a-vis, and who knows but during that lapse into the unconscious the obstinate synapses which block the intelligence center in your cortex may relax, and a path open for reason to penetrate. Such is the way of revelation."

"The release I seek is in oblivion," I responded with a yawn. "Whither away on the wings of this morning?"

"Since the South Pole is under investigation it occurred to me I might see what it has to offer a wayfarer," the Martian said. "And as I can perceive the thought processes of birds it should be amusing to discover the impressions that antarctic explorers make on penguins."

His revelations construed as more mystical than mathematical, the Martian rails at the stupidity of Mankind. How he
would develop the race. Adventures by proxy. The pull of
the inaccessible. Life and death. Properties Jones had that
his corpse lacks. The integrating principle that was in touch
with his cellular structure. Inevitability of design. Justification of analogical reasoning. The Ego speculates about
its abode and the terms of its tenancy. Creating a body for
an Idea. The establishment of an identity-format. Reaction
field of the Self, within.

A PROCESSIONAL of dreams; a phantasmagoria, whose
dramatis-personæ were penguins and white bears, explorers,
neurons disguised as electricians carrying kits of nerve
filaments, vaporous shapes propelling protesting bodies
of men over rocks and ice floes—streamed through my
disordered brain. Never was slumber so distracted by visions.
From my lips I saw volleys of words emerging as pellets of
information. The electricians were rewiring my cerebrum,
establishing new circuits among reflex-arcs: molecules of
oxygen and nitrogen formed an aureole of musical notations
around my head.

I recall snatches of a discussion, in which a penguin and
an explorer debated about companionate marriage and the
divorce problem, in which the bird insisted on the superiority of feathered to human civilization. A walrus and a bear
agreed that, since the South Pole meant nothing in their

lives, no good reason appeared why they should be sacrificed to the cause of its rediscovery. The bear thought the Golden Rule applied to animals as well as to men, but the wiser walrus explained that its engagements extended to Christians alone. And Christianity, he told his friend, was an accident of birth—not a principle.

Two Shipping Board steel hulks, relics of the late war—lying idly at anchor in an inland estuary, commented on a new Ford, flying swiftly along a neighboring road. One said to the other—"And still science denies reincarnation. Who knows but we too, a few years hence may find our old bodies on wheels?" A shadow, that said it was my own psyche, reproached me because I had denied its being, and asked, plaintively, "Who pulls your body out of bed mornings, gets you ready for business, and does all the work for which your carcass draws the pay? *I do,* you ingrate, and never a penny is spent on me or even my presence admitted. Men are fools who have to die to learn who's who in their own organic abodes."

I awoke with a start, looked at my watch. I'd been asleep ten minutes, and thereafter fell into the bliss of oblivion. No further adventures befell until a ruthless alarm clock restored my consciousness at 8 AM.

As I reviewed the incidents of the preceding night I realized that my strange visitor's argument was not without merit. It was straight dualism, but, in the light of recent scientific developments, there might be aspects which justified reconsideration of that abandoned hypothesis. Undeniably, a pair of opposites was present in all conjunctions of matter. Electricity flowed from positive to negative pole. The components of atoms were protons and electrons; cells had nuclei and chromosomes. Invariably, reproduction required the interaction of organisms with opposite endowments. Inclusion of an etheric agency in our schedule did accommodate surplus phenomena now lacking vehicle or allocation, but there was no substantial evidence to justify so radical an assumption. These arguments of the Martians were based on analogies and, though drawn from the operation of familiar mechanisms, were still suspect. Science sanctioned no such testimony.

To suggest that, back of terrestrial appearances there was a master principle accountable for all the circumstances of material and organic forms, might be a bold conception but it was a large order. Its admission meant substitution of a new alignment which would scrap most of the formulas now on the books. To blot out the ascertainments, so laboriously salvaged by search and experiment from the dark womb of nature, on the authority of an unknown voice—was fantastic. Revelations were out of date. Modern society turned mystics over to psychiatrists.

At odd moments during a busy day I re-traversed the train of my visitor's reasoning and made up my mind that, on the whole, his offering savored rather of Swedenborg than of Einstein, and its acceptance would be about as wise as confiding oneself to the custody of a life buoy in mid-Atlantic.

Thus disposed, I awaited the arrival of the Martian, prepared to combat his attributions with such realistic logic as I could muster. Into my cogitations his voice broke, and I noted acerbity in its tones.

"Withers still unwrung, I gather," he began. "All the neuron clans rallied to the defense of the vacant citadel. To weigh the subject-matter offered, according to its bearings as cause and effect, is beyond you. There's a legend, of the days before Babylon: a herdsman, searching in the dark for strayed sheep, was accosted by a pitying angel, who thrust into his hands a flashlight. To the herdsman there was nothing incredible about celestial visitants, but the flashlight smelt of black magic, and righteously he construed the affair as a snare of the Devil. You reject my formula because it interferes with your conventions. Your dumb-driven race clings to its half-witted fundamentals with the fanaticism of idolaters, defending an effigy. To believe, we must see, you declare; yet light your houses and streets with electric current, on which not a mortal among you has ever set eyes. Try to realize that all the realities are intangible. The organ of apprehension and interpretation is the mind, not the hand or the senses."

"Why this blast," I exclaimed. "So far I've offered no objections."

"Because, being insensible to the exertion of energy in the processes of cerebration, you persuade yourself that every perception shares your own limitations," the Martian responded. "Because you may only know what you think by hearing or writing it, you conclude that the mental operations of men are inscrutable. And this, though it is acknowledged, that the radius of the human optical receptor is limited to one octave of the ten in the solar spectrum. There's nothing in the legitimate curricula of science to accommodate the commonplace phenomena of thought-transference, as performed by parlor entertainers, or to explain the extraordinary transactions of hypnosis. Mention either subject, and some owlish sage shakes his beard and goes through the motions of dispelling a heresy. And yet these same sages may spend hours, poring over the disclosures revealed in an X-ray photograph. Assume then, that my visualizing apparatus has the penetrative power of short light waves, and accept the assurance that I have as little difficulty in exploring your cortex as a man looking through a high-powered microscope has in counting the ridges on a moth's back."

"Prowling around other people's brain cells is downright trespass," I protested. "It's indecent. If the development of these potentials take such indelicate directions, privacy will disappear. At least no one will reflect about his wife or his friend save behind leaden doors. There's a saving clause, though—perhaps we shall be relieved of that form of waste-motion—conversation. With telepathy in operation, I presume we could also discard the telephone?"

"No harm in exuding a little optimism," returned my visitor, in his most patronizing tones. "Remember though, that before speech may be abandoned, your people must acquire mental control to know what is in their minds before they hear it through their ears. If you imagine that the glandular spasms which pass here for thinking represent thought processes, consult a psychologist. Most human talk is animal patter—carnivora merely articulating appetites. To conduct consecutive reasoning requires a mind, trained to the practice. And be assured it is simpler to develop muscle than to stabilize consciousness, though physical skill is never other than the application of consciousness to muscle.

"All these are blind thrusts, I am aware; about as futile as discussing evolution with a fundamentalist preacher. Vain though I deem the task, were it imposed on me to hasten the development of this race, I should begin by proscribing your greatest alibis. All those who preached the mercy of God, or engaged in astrophysics, would be chained ear to mouth and condemned to talk each other to death."

"What an extraordinary proposition," I exclaimed. "Due

doubtless to a defective sense of humor, the point escapes me. What do you mean by alibis?"

"Mankind," said the Martian oracularly, "justifies its claim to be intelligent by pointing to its researches in interstellar space, while conducting its domestic affairs in the fashion of the jungle. And it feels free to indulge the fallacy that, in a celestial currency, repentance is negotiable exchange for excess. Vicarious atonement is as egregious a delusion as the idea that calculation of the orbit, or specific gravity of Betelgeuse, confers a charter of civilization on the entire nation whose astronomers plotted it. God gave men eyes to face facts, brains to weigh them and legs to deliver themselves from temptation. Why should He forgive you for misuse of His gifts?"

"If I'd had your opportunities, doubtless I could tell," I replied. "Otherwise what is the cause of this outpouring of lava on my defenseless head?"

"Forgive me," said my visitor more gently. "I'm out of temper with myself. I should have known better than to take a constitution like mine to the South Pole. You must understand that the energy that sustains me is derived from the higher range of light waves and in the cold mists that prevail there, not a ray was perceptible.

"However, I inspected the operations of the unhappy wights who are playing tag there among the ice-floes. Perhaps you can tell me why it is thought necessary to invade the seclusion of a region that has been at so much pains to preserve itself from casual callers?"

"The pull of the Inaccessible," I explained. "A modern equivalent for our forefathers' hunt for the Holy Grail, or Jason's voyage in search of the Golden Fleece—just attempts to relieve the monotony of life. Doubtless there were syndicates behind these ancient ventures with an interest in whatever profits accrued, and publicity before and after, as today. At this period, journalism undertakes and finances the racial adventures, and its return is in arousing competitive fury and securing front-page filling for the dull days when Nature fails to provide a calamity. In the Antarctic, a continent is embedded in ice, in the center of which a focal point invites flags. Surely it is praiseworthy for a publication to set its mark where no other newspaper has penetrated. Besides, the location of fresh promontories, bays and peaks, provides opportunity to confer topographical immortality on those brave fellows whose lives have been sacrificed to extend the frontiers of geography."

"Adventures by proxy seem popular in this civilization," commented the Martian dryly. "I prefer to participate in games rather than to watch them, but there's something to be said for the gladiatorial system, as you have revived it. Though it tends to professionalize fortitude, it does provide heroes for the mob, just as virgin territories furnish tombstones for the foolhardy. Instinctive folk, whose minds are unawakened, regard physical prowess as a phase of divinity. It is but a symptom of racial puberty. As the feet of your kind find the upward curve, this condition will pass. When eyes are turned inward rather than out, and every man realizes that he himself has an unknown continent of being to explore, he will discover more entertainment in winning the franchise of his individual capacities, than is now afforded by the acrobatics of paid performers."

"Then you would turn us all into introspectionists?" I suggested.

"Such practices," my visitor replied, "extend extraordinarily the efficiency of the will. When mind is in power, body is its obedient servant—so, in place of a few overdeveloped specimens, a whole race may become athletic. The authority and confidence of the entity enlarge as it learns the resources of its physical equipment, and of the privilege it enjoys as occupant of so magical a vehicle."

"A touch of Utopia, just to relieve the gloom of the indictment," I suggested.

"Why construe observation as condemnation?" he asked. "Why, if a naturalist incurs no obloquy in defining the characteristics of sheep and geese, should a sociologist be accused of prejudice when he exposes human ignorance? Remember, I speak from the vantage point of a higher culture—if in comparison the Earth's civilization seems crude, and your peoples not far removed from primitive, the fault is not mine. One does not denounce such a society, nor does one condone the stupidity or inertia that prevents its redemption. So don't interpret my judgments as scornful. A hundred years hence, intelligence will have a foothold here, and your descendants will wonder why their ancestors so long cherished the delusion that wars, crime, greed and endless parliamentary discussion were indigenous to human nature."

"Why then delay our salvation just to exhibit superiority?" I interrupted. "For instance, more and better testimony as to the presence of an etheric counterpart of the human body, would be useful. I cannot convince myself that such evidence as you've offered so far, would have converted those skeptical Martian engineers to a notion so far-fetched. As for myself, you'll have to turn up something more substantial and more solid than the theory that this agency must exist because, in mechanisms, the factor of direction or driver is separate from the instrumentality he applies."

"Unfortunately, I can neither enable you to see an impalpable organism, nor the words that issue from your own lips," the Martian replied ironically. "It would be convenient if one could catch the messages from broadcasting stations with the naked ear. If one could but sit with one's back to the screen and assemble on the retina the pictures conveyed by the light beams from the projector, how superior one would feel to the normal movie fan! Optical proof is impossible, so such demonstration as may be offered must be addressed to that rudimentary organ, your mind. Perhaps the most obvious approach would be consideration of the incident of death.

"The corpse of the man who was Jones carries the identical neuron patterns and all the chemicals which, you declared, constituted his character. Jones himself was warm, erect, moved with dispatch, voiced opinions, voted, and made a good living. That cadaver of his is cold, supine, silent and inert. Whatever it was that enabled a man to withstand the pull of gravity and push against wind, come in out of the rain, answer when called, and attend to the business of exhibiting individuality, of a sudden deserted Jones. What fell to the ground was not he, but his remains. Since these are already moldering, it would seem that Jones, in departing, carried off with his personality some underlying structure that supported his body, held together and preserved its parts, and kept all its vital machinery at work.

"But setting hypotheses aside and subtracting that mysterious complex—identity—why not estimate the mechanical factors necessary to the motivation of Jones?

"In the following consideration, forget superstitions as that things happen of themselves, or by coincidence; or that any assemblage of matter in form is accidental, or that any activity, as in the movement and demeanor of a physi-

cal organism, is due to pull of gravity or its own sensitive-
ness. Jones' body was alive, because it carried machinery for
generating the energy necessary to produce that particular
aspect of motion called life. Unlike the average internal
combustion engine in which heat is transformed into work,
the entire vehicle of Jones was animated. He was vitalized
throughout including his hair, bones and protective surfaces
of skin and tissue. Every cell in the insulated circuit of his
structure was engaged in developing the potential needed to
constitute his system a going-concern. In fact Jones' body,
like that of any other animal, was simply a biological power
plant, deriving its current from fuel provided from the environment in which it was located. Attached to this corpus was
an equipment of locomotory and lifting parts, and organs
and appliances which conducted this energy into that variety
of patterns called human behavior.

"And what a superb piece of machinery it is, this automaton, by virtue of whose efficiency Jones was enabled to act as
a man, without knowing how or why he did what he did. The
function of disintegrating and converting food into physiological fuel by digestion; its distribution throughout the
tissues; the oxygenation of hemoglobin and its circulation by
the bloodstream in the veins and capillaries to the billions of
cell-cylinders to which it furnishes ignition; the proteins and
carbohydrates burned and transformed into heat to conserve
normal temperature; the dynamic potentials utilized in the
processes of communication, transfer, repair and evacuation
conducted within the organisms; transmission by the nerves
through the cerebral and muscular systems in supporting
its sensori-motor exchange with environment; sustaining of
posture, and the movements through which are carried out
the representational features of living; operations of chem-

istries in comparison with which the most complicated of aeroplane motors is as crude as the original engine of James Watt! A hundred years hence, humanity may know enough to appreciate the possession of this marvelous instrument.

"However, for all the ingenuity of its fittings and the flexibility of its parts, Jones' body was a dependent. It could neither sustain nor motivate its engines or mechanisms. It had no use for itself. Though it had eyes, ears, nose, lungs and legs, hands and innumerable protoplasmic equivalents for valves, cams and other gadgets, it could not come or go, could not see, smell, breathe, seek, or find its food in the absence of whatever it was that was Jones. It is conventional to ascribe the appetite of this interesting apparatus to an inherent impulse, called 'self-preservation,' and to believe that the irritability of its substance accounts for the variety of its adaptations, but even conservation and excitability are effects, which require energy and support for maintenance and demonstration. They are not so for reasons of their own.

"So the problem offered by Jones' body is akin to that of a steamship. Though outfitted with the equipment necessary for voyaging on all the Seven Seas, she is incapable of moving out of her dock, until a vital element composed of captain and crew, engineers and stokers enter into possession of her parts. They set her screws revolving, and then having had motion imparted to her hull, the vessel is susceptible of direction. Until she is actually under way, her rudder is an incumbrance.

"Some parallel occupation must be assumed to account for the utilization of the corpus under investigation. Inert by the nature and weight of its substance, its movements imply the application of force, their direction the intention and knowledge of the factor on whose behalf the force was applied. Among the properties of this factor, then, must be capacity to initiate, exert and render consecutive the operations of the agencies to which it attaches itself. Since Jones' body was but one of more than a billion now extant, it would be safe to concede that the attributes they had in common represented the tenancy in each of a Principle, in whom these were inherent.

"One may conclude that this efficient Principle was responsible for all the things that Jones did, which his body was incapable of doing. It was the constant in control of that organism, sustaining its form and steering its course. Since Jones appeared as a unit, *it is evident that this actuating and integrating Principle was in contact with all parts of his anatomy,* which indicates *that its faculty of animation and support was extended throughout his entire cellular structure.* As such obligation entails some pervasive texture of conduction, the constitution and arrangement of this system would be the base of the material counterpart or protoplasmic insulation that protects the invisible individual against tensions and pressures antagonistic to its subtle nature. It might help towards realization if one defined this intangible factor as the nucleus, of which Jones' body was the ponderable complement; the content it carried."

"An interesting conjecture," I admitted, "and not untenable, though it provides a lot of additional machinery without altering anything in particular. You agree that the energy Jones used in going about his business was derived from the vicinity, and that the arrangement of his bodily parts governed its use. Being as he was, he was bound to go as he went. I can't yet see that this endowment of an internal twin quickened his progress, or made him wiser or better. The trek of the race up from barbarism, has been long, most of the way on its hands and knees—why deprive humanity of the credit of a great achievement, and say that a Double did it?"

"Throughout the ages," my visitor reminded, "extensive effort has been put forth to prove to man that he was more than his body, but he paid no heed to the information. He ate and drank during many millennia before it was ascertained that he had an abdomen. Knowledge of the adroit methods of that subsurface laboratory is not a century old, nor has it increased or diminished appetites. Now that anatomy and biology have become news it is a dull day in which no medical Columbus appears with an unsuspected gland. There's nothing abnormal about this attempt to define a pervasive internal organism. Like other instrumentalities for maintaining metabolism, it has been in operation since the beginning, and, after it has become a subject of speculation it will continue to function.

"Our Martian thinkers having traversed the ground covered in the foregoing exposition, offered among their conclusions, these postulates:

"All material organisms—including vehicles, machines and sensate bodies are inert, and can do no coordinate work until energy is applied to their parts.

"No material organism is capable of initiating, sustaining or using itself, but requires, for maintenance and direction, the cooperation of an extraneous agent, whose interest is subserved by such support and use.

"Since in itself the human body is without capacity to find provender for its organs of combustion, it follows that the deliverance of such operations represents the potential and interest of an integrating factor, acting on its individual behalf.

"In other words, the being who shaves, washes and dresses your body in the morning—attends to the consumption of its breakfast, drives it to your office and transacts your business is endowed with and exercises faculty of a superior order to the energy generated in that body. Because your Self applies that faculty in an equipment fitted to exhibit its intention, you are a human being. The process is independent of your opinion."

"But I am unconscious of the cleavage you define," I insisted. "The functions mentioned represent the use of muscular energy that was generated by my own body, and employed by it in the furtherance of its individual interest as a going-concern, gaining a livelihood according to the terms of the environment."

"That unconsciousness undoubtedly is shared by your stomach, which is unaware of the identity of the benefactor who provides it with food, and ignorant of its own relation to the system of your going-concern," retorted the Martian. "The distinctions I am driving at might not be recognized, by the average take-life-for-granted thinker, by psychologists or biologists who are ignorant of physics and the arts of imparting motion to matter. It should be grasped by builders of machines, engineers, architects or inventors, who have learned by experience that their function in the undertakings they accomplish is that of coordination—not of creation. The elements that enter into action are their familiars. Material is at hand, force can be aroused. The task is to harness the second to the first on behalf of a third—

the Design. Matter and force, having neither affinity for nor anything in common with design, do not voluntarily yield to its association. Their resistances must be harmonized before their cooperation may be secured. Introduction of an extraneous factor, representing the interest which will be served by the unification, is called for.

"A Catalyzer.

"Inherent in the factor who thus functions must be comprehension of the properties of the ingredients in relation to the problem of combining them, knowledge of the purpose to which it is contributory, and power to effectuate it.

"The room in which we are sitting, together with the apartment house of which it is a subdivision, are supported by the erudition of the architect who delineated on paper the purpose of its promoters, yet the presence of this formula is imperceptible to your senses. It would not occur to you to declare that no plan existed, because now you can neither see nor feel it."

"More argument from analogy," I protested. "Long ago science banned attempts to prove hypotheses by parallel cases."

"It's an old trick in dialectics to dispose of an inconvenient hypothesis by branding it analogy," my visitor retorted. "What is science, if not the classification of correspondences? Forms and structures of the organic world are allocated into genus and species on the warrant of characteristics in common. Recognition of similarities of behavior is the basis of the laws on which your institutions and assumptions are founded. The elements are grouped according to the properties they share. In nature, nothing stands alone, for the same principles are present in every functioning organization. An argument devoted to explaining how things work must be illustrated through working practices. What has been adduced here is within the scope of your personal information, since I have been careful to observe its limitations. I've forced no cards on your mind."

"No, but you have worn the commonplace threadbare with reiteration," I objected with some asperity. "You have told me, from your peculiar angle, what every school boy knows, to prove a thesis which every scientist mocks. How much better entertainment I should have had were you less prudent and had gone further afield!"

"You looked for Voodoo and I passed you bricks," the Martian returned rather grimly. "You have responded in kind. That tribute is to the texture of an understanding impenetrable to reason. However I wish some magic were at my command, so I could lift your mind out of your body and allow it a thorough survey of its tenement."

"That would be interesting," I agreed. "But since you cannot arrange the flight why not give me a bird's-eye view of the situation?"

There was silence for a moment. I could imagine the Martian settling himself back among the cushions of his chair summoning energy for another verbal flight. He began at last.

"I shall assume a developed Ego—not your own, but another's, capable of looking facts in the face. Imagine it then, detached and judicial, hovering curiously above and inspecting the vacated premises. In the engagement it had been conducting, Ego would recognize three factors—itself, its body and an environment which had furnished the scene for the experience. Its obligation, apparently, had been to maintain such relations with this environment as would ensure the safety, comfort and subsistence of this body, during the period of its own sojourn therein. Being cut off from direct association, it must rely on the instrumentalities with which this deputy was outfitted for information about the lay of the land, its provisions, its climate and its menaces. Noting the comfort of its physical circumstances, Ego might reflect that this task must have eased greatly since the period when beings of its nature first began to come here. Then, like blind exiles in a wild country, having to grope their way to knowledge of their own equipment and the fabric and resources of the unknown world around, they might well have been so engrossed in the perilous occupations of keeping alive, that they had little chance of thinking of their origins.

"Free to examine the lodgment from which it had emerged, Ego would realize that only through such a device as this body, could a being of its specific quality preserve foothold, in a region so resistant to its individual character as this Earth. It would examine curiously, the mechanisms by means of which it had derived from the environment the facts that related to its state therein—the set of sense-organs and the end-receptors distributed over the planes of its body—all connected by nerve dendrons with reflex centers in the spine and brain. And thereafter, the reactive adjustment-system of axons coupled to the reticulation of muscles knitted to limb-levers, by means of which it motivated its bulk, either out of harm's way or in pursuit of food; and the proprioceptor system, through which its internal organs registered their conditions and kept in touch with headquarters. Altogether a beautiful instrument, so cleverly sensitized and integrated, inside and without, that it detected and reported instanter to its control office, every change that affected the maintenance of its equilibrium, and returned responses appropriate to the contingencies it encountered.

"'Several of the aspects of an automaton,' Ego might decide, at this stage of the investigation. 'Given an initial impetus, this apparatus seems fitted to do for itself what I thought I did. Obviously, it was designed and built to carry on in this environment, of which its substance is part and parcel, and since it is dependent on the land of its birth for ground space and nourishment, perhaps it is no more than its offspring and subject.'"

"So far, Ego betrays intelligence," I murmured.

"Ego has but opened his eyes," explained the Martian. "Already he has reached the hypothesis on which your savants are now stranded, and he has not yet taken his own entity into account."

"Introspection," I suggested.

"Mechanics," corrected the visitor. "Ego is a pragmatist and as he proceeds, finds there are too many factors outside that formula to allow it standing in any but the court of anthropomorphism. He discovers now that in his absence the plant has suspended operations. We'll say it's asleep. Autonomous functions are proceeding according to rote. Environment is at its old tricks of change, yet, though protoplasm has not relaxed its excitability, and the reflex arcs are geared as before, the recumbent body shows no signs of reacting to stimuli. In fact it is inert—unconscious.

"Assume that the analogy of a telephonic system occurs to Ego, contemplating this slumbering organism so intricately wired for communicatory purposes. Perhaps the afferent nerves were throbbing with messages, but the operator, whose affair it was to interpret and dispose of incoming information through the efferent circuit, was away from his station. In the absence of an incumbent then, the system did no work. This body might be said to be resting, evacuating waste carbon, dissolving lactic acid or recharging its batteries but, as it made no response, undeniably it was unaware of the signals that ordinarily provoked it to action. In fact, it might be a parked automobile awaiting the return of its owner, or a locomotive with steam up, standing on a siding while its engineer, smoking a pipe, lingers for the passing of the express. From all of which, our Ego felt justified in concluding he had exercised, in that organism, functions of the character of driver, and therefore was the agent who set its parts in motion. Then, also, he must represent the purposive factor of the machine, since he kept it on its tracks, controlled direction and held it to the usages to which it was applied.

"Ego begins now to reflect about his abode, and the circumstances that constrained his tenancy therein. How he had entered his body or this region he knows not. The structure grew around him in accordance with laws or plans to which he was not party. Recalling the early years of his sojourn, he would recollect how hard was the task of fitting himself to this organism, the utter helplessness of his infancy, the pains incurred in balancing on legs that would not stand straight, the trouble his arms and hands had, learning to obey his eyes; and how long it took to shape words with his tongue and lips.

"After this period, Ego remembers slowly awakening to a place full of objects and people, and of ways of going about and getting things done. He watched the habits and routines of his folks and copied them; he listened to the sounds by which they communicated their needs and reactions to one another, assigned meanings to these, and imitated them. He knew what hunger was, and thirst, and could himself satisfy their cravings; also the feel of the substances and articles by which he was surrounded. He acquired the freedom of his body-muscles and could run and dance, bend and wave his arms, catch, carry and sometimes come when he was called. He had his own name and began to sense separateness from others of his kind, and, by virtue of his mobility, discovered the limitations, fixations and restrictions of his world. By touch and experiment the child Ego had learned about environment. His education was by dint of friction and collision; his memory—the product of muscular reactions, recorded as ease of doing, obstacle and pain.

" 'Now that I'm outside, looking in,' Ego ponders, 'it is clear I must have been present while that instinctive creature was stumbling about the floor and knocking its head against the furniture. Yet I had no conscious part in these affairs, nor in the processes by which this body grew and developed from childhood into youth and manhood. My relation seems to have been that of a sleeping tenant, round whom a house was built by mechanics who did not know of his existence. Evidently a model inhered in the substance of this structure and my expansion was its unfoldment. As in a seed, the design embedded in the germ attracted the elements it needed for development.

" 'Since I was not privy to these proceedings or aware of the arts this body practiced of manufacturing its material and energy, it seems as though it belonged in a different ordination from my own. It may have been created for my occupancy, but its affairs were outside my jurisdiction. Just how it secreted in its brain the information I gathered and used is as much a mystery to me as how or why I was coupled to its parts. For all that, this body was I. I played in it—learned, loved and hated with it. Mine was the zest and flair of its life. When I worked it sweated. It wept when I grieved, and its face smiled when I was pleased or amused. To my fellows its lineaments figured as my person, yet from this vantage spot, and looking backwards, it seems as though all the transactions of my life and the roles I enacted were performed without my connivance. It actually seems that I was the unconscious victim of a liaison between a human animal and an environment. I cannot understand what it's all about.'"

"Hosannah," I cried, "a new situation—Submerged Self Denounces Betrayer—a fresh theme with all possible chance for comic relief. Casting a voice from the void is no trick at all to a producer who knows his 'talkies.' Here's the flash of a scenario—battlefield, two wounded, bleeding heroes lying unconscious side by side—their Egos emerging from the mortal coils, exchanging views and reminiscences. They blame the civilization their stupid bodies had supported for the tragedy that has befallen. If they'd been allowed a voice in affairs this war would never have happened, and so forth. And though both are sore at life, when a Red Cross Unit appears they are shown scrambling back to their dilapidated carcasses and next are heard begging for water. Or a bedroom scene—husband and wife asleep—twin couches of course—old love turned to hate—their Egos arising engage in recriminations, deplore their union as a mistake of which both were aware, but had been powerless to prevent their animal bodies committing. A ripping chance for dialogue and titles—for instance—'endocrine glands overcome etheric admonition.' Sex stuff flavored with transcendentalism—you couldn't beat it. Now that the stream of consciousness has been dramatized, this idea will go over with a bang."

"You have touched but a stray fringe of a myriad of strange patterns," the Martian returned, disregarding my attempt at derision. "When and if humans realize that they are not mere bodies, but entities individual in volition, with powers to be asserted, they will grow cognizant of the perennial conflict for which their own organisms furnish battleground. Thereafter introspection becomes exploration, in search of impulse—sources and power-transformers. Glandular urges will no longer be dramatized as emotions, or admitted as inspirations. Psychic balance will connote what metabolism now means, and biology will become realistic. The source of adventure will pass from the outside world to the submerged sphere within."

"Picturesque no end," I commented. "New slant on the heaven-on-earth proposition, but unconvincing to those whose feet feel safest on sidewalks. What do you mean, for instance, by perennial conflict and where does it occur?"

"I might explain in a poetic way that it represents two natures side by side, struggling for mastery," my visitor replied, "but it is simply the old antagonism, inseparable from conjunctions of ideas and matter—a symptom of faulty adjustment. Assume that Entity carries the life and the ideas, and is dominant in fact but dependent on body for place, state and opportunity, and you have the elements of discord in juxtaposition for war. One is vital—the other inert and resistant, so, inherently, they are at cross purposes. Under prevailing conditions, organism and entrenchments of prejudice and convention hold off the progress of ideas—but in the long run intelligence will prevail."

"Since all the achievements of mankind represent the triumph of ideas, that is unfair," I objected.

"Recall the obstacles that each has overcome, and I'll seem charitable," retorted the Martian. "If among you there existed even an elementary understanding of the nature of ideas, of their source and the course of their development, you would have an inkling of the character of your own Being and of the circumstances that obstruct its progress."

"Since destiny makes me the recipient of this confidence, I need not invite it," said I, politely.

"I'll tell it as the tale of an adventure in the mind of an inventor," my visitor continued, tranquilly. "At work one day on a problem, a notion uninvited, flashed into his mind. It had no relation to the task under his hand. Another story entirely; a thing-in-itself. He recognized that an idea had occurred to him. He said it was worth thinking about. What followed may resemble the reaction of an oyster to a grain of sand, or the fertilization of an ovum in a womb. Lodged there in his cortex, this idea began to cohere around itself thought-stuff—to assemble neuron patterns, to multiply and subdivide, to develop parts and gather force. Sitting in his laboratory, Inventor smoked and meditated on this chance tenant of his brain, speculated about its growth, perhaps marveled at its vitality and insistence that it be allowed to be born, and later, work for him.

"There are no ready-made bodies for ideas. Whoever has them must create an organism fit for their use. Inventor knew he must fabricate a physical structure, so shaped and equipped as to provide accommodations for every phase of every act his embryo required to effectuate its identity and purpose in the world. Thereafter he drew innumerable pictures of vehicles and when a design was evolved that might interpret Idea's peculiar individuality, he gathered shafts and wheels, cogs, cams, valves and gears, and with mathematical exactitude, set about correlating them in a metal frame to perform the task that the birthing of his offspring demanded. Thereafter, he linked these with a power-source, precisely proportioned to the shape and weight of the apparatus and the needs of the thing in making. Thus were body and energy provided for the tiny invisible that had slipped into Inventor's mind, months—perhaps years—before. Equipped at last, with a material counterpart adapted to its needs, through which to express its particular commission for existence, Idea was ready to be born.

"It might be observed that the apparatus, so carefully set up and put together, was not the Idea itself, but a contrivance to deliver it. For all its dimensions, the identity of the machine did not reside in itself, but in its functions. Its body had no volition, save to stamp out the pattern ingrained in its parts. It had no use, save for that purpose, and its existence depended on the survival of the need that valuated its services.

"On behalf of your appetite for variety—picture a great plant shaded by trees and surrounded by lawns—the lordly domicile of an all-important patented article. Enter and confront symmetrical rows of machines whose revolving wheels are busy turning out a commodity. Inspect the intricate system of correlated cogs and gears installed in each, so neatly adjusted to change and shape the raw stuffs that pour through their frames into an object of need and use, and marvel at the cleverness of the device. A spectacle of human ingenuity you pronounce it, and doubtless envy the wealth that had rewarded the creator of the process.

"Now, traverse my tale of the released Ego and imagine the Idea that, uninvited, had lodged in the mind of the inventor and was the true progenitor of this array of engines— returning from some Limbo of the Thought World to revisit its offspring. Aware of its own role as inspiration and guide, that the conjoined parts were modeled on its behalf, that its image and heredity furnished the design and the coherence which held them in place—it might well wonder at its own relation to these machines and to the fabric that issued from them. Its reflections would parallel the particulars that Ego recalled with so much resentment; and doubtless it would conclude that it, too, belonged in a different category of being from this mental parody. Reality makes no personal appearances here or elsewhere. Circumstances render this a world of substitutes and plagiarisms."

"Shed no tears for me," I announced. "If the originals are as vaporous as you describe, I prefer the imitations. There's a lot of consolation in sight, touch and smell."

"My hallucination," the Martian said. "I cannot rid myself of the obsession that even rudimentary intelligences hate to be fooled."

"It's not that," I explained. "The trouble is in keeping track of the focal points of your argument. It drifts from extreme behaviorism to ultra transcendentalism. You walk off with the clothes of the mechanists and declare they don't fit. What they don't fit I don't grasp. It's not visible, you say, but what would it be if it were? Assume I am I, and, as you suggest, not my body—how is it my body so fully represents what I believe myself to be? It is true that identities vary, but life-patterns don't—not enough at best to make a philosophy about. How cometh the universal deception and the generic commission to be what we are?"

"The trouble with the esoteric cults," my visitor explained, "is that they go too far—with scientific dogma that it does not go far enough, or is erected on defective premises. Throughout these discussions I have railed at the conclusions of mechanists—not at their truths. The fact is that no real progress in intellection will be made by mankind until they comprehend the profoundly mechanistic character of their appearances and actions as exhibited in life. Once this principle is grasped and the further truth that all living organisms are but local vehicles of a Universal order, and that vital existence is only the span required by laboratory processes for purposes extraneous to experience, you'll have a clew to the mystery.

"Consider the vital spark in the tiny body of an infant. From direct exercise of its capacity it is debarred, for, according to the terms of this affiliation, it must register a physical equivalent for every sensation and act it experiences and initiates. As the machine can give out only what the Inventor has provided an outlet for, so the Self may not have consciousness of itself, or of its relations in environment save those it traces within its brain-tracts by sight, sound and touch. Thus, information does not come to it from within but from outside, and what it learns is not what it is, but about the grooves and ruts of the queer place whose obstacles impede its mobility. While it is finding the use of its limbs by feeling its way, the lay of the land and its own separateness therefrom are being secreted on the sensitive plates of its brain in neuron patterns—perhaps in some fashion analogous to the arts by which sound and light waves are caught and set on the receptive surfaces of phonographic disks and celluloid films.

"I often wonder why your psychologists have so slighted the magic of this marvelous machine that all of you carry around without a thought of its amazing gift of converting these etheric vibrations into perceptions and concepts of fact and installing them where they may be summoned again to mind by the merest impulse of wish or need. 'Just a property of gray matter,' they say, glibly, though when one of them sets out to make an appliance of the simplest order, for some trivial trick of timing a movement or alternating a circuit, he must set in a cog, cam or switch for every phase of each change the accounting requires. They lump all the intricate phenomena through which a human being is weaned, weathered and seasoned to the usages of this world, under the tag *'conditioned'* a term as bald and destitute of true content as that other linguistic scrapbag—the *subconscious*.

"What is assembled eventually on the convolutions of the brain, is a working capital of information and experience patterns, all duly classified and correlated in cell and nerve-tissue, constituting a structure, or cylinder, through which the Self's potential responds in words and movements to the circumstances that surround it. Call this an identity-format, and observe that it is a synthesis of the reactions, less of an Ego to an environment than of a sensitized organism to the location which prescribes the conditions in which it must discharge its obligations.

"It is the Self's deputy, built for its habitation and conveyance, and lives by his presence; but it is also the agent for its own processes and reproduction, and must keep its footing on earth to follow all the observances, conventions and superstitions accumulated there by beings of its own kind. In all directions its responsibilities are fixed, whereas those of the Ego, being immaterial and therefore unrecognized, are bound to the minor circuit of the activities represented by the round of such bodily engagements. These he energizes and in a measure controls. The reaction field of the Self is within, but to operate in the world, he too must establish his own patterns.

"*To be known, he must know himself to be.*

"Between rider and horse, driver and motor, owner and

corporation, the same relation subsists. Man ever supplies the interests that guide and motivate, but must confine his demands within the properties of the instrument which is the medium of their effect. Its capacity and his own knowledge limit his freedom. He may have his own will only by making a form, and a way through which to express it. His hours must be spent feeding, tending and repairing his creatures, including his body: So, the round of his life being devoted to the business of sustaining it, and all that he knows derived from the same need, his nature is absorbed by its liabilities, and insensibly he becomes one with what he does—a subject of space, a whirligig of time.

"A reluctant, rebellious slave I grant you, for unconsciously the submerged Ego resents its subjugation and gnaws perpetually at the prison walls. All those impulses called humanitarian and religious arise therein; also aspirations and ideals. The still, small voice is its messenger and when, in the course of their slow evolution, men develop the organ, *Mind*—there will the Self find place for the articulation of its true identity. But that is another story."

There was an interval of silence. Visibly and audibly I yawned.

"If an open mouth signified a receptive brain, I should have no cause for objection," my visitor remarked.

"It's past midnight," I apologized, "and yours is a long tale."

"Bed for you then, and for me, the wide spaces of the Gobi Desert," announced the Martian. "Perhaps through the penetrative power of my eyes I may discover the lair of the first man, so eagerly sought by your scientists."

"And throw a lot of good fellows out of an entertaining job—don't do that," I remonstrated. "Remember the dull last years of the man who located the North Pole—he led a bully life of adventure up to the time he returned with the thing under his hat. Thereafter he could not forget his great deed nor allow anyone else to, and became a bore."

"The point is well taken," admitted my visitor, a twinge of regret in his voice. "There's nothing more desolating than to find what one seeks. It is worse than being presented with what one wants. Happiness is in hoping but not having. Wise men never idly sacrifice the joys of desire to fulfillment. Nor do they pauperize their emotions by forgiving an enemy. Consider my own tragedy—if I had been less successful and perished in space, now I should be exploring the scenery of Elysium, which rumor has it is a delightful state. And if I had never ventured, I should be beside the ancestral fireplace of my home in Mars, in possession of my shape, weight and appetite as well as of my faculties, enjoying my own reputation and conversing, perhaps, with friends who at least could understand what I was talking about."

"I shall pray for your restoration," I murmured sleepily.

"But don't stay awake to do so," warned the Martian as he "thought" himself into space.

Colonization as cell division and multiplication. Human habit patterns conform to traditional usage as among the hymenoptera. Civilization factual and hidebound. The model of all herd societies. No substitute for evolution. Legend of the hawk and the sparrow. *I* discovers he is only the subject of his own activities. Sense of self-preservation as defense of hibernation. Men must die to learn they have lived. Consciousness a force independent of its agencies. Everyday routines as conducted by the unconscious. Separating driver from vehicle, as in the operation of an automobile. Individual attributes shown in the manner of performing standardized functions. Human behavior not biological. Man a member of the cosmic aristocracy.

I HAD finished dinner and was sitting in my library sipping coffee, trying to frame shapes for the questions of which my mind was full, when the Martian's voice broke the train of my ruminations.

"Eventually science will develop enzymes for indigestible ideas," he began, "but they won't be delivered via the esophagus. I do note an intellectual astringency in the rising generation which bodes ill for the superstitions and vested interests that clog the prevailing system. There will emerge a physiology sufficiently realistic to accommodate the actual mechanism of mankind and, though forever there will be a margin of redundant phenomena, at least you'll know the working principles of existence. Before attempting to satisfy the curiosities seething in your cerebrum, and to aid their delineation, I propose a further excursion. What conception does the word 'colonization' summon in your mind?"

"The ordinary meaning," I replied. "Settlement of new lands by emigration from old countries, and so forth—Why?"

"On leaving you last night," my visitor continued, "I decided the Gobi country might be a drab assignment, and hunting the abode of the originals of this race about as futile as listening to baby-talk. So I headed for Palmyra in the Arabian Desert and thereafter hovered around the coasts of the Dardanelles and the Mediterranean, observing the ruins of the varieties of Civilization that preceded the present vogue. All planets are settled in the same terms, of course—by the spur of appetite. It is ever the belly that incites the cortex. Whether migrations originate in exhausted lands or an overflowing population, conquest, trading or even adventure, the stimulus is material—more and cheaper provender—or plunder.

"In whatever terms the efflux be rationalized, the performance but repeats, on a large scale and in a foreign plasm, the familiar process of cell-division and multiplication. The human chromosomes that withdraw from the original nucleus reassemble in the new communal organism habit-patterns to correspond with those to which old usage had accustomed them.

"Consider the case of Brown, Jones and Robinson—depicted in the annals as bold and hardy pioneers who sallied forth across plains, mountains and desert, fought off Indians and marauders, and settled their families in some untrodden outskirt of their continent; in selecting a site for their homes the criterion that guided their choice was the degree of its adaptability to reproduce the conditions from which they had so laboriously extricated themselves. Into the patriarchal framework, without question as to its relevance to the conditions of the strange environment, these free men proceed to fit themselves much as bees, swarming from the paternal hive instinctively set about the manufacture of hexagonal cells and the gathering of honey."

"What else could they do, one may ask, pending whatever exordium is in the brewing?" I demanded sarcastically.

"I am attempting to suggest that most of the transactions regarded on this planet as the results of volition, are automatic," said my visitor. "Your own system, the order called civilization, is as factual and mechanical as that of the hymenoptera. It exists independent of opinion or feeling. It provides its citizens with the primitive conceptions entertained hereabouts as to their place and state in the natural order—even with the contents of their thoughts. What is your thinking, for instance, but reshuffling prescribed cards into new combinations? Your progress, but the accretion of fresh diagrams whose accumulation adds to the subjects' burdens without developing larger capacities for carrying them or sense of the direction in which they are being conveyed?"

"But the system was created by men," I protested. "To have evolved the art of living side by side in great communities, pooling their resources and observing the amenities of intercourse, ranks as their greatest achievement. By dint of our own inspiration and industry we have lifted ourselves out of chaos, and established an order that controls our world."

"Inferior to any physiological order of which you have cognizance, and incompetent in comparison with the disciplines of the hive or the anthill," remarked the Martian. "Curious—is it not, that the scheme of government you vaunt should amount to no more than a bad imitation of the systems established without fuss by instinctive organisms?

When groups of vital beings of the same biological type and subject to similar needs share an environment, obviously the friction induced by their contacts causes them to contrive ways to divide and distribute the necessities of existence, and to equalize physical disparities among their members. Even protozoa begin life endowed with the capacity to sustain it, and though birds and beasts prey on each other, members of the same species observe precedent and keep the peace within their own ranks. Happenings in the lower organic kingdoms are installed in the forms and in the plasms of which the bodies of their members are built. Privilege to participate in the management of living processes represents relief from the compulsion of instinct, but while volition affects, it does not alter the pressure of basic needs. What embitters me is the lack of understanding, even among your wisest members, of the principles on which governments are founded, that condemn your generations to enforced compliance, in what really consists of the maintenance of organic relations."

"Overly cryptic and fatalistic that statement," I commented. "Suppose I admit that humanity, unaware of its abasement and enjoying its fairly delectable world, is in reality a race of dumb, driven cattle—what then? Are there means of deliverance?"

"As long as the question remains academic—none," my visitor replied decisively. "Beings not cognizant of the degradation of slavery are incapable of freeing themselves from its yoke. The life of a bee seems more attractive than an ant's but as the ant is too fully preoccupied to be aware of the aerial privileges a bee enjoys, he is content with his terrestrial lot and satisfied to fulfill the obligations his society imposes on him. Because Brown, Jones and Robinson were not free men, but slaves of heredity, they had no choice when they set forth on their mission of reestablishment, but to reproduce the institutions and customs to which they were habituated. Life to them was a set of patterns, a little round of routines centering about crops and houses, the management of property, and a further anomalous relation with an unknown God whom it was heresy to worship save in terms of a conventional rite. These people mated and produced offspring, who in turn were fitted to the common mold without question of the relevancy of the discipline. They lived and hated in all righteousness, passing along the tradition of their human identity, their property rights and the little stock of knowledge by which they were able to cope with the hostilities of environment.

"You have here the model of all herd societies in which— experiences being parallel—responses are stereotypes. Where reactions are standardized, individuality is obliterated. Among such as these, the free flow of life is clogged by precedent, overlaid by prescription, obstructed by credulity and so dispersed and diverted that the flavor of its reality is unknown to the holders of its franchise.

"Watching, recently, the operations of one of those amazing machines on which newspapers are printed, I noted the roll of virgin paper being clamped in the grip of the revolving cylinders, each of which impressed a content of surmise or information on its chaste surface as, irresistibly, the web was hurled through their steel clutches, to be folded, cut and vomited from a giant maw to be the 'Daily So-and-So.' Thus, thought I, is this human race hurried from the breasts of its mothers into the embrace of a Moloch machine, whose rollers and cylinders are schools, colleges, apprenticeships, institutions; into the matrix of laws and constitutions with all

the flotsam and jetsam of superstition, prejudice and conformity that the rotating Earth has accumulated on its haphazard journey in time and space. From out its bowels drops the
average man, molded in the image of his brethren on whom
every contact has been imposed, whose acts are stencils, and
his reflexes conditioned—whose mind, swaddled like a Chinese woman's feet, is incapable of an original impulse or a
free view of the world he lives in."

The Martian paused. Before I could intervene he went
on:

"Again I am chasing after wind. All this falls off your
mind as water from a porpoise. I am reminded of the fable of
the philanthropic hawk who undertook a mission to preach
selective breeding to sparrows, so they might better defend
themselves from enemies of his own kind. 'After all,' he said,
'we have the air, wings and feathers in common and it is
only an accident of birth that a bird is a hawk, rather than a
sparrow. Watch us, imitate our ways, quit picking up drop-
pings, feed on proteins like worms and slugs, and let every
mother, as she sits on her eggs, dream that her chicks shall be
born with sharp beaks and strong claws. In a few generations
you'll be noble pirates like ourselves, enjoying the freedom
of high altitudes, and our allies in the glorious fight against
the parasitic broods of pigeons and domestic fowl.'

"Gravely, the sage old sparrow spokesman replied: 'Sir, it
would be ill-mannered to doubt the excellence of your intentions, but your offer betrays misapprehension. No sparrow would exchange the sweet and homely usages of the
towns—the easy pickings of the street or the companionship
of men and horses for those lonely spaces of sky frequented
by hawks. You exaggerate our disabilities. It's a smart hawk
nowadays that catches a tripping sparrow, as our mortality

tables prove, and since we are well-found and happy after the fashion God made us, why should we aspire to frustrate His purpose? Tell your brethren that, lowly as our ways may seem from the heights, they fit our build and our spread of wings and, thanking them, we shall cling as long as possible to our good mother earth.'

"The moral of which is that no evangelism, however well meant, can replace mental evolution."

"Aspersing civilization has rather a vogue," I said, "but no one offers a substitute. Here we are parked, the mass of us, with nowhere else to go, making ourselves as comfortable as conditions permit, and in all the things that make life endurable and entertaining, striding ahead of the generations that preceded us. We've developed leisure, golf, an eight-hour day and a five-day week. A lot of power is working for us and there are more automobiles, phonographs, sewing and washing machines, and electrical refrigerators in operation than at any other time in the world's history. We've tagged all the circumstances perceptible to our senses, and have stopped looking for ghosts. This is practical and progressive. On the other hand, you have aroused my curiosity. I concede the relevancy of points in your argument. Our situation is extraordinary. With the knowledge men have amassed about this planet and the universe, it is anomalous we know nothing of our own identity. If I'm not the *I* that has hitherto served as myself—what am I?"

"The commentary indicates a broadening of perspective," my visitor responded, in a kindlier tone. "Before proceeding, let me repeat the warning that, though I may show you how to find what you seek, I can tell you nothing. You ask for specifications—there are only those you can make for your-

self. For instance—who and what at this moment do you believe yourself to be? Forget ascriptions and get at the facts."

"A week ago," I replied after a pause, "I should have referred you to a compact paragraph in *Who's Who,* which supplies a set of physical particulars covering the date and place
of my arrival on this planet, the names of my parents, the
schools and university I attended, the titles of some writings
I've done and my position in the publishing house whose
revenues sustain such state as I maintain. Now, I admit realization that this data is little more than a surveyor's location
mark on a real-estate map. Looking at the premises from the
larger viewpoint, I seem to be in the position of that fabled
ego whose melancholy adventures you related last night. My
life has been what has happened within its span, and its incidents arose out of the circumstances which environed it. I
recognize it was unfolded by these circumstances rather than
determined by my option. The cards I led were in the hands
dealt me. What I had, I used without thought of its source.
And now, contemplating the trackage of my path, I am impelled to ask what agency defined its disposition? The last
footprints derived from the first as dawn broadens into day.

"What am I—you ask—? No other or better than my
memories. I am the sound of my voice, the pitch of my pro-
file, the color of my hair, my possessions, my status in the
little sphere of my authority, the attitude towards me of my
contemporaries, such reasons as my friends have for their
friendship, such impressions of my intelligence as my clients
entertain, the proclivities I construe as characteristic, such
affections as I cherish because of kinship or proximity. Yet
into all these contacts I enter with purpose and passion. I
pass as a man full-blooded and bodied, a factor in my professional concerns; yet now that you demand an answer to

the crucial question—what am I?—the reply must be—the subject of these extrinsic activities. I'm conscious of myself as the unit of interest, the point of attraction; but of neither orbit or direction am I aware. A competence, surety against vicissitudes and then the grave, are my only goals. Yet what else there might or could be, I cannot see or guess.

"You have taken me out of my depth," I added ruefully. "The shore line has disappeared."

"There's ground under your feet if you'll extend them," said the Martian bluntly. "Somnambulism is not a sin, nor am I an evangelist, nor are you on the mourners' bench. Undoubtedly it is devastating to wake up and find oneself in an impasse, but on Mars we say that the friction of one's back on a wall stimulates the mind. In a necessarily factual civilization conducted by rote, the life of a man must be the part he plays in it. Since its requirements and not his nature prescribe his role, he is molded in the terms of its constitution, and is successful to the degree of his capacity to conform to its convictions. Maintenance of the system employs the energies it sustains, so its subjects, being glued to its tracks, accept its mandates as divinely sanctioned. At intervals one of you stirs in his sleep, or a prophet appears, but Inertia regards as traitors or perverts those who would disturb its dreams. What is known as the sense of self-preservation was installed in defense of hibernation.

"My real objection is not to the artificiality of this structure, which in itself exhibits the creative genius of the race, but to the complacence of its members in mistaking a condition of subjectivity for freedom. A system that so constricts the awareness of its subscribers that they must die to know they've been alive, is obviously defective. The self-portrait you delineated was removed from things seen and felt; it was mental in texture; a deduction; not a report. You recognized you were but part of the processes of living, your individuality not inherent, but a standardized version derived from its context. What you had conceived as progress, only the oscillation of a mass in flux—just a glimpse of reality: But that it was perceptible, indicated the uncovering of at least a corner of the organ of perception."

"More literalness would be helpful," I suggested.

"If it were practicable to satisfy curiosity about your identity in ten words, I would," my visitor said; "but where the beginnings of understanding have not been reached, foundations must be established.

"A while ago you defined yourself as the subject of your own activities, but of the peerless equipment that enabled conduct of the relations described, there was not a word. You see, hear, discriminate, learn, exercise will and apply force—you have foresight, control, initiative, creativeness and adaptability—humanity has invested and made over this planet—yet the faculties and instrumentalities through which these marvels are accomplished, were without significance. No wonder that your race is not a whit wiser about its own nature than when the first man set out after food to relieve an ache in his stomach.

"In advance of further excursions, I shall assume as established, the reality of the factor Consciousness, whose properties are awareness, initiative and integration, and that all the phenomena of physical life, from the lowest to the highest, betoken its presence. With consciousness for pole we have a base anterior to phenomena. What you call the survival of the fittest is merely the stabilization of the organic types in closest accord with its potential.

"The magic of consciousness was in the faculty exercised

by your ancestors, who converted their lungs, larynxes and lips into agencies of speech to impart meaning to sounds. Thus they extended intercourse with one another, and established media for the exchange of facts about the concerns they had in common. Its achievements are apparent in the rich store of devices through which the business of living here is transacted. You are the beneficiary of the generations of seekers who preceded your arrival on this sphere, yet with exactly the same nonchalance that you take your body for granted you enter into possession and use of the vast accretion of creative effort represented in the works and appliances of your race.

"Intrinsically, this amounts to unconsciousness. Until you realize the actual character and potential of your Being, you remain no more than a unit of the determining force, blindly exercising its power without sense of Self or a focal point by which to steer a course. In one of their supplementary reports, dealing with this phase of the element, our Martian surveyors remarked—paraphrased as before:

" 'Though the object of the creative labor that marks the progress of man on this planet has been to relieve the hardships incumbent on the possession of a body, its development is shown as outside the radius of his person. Ever directed upon his external circumstances, his faculties have expended their force on his surroundings. Thus it is *not man* that has changed during the ages of his occupancy of the world, but the environment. His is the same organism in which his ancestors fought dragons in days of old, but the surfaces of the land and water have been transformed. Great cities have risen, and high buildings; the sea is furrowed by the keels of countless ships and the air throbs with the hum of passing aeroplanes. Yet man is no whit better or wiser for the facilities that ease his way. In truth he is the victim of these irresistible contrivances, since long years of his life must be spent in learning their use. It may be said that his own stature is dwarfed by the system he and his forbears have unwittingly furthered, because he must submit to processes of conditioning and education before he is fit to draw a living wage. Thus intelligence, breeding in matter, has birthed a monster—and the sleeping Ego is not awake to the fact that he is the bond-slave of a vast and complicated mechanism, which shapes his thoughts and constrains his ways.

" 'This is evident in the constitution of government. Its form and parts—the institutions of law, learning and religion—are prescriptions to regulate the conduct of beings who have no volition and are innately irrational. Yet this structure was devised by men for the use of men, and the order of its adaptation implies exercise of awareness, initiative and integration—the very qualities its definitions negate. It would seem, therefore, that consciousness itself is a force independent of the agencies through which it enacts its codes of adjustment. Its flow is life; its center—the organism it sustains; it functions as instinct or intelligence according to the biological equipment or intellectual status of its creatures, but of itself it is as unconscious as a railway train of the identity of the passengers it carries.' "

"This is disconcerting," I commented with all the sweetness my voice could convey. "Just as I was about to adopt the parentage of this consciousness—suddenly it becomes a subsidiary; a mere current of force, and I am again orphaned. Still, it is good to know that something is doing the world's work willy-nilly, even if it be in the dark as to its own origin or motives."

"The predicament should not seriously embarrass one

reconciled to the hypothesis that Life cometh up as a flower, and that all organic forms are the results of self-fertilization," replied my visitor derisively. "Why refuse to a verifiable force the privileges so generally accorded to a molecular compound?"

"The point is well taken, O Sage," I admitted, "but to one unversed in cosmic equations your explanations are confusing. Do explain how an element with the properties of awareness can also be unconscious."

"Such confusion is inexcusable on the part of an executive directing an organized institution," my visitor responded more placably. "I assume that the affairs of your publishing firm are coordinated according to prescribed formulas, whereby mechanical details that are repetitive are delegated to secretaries, clerks and office boys, while your own attention is reserved for the extension of associations with authors and distributors. Unspecified matters—relations with other individuals and firms—the problems of piloting a going-concern—require your care; internal functions are conducted automatically. You are in touch with this system but do not participate in its movement. If your employees are efficient and loyal you can go on a vacation and forget the shop and its obligations. Thus you are aware, but unconscious, of process proceeding in your absence; as you are aware of the anatomy and physiology of your body but unconscious of the operations through which it develops the energy applied in your work.

"Of the scores of delicate and intricate adjustments involved in the decisions arrived at, you are as innocent as is a swallow of the instinct that impels its flight north or south. You do what you do without a glimpse of the fact that it is magic of a kind, as are the inventions which expedite the transactions of your affairs—telephones, typewriters, steamships, automobiles, radios and computing machines— all magic to a stranger whose culture has not familiarized him with these devices. You do what you do because you are the unconscious subject of conditioned mechanism, which in response to the initial push, revolves on its own axis and conducts its relation with environment whether you are watching it or not. That is why, when I ask who and what you are, the only answer you have to offer is to call yourself the subject of your own activities. I trust I'm disturbing your complacency enough to arouse your curiosity?"

"If I'm but the subject of mechanism whose operations are independent of my knowledge, how may it benefit me to learn its ways?" I asked.

"A child's protest," exclaimed the Martian angrily. "What has changed the face of your civilization in the last quarter century but the growth and application of knowledge? Every fresh acquisition to the total is an accretion of consciousness. Because you are a unit of consciousness, however unconscious, you share the benefit of the attainment; in the same manner that you read by the glow of incandescent tungsten filaments, though profoundly ignorant of the laws of electricity. If, however, it is your will or need to own, personally, any of this erudition, it is necessary to enter the factual texts that represent it upon the plasm of your cortex. Thus, though you do not add to or take from the totality of the knowledge, yet by study you absorb individual title to its possession and can set up its practice.

"Storm, chill, heat and rain are the reactions of a gaseous mixture—the atmosphere of this planet—to the speed of its revolutions and exposure to the sun. You cannot control the installation, but, by observation, weather changes may be predicted. Call consciousness the power to acquire, contain and use information; but information is not consciousness, any more than memory is what is recalled, or the rotation of a shaft is the electricity that impels it. It is apart from all local applications, as unaware of the character of its own potential as yourself."

"That accomplishment you flourish of dissipating a mystery in one breath and intensifying it in the next is most irritating," I protested. "I gather that I am a unit of consciousness and its object. So I am what I do, yet what I do is not I, but a dramatization of the particular circumstances among which I happen to be pitched. But, like myself, the circumstances are an outgrowth of consciousness; so I appear as the victim of the gift which enables me to be aware of them. You'll admit it is rather complicated."

"Not more so than any other relation you conduct without thinking," my visitor retorted. "For instance; you play golf. It's a game, an exercise, an art, and an excuse. What you do is to enact the particular movements—strokes—that represent playing the game. On the links, you exist as a golfer, ranked by your skill at economizing means to an end—making eighteen holes in the fewest number of strokes. The circumstances turn on the physical equipment that enables you to apply energy and direction to a ball through a club. Thus, again, you are the creature of your gift."

"Still, the bearing the argument has on my own circumstances escapes me," I persisted.

"It is an attempt to help realization of the fact that he who is the subject of his activities is slave rather than master," the Martian explained. "His entity being merged with his profession, becomes contributory to its objectives instead of his own development. Yet there is no relief from such servitude until you conceive a self apart from the functions it inspires."

"But there's no precedent for such detachment," I contended.

"On the contrary," he replied. "It is the most familiar of your conventions, but since the point eludes you we must retrace our steps. I assume you are now committed to the axiom that all physical phenomena, including life, are effects of causes exterior to the medium in which they are exhibited. Also, that where purpose appears it denotes an interest with energy to promote it."

"Legitimate enough," I assented.

"Then think of your own automobile," he pursued. "In its organization and use, the principles I have set forth are present. Herein the highways represent environment; the State provides license and traffic law (authority); the vehicle is a machine which converts gasoline into motion and speed to which your occupancy and steering impart purpose. The number and variety of coordinations comprehended in the flight of a taxicab from Wall Street to White Plains neither affect nor occur to you, but all the resources of your civilization are contributory to this accomplishment.

"An automobile is a contrivance to extend the locomotory functions of the user. Being detached from his person without volition or interest in the results of its use, its operations must disclose the attributes peculiar to the driver. This perspective should afford a view of his capacity, as apart from power and apparatus, so avoids the confusion inseparable from organic interdependence.

"Fundamentally, then, Driver is the outfit of faculties that enable him to move a vehicle from one fixed position to a predetermined destination, with due regard to traffic laws and competition; an adjustment which involves the use of sight, hearing, decision and memory, together with the invisible mechanisms through which these potentials are actualized. He is, next, the set-up—the physical frame which develops local energy to convert and coordinate these functions. And last, is his role as a subject of the communal structure which shapes the modes of his actions. His life, then, is the business of sustaining or satisfying the respective appetites of the organizations in interaction, and the tasks he performs arise from the imposition of maintaining a factitious partnership that he created not—neither controls or understands."

"Wherein Driver disappears in a cloud of abstractions," I intervened, a bit frivolously. "How much pleasanter it would be just to say he runs a motorcar because he likes the job, has a brain to remember roads and traffic laws, and supports himself carrying people or cargoes of goods. His life is serving the community, obeying its codes, buying food and paying rent. Of course we are living off each other—taking in each other's washing as the saying goes, but that's the sum and substance of your theorem."

"It's much easier to look at a noble building than pore over blueprints," the Martian returned. "If, however, you undertake the study of architecture, such discipline is essential to understanding. Of course the play's the thing, and it's tiresome to insist on dragging in author, producer, or anything else that detracts from the illusion. For the moment, I assumed you were serious,"

"I was, and am," I explained. "The amendment is withdrawn with apologies."

"At least we've distinguished Driver from Car," my visitor proceeded, tranquilly. "And we've defined the organism and the pattern of actions through which he delivers his work. But is a man something other than his body, his life and his job?"

"Now that you put it that way," I exclaimed, "I'll say that the man is everything and the job incidental. It's not what a man does but how he does it, that ranks him among his fellows, and his disposition is even more important than his character. Personality is over and apart from its possessor. A fair share will take you where angels fear to tread; without any, one is little better than a meal ticket."

"Then 'Driver' would be the degree of affability with which he performed the functions assigned to him?" queried my visitor ironically.

"It devolves on a man to be square in his dealings and keep his engagements, but affability does lubricate intercourse," I explained. "I thought we had subtracted driver from car and were concerned with his individual values."

"If on one side of this equation you posit an invisible entity, and on the other the machinery through which he is committed to exhibit himself, the product of the interaction must indicate the character and quality of his individuality," the Martian argued. "The tangible output is living, which includes not only the preservation and sustaining of life, but also the conduct of work, leisure and intercourse. Living is standardized: It flows in a series of acts—a succession of arbitrary engagements, arising out of the circumstances which environ life. The clew to the nature of the responsible factor must lie in the manner in which he fulfills the routines through which his manhood franchise is exposited, together with such spontaneous disclosures as are outside the contract."

"What does *manner* cover?" I asked. "Does it refer to virtue, merit or their lack, or to degree of efficiency?"

"Motivation of a heavy body in space is a physical, not a moral problem," my visitor insisted. "Assessment of the values under discussion must be in qualitative and not in religious or opinion terms. Driver's professions of faith, or his love of wife and child do not enter into the affair of piloting a car in traffic, or keeping its parts in condition. His function is cerebral—that of coordinator and initiator of movement, for the accomplishment of the purpose which determines its direction. In the execution of the task, such properties are revealed as dexterity or awkwardness; control and decision, or feebleness and hesitation; alertness to grasp situations and celerity of adjustment, or insensibility and obtuseness; courage and caution, or recklessness and timidity; consideration and heedfulness, or indifference and inattention; patience and tenacity, or haste and instability. There are also the traits called temperamental, exterior to action but coloring and flavoring it, such as cheerfulness, amenableness and humor, or disgruntlement and gloom. For the moment, I'm omitting the time multiple with its derivatives of promptitude and punctuality, but these differentials are the standards of measurement by which Driver's performance is estimated, and represent its manner."

"But on these terms we judge every man," I excepted. "These are character qualities. According to the degree that the affirmative virtues are present or absent, we rate human beings on the scale of attainment."

"Precisely," agreed the Martian, "but, by this analogical experiment, we have detached the agent of cause from the mechanism of effect, and shown that the behaviors called human belong in another category from the biological.

Unit-of-consciousness is attached to its body, and operates it in terms parallel to the relation that subsists between driver and car. The real man is not his body, but an incumbent—that conscious entity whose voice may affirm *I am, I can, I will,* which is the title and proclamation of his basic significance."

"For all of which, I find myself no whit wiser or better," I remarked plaintively.

"This exposition does not prove that if your true identity were known you'd be wearing wings, or that your spirit is the reincarnation of Lord Macaulay's," my visitor assured me, "but it does constitute you an incipient member of the cosmic aristocracy, endowed with volition and the capacity to create—with will and muscle for the task of self-conquest and the acquirement of progressive self-consciousness."

"If bewilderment is a sign of development, I'm on the way somewhere," I said.

"A complete suspension of consciousness may help," the Martian suggested. "In dreamland the silent partner has a voice, and sometimes raises it on behalf of his biological deputy. As for myself, I shall meet some rising desert sun, and while the ultraviolet rays are revitalizing my textures, I shall muse on the dullness of self-satisfaction."

"Which means, of course, a loose rein and spurs for your superiority complex," I retorted.

CHAPTER XV: WHAT TO MAN IS LIFE, TO THE UNIVERSE IS PROCESS

Adventures of *I* in search of his own individuality. Was there a reason for his existence? The two interests. Conducting business relations. Materials do not exist save as qualities. *He* unexpectedly lands on Immortality, and Responsibility shows up. Life's joys and sorrows arise from circumstances that accelerate or retard the motions of its bodies. Gold as subject, object and medium. The credit system. Divergent reactions of opposite categories. If someone kicks your dog, where do you feel his foot? The structure of identity. How oysters feel about the tide.

I AWOKE next morning—fortunately it was Sunday—with the words *I am, I can, I will* ringing in my head and began, as one does, to search for the associations of which they were the evocation. Soon I recalled that these were the Martian's affirmation of man's racial significance, and began rather idly to speculate on the meanings that might be attached to the symbol.

Undeniably there was a flavor of paths-to-power literature there. The picture of a smug-faced, small figure, standing with uplifted arm and menacing forefinger, proclaiming the virtues of a cough drop, swam into my brain. Or was he the gifted chief of the Jones-Robinson sales-force, announcing to a convention of go-getters that "it can be done." Our firm's best salesman is a "New Thoughtist" who in a moment of confidence once told me that invariably he "sold" his customer before seeing him. On arising in the morning it was his practice, he explained, to visualize the day's prospects, realize their personalities and points of view and then mentally to interview each, breaking down the subject's resistance until he succumbed to the arguments. This was his real work, he said—thereafter it was merely a matter of taking down orders. Armed with faith in his own power, no one could rebuff him. I asked if his subjects were aware of his method. He told me—no—his talk was addressed at their unconscious minds, which were more intelligent than everyday minds, and that he was scrupulous to respect the interests of his clientele.

This man has pushed several bestsellers over the plate and I remember thinking at the time, what a pity it was that more of our traveling men were not New Thoughtists. Personally, I regarded the disclosure as among those curious delusions the best of us cherish, but did not dispute his reasoning. A man who sells as many books as he is entitled to a favorite bug.

I recalled the superstitions of other men. One of my partners carries a lucky dime and keeps his fingers on it whenever money is mentioned. He has a peculiar ritual for consulting this oracle before buying or selling stocks. Incidentally, he has made a fortune in the market. A friend who is the president of a large corporation, would not think of closing an important contract or meeting his directors unless he was wearing a particular tie, reserved for such occasion. Stranger still—the case of a bachelor banker, head of a rich old institution, who is said to report each night to a large Persian cat, proposals for loans that have been made him during the day. The die is cast according to the tabby's expression—a yawn is no; a blink, yes. He declares the cat is responsible for his reputation for infallibility. Others subscribe to astrological services, that purport to designate good and bad days for concluding transactions, and won't touch a thing that is offered at the wrong time. I remember an author, whose book we had accepted, refusing to sign a contract until two weeks later, because, he said, Saturn was impinging on his Jupiter. And there's a most accomplished man who can neither get nor keep a job because "Scorpio is ascendant in his House of Life."

Not that many of these acquaintances of mine suffer by their infatuations: All have keen eyes for the main chance, are sane investors and live with their own wives. They respect obligations, pay their bills, keep appointments punctually, and most of them so arrange their affairs as to allow three afternoons a week for golf. I've listened to the miracle-tales of Christian Scientists and wondered at the abasement of the minds of men who could swallow such absurdities, but these same dupes are among the shrewdest traders in the lines they follow and, in addition, believe they operate under divine sanction. The percentage of these so-called scientists on a list of business failures is small: They seldom go to jail and rarely figure in divorce court scandals. All this spells good business from the practical standpoint.

Perhaps I had been missing something. There might be another side to the story, and I fell to reflecting on the Martian's argument. According to him, only engineers and architects sensed the responsibilities of life, because they knew and respected the properties of matter and force. It is true that, though I have read a good deal of science and philosophy and speculated considerably as to the nature of things, I have no more conception of my own identity or how I got here than a bird. Was there a single reason for my existence? Or for that of my associates? Suppose they did lead so-called good lives, support their families—subscribe to hospitals, and charities—what of it? When they died they were buried; other men took over their jobs, and their wives and children and the government inherited their estates. But for a slab in the cemetery and an obituary or so, they might as well never have passed this way at all. And, seriously, did their comings and goings make the slightest difference?

The Martian had dropped hints of a Cosmic System exterior to the perception of humans, which governed all appearances here or elsewhere, and that the world was a sort of colossal mill in which vital beings were processed for use. This plant operated irrespective of the sentiments or sensations of the human stuff that passed through its works, and the best break one could get was to watch its steps and participate in its movements. It was a vast frame of relativity, he had suggested; a complex institution like an international manufacturing trust with millions of branches all connected with headquarters and operated according to the same principles. Arrival in a sphere meant that a Being was equipped to make use of the physical apparatus provided for the experience to which he was subjected, and his progress depended on the degree to which he availed himself of opportunity: Precisely as in business.

Two interests were subserved concurrently. What to men was life, to The System was process, he had explained. There were dual crops, different in kind but similar in degree. Insofar as we acquired understanding of the laws regulating the affairs of our jurisdiction, and intelligently applied them, we advanced our own and another purpose. Presumably, this conveyed the idea that promotion in an organization derived from mastery of its details and knowledge of its purpose. Obviously, a man had to learn about his own shop and its objectives before he could run it. I thought of the number of ex-office-boys and former brakemen, now at the heads of large corporations—not because of genial dispositions, but because of familiarity with the machinery from the bottom up. That there was especial merit here, I could not agree. The best one could say about most of these leaders was that they had industry, persistence and push, and attended so strictly to their jobs that they knew little about any of the other worthwhile things of which the world was full. They constituted the heavy bankroll set, that furnished prey for gold-diggers, dealers in "old masters," and angels for theatrical producers. They advanced their own interest, which was getting all the money within reach of their greedy fingers, but left no byproducts that I could recognize.

Take myself for instance—to what purpose, outside my own, do I contribute? In the publishing business I have the reputation of being a "comer." I'm fairly young—yet am the managing head of an old concern that has a national reputation. On graduating with the usual degree, I entered as an apprentice; got the chance because I'd done some writing and had edited the college paper. Also, I was the nephew of a popular novelist. I learned the game thoroughly and, because I liked the work, devoted all my time to it. I'd been there about ten years, when death removed both my chiefs, and no descendants surviving to inherit, three of us, who had been given small interests, took over their holdings—my uncle financing the transaction. We adopted plans the old men had refused to countenance, and revenues doubled in the first year. Since then we have cleaned up our indebtedness and now divide, each twelvemonth, a fairly large profit. Luck has favored, it is true, but we have backed the opportunities that offered with all our force, and feel we have earned what has come to us.

I am trying to figure out some sort of meaning for the Martian's cryptic statement. There is no mystery about the way business is done. Consider our own shop—each of us has his department but each knows what the others are doing and decisions are in common. We take no advantages, and don't indulge in sly or smart tricks; not on moral grounds, but because we are not tempted that way: Nothing esoteric here.

Unless a man has his business under his hat, management of affairs is dualistic. On one side is ownership and control; on the other administration. The manufacture and sale of books or any other commodity belong in a category subsidiary to direction and pilotage. Is there a clew here? Hardly, because these are but parts of a whole. My partners and I furnish motive, cohesion and energy—as of a clock we are the instrument and the mainspring—our employees the works. They contribute service but take no responsibilities. These we shoulder; we provide wages, incur losses, and take for profit what is left of revenues after deducting costs and taxes. We exercise authority; but there's nothing sacrosanct or intellectual about ownership. We are neither wiser nor smarter than some of the people who work for us. Democratic and idealistic, you say? Nonsense— just sane adjustment. Loyalty to the firm, to ourselves and to each other—that is real morality. We are a sound going-concern, with speed up.

Results, personal—that self-satisfaction which is the by-product of successful functioning. On a par with the purr of a sweetly running engine, or the exaltation bred of a long straight drive on a golf course. No chance for any bilateral return here.

Development—perhaps he refers to the effects of work and experience on the individual. There are other assets than money. To myself I seem the same man I was twenty years ago, but I move in a different sphere. I carry information and weight now, but am conscious of freedom. I act with more assurance and use greater discrimination. My perspective is broader. I have learned business economics, something of finance and the credit system—in general the way of the world.

In the ten years of our control my partners and I have changed. Our expectations and enthusiasms have moderated—also our tempers—but we are more resolute and courageous. Of our ability to meet emergencies we are confident, but don't create difficulties by rash experiments. Of course we take fliers, but only after reducing the gamble to the minimum. Our relations prescribe our conduct. We have faith in each other, which means mutual assurance that the firm's interests have preference over our own—that each is entitled to the truth from the others and that all will fairly subserve the common obligation. This extends outside office hours, because our private lives must be so led as not to endanger the reputation of our institution or lessen individual efficiency. Our subjection sits lightly upon us. We feel free to come and go as we please. I suppose the sense of the right to be one's-own-man is a byproduct.

There are outside aspects which count more heavily. Business is the exchange of commodities for profit, and involves the establishment and maintenance of human relations. Out of this intercourse all troubles arise for, as the Martian observed—these are unspecified, being subject to whim, temperament and prejudice. Every man or concern we deal with is a separate problem, whose peculiarities must be remembered and reconciled. So we handle a *variable,* human nature, and our ship must be adroitly steered to destination over this shoreless and uncharted sea whose submerged reefs endanger passage. It is in conducting these relations that one acquires steadiness and flexibility, tact and patience; salient qualities, that are outside knowledge and can only be gained by contact.

Which reminds me of another unspecified element—the sense of right selection. Taste, unlike use, is not standardized but fluctuates. What is good today is a dud tomorrow. The truth is that successful publishing like theatrical producing, or any other business that caters to leisure, is done by guess. Here is not judgment, but instinct. If a flair for what the public wants or can be made to take is lacking in the individual, his force of character is as useless as a thousand dollar bill in a country grocery store. I know a saleable book when I read it—and can give reasons, but not one that would enable someone else to recognize the next that turned up in the mail.

For all of which I'm not an inch nearer knowing what the Martian was talking about.

I fell to thinking of the elements that enter into the manufacture of books, of the variety of processes that separate paper, ink, type and press from the raw material of which they are composed. Paper was wood, ground to pulp and fabricated into a web, to pass without breakage between cylinders that imposed inked impressions on its surface. The lead of the type was dug out of a mine and refined to combine ductility with tenacity. The steel of the press—iron alloyed with carbon to withstand the force discharged through its parts. The ink—viscous vegetable-mineral liquid adhesive yet fluid, subtly compounded for the office it performed.

In each instance complete transformation of the original nature of stabilized products to fit them for the needs of our civilization. Here were selection and adaptation up to date. Undeniably, as the Martian had so often repeated, such conversions presumed the presence of an agent equipped with capacity and information to make them. The idea of a tree changing itself into a roll of newsprint was absurd. Conversely it was absurd to conceive seed, soil, water and sunlight conspiring to change themselves into trees.

I recalled my visitor's description of a tree as a noble invention, and of its efficiency in conducting those exchanges with environment through which it sustained its life. To survive, it had fought a great fight, and winning, stood up proud and beautiful—defying the winds of heaven to disturb its stance. Within the state of its being did it not exhibit qualities men imagined exclusively characteristic of their own species? It had identity, dignity, reserve, integrity; for it was true to itself, and was unmoved by vicissitudes. A man with the attributes of a tree, who served, but held himself as independent and aloof, would be an aristocrat of the race. Yet we wrecked its noble edifice and tore it to shreds to make stuff with which to circulate the frivolous babble of our articulateness.

Such cogitations were profitless, I reflected. Trees were bound and men free. They could neither fight nor run away—only resist, rooted to the spot. In the planetary economy the function of plant life was that of transformer. Out of chemical elements it manufactured the physiological fuel on which insects and animals fed. Plants lived by synthesizing, and extracting the nourishment they needed from sun, soil and water; we, but parasites who lived off their work. At least they were useful to us—of what use to any one are we? Yet everything was interdependent. To assume that this huge food factory, our globe, had no better purpose than to enable us to go through the motions called life, did seem irrational. Literally speaking, we too were transformers, converting the material the environment furnished into goods and utensils appropriate to the needs bred of our state of being, and for whatever invisible cosmic service we exist to fulfill. The changes wrought in a log of wood to turn it into paper were as radical as the original processes which it underwent to become wood.

Isn't it true that the scientists have overstressed environment?—I asked myself. Actually, men subsist by exchanging service and manufactured commodities with one another. Conditions fixed, but independent of location, just as civilization is apart from its members. We are on a plane of our own, removed above our biological neighbors and curiously enough all its appurtenances—our works—are apart from ourselves. On the world's surface we have superimposed a racial order whose constitution is information: And its text is set forth on paper by leaden type and duplicated by means of printing presses—its laws and usages being independent of the comings and goings of its individual subjects. Was life no more than a business of energizing or dramatizing information?

What to man was the action of life—to the System was process!—I repeated. Beef was a synthesis of corn or grass, air and water. What did a steer know about minute steaks or broiled tenderloin? No more than a sheep about mutton or tweed—or a tree about paper. To me, beef was a source of the energy I applied to the publication of books. I did not sit down to dinner to make energy, but to enjoy the smell and taste of beef, to feel out its textures with my tongue and teeth, and to relieve my appetite. In a general way I know what happens to the macerated morsels after they have passed my gullet. They become my kind of physiological fuel and are wrecked and dissolved into their chemical constituents, much in the fashion of a pulp-mill chewing up wood. Process, certainly, and for the profit of him who conducted it. Growth was process and so were education and apprenticeship. Every activity a man engaged in nowadays had a culture of its own. There were no natural movements, even in labor. Pick-and-shovel work had specifications attached to it. The Martian was right—men are little better than animated jobs. Death's sting is less the loss of life than of one's privilege of repeating the motions through which one carries on.

What is process? It implies subject, object, means. One processed wood or rags to make paper. Iron ore is converted into steel by process. It involved changing the texture of raw material so it could be used in work. Work and use imposed wear and tear on textures, so change was to add endurance. A thing had to stand up, be hard, soft or flexible, or hold water, resist fire, force, disintegration or any other of the physical or chemical reagents to which it was exposed. These qualities must be inherent in the original substance; by heat and cold, hammer and tongs, we intensified its atomic pattern to fortify it for our own rough usage. In a sense wood, metal, vegetable fibers did not exist, save as qualities. We dealt with durability, tensility, ductility, resistance, conductivity; and the measure of values was the ratio of these abstractions in the stuffs that contained them. Similarly there were no cattle, sheep or beans—only bodybuilding material—proteins and carbohydrates. One assessed food according to its calories, coal by heat units, and so down the list. Talk was articulated sound.

Given the passage of a man from the womb to the grave—what did he make, en route, beside a living? He accumulated experience. Experience was the sum of all the things that happened to one on the way. It was supposed to fit one for the performance of work. It connoted weathering as applied to lumber or as age to wine. It included marriage, being jilted, jail, inheriting a million dollars, and what one did with the money; being wrecked, charged by an angry elephant—even writing a book. Schooled by experience, it was presumed one knew how things were done and how to get along with one's fellows. Whatever life wrought in the individual was comprised in his experience. If action was process, experience contained the result.

I've been alive for over forty years—what have I gained? The qualities inherent in my makeup have been developed by use. What I had as a boy, I have now, but tested and proven. Reliability, self-confidence, stability, persistence, truthfulness—the sound old bases of character that make for serviceableness in every plane of living! Curiously enough, analogues of the very properties we evoke in material substances, to stand the strains and stresses of use. Imagine consciousness in a ton of ore, dug out of the Mesaba mines, ferried by steamer across the lakes to the mills at Gary, being roasted, smelted, compounded, annealed, forged, and emerging finally in the form of steel rails. If these could tell the story of their passage through the fiery furnaces and rolling mills, it would represent their experience. Process would be education, and their obligation in life affording rigid support to the wheel rims of cars and locomotives. Men had their tribulations, endured pain, sorrow and disappointment; bore burdens. Were the ordeals of life conditioning? For what? Steel rails don't know and cannot see what they are used for, either!

Well, experience did not alter the nature of bone, blood or protoplasmic tissue; so what the action of life processed, was earth's soil, via dissolution of solar energy as processed by man. If permanent effects accrued, they must be registered in that psychic counterpart which the Martian insisted was the actual being of man—the unit of consciousness. But, in allowing the existence of an invisible basic entity, one admitted a fabric capable of surviving the loss of its physical envelope, and virtually accepted potential immortality. That, according to the best current opinion, was unwarrantable. Still, I am not sure that the men who deny continuity to the existence of humans have ever given their minds to a fair consideration of the subject. According to the terms of my thinking, the hypothesis has neither moral nor religious implications, and is independent of any form of opinion. However intangible, consciousness was an element with properties. It supplied a blueprint for life, and endowed it with architecture and rationality. What if the acknowledgment did play havoc with the present scientific structure? According to science, men were better organized than flies and lived longer, but not as long as elephants.

But if one conceded the reality of anything in the nature of a soul—did not one thereby incur responsibility? Responsibility to whom or what? If there be a system, and its standards are analogous to those by which we decide the fitness of our own raw material for use—no man who could face his fellows with an honest record need worry. Trees are not judges of their serviceability to man! Besides, if life be process it implies calculation of treatment and evaluation of results, by different gauges than those applied here.

At this juncture in my soliloquy the telephone rang. I was reminded of a luncheon engagement—and there was just time to bathe, dress and maintain my reputation for punctuality.

*　　*　　*

The Martian's tone, as he greeted me late the same night; carried an inflection of sarcastic friendliness.

"It was a real reconnaissance you made this morning," he said. "I followed telepathically if not sympathetically. There were hurdles jumped that I should have balked, but you did cover country. The flight was of the order of mechanical cerebration, of course, but it indicated that the vibrations your eardrums registered lately had altered the patterns of your brain cells. As I remarked before, strange ideas do disturb tissues like stray bullets. If you can repeat the essay, do so— allowing a latent faculty to exert its own energy, is no more than simple justice. Minds are entitled to light and air as bodies are. The manner in which the human race inhibits the exercise of its greatest gift is sheer cruelty. Incidentally, worrying about responsibilities at this embryonic stage of your development is about as foolish as wondering what costume you'd wear if appointed Grand Vizier to the Emir of Trebizond. A glimpse of reality, like the impression light imprints on a sensitized film, requires fixing. Conclusions leaped at are seldom landed on. When again in your ratiocinations the idea of soul occurs, just remember the homely adage that one does not plough with one's eyes."

"An interval back, you warned that it was up to me to make

my own specifications, and that you could tell me nothing. I follow that lead, find unsuspected facts, and am called a fool for my pains," I protested. "Seems to me I deserve encouragement—not superciliousness."

"Right," the Martian replied. "You covered on the wings of your own mind, ground I should have had to carry you over, so my own task is lighter. The convictions established were individual. Therefore of use to yourself. My objection is that you adventured outside the bounds of an argument whose premises are not yet occupied. Your race is weighted with feet of clay to prevent track jumping. Keep well in mind that men are surrounded by prearranged circumstances; are born into bodies and an environment at given times, and under definite conditions. Whatever process is in the making must be related to the severality and inseparableness of these facts. Think of them as millstones if it so pleases you—within them is the problem and the solution. On future excursions, reckon from here and now and you'll not stray too far afield."

"As thou say'st, O Oracle!" I submitted. "Take your own tack."

"I return to the issue that was left in the air last night," he began. "The proposition we discussed had three factors and two interactions and you had failed to grasp their bearings on one another or their association with the trunk of the thesis."

"Leftovers are seldom palatable," I remonstrated. "Why not a new dish?"

"The next course awaits digestion of the last," the Martian insisted. "The factors in the stipulation were Driver, Automobile, Environment. I detached Driver—let us examine the surviving relation. Environment is earth's mass, gravity and pressures—its field of force. Mobility upon its surface indicates that individual bodies have overcome these resistances. This has been accomplished by adapting the structures of such bodies to the character of these resistances, so they penetrate rather than oppose each other. Thereafter the bodies are equipped with energy for motivation.

"Automobile is an application of this principle. Its parts are so adjusted to environment's constitution as to secure the largest return of mobility from the energy expended. On smooth highways it functions with ease. Roughness and irregularities of surface strain its structure and retard its velocity. Its vicissitudes are such ups and downs. Auto has no sympathetic nervous system or life of its own, and neither knows nor feels its occupational ills.

"It is the man at the wheel, Driver, who is cognizant of what his motor deputy endures. He is a denizen of another world, in which environment is not merely mass and force, but is also the State, its streets, its traffic laws, and the homes and industries of its inhabitants. These inhabitants are also mobile beings, but beings who maintain existence by exchange with one another, according to the circumstances that govern intercourse in the country in which they live. For them Auto is merely a vehicle energized to facilitate their communications and deliveries. The contents of such transfers are the material wants of beings of this caste who, in the transaction of affairs that evolve from their culture, are subject to the vicissitudes incidental to sustaining it. They propel these bodies in furtherance of purposes recognized as advantageous; their experience is derived from the necessity of developing the energy to support their activities and relations among their kind.

"In the body of which it is the incumbent, the role of Consciousness parallels the relations between driver and auto. Its joys and sorrows arise from the circumstances that accelerate or retard rotation in the field of its orbit. The nature of the circumstances inhere in the environment. Its tools, institutions and conventions furnish facilities and obstacles to transmission. Consciousness is passenger as well as driver—subject as well as medium. It interprets, classifies and coordinates the incidents of the journey, as bearing on the progress of a vehicle discharging an obligation. The field of its own experience being the body it inhabits, through the machinery of this deputy, it synchronously registers the reactions of its unit to degrees of attainment, and it does so in the terms of intentions and expectations, satisfaction or disappointment. Note the association here between energy expenditure and emotion."

"Intentions and expectations! It is said Hell is paved with them," I interrupted, jocularly.

"And the Patent office with miscarriages," retorted the Martian. "Bad driving is not indigenous to this vicinity alone, nor are abortive inventions, misjudgments or errors. All planets are strewn with the remains of prehistoric monsters, which were more interesting as experiments than effective as survivors.

"The task of dovetailing cause and effect, and adjusting force for function is not much easier in one place than another. It is consoling to remember that an archangel's knowledge of the principle and ingredients of cold light would help him but little in producing it for use on earth. Magic is just uncommon knowledge, and miracles—demonstrations of laws not yet entered in science's statute books. In a universe in which every happening is an experience of consciousness, there can be no losses. Failure is as educational as success, provided it does not abate the courage of convictions. He who wins, opens for himself no more than larger fields for expenditure, wherein slip may mean smash, instead of stumble."

"Wise stuff, Master," I interrupted. "Your saws would adorn any copy book. Our own 'opportunity books' sell well, and I've delivered success talks myself to sales conventions. In the meantime, the diverse properties of consciousness elude my grasp. It is the devil, the deep sea, the angel Gabriel and whatever else is or is not. For the life of me, I cannot reconcile all the similarities and differences you reel off so glibly. How can the same element be both subject and medium, or apply divergent standards? How can one possess and exercise a faculty and yet remain ignorant of its reach or existence?"

"Think of gold, currency and the credit system," my visitor suggested. "Gold is an element stabilized by its rarity, and the yardstick for exchangeable values. Whatever is made of, or derives from it, embraces its attributes. A dollar is a unit of gold. Its worth is inherent—its degree defined by its purchasing power. Currency is deputy gold, whose validity is guaranteed by the government that issues it. It is not the paper but the sign manual it bears that the grocer accepts for his goods. Credit is humanity's organized faith in the will and ability of its members to redeem their pledges in gold or its equivalent.

"Thus gold is subject, object and medium. Though it exists in itself, of itself it is ignorant. It has neither morality or prejudice. It is where it is found, goes where it is taken, and disappears in investments but, in recoverage, reverts to its source. Since all work is interpreted, appraised and returnable in its terms, it is the measure of the success or failure of effort to achieve purpose. It gilds with its glamor whoever discovers, makes or hoards it. Identities are based on the ownership of its power and expanded by the means it commands. Aspiration for its possession is the fulcrum of emotion—so to have it is the token of happiness, and its lack is grief.

"Here then is a familiar of your system endowed with most of the characteristics I ascribed to consciousness. If you will but explore the diversity of its significances in your own mind, the obstacles to comprehension may be removed.

"Or, take credit: It is a frame for coordinating the variabilities of conscious mobile beings. Though the measure of values is still the gold yardstick, its terms are qualitative instead of quantitative. Its standards are constants, such as reliability, responsibility and precision, which extend into honor, fidelity and truth. So your credit covers more than will and ability to pay, for it includes as debit, the individual's attitude towards every obligation he incurs in the business of living. Here then is an intangible that pervades all relationships; of it you are subject and medium; yet it is apart from and ignorant of your existence and still conditions your activities. Its invisible government classifies and records you, not as a man among men, but as a good or bad risk.

"Or there's the principle of silent partnership," my visitor went on. "The brokerage firm of John Brown & Co. operates with capital furnished by the father of a junior member, who has not been told of the arrangement. The lender gets security and interest on his money; the son—training and experience. The same fund serves as wage for employees and investment for the boss.

"As to variation of standards, an income which seems to you large would mean but pocket money to a Captain of

Industry. Last week I listened-in on the moanings of a disconsolate personage who had lost ten of his thirty million fortune in a stock slump. He was practicing all the small economies that occurred to him, and distributing the ill-luck among his relatives and creditors. Do try to remember that the same principles repeat themselves in every transaction, however diverse the circumstances. What your world needs above all things is some sort of serum to dissolve the air and watertight neuron-compartments, in which the accumulated knowledge and wisdom of the race are now locked up."

"I begin to follow some of the divagations of your protean element but still can't understand what bearing the experience of a motorcar on a highway has on the relations between 'I' and my body," I pursued.

"Analogical only," said the Martian. "I'm simply converting the commonplaces of cosmic operation to the terms of your mind. I'll try again. Punctuality is among your fetishes and invariably you are in the firm's office by 9 AM. Between desk and home there's an interval of thirty blocks. Depending on rising-time—you walk or ride. If walk it is, your purpose is conveyed to its destination on legs and feet. You furnish the route and control the speed. They do the work.

"The environment presents itself to your sense-organs and you are aware of its content of habitations and fellow passengers. You obey traffic laws, avoid colliding with the other occupants of the sidewalk, and perform all the maneuvers through which the piloting of a human body on a crowded city street are accomplished. All these contacts are immediate and personal because the apparatus through which they are conducted is coordinated with the unit of consciousness that initiates, classifies, records and interprets them—not in mechanical or psychological terms but as normal application of its power to do what it does.

"If time presses, you invoke supplementary energy by calling a taxicab. Therein, across an equal interval of space, along duplicate thoroughfares, you are rushed to your destination by a substitute power, which both relieves your legs and preserves your reputation. The taxicab is in contact with the same environment, encounters parallel interferences and is subject to the same light-vibrations which you synthesized as information—all without awareness of its service, of your weight, or of the subtle appliances by means of which your will was transformed through the driver's ears and hands to its ignition and transmission systems.

"So, without realization of any of the interactions inseparable from the movement of a heavy body across a field of gravity, a purpose was conveyed to an office door and released to work out its destiny."

"If in pursuit of this punctuality I am jostled by a rough, or a careless driver runs into my taxi and I fly into a rage—who is angry?—my consciousness, or my body?" I asked. "It can't be my consciousness, because its own equilibrium could not be shaken by the strains and stresses of its vehicle. And body is no more than a protoplasmic envelope. Yet some one is threatening to punch someone else's head."

"If someone kicks your dog, where do you feel his foot?" asked my visitor derisively. "Not on your own shins, surely. The injury is to something that neither you nor anyone else ever saw; your structure of identity. The taxicab, into which the vehicle of the boob driver crashed, emitted no protest. Neither you nor its driver was hurt physically, though one of you struck the boob and the other called a policeman. What did the rough disturb in brushing against you? Not consciousness—since that is not tangible. It was the sacred territory of your arm and leg he invaded. The boob interfered with a vehicular right-of-way. He was taken to a police station nursing a black eye; the car was hauled to the nearest garage. You denounced the awkwardness of the rough, and admonished him to keep out of your path.

"Such affairs are unknown in spheres in which gravity and purpose never cross tracks. When two mobile material bodies in transit impinge on each other's orbit, and collision occurs, it is a clash of opposing forces, and heat is engendered. If neither is equipped with sensory apparatus to measure it, the atmosphere absorbs the effect. But if both are organisms integrated for pilotage and freighted with purpose and destination, their interests have been thwarted, and another element is involved. An interest is a factor with values attached, and betokens the presence of a faculty of appraising, holding and protecting its own estimate. Since such appreciation is based on the potentials of consciousness, it is in the terms of consciousness that the damage is assessed."

"Undoubtedly you know what you mean but still you have the advantage of me," I put in. "Whether the nature of such intelligence as I exercise in transacting the affairs of my life is conscious or unconscious, I am unable to judge. With all due respect to the excellence of your argument, it seems to amount to the same thing. I know that I get by and behave; and do both rather well."

"You get by on the current and behave by prescription," replied my visitor contemptuously. "The rules of the game ordain your plays. Ad infinitum; you deal and shuffle the same cards. Where games and cards came from—how you got to the table—and where you go afterwards—are of no concern. Oysters feel that way about the tide. The real flavor of life is in the satisfaction of curiosities. As well be dead as never to wonder or explore."

"Forgive me and call it a night," I begged. "Truth is, my mind is on its last legs and you've forgotten that there's a morrow."

"Granted, on all counts," my visitor agreed cheerfully. "Besides, there's a mass-meeting of mystics tonight—somewhere in southern California—and mayhap they'll let me make them a speech."

Dispassionate consideration of the phenomena of hypnotism. Only mind can measure the imponderable. The uncontrovertible facts: you are here, and you know it. Functions consciousness contributes to organism. Significance of the mechanics of a simple action. The problem of etheric exchange. Perception as factual as enunciation. How human beings overcome their isolation and insulation for the purpose of communication. Identity of the Universe resides in its unity, and is expressed in self-realization. Our Cosmos as the embodiment of a Logos whose obligations lie in the preservation of his own entity and orbit. Men as agents for the maintenance of His awareness. Go look for your own soul.

"What luck?" I began next evening as soon as the Martian had signaled his arrival. "Did the mystics applaud your oratory?"

"I did not raise my voice," replied my visitor mournfully. "That there were many mansions in the Father's house I knew, but never dreamed the number of rooms they contained. If Babel was the confusion of tongues, out there it's the profusion of faiths. That territory is a lesser Tibet, and every second house is a lamasery. I soon got lost in a maze of hidden ways and upward paths, and withdrew to the silences of Death Valley to regain my wits."

"You were successful, I hope?" said I politely.

"It might be doubted, since I've returned," he replied with equal and opposite sweetness. "Truth is, there's a trace of madness in my family—one of my ancestors was confined in an asylum to prevent him dissipating his fortune, trying to fill a bottomless pit. It must be that contact with your mind has revived the taint and it is revealed by the continuation of this argument."

"As long as it's neither love nor a desire for my salvation that drives you to these extremes, I'm satisfied to listen," I assured him. "You had just finished pulverizing me for suggesting that whatever consciousness I exercised was by inadvertence. Go on from there."

"That's the trouble," said my visitor. "I might as well be talking temperance to a prohibitionist. From the drift and tendency of your comments, it is clear you are still far from grasping the everyday reality of the potential I'm attempting to exposit. That psychic counterpart, stipulated as the medium through which the Self functions, still swims in your mind as the figment of a theory, rather than a fact of the significance, for instance, of reception and condensation in radio telephony. Do try to realize that we are dealing with phenomena which are inexplicable until adequate premises have been set up to account for their workings. Material for such generalization has been accumulated. For instance, it is extraordinary that conditions disclosed in the hypnotic trance, the effects registered in anæsthesia, and dissociation as in sleep have not indicated to your pundits that the operating factor in a human organism must belong in a different category from the physical machinery of its normal awareness and response. However, among one-dimensional thinkers, for whom observation and verbal description are ends in themselves, the exploration of lateral relations is not encouraged."

"But hypnotism is a commonplace," I objected. "It has

been studied to exhaustion. Whole libraries are devoted to the subject and a technic for its use perfected."

"But seldom, and then covertly applied," returned the Martian. "I am not interested in trances, as such, but in the concrete elements affected therein. Dispassionate consideration of hypnosis proves the contentions I've been elaborating. If, by mechanical or physical means, there can be induced in a human being a state in which his *I* is dislodged, and control of his organism usurped by another, surely there is demonstrated an *I* factor distinguishable from the machinery that normally responds to its reflexes. If the usurper can by suggestion, cause this machinery to perform its routine responses such as going through the leg and arm movements of swimming if told it is in the water, or reproducing the facial distortions through which it is wont to represent grief, anger or amusement—is it not evident that it is an autonomous motor-unit whose own system carries the behavior-patterns ingrained by its experience contacts; and that these may be energized by another than the incumbent who had installed them in its neuron fibers? Since, under such extraordinary circumstances, this system accepts and transacts, without protest, whatever vagaries are imposed from the outside, one would be justified in believing that it does not itself exercise the powers of cognition and judgment it ordinarily exhibits.

"If this autonomous unit is capable of forging in its own tissues the mark of a burn, as reaction to a whisper from the usurper that the pencil he presses on its wrist is red hot, it must be admitted that the perception of reality, which usually inhibits such illusions, resides with the incumbent and not in its system.

"Since in the hypnotic state the cerebral, muscular and

visceral systems of the inert subject's organism continue to
function, and its physical contact with the environment is
unchanged, the impingement of their respective energies
on each other cannot be the source or motive of the intercourse ordinarily maintained between them. If the parts of
an otherwise insensible organism return their habitized responses to impulses which have not passed over the conductive thresholds, it is evident that there are other paths to
the mechanisms of its central nervous control than those ordinarily activated by mechanical stimuli. Since rational use
of a human organism, together with right application of its
faculties, depends on the presence of a conscious incumbent,
and are suspended in the absence of such a factor, it is fair
to conclude that this capacity must be inherent in his constitution, and denotes it as of an order and character superior
to—and separable from—the physical instrument whose vital energies it sustains and directs.

"Now I have touched on the most obvious phases of hypnotism, omitting the more upsetting phenomena of that su-
per-stage, called somnambulism, in which the strange faculties of lucidity and telepathy are evoked. For none of these
aspects have prevailing hypotheses accommodation, and, until the lacuna is recognized and a new assignment of values
agreed upon, the mental evolution of the race is estopped."

"In other words, we are to substitute intuition or revelation for research—meditation for experiment—and the
séance room for the laboratory," I sneered.

"Nonsense," my visitor returned, "extending conceptions
does not alter conditions. The relations between body and
planet are fixed, and remain the same, whatever the viewpoint. I do not dispute the findings of the biologists, as bearing on the physical geography of the human system, or the

assurance of Behaviorists that the life-story of a man is the biography of an organism adapting itself to an environment. I do insist that cause, coordination, architecture, tenancy and motivation are outside their pictures. Right understanding of the problem requires that the person of that which perceives, feels and wills is given factual significance, quite different in nature from the body, whose sensations it recognizes and interprets.

"But by what instrumentality may an imponderable be assayed?" I asked.

"By the most efficient and unfamiliar of all the tools of men—the mind," the Martian replied. "Life operates in the open—and as the mysteries of creation are exemplified in every structure, vehicle and calculation used here—surely it is practicable for an adult intelligence to disentangle its principles from its practices. Set up an imaginary fixed frame, external to yourself, and triangulate your own movements."

"But how does one begin?" I invited.

"By forgetting for the moment about test tubes, scales and spectroscopes," my visitor said sharply. "Start stocktaking by positing the two uncontrovertible facts. *You are here, and you know it.* That knowledge is consciousness. Go back a bit. The content that consciousness is aware of is not of itself, but of the environment in which it awakened. At that awakening it found itself in a body through whose organisms it established contact with that environment, and its experience of life was gained through the movements it stimulated to maintain the existence of this body.

"We start then with two interactions—between consciousness and the body it occupies—and between body and this environing theater of its operations. Thus the body is the intermediary, through which an individual consciousness acquires that information about the world which enables it to live there. Since the bodily activities through which this information is derived are initiated by consciousness for its benefit, it must control the energy which motivates them. So we may say that consciousness is the *source* of the energy developed and applied by its body.

"Since the processes of fertilization, cell-division and multiplication by which matter was disposed on the embryo in the womb are dynamic, and its mobility and growth thereafter are products of energy, presumably the phenomenon Life is the token and expression of the presence of *a unit of the element Consciousness.*

"Accept body, then, as a vehicle, equipped to accommodate the functions of consciousness, a mobile agent, in environment, a stabilized field. Deprived of direct association with the region of its sojourn, the contacts and communications that consciousness may have are at secondhand and through this deputy.

"Confined to location by the weight and range of its physical medium, what consciousness learns about life is a record of the reactions of a human body, in being adapted to the pressures and resistances the world opposes to its mobility, appetites and needs. To these ordeals it contributes initiative and pilotage and order.

"If these conjunctions are difficult to visualize, transpose consciousness and environment to the terms of an Atlantic voyage. You are passenger, steamer is body, and ocean the field of operation. You are aware of this medium but not in touch with it. The hull of the craft contacts the resistances that the water presents to the transit of a heavy vessel. The tossings, pitching and shivers through which this hull registers stresses inseparable from the clash of energies in the encounter, you interpret as they affect your own equilibrium—as they further or retard the fulfillment of individual purpose. So the steamer appears as a traveler's accommodation for an excursion in an environment for which his own organism is not adapted, and wherein translation of purpose and modifications of course are discharged by captain and crew, whose vital governing function, a passenger takes for granted, as beyond his jurisdiction. Thus, your relations with the ocean are conducted by deputy, and the reactions are wholly internal—determined by your physical state and the conditions of voyage.

"When I contemplate the amazing intelligence exhibited in the architecture and organization of such great vehicles as those you propel in air and water, I marvel at the obtuseness of your philosophies. When every motive structure is adapted both to environment and to the exercise of consciousness, and so clear an understanding is exhibited of the principles in accordance with which direction is stepped-down from mind to mechanism, your failure to realize the inevitability of parallel agencies being present in all vital organisms must be due to some innate mental astigmatism. Since all inventions and appliances of men are dualistic in origin, design and development, and carry, in separate compartments, machineries for internal guidance and external administration, why assume that plant and animal creations achieve form and behavior without an analogous equipment?

"In a world in which everything that moves sequentially functions by virtue of the energy its system enables it to transform, why imagine that particular shape or identity-patterns may be unfolded without specific instrumentalities of contact to time and proportion and deliver the power that defines and sustains their delineation? The magic of tree

and flower, and all the wonders of growth and development
are exhibits of consciousness in being. However small the
degree of its self-awareness—rest assured that, where life
shows—consciousness is domiciled.

"Think of an acorn—implicit therein are the design of an
oak and the power to be one. It is a microcosmic storage-cell
which, set in an electrolytic medium called the soil, induces
the currents that dissolve the fabric of its kernel and deposit,
on the diagram of its nucleus, the material constituents required for integration in time and space. It emerges a tree,
of the order its format designated; a sturdy going-concern,
competently engineered for the conversion of sunlight, air
and sap into roots, trunk, branches, leaves and seed. In the
great economy of Nature it is part of the giant filtering and
fixation system through which air is cleansed of the exhaust
products—of the breath of men and animals—and within it,
chemical substances are prepared on which mobile beings
depend.

"In the constitution of an oak are concentrated the tech-
niques of the arts and sciences, which humans have learned
so laboriously to apply to the work of their hands. Its form,
proportion, anchorage and internal organization are engineering and architecture; the disposition of the matter on
the form—the art and skill of the builders; its usage of energy, mechanics and thermodynamics; its capacity to transform and combine elements—operative chemistry. Since in
all the works of Nature, her structural and motive problems
are the same as those which human inventors and craftsmen
grapple with—and in her solutions the same mechanical
principles appear—is it not obvious that the same potentials
are present in all creative operations? Because your knowledge is tabulated and Nature's unwritten, why conclude her

fabrics to be wrought according to different laws than those which govern your own practices?"

"To accelerate progress," I said, "certain postulates apparently essential for the development of your argument shall be allowed if not conceded. Though it be biological heresy, I'll agree that all animate organisms must be bipolar in structure and have psychological as well as physiological systems; that these are opposed yet interdependent, but separately articulated formations, and that it is their contact which induces the flow of the current of life. All of which does not change my outlook, nor help me to conceive consciousness as a reality. What, literally, is its part and place in the set-up?"

"Think of it, to begin with, as the power which initiates and effectuates that interchange with environment which conditions the maintenance of vital organisms," the Martian explained, as patient as ever. "Obviously, the Earth's surface furnishes neither the light that illuminates a food-source, nor the perception that recognizes it: Nor energy nor an agent to convey it to the cell, mandible or mouth of the physical structure calling for provender. Just remember that all is not nitrogenous that comes in the way of a tree's roots. Also, that matter does not rearrange its molecules to fit the variety of viscera that consume it. Set down then, as further attributes of consciousness, the property to recognize, remember, and select and thereafter to seize and utilize the especial nourishment which individual systems are equipped to digest. It is significant that no one has yet made an engine that knows the kind of fuel it needs and goes forth and finds it.

"That's in general. Biology furnishes all necessary specifications as to the human organism as structure and going-concern. Let us again consider it as a tool, and construe some commonplace action according to the principles of mechanics and physics present in the construction and motivation of vehicles. Review, for example, the operations involved in rising to your feet, crossing this room to a book shelf, picking out a particular volume, turning to a given page and reading aloud some reference, say, to the theory of the survival of the fittest.

"Perfectly simple of course, and no sooner said than done. Thus, an impulse released the energy required to overcome the inertia of a solid body weighing 165 pounds at rest in a chair, to transfer it a distance of fifteen feet; and, a purpose coordinated the instrumentalities employed in the transaction. The performances contained these capacities: to detect printed symbols on the backs of books by means of light-waves from an incandescent bulb; to lift an attachment of bone, muscle and tendon, aim and propel it to a specific spot, and displace the volume; to alter the relations of these several heavy bodies to the lamp; to convert black diagrams reflected from a white page into pictures and words; thereafter, to transpose these words to harmonic intervals, impose them on an air current, project deliberately, recover as sound sequences and simultaneously reintegrate and recognize as the equivalents of the parallel optical and perceptive record.

"Note that this series of dynamic deformations were predetermined in a cerebral mechanism that shared the properties of radio-tubes, photoelectric cells, and a microphone— in order to change light and sound-waves into electrical impulses and condense them to pictures and words. Also, that this mechanism was charged with purpose and a knowledge of the subject under discussion, of the location of the book, the significance of the symbols on its pages, their bearing on the issue, and how to utilize the complicated apparatus through whose parts these subtle motion and sound designs were delineated and delivered in actions. And that light was the medium through which the several contacts in the transaction were established. Observe further, that the work medium (the body), is a primary power plant that generates the energy it consumes in maintaining its posture, conveying its movements, conducting its vital processes, and for the electronic exchange with etheric vibrations through which it is enabled to see, hear, feel and speak.

"Unlike the average machine, the behavior of this tool is unpredictable. Its power and aspect alter with the circumstances it encounters. Suppose that, en route from chair to shelf, the body is deflected by an obstacle, or its aural receptors detach vibratory sequences that disturb its equilibrium (condemnatory criticism); thereupon its structure undergoes physiological changes—the beat of its heart is accelerated—its lungs draw in a larger oxygen-draught for faster combustion in the cells of its frame and its surface registers muscular reactions to such interference with its mobility and sense of proportion. These are automatic effects, induced by glandular stimulation which modify the chemical content of the organism's blood stream, increase the temperature and pressure of the system, and cause it to develop extra energy which is discharged in violent gestures or words—all bearing on the terms of the resistances encountered.

"Returning now to the problem as a whole—we have here a simple performance, whose objective aspects are represented by the room and by the body in transit. On the surface it is meaningless. To interpret what it's about, requires knowledge of the motives served and the circumstances that inspired the interactions. None of these is within eye-range. The actual progressions occur in an invisible sphere, which transcends body and room, and includes quantities and interests negligibly affected by gravity and pressure. Exchange within this environment is etheric—being in the terms of *light, sound and induction:* And by means of light, sound and induction all physical adjustments in intercourse and communication are disposed; so the foregoing, and other activities incidental to the existence of the human kind, would appear as the reactions of *etheric* entities, attached to bodies; compelled by this exigency to accommodate their beings and their vehicles to the conditions prevailing in the terrene to which they are confined."

"Labeling your intangible is helpful, of course, but a tag is not a proof," I objected. "Say that to a biologist and hear him laugh."

"As well talk of light to a mole, of vitamins to a butcher or of calories to a coal heaver," the Martian retorted. "When a man's job is his life, his horizon is limited to its radius. But what's mystical here? Given an act—if the factors in sight lack the motive, power and the parts to explain either its initiation or completion, is it not logical to seek elsewhere for a quantity capable of its accomplishment? In this instance, body and room supply machinery and foundation; but, while their juxtaposition occasioned the ensuing movements, neither one of them started, developed, or coordinated them.

"A missing factor carried the purpose, together with awareness of the embracing circumstances and shaped, timed, energized, observed and reported the set of motions which effectuated it. Since these are definite properties they must be characteristic of an element that exerts them. Since the medium of the stimuli to which these operations were response was the *ether,* it is fair to assume the constitution of the missing factor to be of like nature—*etheric.* I supply no other than a causal corpus for effects biology does not consider."

"But you introduce an undefined and indefinite element to take up the slack," I objected. "You set up a center of consciousness apart from the center of gravity, and further confuse the issue by involving mechanics beyond the field of our precisions."

"But you are exercising daily the faculties enumerated," protested my visitor. "These are no occult rites. Instead of supplanting your precisions I'm enlarging their field. In mechanics and law, it is taken for granted that direction and effector-centers are disparate. Captain is not ship, nor is driver the motorcar. Both apply motive through steering gear. Perception is as factual as enunciation. Identity is as much entitled to fabric and a form as is the body through which its expression is affected, though the latter is maintained by organic change. Surely it is time to enfranchise the so-called subconscious and to rescue from healer, practitioner and quack, the application of high potentials that superstition relegates to the supernatural."

"Perhaps I'm inhibited mentally," I interrupted, "but your intangibles leave me gasping. I don't grasp their significance. The truth is that your approach to the subject is from a plane beyond my understanding. We lack common denominators."

"It's hard to adjust a cosmic vista to a local viewpoint," my visitor replied. "Still, difference of focus does not affect the problem or alter the facts. We are both looking at the same world and at that autonomous motion among organic forms, called life. As a spectacle it is overwhelming and meaningless but while no motive is discernible, the spheres in their gyrations seem headed somewhere, and it is reasonable to presume the pressure of an underlying purpose or need, sufficiently great to justify the energy applied in its delivery. The problem is, first, as to the place and function of human beings in the totality of the operation, and thereafter, what's in the making? Let us examine a subsection of the general procedure that assembles as a situation, and from its content and arrangement try to deduce its bearings.

"It is taken for granted, that it must consist of all the separate integers—men and women, furniture and locality—included in its dimensions. Also the surrounding circumstances, such as air, light and gravity. That the vital units are specific designs—have form, weight and are self-motile—need not concern us for the moment; but we'll agree that the action does not start until all the elements of which it is blended are gathered in a given place, within sight, touch and hearing of each other. What happens thereafter must represent interactions among the factors in communication.

"These are conducted through physical mechanisms; the unit bodies in contact, whose movements and speech are in response to ordinary stimuli. The medium of these relations is the atmosphere that interpenetrates and segregates the participants. As they are sensible of each other's presence, it is obvious their equipment includes appliances that enable them to intercept, register and interpret differentiations in light and sound waves set up by their several physical movements. We are entitled to assume that an interest common to these integers is in development, and that alterations in their state and place, their gestures and variations of expression, and the sounds they emit conspire to proclaim and advance it. Since all such sounds and movements are timed and ordered, and are significant, they must reflect mutual understandings separately arrived at, and may be construed as a system of signals by means of which they overcome their isolation in space and the insulation of their frames.

"As isolation and insulation are conditions of the existence of these bodies, yet have been surmounted by this system, there is indicated *awareness* of the circumstances and resistances involved: Also capacity to invent instrumentalities through which to penetrate them. Since such faculty of adjustment denotes the presence of consciousness, we may posit the dramatis-personæ in our situation as individual centers-of-consciousness, and their articulated activities as a technique for communicating perception and recognition of each other's place and state, and as a means of meeting their statutory liabilities. The currency they exchange is information and work.

"But Consciousness—like its auxiliary, Light—is not what it embraces, nor who shares it, but acts as a catalyzer, through whose potentials its satellites become aware of their relations with the Universe and are enabled to convert the resources of an environment to their needs. So it is the property by which men cognize, retain, compare and conjoin; but it is *separable from the matter of memories,* though essential for the identification and unfoldment of experience. Ascending now from the particular to the general, the basic interaction behind the phenomena described would appear as interchange between consciousness and the subjects in which it had invested itself and through which it expresses its own continuity.

"Though this, from the local viewpoint, may seem the significant aspect of the problem, it affords no frame for the circumstances and setting of our vital integers. In the stipulation light, air and gravity were specified as elements in the situation under examination, and as these forces condition the operations of which human beings are conscious, they must be assumed as contributory to their racial existence. In this perspective, simplicity vanishes, and there emerge the outlines of a complex relativity that enmeshes all the ethers, matters, energies, categories and behaviors within its dimensions. From being Lords of Creation, our integers are reduced to the level of cellular multiples in an organization, that not only provides the form and ingredients of their bodies, but keeps them alive with its breath. For man's lease of life, though it be protracted beyond the Psalmist's three score years and ten, is renewed every three seconds through his lungs; and the range of his actions is as definitely fixed by the weight and shape of his organism and location as those of a locomotive by roadbed and rails.

"On the strength of these findings Science offers man as a biological exhibit, the end of a chapter of evolution but of no greater significance than his surroundings and with no bearing on their disposition. Yet this affirmation that human beings actually belong where they occur concedes to the relativity-complex itself, the functions of life and consciousness, and as the potentials of matter and force do not intersect without subvention, we are entitled to posit—behind its mechanics of evolution and adaptation—an Intelligence reforming its patterns to accommodate the growth of its local self-awareness. Thus our integers regain status and appear as neurons in the cerebral system of the planetary entity Mother Earth, whose individual thinking and planning are objectivized through their medium; as among men, thought is conducted in the brain, and converted into action by means of their bodily parts.

"In offering vital phenomena in general to represent the outward activities of a subjective factor-of-the-Whole, there is set up an adequate cause for the effects in evidence. As every mechanical organization is of itself proof of a directive Intelligence, it is logical to opine that the sphere which conveys human lives is also the materialization of a controlling and sustaining Will, in whose own self-consciousness its inhabitants participate. By reflecting on the character of the processes through which your individual being is sustained and motivated, the pertinence of the hypothesis may be realized.

"Since we have hazarded so far, let us broaden the perspective and take the Universe, or that department of it in which Mars and the Earth rotate, as the subject of a larger conjecture. In the nature of things, it would be a Whole occupying the field of its dimensions, containing its own center of gravity, materialized in its stellar satellites and their planetary progenies, and maintaining the order and orbit of its establishment by alternations between its magnetic and electrostatic entities. The identity of such a Being or institution would reside in its *unity,* and be expressed in *self-realization.* Since its mass could be no other than emanations and concretions of its power-to-be, its atomic patterns and architectonic form must be multiples of the same Self, repeated throughout the expanse of its manifestations. So it would be an aggregate of self-images, cohered in units and unities of all varieties of magnitudes, integrated and energized for cooperation and intercommunication and controlled in the interest of the maintenance and enhancement of its own Being. Therefore it would be both self-conscious and conscious of its physical corpus, which would imply the pervasion of the composite with self-awareness, and agencies for its functions of realization and articulation. The inevitability of a parallel organization, a cerebral system for the conduction and administration of such perceptions and information, and their application to motivation and direction seems obvious. Nor is it unreasonable to assume that its vegetative growths—that all the vast succession of life forms throughout the ascending scale of consciousness—serve as the physical instrumentalities of *subjective integration*.

"Here is material for a conception of our Cosmos as the embodiment of a Logos, or Hierarch of space, whose physical organism is the galaxy of stars swimming in His magnetic field—your heavens. The ebb and flow of His consciousness, inspired as cognition, and respired as *re*cognition—contracting and expanding the ethers and cells of the pairs of opposites in the organization, maintain the continuity of His life. From these arise the initiation of the processes of interaction and exchange from which are derived the energies that rotate the machineries of His spheres. So the indrawn and outgoing breath of the Great Entity are the pulse and rhythm of His consciousness, vitalizing and renewing the grip of His will throughout the orbit of His creations. And from center to circumference, this systolic and diastolic movement is reciprocated in the harmonious and consecutive revolutions of these terrestrial auxiliaries, recalling and recording their identification with the person of their creator and lawgiver.

"Supreme within the domain of His individual Self-consciousness, the charge and obligation of this Great Entity would lie in the preservation of his own orbit, and his relations among the multitudinous galactic personalities that people the Super-Cosmos. Amid these he must keep his isolation, and his course with regard to the laws that prescribe the movements of equivalent federations in space. The degree of his will and wisdom would have, for its measure, his power to maintain the precession of his organic satellites, and his capacity to enforce observance of the equities and exigencies of celestial traffic.

"Against this colossal background, the integers in our situation may seem dwarfed to the dimensions of infusoria, but of their relationship there is no doubt. The character of their role is resolved as that of minor agents for the unfoldment of awareness. They are units of consciousness, embryos of the universal pattern, molded in the image of the Great Self, and set up in environmental substance as stations of its transmission and articulation-systems. The degree of their attainments defines their place in the scale of being. Though mobile and self-supporting, their self-knowledge is limited to the organisms of which they are the incumbents, and to information bearing on the affairs of maintenance, shelter and communication in the spheres to which their lives are committed.

"Striving in that unhappy stage of evolution between the animal and the child, their consciousness emerges in the creative faculty exhibited in their domiciliary adjustments, the accretion of facts about their place and state, and in the extension and speeding up of instrumentalities of intercourse and transport, as in language and traffic. Of origin, lineage and relation they are ignorant and suspicious, while of the great subjective force, whose breath in their nostrils is the source of that synthesization of ether and matter called living, they know as little as the beasts of the field. Yet their existences are led in the shadow of the Great Awareness, from which arise all the discontents and conflicts that beset this scattered race, together with the hopes and ideals that inspire its aspiration for harmony and the peace of understanding."

"I feel like quarry of the 'Hound of Heaven' at the close

of that immortal chase," I murmured wearily. "Whether my weakness is response to the iteration of your argument, or is mere exhaustion, give me time to decide. I gather that my status has been elevated from that of a visceral cell in the cosmic constitution, to the proud role of a neuron in its cerebral system. I was Tom—now I'm Jerry—but still ignorant of any literal ancestry. As orphaned as ever, in spite of your flow of matter and force, and the invocation of the Cosmos. Secretly, I've been hoping throughout that you'd legitimatize a soul for me."

"Seek and ye shall find is the universal watchword," the Martian replied. "On entering this earth some decades ago, you were endowed with legs. The early years of your local career were spent in learning their use. An individual existence was established to your satisfaction, by collision and friction. Thereafter you began to *be* what you discovered you *had*—a body with faculties, eyes and hands; so your title to encumber space was founded on its occupation and use. Identity, thus naively originating in localization, was magnified by extending its surface—one was one's possessions. In this vicinity were traditions of God in a heaven and of his bounty; but, since survival was secured by search and seizure and one fed oneself—these were mere folk lore. Here come I and, purely by dint of friction on your eardrums, awaken doubt and curiosity as to the character of your tenure. I suggest that there are more worlds than you see. Since changing the angle of vision would upset the bliss of your ignorance, you argue that I'm pulling wool over your eyes—not opening them. However, I've aroused a suspicion and in return you are disappointed that I don't hand you a soul! I'm not Santa Claus, my friend. Go look for your own."

"But not tonight," I protested. "At this moment I need a

sleep more than a spirit. The search will have to await a new sunrise."

"It will take the balance of your life," the Martian said. "Remember, when you go forth, that it's no rainbow trail but the world's hardest trek. Follow any one of the leads I've blazed to its end and I'll promise that your Self will be there to meet you. If in your cogitations additional light is needed, mentally page me in Death Valley."

Tribulations of a bestseller. Cosmic speculations in a smoking car. Looking the facts in the face. The rough frames of
living. Men, servants and victims of their circumstances;
their identity geographical, their institutions, outgrowths of
economic need. Life's meanings, external to mediums and
motions. Functions of an Intelligence factor and how they
are conducted. The Power to Be, and Being. Has the Universe an invisible government? Phases of reality. Man lives
off the equilibria he disturbs. Expansion of understanding
as the means of altering relations. To be what I am, more
wonderful than to do what I do. Bird and cage. Life an artifice. Human behavior as electrolysis. Futility of progress
without comprehension. Inequality and determinism. Is
there a Book in which the Fates of men are written?

A BESTSELLER who had fled to Atlantic City to be delivered
of his latest offspring found the accouchement harder than
he expected and sought editorial midwifery. There was a
night letter from this prodigy on my desk next morning.
And I must come at once.

Such service is in larger demand than the laity suspects.
The pangs of book-bearing are often beyond the control
or endurance of authors. Characters behave like ungrateful
children, grow unmanageable, refuse to stay in their parts,
catch cramps or anemia and even die. Plots clog, lag, develop
kinks that defy unravelment or get lost in a jungle of de-
tail. Tribulation being futile without an audience, a publish-

er's first aid is summoned. He may officiate as sympathizer, guide, surgeon or dummy. Some writers are literary hypochondriacs and need humoring like doctors' rich patients. Others require advice either for controversy, or to disregard. In opposing the opinions of others one consolidates one's own. Still others use editorial consultation to vocalize their plans, thereby hearing what they are thinking about.

There's nothing more provocative of pessimism than involuntary exertion. That the predicament of this official friend should compel departure from my settled ways and plunge me into the bastardized glitter of Atlantic City, struck me like a call for more margin; but since we served each other's pockets, his claim was a summons. Hastily I cleared up my routine and took the best train there. En route, I promised to dispose of a manuscript that had split our readers like a racial taint (their reports being either blasphemous or worshipful), but as I settled comfortably into my chair in the parlor car, I fell to thinking about consciousness and the cosmos, and to puzzling as to the character of the relations Galactic Entities exchanged in the infinitude of space. The high astronomical sharps had already mapped a million of these systems, disposed along a diameter of several sextillions of miles, and since they were uncommonly careful of each other's orbits and rights-of-way, they must be observing some sort of a commutation code that governed their precessions. Doubtless they had a super-civilization, and on coming into conjunction, swapped greetings across the light-year chasms that separated their individual organizations. Exchanging how-do-you-dos under such magnificent circumstances savored of absurdity; yet, as I understood the Martian, their problems were but enlargements of our own.

Even if they be self-conscious and know exactly what they

are doing and why, it cannot relieve an iota of the responsibility they sustain of keeping their parts behaving aright and in proper relation to one another. When I ask a man how he is feeling, it is merely opening up communications, because I don't especially care how he happens to be, unless the state of his health affects some interest of my own. He is the custodian of his body—I, of mine; it is our business to keep these organisms in functioning condition to maintain the concerns through which we sustain our places in the world. If he is losing his grip I may express conventional sorrow but should not hesitate at taking over his burdens and assets if, by my doing so, the firm's importance were enhanced. As above—even so below! I wondered if the law of the pack did extend into higher altitudes. Or whether the great entities turned, in their courses, to help a stumbling brother?

The importunate manuscript was jettisoned and I moved into the smoking car to pursue my musings more comfortably. Idle speculation, of course—day dreams—but my mind was full of the Martian's gospels.

Though I had but half admitted it, I knew his arguments were not negligible. They presented a problem that had to be grappled with. According to the best authorities—I—my body—is a machine; a type of internal combustion engine, in which a life is being conducted for no reason whatever. That is, the life is derived from the body which is derived from the environment. Because the body is here, and I find myself within it—just to relieve its hunger pangs I am loaded with the job of keeping it in air, food and shelter. Without *me* there is no body and no life—so the entire episode turns on my presence in a body. Does anyone know the nature of the obligation which prescribes that I shall toil and sweat, in order that the combustion processes of an engine, which

I happened into by accident of birth, shall be maintained? There's no intelligence here.

Considered dispassionately, this situation includes three separate elements—I—the body that lives by my work and the life that is its product. This life is the registration of a series of external acts that owe cogency, continuity and visibility to my person. They are related to the conduct of the occupation to which my energies are devoted. Physically, they appear as the movements of one walking, sitting, talking, listening, reading, eating and sleeping. Suppose a detective followed my routes and watched my processes— how much could he gather as to my character or the arts of the publishing game? Nothing. As to my disposition he might hazard guesses, based on the manner and speed of my performances, and the demeanor towards me of my partners and associates. The meaning and purpose of our collective activities are as imperceptible to outside observation as the content of our thoughts and the forms of our plans. Yet, with no more than a word, a signature or the turn of a hand, we set in motion energies that change the nature of thousands of tons of raw material, start great machines revolving, and contribute to the wages which buy food and lodgings for hundreds of fellow beings.

We make and sell books—some factual, more fictional. We live as agents for verbal transcriptions of the doings of men and women in vital relations with one another. Valuations therein are determined by the degree of realism attained by the transcriber, and according to the manner and symmetry of his narrative. So the field of our action is an artifice of civilization—the made-ground of the literateness of a population.

But for the inventions of language, paper, ink, movable

type, the printing press, the educational system, post offices and railways and a thirst for more knowledge, I and my neighbors would be dumb brutes chasing other beasts for provender—domiciled in caves and ignorant of the nature of our being—unaware of our own powers or the wealth the environment had stored in readiness for our needs. What actually conditions our present existences is the mass of this information, which lives by being circulated, and whose product is registered in the works that men have wrought on this planet. The sum of this knowledge is the collective consciousness of our world, and in this system my identity appears as that of a tool for its transmission. From that service is derived the wage, which I exchange with environment for the food, drink, shelter and space required to maintain my station.

On these terms, without being less of a body, I become more of an entity. Instead of my life being merely the routine reaction of an organism to an environment, it is revealed as a function of a Consciousness-of-the-Whole, whose properties and powers it shares to the degree of my capacity to comprehend them. True, I know no more about myself than before, but there is opened a vista of external relations that justifies my existence and aspirations. At least there is here an intimation that, in the Great-Scheme-of-Things, membership in the human race has more than a material significance.

That there was a transcendental ring to this reasoning, suddenly occurred to me. Prior to the advent of the Martian, the universe had never entered my calculations; nor is it much more to the average man than the scenery of skies and stars. Our world is an everyday reality in which life is the business of sustaining it and food and place are the rewards.

Some billion and a half of humans, clustered in a few fertile areas on the surface of a planet, traffic with one another for means to stay where they have found themselves. Their necessities and privileges are prescribed by the character of their organic parts. During the ages of their occupation men have invented means to accommodate their natures to their surroundings and, more recently, have discovered how to supplement their own powers with natural forces. If this has eased their way, it has intensified their activities; for their requirements have increased with their facilities for satisfying them.

We know more about our bodies and the kind of world we live in than our ancestors knew, but our philosophies are still grounded on the relief of our physical necessities. Our institutions, like theirs, are outgrowths of economic problems and are based on the stabilization and protection of the race as food growers and consumers. Our governments are mere agencies to defend us from one another and against outside encroachments, and our behaviors are specified by law and convention. Our classifications and distinctions are determined by mechanical circumstances and outward appearances. The identity of a man is fixed, first by geography and parentage, later by the particular way in which he exchanges his energy for provender and shelter. He is, further, the inhabitant of a city, a state or province and, simultaneously, a member of the corpus of the nation that enumerates him as a unit of population. Not even his individuality is his own, because as a citizen, he is the subject of his nation—shaped and reared to fit its services and utilities. Its schools are mills in which he is molded to a pattern—clipped and rounded for smooth conveyance of its customs and enactments. Since all stimuli are stereotypes, and responses habitized in advance, how can a man be other than he is—the servant and victim of his circumstances?

Unconsciously, I stood up, sat down, resettled myself in the chair and looked out the window.

This motor-vehicle adjusts itself to strains and stresses, I mused. It's the carrier, sustains the shocks and its response is its own adaptation to environment. *I* interprets, as in this instance, what my apparatus registers—not as an independent entity—but in the terms of a Whole, engaged in a task to which *I* furnish initiative and motive.

Motor-vehicle is body, environment is earth and I am *I*—trafficking with my species according to the conventions evolved for the welfare of our lives. What of it? Just—I presume—that to control circumstances one must master the conditions that compose them. One leads or follows—bids or submits. Slavery, probably, is inertia or the lack of will and courage to be free.

If I confide this thesis to my partners they'll argue, "Suppose it is true—what's the difference? Your body represents your *I* for all practical purposes and that's as far as we need to go. As long as your opinions don't interfere with business, entertain as many as you can carry." That's what I'd say, yet I'm convinced that there are bearings here which, if we understood, might sensibly alter all our worldly relations. Wherein and to what end? But this stuff is as ancient as the human mind and these are old-time philosophical paradoxes. The values, so far, are my own. At least it is clear that, from the level of its transaction, Life is what it appears to be—the familiar struggle for existence among organisms equipped to conduct it, and its incidents are no more than the activities generated in the process of sustaining it.

But these aspects broaden with the perspective of the

observer. In its entirety, Life is exhibited as a function of the Universe. Light and heat are radiated from beyond our shores, and sight and sound borne from one man to another on etheric waves. And, sublimating this interplay of forces, appears an integrating factor I'll call Intelligence, an intangible—which endows individual beings with capacity to synthesize the various elements that surround them: Because of it they are able to motivate themselves, to maintain unitary existence and compose pictures of the world and their relations. The degree of its inherency determines rank in all species that exercise it and doubtless forms the basis of identity. Human outfits and obligations are ever the same, but performances are unequal, and we ascribe such inequalities to talent or aptitude; terms which have no biological meaning, but refer to quality and to power of comprehension and application—other attributes of Intelligence.

I began to sense the point of the Martian's insistence, that no direct examination of its mechanisms enabled one to determine what Life was about. Its meaning must lie outside the media and the motions through which it was conveyed; just as the meaning of a cornfield lies outside its appearance and the growth of its stalks and ears. Obviously, Life's incidents arise out of the processes of preserving it, but could one guess the direction of a steamer's course by watching the rise and fall of her pistons, or the revolutions of her shafts? There is a standardized organic model for humans, but no two men get the same results from the use of its parts. There are ugly geniuses and lovely morons.

In a jammed subway car the sole visible differences are between the sexes, the sitters and the standers, and—though all are headed the same way—each has a different destination and a distinctive background.

What was proved by it? No more than that some were better fitted than others to conduct life. Could a good man help being good? Would it not be harder for him to do evil? To be a holy man in Russia today is to invite imprisonment or death. My own virtues represent personal bent and preference. Such success as has rewarded my industry and devotion to business, I regard as fairly earned; yet, two tricksters who filched fortunes by fraudulent representation keep ten times my state, in palaces around the corner, and are courted in select coteries to which I am ineligible. If the object of life is securing ease and a prosperous old age, neither integrity nor dishonesty can be proved handicaps to its attainment. There is one's attitude to one's self. If ever I saw self-satisfaction it radiated from the face of one of the aforementioned tricksters, as he paraded down the Avenue yesterday arm and arm with his two handsome daughters.

But this is twaddle—however amorphous, there's an instinctive code; and between ourselves, we know who keep faith and who do not. Most do, in the things that matter. The great society is that of honorable men. It has no nationality, constitution, dues or passwords; but those who belong recognize its fellowship and among themselves, exchange credit with confidence. That is one conviction which lends sweetness to life. What disposition has protoplasm, I wonder, that makes for truth and loyalty as exhibited in human behavior? The law of the cell is the law of the pack; appetite has no other goal than repletion, but hot blood knows no more of anger than scales know of weight. In practice we don't attribute properties they lack to things or machines; but, according to the current philosophies of mechanism, what we are, what we do and how and why we do it are all of a piece.

"There's a residual self," says the Martian, and I can come

by it if I look hard enough. Presumably it is that Intelligence
factor, isolated a few moments back. Well, I pass for being
intelligent, at least I distinguish between impulses, interests
and objectives, diagnose conditions, choose among alternatives, and, with fair success, coordinate means to an end.
These are internal processes conducted in my mind, often
below the threshold of awareness, with material registered
in memory. The procedure is a recalling and reviewing of
facts and precedents bearing on the problem in hand, clas-
sifying and rearranging data to fit some new pattern, or re-
adjusting an old one to altered circumstances. The theater
of these rehearsals is my cerebrum—a mysterious tract, automatically stocked with neuron-records corresponding to
my experiences. In so far as the circulation of my thought
is confined to its cells, nothing outside is affected. When I
speak or act, I enter the medium of the whole—the external
world, into space, which is the area of physical communication; and therein, by refraction and stimulation of light and
sound waves in its atmosphere, I extend information to my
spatial compatriots in range and tune with such radiations,
as to changes in order and circumstance which I desire to
bring about. The field of these changes is subject to gravity
and pressure, so alterations of material states herein are disturbances of equilibrium, and require energy adequate to the
inertias and resistances involved. This energy is furnished by
the organic system in which I am present on the scene, my
body—whose constitution reflects and reveals my purposes
in visible motion patterns. In turn, these spring from, and
are shaped by—the occasion of a body in an environment
to which it is adjusted; but though it is *I* who inspire, coordinate, start and steer the acts through which its processes are maintained, these appear only in the inflections and

variations of its motor equipment and in the movements of the objects or instruments to which stimulation has been extended.

Thus *I* am in attendance by proxy, as the Martian said, and so far as my neighbors and I know, am no more than the body in which I am invested.

This condition further supports the existence of the two fundamentals, which my visitor declared were the bases of dynamic phenomena. One, I should say, is Intelligence containing the *Power to Be*—representing cause. The other—inert matter—the stuff in which it manifested its Being. The potter-and-the-clay thesis. The first was organizer—the second, what it organized. Thus the appearance of life was the interaction between the two elementary forces. Intelligence molded the forms required for its expressions, and motivated the movements through which they were energized and extended. Each of its incarnations made a whole, functioning inside and outside the orbit of its assembled parts. For instance, atomic elements and corporations. The former consisted of positive nuclei neutralized by negative electrons; their identity in the periodic table deriving from the quantity and arrangement of their constituents. A corporation was an enlargement and dramatization of the atomic model. A unit of force, the organizer, conjoined with his own other units, to create the nucleus of an institution for making and distributing a commodity. Purpose and design figure as the causative but intangible quantity. Materialization follows—incorporation, franchise, plant and employees—the electronic complement. Collaboration between executives and administration generates internal energy and results in product. Thus the *positive nucleus* imposes the form, and initiates and sustains sequence and continuity. "Process" is in converting and reforming inert substances, by application of hands and machines. Its sum is a commodity. So the life of the institution is energized. It is supported by interchange with the world, outside its distinctive integration.

Sounds Martian and metaphysical, and a long way from home. Still, here am I—in a body meticulously adapted to place and state. A body that no man designed, though each man grows his own version of the standardized model. I am supporting my being and piloting my way, in accordance with provisions for finding it; operating this stabilized entity in an ordered and organized world—which is a unit of the solar system, that itself is an integer in the giant consolidation in whose unknown dimensions it is incorporated. In a relativity so methodically and mathematically proportioned, I can't be a foundling. My existence must somehow be contributory to its processes. The architectural and mechanical principles of the structure in which I function coincide with its specifications. However minor my intelligence-quotient, I can conceive and observe this universe, and at least hazard a guess as to its workings. The human species molds matter in form, energizes its devices, bridges space and computes and keeps time. *These are the faculties of creators and must denote rank in any community of their genus.*

But if the structures by means of which we coordinated and conducted life originated in, and were derived from— the exercise of human intelligence, and if they literally represented the minds of the race, must it not follow that the living organisms, which we used but did not and could not make, are also fructification of designs? The Martian, I remember, claimed that whatever had form, operated consecutively, and nourished and reproduced itself was an invention; and that, in however minor a degree, *consciousness abided in it.*

Here was the path perilous. If I accepted this presumption, I must admit the immanence of an order of mind and an ordination—external to our own and coincident with—all that is within and outside our immediate world. This meant an invisible government, devoted to the control and administration of the persons and affairs of vitalized and motivated organisms; a dominion-of-the-whole, articulated for the conveyance of the interests of its own state. Not only must the kingdoms of living things be its diminutive models and subjects but, it would appear as designer and pilot of the constellations that keep their precessions in space.

This is the argument of design, I recognized, like analogy, discarded by modern science and philosophy as an untrustworthy tool of ascertainment and logic. But if the findings of archaeology, paleontology and geology are inductive, and therefore arguments of designs (and it seems that no scientist rejects them on that score), why is the method not an efficient weapon of ratiocination in a wider field? Once one admitted equilibrium and change—granted that mass can be motivated, one posited an outside agent, who aroused and applied the energy required for the displacements that occurred. If this agency is invisible, there is but one way to trace and diagnose its character, and that is to observe and record the course, aim, reach and goal of its projections. The composite of these activities is the material evidence of its purpose, of its degree of accomplishment; and must represent such agents' inherent knowledge and power.

Before us is the cosmic spectacle which, despite its immensity, can be no other than a large-scale power plant in operation. Its systems are punctual; they preserve alignment and position in space. Since they have a common axis, we are justified in assuming relationship and that a unified interest maintains their rotations for some ulterior end. At least, we are entitled to go as far as a man may, who watches the revolving spokes of a giant flywheel.

A windmill swam into view, as the train swung round a bend in the track. Instinctively, my mind accepted the picture as indicating an evocation of power by knowledge, deduced the presence of beings possessing attributes enabling them to apply both, and my curiosity was excited in wondering only as to the particular use the owner made of its force. Had I been an engineer, I should, in addition, have mentally defined the structural and mechanical parts of the apparatus, contrasted it with other appliances for catching and converting wind pressure into energy, and doubtless would have entered into economic computations, comparing it with electric or gasoline motors as a source of power capture and conversion, etc. Anyway, human habitation and culture were connoted. The fact is that most mental associations are arguments of design, and though the method be inexact, all immediate interpretation of stimuli are expressed in its terms.

I am beginning to understand what the Martian meant when he objected that materialistic philosophies failed to realize how wholly mechanical are the processes of conducting life. Actually, we ourselves and our companionate species are byproducts of chemical reactions for which our own organisms furnish the apparatus. Civilization itself is reared on the combustion of oxygen, and its discharge as carbon dioxide performed in protoplasmic cells. To the varied modes of generating this energy we contribute nothing. Frame, setting, forms and parts are prescribed. Even the will to live is set up and enforced by organic pangs. Here is every aspect of an organized plant toiling twenty-four hours a day and involving in its operations interchange among the etheric and molecular elements of which our worlds are conjoined, whose sole apparent output is that little span of participation men call their lives.

Something else in the making? Probably a familiar of experience, conducted on so large a scale that its outlines are beyond our perspective. We don't really see things as they are, but as we've been taught to look at them, and so miss details and phases to which we've not been introduced. What differentiates our own lives from those of our aboriginal forefathers, who operated with identical faculties—and certainly had a much harder time of it than we do today? We enter a world that knowledge has shrunk to our mental dimensions—for during the period of men's occupation, they have classified, charted and measured its spaces, named its lands and waters, explored and listed its resources and trapped and confined its forces to drive their machines. Altogether, they have profoundly modified their relation to their habitat. The weapons of this conquest were language and tools. One enabled men to register and exchange facts that bore on their situation; the other to overcome and regulate the resistances arising from untoward associations.

Considering the appearance of our earth today, with its many inventions, one might be persuaded that the Creative Spirit having adapted man to his environment—had jumped outside and reversed its action by adjusting the same environment to accommodate his needs. On this theory, everything we make, that has an existence of its own external to ours, is an evocation of the same principle that organized us, our world, and all the other bodies it contains. Thus, humans would be parties to an evolutionary process, pursued through the agencies of their hands and brains, in whose profits they participated—even if they lacked understand-ing of the proceedings. At least, the supposition furnished an amusing explanation of that ignorance of identity which makes us the unwitting puppets of our inherent powers, and leaves us victims of the magic that is wrought through our means.

What most of us get out of Life is but the temporary use of its utensils and opportunities. We have to habituate our bodies to action and our tongues and lips to speech before we can carry on. Thereafter comes the business of transfer-ring to memory the symbols and diagrams in which commu-nications are couched, together with the vast technic of law and conduct to which conformity is obligatory. We pile into our heads volumes of information inapplicable save to our present conditions, and, when the end comes, are no whit wiser regarding the only thing that matters—what it has meant *to ourselves*.

Here am I, again attempting to penetrate what it is all about, describing circles without touching a single reality.

What do I mean by reality? Well, this chair is real, and the floor and walls of the car, the landscape flowing by at fifty miles an hour—they are real enough. So is this body that sits in the chair, my hand that feels their outlines and surfaces, the pane of glass through which I look, the ciga-rette I'm puffing and my nearby neighbors—smoking and talking. But is reality that alone which possesses weight and volume? A silhouette has neither. If, suddenly, here and now, I suffered a paralytic stroke—though still in the same place, I should lose consciousness of the facts that surround me. Yet the weight, volume and structure of my parts would be unaltered. A minute displacement of brain-plasm suffices to dislocate my relations with the world outside. Physiology

covers all the details of the injury, but offers no specifications as to the Ego whose capacity to appraise and motivate
circumstances has been suspended. It would be fatuous to
declare a chauffeur out of commission because the steering
gear of the car he drove had jammed.

Truth is, we have never clearly formulated and separately determined the elements combined in human action. In
accounting for our doings we lump together subject, object,
location, energy, apparatus, obstacle and time—so that individual achievements are little better than unconscious cerebration. When it comes to business and mechanics, guesswork is excluded and mathematics applied. Cause and effect,
and every phase of every part required in conjoining motive
to delivery, has its separate definition or design.

In the unwritten canons of mechanics is perhaps the
shrewdest estimate of what heads and hands are equipped
to supply that cams, shafts, levers or gears can't be made to
return. Only a man can stand still, start and stop, turn and
reverse, pick and choose, find and hold a course, change gait
and speed—all without changing gears; avoid obstacles and
rise to emergencies, keep time, hit a mark, reach a destination and explain his ways. His body must be an instrumentality outfitted for deliberate or instantaneous adjustment to
the exigencies of action in space and time. Individually, we
may figure him as the capacity to comprehend relationships
in this complex, and to adopt its contingencies to the maintenance and progression of his own status.

Man lives off the equilibria disturbed by him. He is the
computer of distances, measurer of the hours, apportioner of
means to ends, judge of the values he produces.

Obviously, a factor with such attributes is of a diverse
order to the forms, materials and circumstances which it

embraces, and through which it establishes and supports its presence in an environment. And, since it is the protagonist of what it promotes, may fairly be assumed to be the subject of its experiences.

Now I emerge as a unit of understanding of my own situation in time and place, plus an ability to extend it. And this body is the seat of my capacity for realization—the means of keeping in touch with the matter of the situation, and the generator of the energy required to maintain and change perspective and position. The results of my tenancy of a given location would be registered in the enlargement of my understanding, which, by broadening my outlook, would alter my relations to environing circumstances. Inference would appear as the agent by which men expanded their horizons; and knowledge, as its physical equivalent—exchangeable in the terms of the product, "information." Evolution, then, figures as the process of extending the area of associations and meanings, in the material world—the re-adaptation of vehicles to alterations in perspective and value. As we do in the cases of motors and aeroplanes.

That's an abstract of the way things do happen, I decided after an interval of reflection. I arrive here a unit of capacity to understand; but without data to go on. I am attached to a body, with instrumentalities to open up communications with a strange vicinity and represent its aspects and provisos to my consciousness. I discover myself enmeshed in a cellular complex, in which it is necessary to assert mobility to predicate my status. So I breathe, and thereby animate my body and, by kindling its energies, learn the degree of my freedom—my geography. I am instructed upon the terms of my material relations by friction.

To carry on according to the code of our engagements,

both I and my body have to be conditioned. What I may cognize, must be gathered through its senses, and my conceptions of our mutual situation are expressed through its organs and limbs. *I* am educated; *it* is trained.

Information nourishes *my* being; *its* fires are sustained with food. *I* establish my individuality and power by organizing ways to supply *it* with shelter and provender. *Its* structure accommodates both our natures, but the planet furnishes the terms, properties and theater for performance. *My* role is manipulative—managerial; administering the fluctuations of an ever-changing relation between an organism and an environment. The actions *I* initiate are responses to *its* reactions to circumstances and to the terrene: They are reflected and reported to my imponderable awareness centers by its automatic system of nerve conduction. On the plastic surfaces of this brain-plasm are registered the tensions, pressures and resistances incurred by *its* modulations and mutations, together with the internal strains incidental to the operations of its automotive machinery. *I* plot our course by deduction, as does a mariner in navigating a ship on the high seas.

This description of the character of our associations fits many familiar situations, I admitted. The *I* is the fighting chief in the conning tower of a battleship in action—regulating speed and direction—aim and gun discharge, according to positions relayed to him and returned by telephony and telegraphy. Or, it is the commanding general at headquarters apart from the scene of action, deploying armies against an enemy's forces to conquer his resistances. Out of sight, touch or hearing of battle, he follows and orders its movements by message.

Being *I* involves the existence and operation of machineries far more intricate than I suspected. In truth *I'm* an ex-

traordinary phenomenon and the things I do, without greater effort than an impulse, are amazing. This flexible body of
mine is not only adjusted to the modes of the environment,
but to my moods. I walk, run, stand, sit, gesticulate, talk; all
without considering that every turn and twist of structure
is a deformation caused by the application of force—alterations of equilibrium that cannot be described justly, save
in the terms of mechanics. Reclining comfortably here, this
plant goes on manufacturing the energies required by my
brain for the thinking I'm carrying on, energies to keep a
heart beating and blood circulating—all so secretly that I'm
unaware of the chemistries and conversions involved in the
performance. I'm commencing to agree with my invisible
friend's theory that *to be what I am* is far more wonderful
than to do what I do.

My role at the moment is that of observer. Though the
processes of reviewing and comparing take place in my cerebrum, and the subject-matter under consideration are records of my own life—inscribed there by actual contact—my
attitude is that of an analyst toward an object detached from
his person. Without dismounting from my body, I can look
it over, examine its works and speculate about my association
with its parts.

"*I*" is thinker and actor conjoined. The same language covers their work but they use different idioms. "*I*" thinks with
words, pictures or symbols, but to act must employ speech,
gesture and locomotion. This body is the medium for the
two operations—the patterns of the second series being set
by the first. As thinker, *I's* range is the universe and encom-
passes innumerable possibilities but *he* may deliver to this
world only what the parts of this corpus are equipped to
produce and habitized to express. It holds *I* to the earth and

to the job of satisfying the variety of its appetites and needs; also to conveying its shape and weight across these fields of space. That Tibetan was right. "*I* is a bird and its body is a cage."

Picturesque but misleading. This bird is in the cage, and, so far as I know, has no factual existence external to its accommodations. Why assume that it is other than it appears? Or that things can be different from what they are? Literally speaking, this body of mine is as definitely a property of the environment as is the food it converts into energy, or the information that must be absorbed by it to function. Its own conditions prescribe the character of its activities. But, on the other hand, a man's place in human society is not determined by his organism or its location, but is based on the returns of his tenancy. In our unreasoning way, we take gifts for granted. We judge by performance and product.

I'm examining appearances and experiences. Does the power to think derive from the matter of the thought? Not more so, I'd say, than a newspaper is the fruit of the press that prints it. Curious—this double aspect that pervades all our affairs! Everything is itself, plus something else. Eating is the process of energizing a body. Exercise is to aid the delivery of its functions. *I* am en route to Atlantic City—not to be carried there—but to fulfill an engagement. Iron is converted into steel to strengthen the fabric of a substance, the better to sustain the energies and contacts it is required to endure. One plays games for pastime, to apply one's wits, to win supremacy, or a wager, or—all together. Try to deduce the rules of golf by watching a man on the links!

But this is tail-chasing. There's nothing inconsistent or mysterious here, if I cling to premises—now soundly established—that what happens is the sum of the factors conjoined to procure its occurrence; that elements don't lose their identity in becoming compounds. A skyscraper is not alone its spatial dimensions and the business domicile of its tenants, but the container of the arts of the architects and contractors who collaborated in its organization: It is the labor of the artisans who assembled and erected it, and the steel, stone, wood and glass that compose its substantial fabric. On other planes, it is the realization of the builder's aspiration, an investment of capital, the asset of a corporation, a valuable frontage and a source of civic revenue: And it is all these things at the same time that it is a going-concern. Incidentally, two years earlier it was no more than an idea in mind and a hole in the ground. Such metamorphoses are so familiarized by repetition among us that they are taken for granted, as commonplaces of commercial routine.

Let's try it this way: human life is the pattern described on the earth's surface by the motions of Beings in bodies. The bodies owe their existence to the Beings, and their form to the circumstances of their installation. They are conditioned by the qualities of being and the exigencies of place. Thus they are media—links between opposite worlds, and their movements are phenomena arising from the interaction of two jurisdictions.

A body may be termed a device for maintaining the nature of Being in the state of matter, in which the latter furnishes the terms and the former the principles. Or, one might say, body is a frame that consciousness has contrived for its communications in space.

An accommodating hypothesis, we conclude. It can be transposed to fit an automobiling by substituting car for body and driver for being. Circumstances of installation mean no more than adaptation of vehicle to highway, carburetion to atmospheric pressure, and starting, stopping and steering gears to the hands and feet of chauffeurs. Interaction of two jurisdictions covers performance, and implies relation of direction to system of motivation. In fact the theorem contains any and all operations whose accomplishment requires the application of power to tools. The form of a utensil is based on the anatomy of its maker; its significance is derived from his needs. Implicit in its design are perception of need and accommodation for use. Again, use appears in another category, because it involves subject, object, shape, urge and fulfillment. Among men, energy conveys process and consciousness synthesizes and registers actualizations and continuities. But the profits of effort redound to the ease and glorification of body, where, indeed, as long as one does not examine the antecedents, they legitimately belong.

But, according to these premises, consciousness figures as no more than the dominant adjunct in the totality of an operation which involves a variety of processes and parts, and emerges outside as human conduct. It carries the principle of whatever determinant there be, since organic energy is undoubtedly electromotive force whose flow is induced by differences in potential between an electrokinetic entity and its electrostatic opposite, but its circuit is confined within the individual body that develops it. Given the installation, consciousness contributes—automatically—the synthetic functions that constitute awareness. It reacts to external stimuli—etheric and physical—and registers changes within and on the outside of the organic structure of which it is the positive factor, as they affect the integration of its mass as a whole. By means of its nervous and muscular adjuncts, it responds by altering the relations of this whole to the resistances evoked by the mobilization of its members.

On these terms one might construe differentiations in personality as representing variations in the strength of positive
and negative charges—behavior, as electrolytic. Or, compute
character in units of force, as power and resistance, and figure individuality as valence. Substituting a kinematic rating for an intelligence quotient would supply us with sound
standards, and relieve many uncertainties. Far-fetched, of
course, but the conception of some analogical polarization
afforded a pseudo-anatomical format for that *unconsciousness*
which Freud and his ilk have improvised—that porcelain
depository for the wealth of sporadic complexes to which
men's mechanisms are subject, and for which biology provides no stowage. And what a relief it would be to literature
and life, if the nebulous vocabulary of psychoanalysis were
superseded by the precise terminology of the electrician and
the chemist, and the stream of consciousness interpreted
by amperage and voltage. Romance thereafter could be set
forth in mathematical symbols and the eternal triangle denoted through equations. At least it would be a setback for
the prevailing sex-motive.

In all these shufflings *I* drifts further abaft. Whatever *it*
is that is doing this thinking, is revealed as little better than
the hub of the mechanisms through whose processes a life is
being conducted for him. All his circumstances appear fore-
ordained and dependent; appointed as to organism, parentage, tradition and surroundings. An infant is not regarded
by his progenitors as a person but as raw material for a social
unit. He does not belong to himself but to his situation. The
contents of his consciousness are as completely determined
by the conventions in which he is enfolded as his comprehension of his own body is fixed by the shape and confines
of its parts. In due course he is initiated into the sciences

of communication and nomenclature; learns the use of his mouth, tongue and lips as instruments for setting up and projecting language; the use of other loose and more or less flexible members, to express sensations. Thus he is ushered into the *word-plane* and becomes aware that persons, places and things are not only forms with volume, but have names. And he may go on through the years of his days without suspecting that the entire structure of his conceptions and the mode of his actions are as artificial as the streets, the houses or the motor cars about him.

For who is to tell him, that his career from birth to grave, is stipulated and classified by the character of the conventions and inventions, in and by which it is carried on?

When for a moment I stop to consider myself, my clothed body, this train in which I'm hurled so speedily through space; when I envision the towers of Manhattan in the background of my mind, and the convenient classifications of signs, symbols and sounds through which I can depict every phase and shade of my physical and conceptual reactions to these wonders, and explain my opinions, both to myself and to my neighbors—I marvel at the range and flexibility of man's greatest achievements—*Language*—this triumph of mechanical cerebration of which we are the heirs and beneficiaries. That we so glibly take for granted our relations to the vast congeries of organizations and mechanisms, in whose creation and development so few of us have either part or understanding, is surely the sublimation of folly.

The mystery in the background of Life is not that men do as they do; it is the frame, circumstance and fact of their existence. Curious—our dependence on conditions we neither control nor understand—for food, raiment, light, air and place. We are domiciled and rationed. We see, hear, feel and think by dint of the equipment provided for the guidance of our hands and feet in the obligation of staying alive. In the fervor of new undertakings our generations forget that they are mere pensioners of an ancient bounty, and that neither to the machineries of their bodies, nor to the constitution of the environment, do they contribute more than use. The discoveries hailed so enthusiastically are but disclosures of primordial provisions for the upkeep and operation of our kind; and our inventions but re-adaptations of old processes to altered positions.

Undeniably there is progression—but in what direction? It is not in organism or earth, but in knowledge of the nature of both. We apply less muscle and more energy than our predecessors. A lot of burdens have been shifted off our backs and loaded on machines. Our communications have been facilitated—the globe is now the field of the race, and we go swiftly over land and water where our purposes or our fancies take us. The air has been made a medium for the distribution of words, music and cargoes. This implies a vast enhancement of the scope of human motility, based on the accretion of information about ourselves and our surrounding circumstances. In broadening our horizons we have extended our orbits.

Great work—undoubtedly, but what is the racial attitude to this increment of new knowledge that has been conferred on it? For the most part that of spectators. We are lookers-on at a game that is being played by professionals. Our world is changing before our eyes without affecting our bodies, our habits or our dispositions. This accumulation of ascertainments is outside our physical persons and but amplifies our needs; for we must absorb enough of it into our brains before we are fit company for our contemporaries. In truth we have

increased the tempo of life without adding to our understanding of it. We have more of everything—including more
to do—with less to say about it. Actually, we are submerged
under our encyclopedias, staggering beneath facts with no
better yield from them than our forefathers gathered from
the scanty stock available for living in their own generation.

To think of our world and its inhabitants in terms other
than are registered by our senses is nearly as difficult as it
would be for a needle to find itself in a haystack. I begin now
to appreciate the extraordinary value of the Martian's testimony. To him, Life denoted cosmic operation, and the planet together with its population of vitalized organisms—was
just machinery for its turnover. Elsewhere, throughout the
galactic expanse, the same principles controlled—but forms
varied with the pressure and tensions prevailing on the stars
and planets whose coordinated entities constituted the body
of the system. What was being conducted he construed as
the life of an individualized Self-consciousness, stabilized
through the medium of its own objectivity, and realized as
an integrated unit Self.

Perhaps the upshot of my own cogitations does point in
the direction of a parallel hypothesis; but to sense and feel
my actual being, and to regard all the friendly interchanges
with my fellows that engage and color my life as but drama-
tizations of solar processes is more than I care to swallow just
now. True, it did help fix my identity, though emphasizing
my insignificance. To know oneself for a cell in the loose-knit
cortex of a god was doubtless flattering, even if it did diminish the area of self-determination. My freedom disappears
in his bulk. But was this freedom ever more than delusion?
Not so long ago I demonstrated to my own satisfaction that
men were but units of the states, nations and civilizations

whose populations they composed. Now I'm figuring myself the citizen of a larger dominion, in which rank turns on the degree of individual understanding, though participation continues to depend on service.

And, indeed, there is nothing unconstitutional here. Am not I, too, an individual consciousness, whose occupational sphere is the body I keep according to the current conception of my relation to the circumstances that environ it? Enlargement of this conception does not alter my relation to the circumstances, but does affect my position with regard to them. If I change from tenant to owner, my domicile becomes an investment instead of a leasehold and my title insures me the right to control the holding and improve its premises, but I have only extended the conditions of tenure. I remain a member of a community and a vassal of the State which is supported by the taxes it exacts from me.

Interesting—undoubtedly—but too vague and remote for home consumption. It has no standing in my mind. Yet I've wandered around and been told enough to have established some implications in regard to that Self who, the Martian declared—could be discovered, if sought with sufficient zeal. Whether it be *a* or *the* Self, some agent there is, with properties that the known chemistry of my body does not contain. It inheres in my disposition rather than in my actions; which may well be, since the latter are constrained by the type of the organism that delivers them. Yet it designs their pattern, initiates and modifies their character, and is affected by results. Its interests are bound up with those of the structure it animates.

It is supple, suggestive, and expansive; is irked by confinement, yet molds itself to the body to which it is contracted and adopts the tone and color of the society that enfolds it. It is sensitive to change; essentially curious and vagrant, is that which coheres, retains and reacts; it has its own ebbs and flows in inertia and enthusiasm; it has no individual convictions; its capacity is to absorb, ingest and apply the information it gleans from the experiences it inspires and incurs. It functions as pilot and operator and is the source of the movements and communications men engage in and enjoy. It seeks and requires light for development; conceivably, is itself sustained by etheric components in the air decomposed in its lungs; and appears to be insulated by the organism which is the station and conductor of its power.

Qualities that the dead lack and the living hold, characteristic of the human family and, according to my visitor, typical of the element Consciousness which he declared was ingrained of awareness, initiative and integration.

On these terms one might conjecture life to be the colonization of an environment by agents of consciousness, and its terms to represent the conversion of local conditions to the needs of the invaders. The ascending scale of vital forms could denote rank and degree in its army. The structures and institutions established for their accommodation and government—improvisations modeled on ancestral memories, adjusted to contingent circumstances.

Colorful but unsubstantial.

It can be set down, however, that man *is* a unit of this Element; and the organism in which he is domiciled, a type of motor vehicle adapted to the functions of transmitting and maintaining consciousness in this vicinity—which again leaves one holding a large generality without affording a glimpse of the particulars.

For why should these units differ so radically from one another? Human bodies are identical in pattern and substance,

share the same space and air, are yoked to the same obligations of protecting and sustaining their own lives; yet, in
forcefulness, capacity and disposition, no two men are alike.
It is not through the multiplicity of occupations that distinctions and discrepancies declare themselves; for, where
conditions, materials and apparatus are uniform, operation
and product must belong in the same category; but in the
character and manner of use. Thus it is not what men *do*
that is significant—but how, how much, and in what order
and spirit. In the final determination of a great individual's
career, his beginnings figure merely as incidentals. His status is that which he affirms and achieves in human society.
The resistances encountered in the attainment of the place
his power or talent enable him to take, are but rungs on the
ladder of an inevitable ascent. Nor does failure or success
turn on physical attributes; for, though health and strength
aid continuity of application—illness and debility handicap,
but do not affect, the delivery of specific accomplishments.

Must consciousness also be entered in the realm of determinism? Are stations in life, aptitudes and professions fixed
in advance? Is there, then, a Book in which the fates of men
are written, and all we do but enactments of the roles assigned to us?

Yet why balk at determinism? It begins in the womb. On
what selective principle do the protoplasmic cells in the ovum
segregate and assort themselves to the visceral, muscular and
cerebral systems of the embryo they form? Are they born to
the parts they take, or is each individually conditioned for its
post in the organism? Cells live and move, have their little
day and their own being, yield up their properties to the
structures whose bone and tissue they compose, and serve
and die in the maintenance of its metabolism. What may a

cell know of the functions it conducts—or of its place in the scheme of things?

The gait of the train slackened. I felt the touch of the car attendant on my shoulder.

"Atlantic City in ten minutes, sir," he reminded me.

I arose with a start, shuffled unsteadily back to the vacated seat in the parlor car, resigned myself to the ministrations of the porter, gathered my belongings and refaced the world of reality, the world in which men were men, and worked for their livings and were not mere units of consciousness, wrapped up in helpless, self-sacrificing protoplasmic tissue.

And the thoughts that formulated themselves in my mind were concerned with hotel accommodation, food, drink and the character and extent of the literary ailment which had taken me so far afield.

A moment later I espied my invalid restlessly pacing the station platform, and realized that there was trouble ahead.

CHAPTER XVIII: THE CHARTER AND CONSTITUTION OF
IDENTITY

Minds play tricks on their owners. Development and operations of an unpremeditated talent. Dual structure of man.
Life, the product of machineries organized for its delivery.
Role of the individual prescribed by organism and defined
by public opinion. A plot with all creation for accomplice.
Looking and Listening-posts of the All-Consciousness. We
are not party to the conditions that enfold us. Characteristics of the Ordainment external to our senses. If the Universe is a unity, events are fulfillments of purpose. Commercial practices as analogues of cosmic mechanics. The process
of evolving executives. Man's career, the dramatization of
innate tendencies. Mother Nature attends to her exchanges,
indifferent to controversy.

FORTUNATELY my client's predicament was not a problem.
It was sympathy he sought, not aid. The flow of his narrative
had ceased. He said his mind had run dry. Of a sudden and
without warning he found himself bereft of words and ideas.
He had examined his conscience and his conduct, found both
blameless and thought seriously of consulting a physician. In
the meantime was there a reliable mental aphrodisiac? He
nearly wept on my shoulder.

I knew the symptoms. Health, industry, appetite and golf
game unimpaired, but cerebral routines inhibited. A mysterious ailment apt to overtake persons who function through
words, figures, pictures or symbols—brain workers—due, as
I now saw it, to an interruption in the currency circuit be-

tween entity and organism. Doubtless something to do with the photosynthetic processes through which the exchange between response and stimuli is affected.

It was useless to take the disturbance to a doctor, I explained, since the medical profession was provided with neither understanding of the quantities involved or tools wherewith to readjust their contacts. Psychiatrists and psychoanalysts would transpose the phenomena in the terms of their own abracadabra, for a fee; but though his vocabulary might be enlarged no relief need be expected. Personally, I preferred Astrology, which if one granted the premises had a remote physical bearing; yet its significance was meteorological rather than remedial. There was faith-healing, of course, but one needed faith to find a healer and if one had faith enough, healers were superfluous.

What's amiss, after all? I demanded. The condition is common enough. Minds played tricks on their owners, and without rhyme or reason, turned truant. Expostulation was vain; remorse aggravated the malady. Better defy it, take his laurels to Paris and tap good liquor at the fountain head. Or, accumulate fresh backgrounds in Alaska or the Canadian wilds. Just be indifferent to her, and before he knew it his Muse would be begging forgiveness. Both would be the better for a vacation.

We had strolled the Boardwalk, explored the pier, observed our compatriots absorbing the raucous glamor of the settings, agreed that the fringe of giant caravansaries were sound exemplars of the architectural style of baroque-hippopotami so popular for resorts, remarked on the reliability of the ocean as a source of increment and, of human credulity—that it was the most negotiable of securities. In brief we gave free rein to our superiority complexes and whetted excellent appetites for dinner.

Of which we partook in peace. It was unnecessary for my friend to retell the story of his life. His was one of those un-premeditated talents that had broken unawares upon the un-furrowed life of a sales-executive in a western factory. There was a respectable social background, some years in a state university and a bit of humdrum success, and then this sei-zure. Impelled by some force, he knew not what, one night at home after supper he seized paper and a pencil and began to write. In the course of a month, a novel accumulated under his hands and his amazed mother dispatched the manuscript to a publisher. Plot, scene and dramatis-personæ were extra-neous to his experiences. The style was unlabored and color-ful, and though the tale had neither nature nor truth, it was the stuff of romance and sold a hundred thousand copies in a season. This miracle occurred ten years ago and, at decent intervals since, had renewed itself. It was as though he had struck oil in his own back yard.

The stories wrote themselves, he had confided. All that was necessary during the period of conception was to sit still in a quiet room at a desk. His career had begun on a dark evening in November before an open fire—and annu-ally thereafter, at the same time, the yearning recurred. No thought processes whatever, or research. When the flow set in he turned out 1,000 words a day, never more or less. In due course the tale spun itself out without strain or effort. Nor was ever revision required. It was his custom to read each morning's installment after it had been delivered, and often, he confessed, he wondered how his heroes and hero-ines could possibly be extricated from the predicaments into which they had been plunged. Always they were righted legitimately and ingenuously, and led to the altar in the concluding chapter. An amazing business, altogether.

Being neither of an inquiring or inquisitive turn, my friend had never investigated his gift. It was a sort of special providence attached to his person, and far be it from one so modest to question the pedigree of his benefactions. So he felt there was something capricious in the misfortune. It was as though he had been betrayed by a fairy godmother. However, while it lasted, the relationship had been so fertile that he was provided against its dissolution. In its own right his was a thrifty soul and there were dividends enough to keep him in cakes, ale, and a Park Avenue duplex if he never wrote another line in his life.

As I had begun to realize, it's not as simple a world as the best authorities make out, and there may be possessions as well as obsessions. Celestial cuckoos lay foreign eggs in improperly insulated cerebrums, and birds of strange plumage emerge from domestic nests, to the disturbance both of ornithologists and publishers. Anyway, authors, like gold, are where you find them, and the best are seldom accountable for their product. Like millionaires, they are born, not made, for it is what is inlaid in the seed that comes forth in the flesh.

I left him late that night—reconciled if not rejoiced by the prospect of a vacation. What his mother would say bothered him, and he was a bit troubled over the disappointment of his "large public." I consoled with the suggestion that the suspense might augment the demand for his works and perhaps double the sale of the next volume. At any rate it was the part of wisdom to acquiesce with a forced conclusion.

In what dark realm of the unconditioned the next eight hours of my life were sped, I know not. It was a spell of oblivion in a comfortable bed, unbroken by dreams, and I arose out of its shadows with replenished energies and a mind clear of vapors. There followed an interval of breakfast and farewells, and I was back in a new parlor car tingling with resolve to fight a way out of the perplexities that had swamped me on the down trip.

What is, *is*, I insisted to myself, and its components must contain the secret of what's in the making. I've followed some distance along the Martian's trail, but who's who and why still elude me. Best plan is to set down the ascertainments so far established, and find bearings.

What is a man? His body; his consciousness of that body, of his fellows of the same genus, of the environment in which they are installed, and of the power to move therein.

What does he? Acts. Maintains the life of this body by means of exchange with environment and intercourse with other human beings.

What is a body? The seat of a unit of consciousness—a locomotory organism equipped to generate the energy required for the sustainment and communications of its incumbent.

What is consciousness? An element whose power constitutes the positive pole of the organism in which it is placed—whose reaction to etheric stimuli and atmospheric gases through the medium of that organism kindles the phenomena of life and awareness.

That goes for a seed or an ovum cell, as well as for a man, I reminded myself.

From consciousness, then, we derive the matrix—mobilization and motivation of the vital organisms which inhere as structures and going-concerns—by virtue of its properties of integration, initiative and awareness.

It is through his consciousness that a man is enabled to perceive and appraise his individual relations to the circumstances that environ his body, and to take due measures for the relief of the needs arising from the liability to preserve his position therein.

A man's life, then, is the product of the machineries organized and combined for its actualization; he contributes to its maintenance his understanding of the kind of food and treatment required to conduct the operations of these machineries. It would seem that our relations to our bodies parallel, in general, those we bear to power organizations, such as locomotives, automobiles and manufacturing plants which we create and use, and for which we provide housing, care and fuel.

Neither the designs of men's bodies or the circumstances of the planet have altered during the period of human occupation, and change has been confined to the betterment of human habitations, tools and associations. The growth of these betterments is due to the advancement of knowledge of the principles that regulate the affiliation between bodies and an environment. The acquirement and application of knowledge are functions of consciousness. It follows, logically, that the creative works of the human race are due to the exercise of its potentials.

Knowledge is the totality of facts accreted by consciousness and set down in symbols about men and their habitations, during the ages of planetary colonization. This store of objectivized information—which defines causes, effects and usages as bearing on the regulation of human conduct and work, is the racial inheritance, and defines the significance of an individual unit in the locality to which he is committed by birth. So he awakens to the identity and opportunities prescribed by his civilization; his destiny is framed by its modes. Thus, the character of his experience is conditioned by the circumstances of his nativity. Be his role that of slave, Hottentot, Chinese Mandarin, Bedouin, American Citizen or Frenchman, his life must be enacted according to prevailing properties and terms.

The situation, then, contains these elements: the Earth, a stabilized organization rotating among other material bodies of its kind; Humans, standardized organisms equipped to pick up the energy applied in sustaining unitary existence on its surface; Knowledge, specifications covering relations between organisms and earth with regard to the initiation and maintenance of these relations; Consciousness—the coordinating element which integrates, animates and uses individual organisms through which its units sustain their habitation of the Earth and maintain place and association.

So far as my own entity is concerned, this set of circumstances is independent of me and subsisted prior to my appearance therein. *I* brought nothing here, save capacity to kindle the germ of a particular type of organism; to grow, inhabit and apply its mechanisms to cognize and carry on an individual life. Every condition of this occupation was prescribed; the form of my activities by the shape of the parts through which they were issued; my viewpoint and opportunities—by the social and economic status of my parentage.

Physically, then, I am the product of the conditions converged for my birthing and, subsequently, of the circumstances that surrounded my childhood. My mind developed in the mold of the version of the world and its works compiled by my parents and accepted in their social environment. My realities were theirs, because I could not know more than what I saw or was told. So I took what was given, for granted—as the right dispensation for one of my worth.

Individually, I am the sum of the impressions insensibly engraved on my cerebrum during the years of residence here as to the place and state of my nativity, and my sense of power to cope with its problems. This forms my personal picture of life and is the structure of my identity—the man that I feel I am—that I affirm, and impress on my fellows in the give and take of existence. It is not a fixed conception, because it varies from day to day, but an anomalous compound woven of memories of my activities, my associations, my expectations and doubts, and of effects registered external to my own being in that milieu of which I am part, but whose interests are separate from my own.

This body of miscellaneous recollections, ascertainments and expectations has hitherto constituted the working formula of the life I maintain according to the ordained conventions of my vicinity. Save for the Martian's interposition, I should never have dreamed of questioning its validity or sanctions. From this new angle, its artifice is obvious.

There was a moment's pause in the flow of hypotheses. I became aware of the immediate world of New Jersey registering itself on my optical lenses—insensibly translated into landscape and disparate features—each with its place, ideology and name. A brilliant morning, in which shrubs, trees, gardens and houses showed clear in the light refracted from their contours and surfaces. As I gazed at the flying visions filmed on my attention, there surged into my mind a wave of bitterness at the realization that the sensations these pleasant prospects aroused in me were automatic, and—like all the other functions I exercised—purely mechanical.

No recourse remained but to regard myself as an artificial

product, conjoined of the properties of the elements integrated in my organism and set in motion for the establishment of its own verities as stereotyped by the ordainment that had bred and delivered me. In such an allocation, the activities I thought inspired by individual choice appeared as the ways through which it affected its own ends.

I had but taken the paths along which its needs had impelled me as do corpuscles coursing in veins. I might solace myself with the theory that I was a tool of this mighty power—honored by the privilege of its livery; but, since I was ignorant of its being and my own relation thereto, it was clear that, for all our pretensions, men must stand low in the scale of its structure.

So that's the situation, I exclaimed to myself. As a man lives on the outside of his person, what he discovers about himself must be gathered from the spectacle of his own body making its private way in the world. His role is prescribed by public opinion, and he conceives himself to be what he sees and feels. He is forever accumulating additional evidence about his relation to environing circumstance, erecting fresh pretensions which issue in new objectives, being cast down or exalted by success or failure, and ascribing to misfortune or luck—the results of his ventures. Naturally, his joys and sorrows are engendered by the hopes and fears bred of his uncertainties. These, too, are registered by external physical associations, reacting as internal strains and pressures within the system they affect; verbalized according to the current ascriptions for the sensations aroused.

Similarly, he embroiders, with cryptic significance, the processes and machineries that endow his organism with the potential of reproduction, and rears the structures of his happiness and shames on the satisfaction, denial or perversion of instinctive stimuli. Instinctive, too, are the attractions and repulsions germane to the motions and contacts of electrified bodies in a magnetic field which, in the vernacular of the species, are articulated as affinities and dislikes, as loves and hates. His occupation expresses the bent of his tendencies in the best terms he can find to accommodate their leanings. Since it is impossible for him to pierce through the clouds of expectation and illusion that befog his passage, he is incapable of disinterested self-knowledge. A plot, if ever there was one; but with all creation its accessories and accomplices. Here is evidence of purpose, plan and integration, developed according to principles so ingenious that the participants are kept unaware of their roles—yet furnish the initiative to forward them. Arguing about the matters and circumstances of which this design is compounded is as futile as it would be to attribute the action of a drama to the theater or to the scenery and players that unfold its progressions. All are but properties of the producer, lent to the performance of an author's improvisation. As indeed—though they don't realize it—are the substances in which inventors mold vehicles for the articulation of their devices. So, to say that these conjunctions of worlds are either the elements of which they were generated, or the forces which cause them to revolve, is equivalent in reason to declaring that a communication is the paper on which it is written, or an artist's palette is the picture whose texture it supplies. What we call Nature's laws can be no more than the working formulas of an ordainment, in which both the subject and the stuffs of its enactments originate.

A cigarette was lighted and smoked. I became aware of the motion of the train, of fellow passengers reading newspapers or conversing, of stray words and phrases—the mundane world and its members going about their own business, curiously heedless of the magical faculties being exercised in the accomplishment of their communications. Chemically, each was a compound of qualities and properties loosely arranged as an individualized element in human society, stabilized in some matrimonial and co-partnership relation with elements variously charged: or sought new unions to more effectively balance their exchanges. Probably everyone has an atomic equivalent in the periodic table of being, denoting specific place or range in the scale of human development. Nature is given to such parallels, and advances her effects by magnifications of the same architectural principles. It occurred to me that it would be amusing to assign characters to a selected group of gases in a flask, and make a drama out of their behaviorisms and the molecular combinations they formed among themselves. Consider the aspects of sodium and chlorine atoms flying into each other's arms and calling it love at first sight!

Skipping around among conjectures won't land me on standing room, I reminded myself. Nor are my personal responses to the facts disclosed pertinent. While hazarding a lot of assumptions I seem to have stumbled upon a couple of premises. One certainty is that it is impossible to rationalize the phenomena in sight from the basis of the man on the street. The other, that I can detach myself from my body and environing circumstances, and survey them; which indicates a potential within me, capable of that office. While the exercise of this power has enlarged my perspective, thus far it has no more than deepened my confusions. Instead of an *I* transcending this environment—my stature has shrunk to that of a coin in its currency. My identity is based on its evaluation, and I furnish no more than motive power for its circulation. And, still further obscuring a situation already unendurably complicated, in the picture that is now forming, the Universe appears as the background.

Yet, since in this adventure it is my illusions that are being dissipated, perhaps it is a warrant that I'm emerging from shadow-land. As long as I accepted for realities the processes that insensibly I conveyed, I was the victim of appearances. The image of the man I thought I was has faded, but the survivor is traveling in a broader landscape than he had ever dreamed of. However insecure the footing—at least there's ground under his feet. And, curiously—a sense of freedom as of one released from shackles.

More is involved in this new orientation than immediately shows. How did I arrive at it? Not through unconscious cerebration certainly, rather by drastic self-analysis. What has changed? Physically—nothing. I am in the same spot, place, body and clothes. Perhaps the mere act of looking inward, instead of out, establishes a different focus. A lot of old anchorages adrift, for all that I have no more than raised my eyes. There's the gist of it. It's my mind that has stirred; and lo—strange horizons loom.

Since in the human makeup the one unmoored element is consciousness—it must be that which has awakened; it can be extended, said the Martian. It may have no convictions of its own; so is confined to the evidence the individual self-interest exposes it to; but out of further information it may frame larger patterns, and with equal facility, unscramble old ones. Since it is the power through which understandings and opinions are reached and changed, yet must be aroused to activity—perhaps the ordeals of life are means to awaken its potentials. Presume an entity endowed with a capital of perception, fortitude and ingenuity committed to earth in a human body and refusing to function—what happens to him? Pressure of the environment, of bodily pangs and his crowding fellows, all sting him to action. He must move or be crushed, find food or perish, conform or be outlawed. He is goaded to realization of his inertness by pain and punishment, labor and sweat—to learning how to relieve his burdens by taking stock of his predicaments and abilities. Whether the curriculum be that of the jungle or the metropolis—effort is inescapable. Flight is incarnated in wings, but fledglings must learn to fly their own.

In a world of artifice and calculation such as this is revealed to be, whatever is must be significant. Yet, perhaps nothing is being proved, beyond the adequacy of the machinery to carry on consecutively and continuously the life of the Universe itself. Maybe each of us is a looking and listening-post of Him whom the Martian calls the All-Consciousness, contributing a moiety of seeing and hearing to the sum of His self-awareness. Human radio sets—so to speak.

Assuming our role in the complex to be no more than that—what possible use could an Hierarch of Space make, of the kind of news that is manufactured here by his subjects? Our incidents grow out of biological, geographical and occupational strains and stresses. We look at life through the spectacles of our interests, which include our personal attitudes to the problems that affect them. Therefore aspirations and opinions voice ambitions and appetites. For the most part minds are in their owner's or someone else's pocketbook. We follow our noses like dogs after bones, or bees scenting honey. The game is to keep moving, preferably avoiding collisions, but practically to enlarge our possessions and powers. One lands where one is headed—or succumbs to the pace. Survivors demonstrate ability to survive. Age may provide wisdom, but is more likely to engender apathy. Unless we are tearing at each other's throats as in revolution or warfare, it's no story of more than domiciliary concern that goes from here to the stars.

Life is like that, its episodes being no more than germane to keeping its fires burning. Again, my reason reiterates that it is the circumstances, out of which the trifles that are called events evolve, which are strange and important; and that one must dismiss as delusion, the idea that human existence is about anything that shows on the surface.

The fact is plain—men are not party to the conditions that enfold their attendance in the environment in which they appear, and therefore must be the subjects of whatever power and jurisdiction provided the accoutrements and environment for their presence. Agents thus encumbered and commonly ignorant of their own identity, are neither free nor responsible. As the Society into which they are thrust is trammeled by the same obscurities and handicaps, it is reasonable to infer that there may be a relation between the state to which they awaken and the purpose that installed them there.

The same tasks confront all our populations. The problems that plague rulers are only enlargements of the diffi culties that perplex individuals. Throughout the world governments strive to insure their people's food, shelter, peace, order and freedom. Since these are only attainable by unfolding the resources of environments through developing the stability, skill and industry of their subjects—their character, knowledge and culture—it might seem that, through the disciplines enforced by our circumstances, we insensibly make for the ends of those who sent us here.

What may a man take out of the world in leaving it that he

lacked on arrival? Only such alterations as have been wrought in the degree of his consciousness, by the compulsion to exercise it in the solution of the complications that beset his passage. Maybe self-knowledge is the aim of attainment, and our trials and tribulations but weaning and weathering for some larger life, when we have lifted ourselves off the lap of the gods and taken over our own dispensations.

Once concede a holding organization, whose dominion is external to our senses—we must assume that all phenomena in sight are conditioned by the submerged constitution of the Whole. Since it is in motion, and we must move to sustain our own positions therein, obviously—like ourselves—it lives through the momentum it sets up among the organic parts of its entity. Since it is a physical fabrication, its corporeality is the development of a design and, since apparently it is self-contained and maintains itself, it fulfills the purpose of the creator who had the will and power to evoke its being. We must infer that the order observed by its members is necessary to the preservation of its integrity and position; that the causes and effects arising within the confines of its dimensions emerge from the circumstances of its existence; that the forms it has established are appropriate for its expression. As in the case of a man walking down the street, or a motor coursing swiftly along a speedway, or a dog chasing a rabbit—what happens is the product of the means conjoined to achieve it; so we may take it that the Universe is as it is, because it was built to do what it does.

But in essaying to define an organization of the type of the Universe or, indeed, any object or person as apart from oneself, is not Consciousness itself affirmed—and an individual awareness set up? As both Universe and its observer are alive, and are sustained by etheric and physical exchange with each other, they must belong in the same order of Being.

In a general way, then, the individual might be a small and dependent universe; a coordinated consciousness and body, applying the first to the maintenance of the latter; acquiring through its medium, a standpoint from which to cognize his personal and spatial relations and to find the means whereby to preserve their alignment. One's status in the Corporation-of-the-Whole, would reside in the breadth of his recognition of his personal estate therein, and realization of the obligation incumbent on him to conform to its nature. Corresponding, one must admit, to the civic relations that we bear here and now to national and international institutions of government.

Presuming that parallel principles hold true in the large units and the small, there is ground for conjecturing that the Universe itself, like its vitalized constituents, is a mechanical structure generating within its anatomical framework the powers that motivate its parts. As the lives of men are kindled and sustained by interaction between their consciousness and their bodies so the Great Entity supports his own existence, cognizes and controls the order of his cosmos by the interactions he sets up and maintains through the congeries of vital organisms that people it. As the neurons of his cerebrum form the thinking apparatus of a human being, that being is himself a neuron perhaps, in the cerebrum of the All-Consciousness.

There's a conception to set the teeth of both scientists and theologians on edge, I thought, but it does have commonsense aspects which might commend it to practical minds. It allows me to predicate a government of the Universe— extending throughout its dimensions, charged with the operation and administration of its far-flung stellar systems together with their populations of animate organisms; managed in the interest, and ruled according to the purposes of its Founder; administered by a personnel graduated from its membership of individuals. Even as in the British Empire or the USA. Since there's an immense body of phenomena to be accounted for, which none of our ascertainments can explain—presumably the minds and powers of these executives are kept busy harmonizing spherical relations and etheric exchange, together with supervising the operations of the laws and processes by which units of consciousness are produced, assorted and set-up in frames. In some arcanum exterior to our vision are shaped the materials, images and occasions of our small lives, and we strut their courses without a suspicion that what appears as the workings of chance is the registration of design.

The Martian is right. There must be a stupendous amount of millwork, sifting and adjusting going on behind the scenes, to produce the effects in evidence. Once lodge in the mind the theory that the universe is a unity, accident goes out the window. One is forced to assume regulation, direction, policy, promotion and police power—the invariable features of government. Events, thereafter, become the fulfillment of purposive operation—the execution of the law. This is Karma or fate, the basis of oriental acquiescence. Yet it but challenges the curiosity of an occidental who recognizes that there are other subjects for meteorologies than the weather. Life becomes more interesting because of a new mystery.

If I were to hazard these audacious conceptions to a sympathetic friend, on what realistic grounds could I urge their plausibility? I might suggest to him that the principles which rule local commercial practices are probable if remote parallels of the logic of cosmic mechanics; and, for confirmation, ask him to examine the constitutions and usages of our multimillionaire corporate institutions and note their verities and procedures.

All such organizations are aggregates of units of force and consciousness welded into autonomous wholes, driven by strong wills—revolving on their own axes, so to speak—and insulated within their dimensions. Each has purpose, plant, orbit—and supports itself by exchange with its customers. In engineering and operation each duplicates a vital organic system; for direction is by report, and action is in function and change of position in response to stimuli. Furthermore, all are managed by a personnel of executives and employees on behalf of the owners, and evolve domiciliary civilizations based on the maintenance of order among their parts, and the fulfillment of the service for which they exist. In their attitude to labor they are devoid of sentimentality.

To Standard Oil—for instance, or to the US Steel Corporation—a man is not a son of God, but an item of inherent energy that can be converted to its use. In its service he begins as an apprentice, absorbs the subject-matter of its operations by being immersed in their routines and picks up its vocabulary and convictions on the same terms. His individuality is swallowed up in its bulk but he is the conveyer of the processes conducted through his means. The substance of his learning is how to maintain the volume and speed of its traffic and communications. If his mind acquires the same, or a greater momentum, he is inducted into the ranks of its management. Thus, advancement turns on the degree of an ability to assimilate knowledge and apply it to action, and in the exercise of his potentials, a man establishes his individual rating.

Nor do these great institutions presume that the human units entering their shops are better than morons. Jobs are organically determined. Prescribed routines are attached to posts—as in protoplasmic structures—and work is forwarded if specifications are delivered. But masters are alert for signs of intelligence among their staffs and whoever shows it gets scope for its evolution on behalf of their interests. Marked for executive development, he is advanced, by successive changes of position that expand his knowledge of ways, means, and processes, and is harnessed to larger and harder tasks to extend his understanding of practices and policies. He is inured to the exercise of discretion and responsibility, by independent command of outlying stations. Always he is being watched, weighed, timed and judged. Gradually he transfers his sense of self to the cause of the institution; thinks and acts through and for it; and the matter of its dispositions becomes integral with his flesh and blood. If he be endowed with reach and push as well as grasp—he is intrusted with the insignia and emoluments of high office, and controls where he formerly served. But he is no longer his own man, even in private, for he belongs to the corporation-as-a-whole, and must uphold the dignity of its magnitude.

In theosophic and occult methodology, such discipline is the path of attainment. In business circles, it is merely the way to the top. Thus do conditions and considerations tend to repeat themselves in far distant fields.

Also, I'd ask him to note that morality in a great commercial system, is never an abstraction. Virtue is in service to its interests; religion is loyalty to its purpose and its captains. Steerage of material structures in motion requires obedience to the authority vested in pilotage. Sin is in rebellion, treachery or blunder, which delay or abort deliveries. But discipline is purgative rather than punitive, because discharge is more economical than prosecution. Since all values are in sight and within reach, no employee imbibes delusions about his state or nature. Status and development are mechanical, and according to precedent. There are ladders for ambition. The man who fails knows who is to blame. To attribute his woes to the boss would but excite the derision of his fellows. And Love?—it is nepotism.

What is acquired under such systems is knowledge of the principles and practices that regulate the conduct of life. What develops through resistances surmounted are self-confidence and self-control; what is augmented—the senses of power and responsibility; what is enhanced—understanding. Qualities that are the ideals of all citizens and adjustable to the exigencies of further experience and, curiously, parallels of the very properties we induce in the fabrics of material substances by process—since they correspond, generally, to durability, tensility, resiliency, flexibility and conductivity—characteristics that are due to changes in atomic patterns matured through the offices of furnaces and rolling mills.

Further presumptions may be based on the hypothesis of the universe as a closed system, within which the unitary consciousness is passed through its various stages of integration and stabilization on behalf of the Ordainment to which its functions are correlated and contributory. Inevitably, its structural development must be regulated by laws that parallel the intensification of atomic patterns in material substances, for, I take it, that consciousness is etheric in essence, and the medium rather than the cause of the phenomena it registers. Since our own environment is filled with its allotropes, in all the shades of development from aborigine to adept, and its potentials as manifest in individuals, so diverse in kind and degree, it is safe to believe that what is fortified by exposure to the rigors of experience is its nucleus; and that varieties of types spring from the degrees of its charge. Presumably, it evolves through successive mutations; gaining momentum in its progressions and, eventually, the power to expand the germ cell of the human genus and develop its frame and texture.

It would emerge in the disposition of the being whom it awakened to life and would mature in the heightening degree of his capacity to deal with planetary circumstances. Its inherency would be revealed by the virility, speed and range of reactions, as exhibited in the patterns of his occupational activities, as reflected in his interests, inclinations and sensibilities, and as emanating in the influence he exerted in associations: all these, of course, modeled in the matters and fashions of the environment, and in the tone of the racial society in which his body happened to be born and grow.

Thus, his career would appear a dramatization of innate tendencies; construed according to local conceptions of the role of his genus; conditioned and constrained by the deposit of stimuli and response records automatically accreted in his brain by the senses, nerves, muscles, glands and blood of a dynamic organism, bent on fulfilling the obligations of its own nature as a going and reproducing concern.

In this view and estimate of the constitution of the human kind, it is not strange that men have sought behind the veil of their senses for some cause, source and aim for their circumstances and detachment. Assuming that all states and emergencies are stipulations for the development of the unitary and the racial consciousness, perhaps these very conditions are stimuli, set up to awaken the potential of curiosity.

It was man's hunt for the secret of his being that aroused his imagination, and gave us that rich tapestry of myth and tradition which is our most delectable heritage.

To dub as superstitions, those early flights of intelligence seems from this premise a sad error of scholarship. For it was true instinct of their own intransigency that bred our ancestors' conceptions of superior beings of their own kind who had made this crude and hostile world and could be persuaded by prayer and sacrifice to temper its stresses. Personalized as idols in clay or stone, and endowed with the virtues and valors their human creators lacked, in them were integrated their ideals of governance and behavior. It was no great step thereafter to fashioning the laws of social intercourse and survival into hieratic writs and regarding their enforcement as divinely sanctioned. Since the beginning, it has been easier to command than explain, and magic has ever been more convincing than reason in the imposition of morality on the conduct of men.

There exists no stronger testimony of the fertility of the human mind than the galaxies of Olympians with which the passing generations have tenanted their heavens. In defense of this inconstancy, let it be said that it is theological patterns that have altered during the ages and not the vital textures of hope, faith and belief.

Never for an instant, throughout the long history of humanity's adventures in search of a soul, has Mother Nature relaxed her grip on the bodies, muscles and hands of her offspring. The processes of exchange within environments, the ceaseless conjoining and turnover of matter and force, and the transformations and evolutions of forms and powers through which it would seem the physical life of the universe is sustained, grind on relentlessly, indifferent to controversy and apparently heedless of results.

Well may men wonder, as they contemplate the machinery of the organized entity whose dimensions and authority enlarge with the expansion of their own cognitions, what their part may be in an institution whose precessions are so stoutly insulated against interference.

For all the handicaps and obstacles along the way what a harvest of accomplishment stands to man's credit! However blind and insensate, he has built up an order of living and a literature that is honorable to his great heritage. He has made himself at home in the air and under the sea, explored, measured and named the salients of the earth and the skies. Thousands of his kind have sacrificed, for cause or brother, what is conceived as their most valuable possession—their lives. For all our derelictions the truth is held high here, and more loyalty is extended by the race than is due the individuals and governments to whom it is given. Slowly but with increasing momentum, the growing flood of knowledge is being circulated and applied. Here, at least, the lot of the average men is larger, safer and more endurable than before in history. Human rights have ascended, and, though justice is not evenhanded, it is ever harder to buy, and mercy is appearing in the mantle of wisdom.

Out of the innate capacity to perceive change, recall precedents, recognize resemblances and compare results, there has grown a structure of knowledge which may yet set us free. Though our emotions may be no more than glandular reactions, and our attachments and devotions mere electrical phenomena, they have supplied poetry, romance, color and nobility to the lifetime of a race that would indeed be drab and mechanical without their solace.

Cerebration ceased. Peace settled upon my understanding and, curiously enough, I recalled the neglected manuscript that reposed unread in my portfolio. Soon I was immersed in a swift narrative and in alternations of amusement, irritation and pleasure, spent the rest of the journey.

"Another half-witted genius that has fallen into a clover patch," I commented to myself, as the train drew into New York. "At least he's tapped some stream of consciousness and got it flowing in his tale. Unconventional enough, and there's trouble in it—but it will go big. How he is to get this girl out of the net she's now skewered in is a puzzle, and I'll have to wait till after dinner to find out."

CHAPTER XIX: THE TASK OF LIFTING ONESELF OFF THE KNEES OF THE GODS

Return of the Martian. Unrest, the growth of the collective consciousness. Secrets of the Universe embodied in its structure and behaviors. Nothing exists of itself. All creations, achievements of will. Our cosmos, the embodiment of Him who conceived and had the power to make it. Man's identity as a link in the transmission system of the universal mind. Our world a laboratory for the quickening of individual consciousness. The technic of self-observation, as means of stabilizing the entity in the center of consciousness. Building an internal order. Opening a way to the hidden springs of the human organism. Even miracles depend on mechanism. Character and privilege of the developed man. Struggle of humanity to grasp the reality of the Soul. Martian views of immortality and of religion. Belief in a God, not faith but intelligence. Retirement of the Martian.

At home two hours later I was so deep in the queer book's contents that when the sardonic chuckle of the Martian fell on my ears I did not look up.

"Is it a trance or entrancement?" I heard, in the brittle timbre of his tones, and awoke with a start. "Back from Death Valley," continued the unmistakable voice, "to reclaim your attention and resume your education."

"I've gone some distance since our last conference," I said, noting a graciousness in the greeting that had been absent in our previous passages.

"I followed your explorations from afar, and urged their

inclinations a bit," he returned. " 'Twas was a winding trail you stumbled along, and rough going. Often better foot than head work, but you stayed on the ground. Under the circumstances, a little transcendentalism is pardonable."

"Your argument may have colored my conclusions some," I admitted, "but I reasoned with my own materials. If it had ever occurred to me to stop in my tracks, look and listen—I'd have landed on the same principles. What bearing these can have on my life does not yet appear, nor how such a thesis can be verified outside the mind. Lifting the scales from my eyes leaves me more patient and tolerant—nice qualities, but hardly potentials. Knowing the rules is essential for good playing, but helps little towards improving a player's game."

"There's always been a market in your world for wisdom," my visitor replied, "though nowadays the article is no longer being sought of prophets or philosophers, but is monopolized by practical men. Of course that betrays the materialism of your populations, but also a better general understanding of their own situation. For instinctive people, who live from one day to the next, too much ease or prosperity is debilitating. It takes their minds off themselves and away from their problems, so aborts the progress of races. For the future of humanity, according to prevailing dispensations, revolution is more salutary than contentment. The common lot is always deplorable, but it can only be changed by being perceived to be unendurable. By innate endowment, man is a thinking animal. Having now become literate, there is fodder for his consciousness and words for the articulation of his feelings. So the processes of classification, comparison and rejection are today in full cry, and the air is filled with the clangor of antagonistic conclusions. Yet, how much better than silence, which is more often dumbness than restraint.

What really is being exhibited hereabouts is the growth of the collective consciousness through exercise. The unrests that follow in economics, sociology and government are but the adjustments of its bodies to larger convictions. Internal tensions released as are geological spasms. Mechanical cerebration equals instinctive culture. Like the Universe, individual societies advance through the motions set up among their parts."

"That, O Sage, might have been said by myself," I objected, "and it does not answer my question."

"Right," the Martian responded, "though not on the day before yesterday. Is increase of understanding not in itself a return for the effort that attained it? Since you arrived at an hypothesis of what life is about, should not that improve the living of it? Half the work of getting anywhere is that of deciding on an objective. The efficacy of prayer lies in the formulation of the hope that inspired it. The man who returns to your desk tomorrow morning has lost most of his delusions and so will waste less time. At least he has the power to know what he wants before commissioning someone else to get it for him. Rough but profitable results, even if you don't appreciate their value or grasp the processes of acquirement."

"The latter's the point," I confessed. "All I accomplished was to tear down a dream fabric. How to assemble a new structure or give significance to the old patterns is beyond me."

"When a man realizes that understanding is no more than the better half of conviction," he replied, "he is ripe for development. For practical purposes then, that picturesque mental excursion of yours meant nothing. Mapping and traveling—like planning and building—belong in different categories of endeavor. Making a new start requires returning to the point of departure, and in this instance involves me in recapitulating and stabilizing premises—and you in listening.

"Visualize two interpenetrating concentric spheres, having the same orbit and in synchronous reciprocation, whose opposed oscillations engender the energy that effects and perpetuates their motions. Together they constitute a trinity, THE WHOLE that is our Universe. All that it contains conforms to the same principle and pattern.

"The secrets of this Universe then, are embodied in its structure and in the forms and behaviors of its inhabitants. Small units are in the image of large ones, just as the sequence ascent in the table of the elements arises from multiplications of the same electric charges.

"Idea and purpose are primary. Strong wills summon, arouse and array force to compass their objectives. They impose form on force to frame, regulate and maintain their currencies. Matrix, mold, motion and circulation. Energy is gathered to centers in accumulation and discharged towards circumferences. Production, distribution and reproduction. Awareness and initiative are forever external to force and form yet supply coordination, support and significance.

"Men, corporations and universe are all of a piece. Their embryos in development duplicate the same rhythms. They start with some seed or unit of consciousness enfolded in which are the potentials of awareness, initiation, integration and self-sustainment. Pressure to expand becomes the will to express. What is revealed in the materialized form is the architecture of the ideal that was predisposed in the seed. Its magnitude is the measure of the will that propelled it into being.

"All creations are devices for work; means to ends. What is seen, heard and felt has been wrought, sent forth and is returned. Nothing exists of or for itself. All principles and things are relative and contributory. Every vehicle and tool made under the seven heavens is shaped for reciprocation with the parts and needs of the user. Use derives from need; need from appetite, which is dynamic demand. What persists and functions profitably does so through exchange among the integers of its organization. It is the Whole, that sustains the identity and status of its being—its Entirety that attains fulfillment.

"Let us assume that the Universe had a beginning, was born of time, grew by degrees and matured in its present terms; much in the way men, trees, governments and corporations start at scratch, evolve into systems, and gradually consolidate their potentials into principles that regulate the performance of their routines. Before this colossal aggregation of worlds appeared, there must have existed a Being in whose consciousness it was conceived and planned, and whose will was powerful enough to embody, energize and motivate his design. That which was developed thereafter, through force, in form, can be accepted as constituting the identification and instrumentality of this Being's purpose— his embodiment—and therefore the medium of his will. All subsequent activities and proceedings, as derived from the same source, may be taken as phenomena incidental to its accomplishment. Thus we are entitled to say, that the creator lives, and moves, and has his being in the unity of his works.

"Note the natural courses of unfoldment: all creators follow parallel practices. The substance of their thoughts and the media in which their ideas and inventions are reproduced have different polarities and pitch. Your own manufacturing and governmental institutions are devices to provide for conditions that arise from the presence here of human organisms that require food, shelter, light, heat, transportation and other perquisites to traffic with one another, and to sustain their lives and communications on this planet. They originated and were modeled in individual minds, as solutions of their own problems and those of their neighbors. Each is maintained by an operating organization, separate from the premises, plants and processes charged with delivery of the product or service which rounds out its cycle of significance.

"Without such abstractions as constitutions, charters and laws, and executives to administer them, civilization and business would be at a standstill and your race would revert to barbarism.

"Take it for granted, then, that in every objective, autonomous unit, the same pair of opposites—contraction and expansion—are engaged for energetics; that form is frame and matrix; and response, reciprocation—with consciousness furnishing the applicative functions of perception and adjustment in consonance with whatever cycle of the whole its particular system is centralized in and attuned with.

"Whatever kind of exchange our universe is engaged in with its neighbors it is fair to presume that its material affairs fall in the same categories that prevail here; that it is provided with some system of sense and nerve conduction by which its center-of-consciousness keeps track of motion and change within its expansive circumference; with mobile agencies to make adequate response to disturbances affecting its metabolism or equilibrium. Your guess that the reportorial and cerebral functions of the great Being are effectuated by the vital organisms with which the surfaces of its satellites are invested, is reasonable since it is through parallel agencies that your own mechanisms are piloted and repaired. And further, on the same basis, you may predicate the presence of a working personnel of executives and administrators higher in scale and wielding larger powers, whose knowledge of the processes by which the organization as a whole is operated, enables them to participate in its management.

"However far-fetched this proposition might seem to skeptical minds in your vicinity, all would scout the idea that large scale systems of traffic and communication could possibly effectuate their purposes without authoritative supervision and control. After all—presidents, directors, superintendents and foremen are of the same clay as their subordinates and differ from them only in the degree of responsibility. Since advancement in the ranks of your peoples turns so definitely on an individual's power of applying intelligence to work, and as this is reasonable—why should anyone imagine that other principles prevail elsewhere?

"Life is the reciprocal pulsation of the universal Consciousness in exchange with its coordinated constituents. Man's true identity then is that of a link in the transmission system of the universal mind. His body is one of its perfected instruments of induction-conduction. The unit consciousness that motivates within his being may be imaged as an individual agent of the great Executive serving to the degree of his understanding of the processes being conveyed, and enlarging in status with the extension of his vision and of his capacity for participation in the cycle of its engagements. As here, there.

"Or, if you prefer other correspondences—think of your world as a laboratory for the quickening of individual consciousnesses. Or, even an educational institution—an Academy for souls. In laboratories, molecular constitutions are altered to release properties or enhance qualities, all for purposes ulterior to process. Education steps up the development of minds by charging them with a content of information as to the significance of things as bearing on individual sustainment, and for the right conduct of social relations. Graduation implies maturescence of capacity to take over the custody of the individual being.

"The next step is to digest and realize the bearings of these foundations on your own or any life. Herein lies the chance to contribute to the Universe—to lift yourself off the knees of the gods."

"That's what I want to be about," I agreed, "but where to start from or how, I'd like to be told."

"It will help if we go back for a moment to the old theorem," the Martian proceeded. "The business of human operation requires three factors and contains two interactions. The factors are consciousness, organism, environment. One interaction is between organism and environment; the other between consciousness and organism. Organism is environment for consciousness. Assume organism and environment in equilibrium. Enter consciousness, kindling life, motion and change. Environment's resistance reacts on an organic medium whose fabric is sensitized and wired to convey external variations of pressure, light, heat and sound to the photoelectric brain that transmits them to consciousness which reacts to maintain the stability of the structure with which it identifies itself.

"The yield of these automatic interactions is instinctive behavior. By exploring this submerged relation and articulating its structure in mind, its potential may be raised to the grades of self-control and ownership—a rebirth."

"It is impossible to fill a prescription to which no quantities are attached," I protested. "Some nearer approach to a program, please."

"Not long ago," he explained, "you described how the picture of that Self which is the structure of your identity was assembled, thrust upon you by the world, picked up piecemeal from your parents and contemporaries forming a growth of acceptances accreted without effort much as a ship gathers barnacles on her hull. Resurvey these premises as though you were detached from them and establish the facts for your own account, remembering always the mechanics involved."

"Mechanics," I repeated.

"Obviously," he insisted. "If at this moment I were to asperse your integrity or parentage, involuntarily your body is transfigured, its posture stiffened, its nerves and muscles contracted, its heart beats faster and its eyes blaze. Yet the earth has not stirred nor is any interest of the organism affected. It was this identity structure that reacted to my insult, and since the physical deformations that ensued were mechanical it must be in touch with the nerve centers that released the energy which automatically converted you from a passive to a fighting animal.

"Here, then, is a subtle system that exerts pressure by way of response to what stimulates or resists its inherency, whose ramifications must be charted and recognized before knowledge or command of its forces may be established. Think of it as the matrix of man's body whose fabric carries his memories and his racial inheritance and is the seat of his will, and accord it machinery commensurate with its functions.

Seek for the valves and levers of its controls. While rated as unconscious it remains unpredictable, and you're a drifter at the mercy of unknown currents."

"The victim was led in front of a stone wall and invited to describe what was happening on the other side," I reproached. "There's neither body nor handle to that proposal."

"Both await identification," the Martian proceeded. "Agreed that an action is the sum of the elements engaged in its effectuation, it is obvious that what you do comprises set-up, motive, design, energy, supervision and fulfillment. If each specification is not entered and followed in mind, performance is no better than mechanical response to the stimuli that evoked it. The trouble is that you have not yet grasped the fundamentals involved in your own conclusions. Here you are alive and in possession of faculty—now exactly what do you know about yourself save what you have assumed and I affirmed? You are not on your own feet."

"Granted again," I agreed.

"Then work on the subject-matter at hand," he pursued, "the body of your immediate occupation. How does it do what you do, in what manner and why? Observe it dispassionately, objectively, phenomenally. Make a transcript in consciousness of its appearance, posture and acts, how it moves and what motivates it. Mark its changes, what urges it to wrath, grief or laughter? It thinks. Of what is that thinking composed? And how and why are particular decisions determined? It may help you to learn which interest your actions serve—your body's or your own—or an interest hitherto unsuspected. That would be illuminating.

"Through its tongue and lips you convey opinions and convictions. How did you capture and install them as invest-

ments of your personality? Have you ever listened to yourself speak, to catch the tones of your voice or the architecture
of your sentences? They emerge framed, energized, spaced,
cadenced. Having as a child accomplished the feat of training the nerves and muscles of larynx, pharynx, tongue and
lips to convert a current of air from the lungs into a verbal
communication, it would now be enlightening to reexamine
the processes. Quite often you are ignorant about what's in
your mind until it comes to your ears by way of your mouth.
Who sets up the words your lips frame, and how did they
reach your tongue?

"Remembering that every one of the countless movements through which a body carries on a life is an artifice,
an action-pattern shaped to a purpose, that it was learned
as an artist learns his technic and has correspondent neu-
ron-patterns through which the energy that motivates it is
delivered; now try to follow the trails of some of them and
occasionally to change their direction.

"Then there's that interesting fabric—your structure of
identity—the personality portrayed and affirmed by your
words and deeds—has it a definite outline? Does it exist as
a factor independent of what affects its material concerns? It
would be worthwhile to discover the truth about your own
personality. No psychologist can tell just where the members
of your species keep their courage, honor, sense of justice,
charity, reverence and so forth. Undeniably these virtues
are verities. At least their evocation disturbs equilibrium—
which of course requires the discharge of energy. Think how
useful it would be to learn their sources and associations;
and, of the privilege of being present in mind at the transaction of your own affairs.

"And there is the matter of emotion—of love, especially.

Apparently this term has a different connotation for whoever uses it, since it covers the whole gamut of human and divine relations. Does it for you describe an organic reaction that may be relieved by embrace and exchange, or is it inspired by admiration, obligation, fear or reciprocation? All men and women are said to seek love—how helpful in finding it, to know what one wants. Dispassionate examination of your generosities may reveal another beneficiary than their subjects. Self-indulgence has been known to disguise itself as kindliness; as even inertia or indifference is often paraded as self-sacrifice. Since the object of self-observation is information, no judgments need ever be entered, so, neither criticize nor commend, but keep tabs on the counting.

"One might protract ad infinitum the list of things men don't know about their natures and which can be discovered only by watching their own bodies in action, but why persist further? Admit that I've offered something to do with your mind besides the tasks that evolve from its professional vocation of filling a stomach and exercising limbs!"

"It never occurred to me to look at myself from that standpoint," I granted.

"Your neighbors and friends do," the Martian reassured. "And you are not in the habit of accepting neighbors and friends at their own valuations. Now that you are aware of an instrumentality for self-examination there is afforded the inestimable privilege of seeing yourself as others see you. The process may denude you of hair and heroism, but what remainder survives will furnish a pivot from which to reckon further adventures."

There was a pause.

"Somehow I can't fix my mind on the process you suggest, or follow either my thoughts or my own movements,"

I confessed. "It wanders; it won't stay put; it flies hither and thither. What's the meaning of that?"

"If the stream of consciousness is to turn the mind's wheels it must be channeled within banks," he advised. "If it be hard to control—gain courage by remembering how long it took the inventor of the internal combustion engine to find the exact mixture of air and gasoline vapor to concentrate in a cylinder—and how to make and adjust the spark that explodes and changes it into the force that turns car wheels. Run over the story of electricity—of the countless experiments that preceded the capture and conversion of that mysterious power into light, heat and voltage. Since the Self's potentials are factual, they are there for the finding, and happily, the resistances overcome in the search reinforce the will of the pursuer to attain his ends."

"I must be dense or dazed," I pleaded. "Your statements make sense but I cannot get a mental grip on what they imply."

The Martian sighed, but went on patiently:

"You defined a man as his body, his consciousness of that body, of its planetary relations, of the ability to move therein. On one side of this theorem posit capacity of awareness; on the other its subject-matter. Object is maintenance of the coordination of consciousness and body whose sum is an individual existence. The point I'm making is, that failure to allot their respective values to both coefficients, has aborted consciousness. Denied place and prerogative in the organic scheme, it establishes no operating center for its attributes of identification, interpretation and exchange. It submerges as the unconscious and functions as instinct, intuition, imagination, inhibition or along any other avenue of doubt, fear or guess instead of as self-consciousness. Thus, the individual entity, lacking internal integration, develops no significance, takes his law and conduct from the outside and appears as what he does rather than as what he is. Figuratively, it is as though one refused to see out of one's eyes and guided one's steps with a cane. Or, as if a mariner rejecting compass, tiller, sextant and chart entrusted the navigation of his craft to wind and current.

"How to stimulate this potential to take on positiveness is the problem. It is in close touch with its own body. By offering it that body as the subject of its awareness it is given an exercise peculiarly adapted for its own articulation."

"Why setting a watch on my own movements should have that effect, or prove enlightening, I can't see," I objected impatiently.

"Yet, if a golf expert urged the practice of driving before a mirror to follow the swing of your shoulders, it would merely be to enlist your intelligence for the correction of your faults," my visitor reminded me. "The technics of mechanics and of the arts are derived from observation. So is the structure of knowledge. In becoming the subject of one's own attention the cognitive potential is attached to its immediate premises and from a fresh angle gains awareness of its body performing the series of activities that constitute its routine reactions to environment and society. Its motive processes of comparison and selection are kindled and new cortical records registered that retard, accelerate or reverse subsequent response to stimuli. Insensibly, the individual's viewpoint acquires that sanity and detachment which, thereafter, enable him to act advisedly. That is, precisely to adapt his words and deeds for the ends at which his evolving self-interest directs them. What is achieved, mechanically, is restoring an aberrant entity to its right field, but the important result is to stabilize organic control where it belongs—in the center of consciousness."

"I begin to see what you mean," I admitted, hesitatingly. "But what does it amount to?"

"Being fed the right food for its development, consciousness starts to function on its own terms," said the Martian. "It accounts for its state, and differentiates between its potential and the properties of its organic auxiliary. Reacting within its own medium it begins to be self-conscious. Gradually it builds up an internal order and economy, accreted out of its assessments and experiments, and re-knits its control mechanism in correspondence with its findings. Thus the old vague identity structure is replaced with a realistic pattern. Individual standards become objective. Intuition and impulse are suspect. Behavior issues as weighed and measured response to what evokes it. The entity having grasped the facts of its integration, recognizes itself for what it is and proceeds to readjust its expectations and its organism for better reciprocation with environing circumstances."

"That's the return of everyday wisdom and self-restraint," I objected. "It's just the attainment a man is educated to mature out of experience."

"Wisdom without comprehension of its own ways and means is little better than instinct," he advised. "Given fair conditions, what's in the seed comes out in the life, but that may be charged to heredity and environment. A mathematical prodigy can extract the square root of seven integers while you are adding them, but does not know how he arrived at the sum. There's no satisfaction in the possession of gifts that appropriate your capacities for their own preferment. Do try to realize, that precision and control, sequence and consecutivity, which are the ideals of motivation and duplication, are never achieved save when the applicator is armed with complete knowledge of subject and object. Men are successful mechanics, architects, engineers and navigators because they operate with due cognizance of the laws and relations that must be accurately coordinated to beget their purposes."

"Am I to conclude then that beauty, prowess and goodness without privity and understanding are but happy accidents, and establish no record?" I demanded.

"Surely the aphorisms of your race that virtue is its own reward, and that honesty is the best policy, dispose of that problem," my visitor responded. "In your own case, for instance—born sound of wind and limb, of God-fearing parents, habitized to law and order—what chance had you to go wrong? For you, the way of truth and honor is the primrose path. If what's bred in the bone comes forth in the flesh— credit for whatever attainment you've achieved is surely due the progenitors who sowed what you've reaped."

"I've resisted my share of temptations," I insisted, angrily, "and earned all I've made. That's far-fetched."

"On about the same terms that capital returns interest," he snapped. "No blame attaches to your vassalage and no glory. But, if a man's life is no better than the fruitage of his ancestry conveyed along the trackage of his world, what has he to offer at the end for graduation into any other state? Nothing of his own making."

Before I could utter the objection that rose to my lips— the Martian said:

"Wait!

"For all my arguments and your own rationalizings," he went on, "your mind has not yet grasped the fact that Life is no one's private affair, but a function of the Universe that has provided the machineries and support for its own maintenance. Your sole birthright therein is an equity in one of its service bodies and though privileged to cooperate in the processes of this Ordination you have no greater claim on its consideration than is warranted by your knowledge of its affairs. Some inkling of this dependency having penetrated your understanding, why this persistence in futile disputation? In view of the immensity and grandeur of the institution, of what concern are the delusions or conjectures of an anonymous tenant? I offer no tickets to paradise. My purpose is to supply material for utilitarian development that may lead to the betterment of your lot. Once more then, let us review the facts as they affect your own relation, remembering that the God I referred to is the maker and ruler of the corporation of Being, and not a theological conception.

"That human existence is conditional on its maintenance, is fundamental; also, that the kind and degree of that maintenance depends on an individual's understanding of the problem in his own case, and his power to solve it. That power, the structure of the body and his awareness of the circumstance which environs it, are extraneous to their evocation, as that evocation is to its cause.

"For instance, the constitution and organization of a factory are extraneous to the craftsmen who work in it and to the owner who administers it. It is inanimate and they vital, but sustenance for their vitality is derived from the interactions they set up among its machines. To the coolie who purchases a quart of kerosene in Shanghai, the immanence of Standard Oil is imperceptible, but in return for the light it sells, he helps support its system. Thus, unwittingly, he contributes to the improvement of the world's health through the Rockefeller institute of medical research.

"As to creation, we are agreed that a being endowed with the creative capacity is obliged to go outside his Self to exercise it, and must use materials that will take and hold form in order to demonstrate that he is not only what he affirms, but, by the activities he is able to induce in his embodiments, to sustain and make consecutive an existence of the type he has chosen for his expression. Thereafter he exists *both* as himself and as his creation; as the organizer and head of a corporation is himself and what he has built—that institution whose own activities sustain itself, maintain his idea and his status as its creator. Again, the pair of opposites, positive and negative charges, combining to make an entity or element, maintained by interchange.

"Now think of the Universe as an organism for conducting the life of its Creator who has materialized his conception of Himself in the form and nature of the worlds perceptible to your senses. It includes all that moves sequentially within its orbit, and, as in the instance of yourself, the individuality of the Creator, though it pervades them, is external to His works. A man, then, must be a unit of the body of his Maker. In sustaining his own existence, he contributes to the maintenance of the source of his form and power; his ability to be aware of his relation in this complex is the Creator's means of supervising and ordering His individual progressions. Man gains his living by duplicating the same principles, and coordinates his work with his consciousness-of-Self by exercising the native capacity to frame, manage and observe his operations. Since to this partnership he furnishes nothing of his own making, and his connivance is involuntary, he ranks but as a tool, and is without significance save a dummy.

"As in any mundane institution, degree of participation can be changed, but to do so a man must turn *positive*, learn the character of his integration and, by comprehending its constitution, do, for his own account, what was formerly automatic response to its exigencies. The secrets to be developed are buried in the body of his incarnation, that complex and beautiful organism designed for his occupancy. By analyzing the processes through which the affairs of his living are conducted, this individual sets up friction between consciousness and organism—an entirely new interaction—and from it is begotten a Self, the knower, whose perceptions being detached from the mediums of its generation, is capable of learning of its parentage and circumstances. Being nourished by self-observation, its texture of content is the knowledge it has gained by exploring its own resources and relationships, that emerges in expansion of understanding and revision of position. Like the escaped soul whose symbolic adventures I narrated some nights ago, it discovers its own potential to be the dominant in its physical associations, and assumes direction of them on behalf of its responsibility. This is rebirth—the first step in the attainment; of self-consciousness. Having by its own efforts possessed itself of the means of material existence, the egoic entity has asserted its prerogative. *It knows itself to be its Self.*

"Though the form of this statement be unfamiliar, it is an abstract of the principles involved in the attainment of any technic of the arts or crafts. Rehearse the processes by which a dancer converts his limbs into mediums for the execution of rhythmic patterns in time, or whereby a Paderewski, induces his fingers and arms to reproduce sound patterns from a piano, or whereby a woodcarver imparts exactitude to the movements of a chisel.

"In each instance, will and mind are concentrated on the body-members concerned to make them effective mediums to translate external subject-matter from an intangible to a perceptible form. Objective, and standard of performance pertain to the interests of the applicator who evokes and recognizes them, but because he does not appreciate the separateness of his own role in the proceeding, his identity is merged with its product. He becomes what he does. His personality is not that of a human being, but of the degree of his skill. Thus your societies are mechanical soviets in which the existences of individual members are founded on their contributions to the conduct of collective interests. The true being is sabotaged, and culture is a cul-de-sac.

"Compare this inhibitive curriculum with the development of an entity who, having perfected integration with his body by surveying and possessing himself of its resources, is *at one* with it. From the mechanical mixture of consciousness and organism which was his original state, he has evolved a chemical compound, a unit of the element *Man,* capable of that perfection of adjustment which is the return of control of medium and circumstances: As, for instance, is conveyance, in an exact period of time, of a 60,000 ton ocean liner from a pier in New York to its appointed berth at a dock in Southampton.

"Having remolded the body of his inheritance in the image of his consciousness, such a one can enter single minded upon the activities that are accessible to his potential and its estate. Knowledge of his origin has made him party to its obligations, but having acquired control of his vehicle, he can recast his behavior and originate new experiences either to test his powers or extend their orbit. Thereafter he may grow in status and wisdom and, having attained maturescence, enjoy that fullness of life which is the fruitage of right use of its opportunities. But however high the degree of his culture he may never free himself of the responsibilities of his nativity. He belongs to that generation of the species to which he has been committed and his powers are allotted to the development of its material and spiritual constitution. Nor is he exempt from the conditions of his tenancy. Enlightenment relieves but cannot remit the tensions of maintenance.

"As I explained to that Tibetan sage, man is a conscript. His is the power-to-be, but the frame and investment of that being belong to the Ordainment which supplied them as means for its own correspondences. What such transcendence as I have defined reveals to the entity who earns it, is the dimension of his subjectivity. He discovers himself a relative among relations; a cell in the structure of his Creator. By becoming united within himself, he has bettered his conductivity as an instrument for the transmission of the eternal forces. Thereafter he is responsive to the rhythms of the Universe-as-a-whole, as well as to the groundswell of the earth and his fellows. As in your instance of the employee in course of promotion, his advancement is on behalf of the institution that has enlisted his intelligence. The qualities developed in its service are absorbed into its constitution. Eventually, he exchanges his identity for its own. That, perhaps, is the significance of the words of your Christ when he said, 'Whoever shall lose his life shall preserve it.'"

"I catch the drift," I said, as he paused, "but there are rather more geography and physics in your statement than can be swallowed between two breaths. I'd like to know what is covered by survey and possession of the body's resources?"

"Has it never struck you as curious that from the same body each member of your race elicits a different response," the Martian replied. "Think of the variety of human attainments and experiences, and realize that all were recorded through the same type of organism. Consider the mysteries of clairvoyance, of telepathy, of prophetic visions, of the miracles wrought on themselves by disciples of Yoga, of faith healing at Lourdes or as practiced here by Christian Science, of the suspension of animation as achieved by 'fakirs,' of the mystic revelations of the Saints; of abnormality in general—the strange dreams induced by narcotics, comatose states as in anæsthesia or in hypnotic trance, that constitutional change which occurs in 'presence of mind' whereby an individual is enabled to act swiftly and deftly in danger. For none of these phenomena has your science accommodation or explanation. What hidden springs are tapped by the genius, the mathematical prodigy, the adept, the healer?

"Such properties must be contained in the body that produces them. Entering into possession of them, as in acquiring the use of other faculties of that body, is the return of that outlay of research and application which has been described. The profit of their pursuit is undeniable. Could the average man command that control of his own organism which flows to obey the alien will of a hypnotist, how vast the enhancement of his strength and endurance! And of his ability to resist pain and repair injury. Could your consciousness unlock and win access to the annals of your own life photographed and inlaid by light and sound on the plasm of your brain, what a wealth of data for comparison would be available for thinking. Some men have encyclopedic memories but don't know the source of this gift; yet memory is but another phase of mental mechanics whose mastery is on the path of attainment."

"Desirable as it may be, is not this approach to the new freedom rather from the esoteric angle?" I inquired cautiously.

"If so it be, why not?" the Martian demanded. "To decry valuable experience because it negates a creed or a hypothesis, is folly. Worse: it is sentimentality. There's a body of belief and ascertainment called occult, containing lore available for wider distribution that may quicken progress—why not find and use it? True, its votaries are as superstitious about concealing their knowledge as are your scientists in proclaiming it fraudulent, but facts are facts. To sneer at any faith that has a record of marvels to its credit, is provincial. Intelligence come to her own, will rather say at a Shrine, that here an unmapped power operates, than that the worshipers suffer from hallucinations. Even miracles depend on mechanisms. Working one requires stepping up the high energy discharged in performing it."

"You open doors wide to mumbo-jumbo and hocus pocus," I interjected.

"Not wider than they yawn at the moment," he retorted. "Superstition is compounded of fear and bigotry, and deception trades on it. Fear is the root of distrust, just as incredulity for the most part is in refusing credit without investigation. On the one hand faith is contemptible, but the usages of salesmanship, banking and advertising are founded on its existence. These foolish confusions will never be resolved until men realize that they belong where they are, that they exist by arrangement; and that the Universe is behind and speaks through them. It's only the anonymity of Nature that is fearful. Give her a name and a place and she turns from enemy to friend."

"At last a little light on the horizon," I commented.

"There are magnificent possibilities," my visitor affirmed. "A right man is the master of his being; his body is his abode, tool and obedient servant. Of himself and of its processes, he is ruler. He is present in person in all its actions and these are the consummation of his will. No endocrine ferments arouse his passions or corrupt his judgments. The voltage of his consciousness is impressed into the work of his mind and hands. The play of stimuli still reaches him, and his senses show him the world and its ways, but, having banished the fears, hopes and incertitudes that obscured his vision, he is no longer the slave of suggestion, of habitized response or synaptic hesitations; nor of organic loves and hates. And since he meets them on his own terms, the hostilities of the environment are but obstacles for the development of his resistances.

"To such a one, Life is a glorious opportunity. It becomes an interval of travel in a noble vehicle, through whose reactions he is privileged to experience the sights and scenery of this beautiful, luxurious planet; and to taste, smell and partake of its delectable resources. He grows to be what his Creator intended him to be. In learning and conforming to the laws of the Universe, he has acquired the control of its instrumentality. He enters into the spirit of its undertakings, joyfully fulfills the obligations of his part and insures his own future usefulness as helpful to the management."

I clapped my hands enthusiastically.

"That's more like it," I announced. "It's the first glimpse of a colored prospect you've yet vouchsafed. Almost I am persuaded to take up a cross and follow."

"Alas," said the Martian, "what I have depicted is easier told than achieved. And it's an old story. All tales of lost elysiums, of sleeping beauties in enchanted castles, of the search for the Holy Grail and a hundred other antique legends are allegories of the struggle of men to grasp the reality of the soul. The same motif pervades them—some hidden secret of origin or identity, that may be found by long, hard seeking. The Tibetan, whose speculations I set forth, was satisfied he had found the path, and was on the way to attainment. What is fresh in my statement is only the pitch of the narrative. Ancient Egypt, Chaldea and the Greece of Pythagoras and Plato, sensed the same realities. The seers of those civilizations taught that man is not his body. The miscomprehended mission of Christ was to proclaim the same certitude. It is the theme of occult philosophy. Strands of the ancient wisdom underlie the life of India.

"But this is a practical age, and prophets, if they have not the tongues of financiers, are unheard. For oracles you have the scientists, who have lighted and motorized your world and made life so much better worth living by multiplying the appliances to live it with. Still, I have shown you the way that we on Mars have found and follow. As I said in the beginning, it has made the later years of our sojourn on that planet peaceful, profitable and entertaining."

"It may be an intrusion on the solemnity of your mood," I ventured, "but I'm curious to know if there are religions on Mars. And do its peoples believe in immortality?"

"Religion, yes," he responded a bit wearily, "but no Theologies. Since the Universe is the embodiment of the will of its Creator and exists as His individual being, His All-Consciousness is the sum of all the units of consciousness through whom His Self-Awareness goes forth, is transmitted and returns. Since the life of this great Being is consecutive and continuous, and is maintained by means of its units— perforce they share its nature. Since, of all the factors and elements, consciousness alone is capable of persisting, and of being enlarged and extended, and as its units are unequal in the degree of possessing it, it may be taken for granted that its potential is being stepped-up by exposure to experience; that it is developed through successive plunges into incarnation much in the manner you described the employee absorbing information by being immersed in routines.

"But its evolution is on behalf of the System that attends to the tempering and annealing; so the gates of death merely open upon another life here, or elsewhere, with, perhaps, a higher and a harder curriculum, if the mettle of the subject has gained resiliency in its last adventure.

"As that hypothesis informs our Martian councils we are mindful of our steps, and of our responsibilities to one another and to the cause of our being. But, since we conceive a God who, however busy, is never solemn; who, as demonstrated in His works—has imagination, humor and a friendly and forbearing interest in His creatures—we do not fear Him. We like to think of ourselves as custodians of His concerns, rather than as charges upon His mercy. Thus, prayer among us takes the form of reporting to Him the details of our experiments in understanding His ways and His works; and of laying open our minds to the whispers of His wisdom."

"To that kind of a religion I could subscribe myself," I declared.

"Any kind of a religion is better than none at all," my visitor affirmed. "It is the urge of ancestral relationship, the voice of transcendental patriotism, and any of its modes are attunement to the higher etheric frequencies. Belief in a God is not a matter of faith, but of intelligence. The kind of God you discern depends on the degree of your intelligence. The further it penetrates—the greater and nobler and more magnificent the conception of His divinity and power that possesses you. I have laid out a path which, if you have the will and tenacity to pursue it, must increase your efficiency and enhance your self-confidence. But, as your steps grow firmer, your eyes will be opened to wider spaces and your heart grow humble in contemplating the immensity of the Universe, the length of the path, and the disparity between your tiny power and its magnitude. However—be on the way."

"That's not a farewell?" I asked, for I had noted that my visitor's voice had faded to a murmur.

"For the time being, yes," he replied. "In my solicitude to deliver you from organic thralldom I have exhausted the slight fabric of my own vehicle. At any rate, I have spread a feast of fact that it will take your remaining years to digest; and, into the bargain, have provided an occupation and a technic that will engage and enlarge your interest in life. In seeking for that buried treasure—your Self—never again need you know a dull moment."

With difficulty I caught the Martian's last words. They seemed to recede as if coming from increasing distances. Then I knew he had departed.

Thus came to an end my greatest experience. I have not heard again from this strange visitor. Perchance he is restoring, in some African or Australian desert, the energy so generously expended in my education. He may be derisively whispering of our civilization into some attentive ear in California, Queensland, or the Soudan. One day he may return and survey the work he wrought on my premises.

He will be welcome. I hope I have not obscured his teachings.